Also by Anne Rice
Available from Random House Large Print

**Prince Lestat**
**The Wolf Gift**
**The Wolves of Midwinter**

# PRINCE LESTAT
## AND THE
# REALMS of ATLANTIS

# PRINCE LESTAT

## AND THE

# REALMS OF ATLANTIS

## The Vampire Chronicles

# ANNE RICE

RANDOM HOUSE
LARGE PRINT

Published in the United States of America by Random House Large Print in association with Alfred A. Knopf, a division of Random House LLC, New York

Cover design by Oliver Munday

The Library of Congress has established a Cataloging-in-Publication record for this title.

ISBN: 978-1-5247-7461-5

www.randomhouse.com/largeprint

FIRST LARGE PRINT EDITION

Printed in the United States of America

10 9 8 7 6 5 4 3 2 1

This Large Print edition published in accord with the standards of the N.A.V.H.

THIS BOOK IS DEDICATED
TO

The undefeated and retired
babyweight champion of the world

and

Mitey Joe,
without whom the book might not have
been born,

and

my old friends,
Shirley Stuart and Bill Seely,

and

friends and fellow writers
of my Northern California days:
Cleo, Maria, Carole, Dorothy, Jim, Carolyn,
Candy, Lee, and others

and

once again,
to
the People of the Page
who give me so much more than I can ever
give them.

Remember him—before the silver cord is severed,
and the golden bowl is broken;
before the pitcher is shattered at the spring,
and the wheel broken at the well,
and the dust returns to the ground it came from,
and the spirit returns to God who gave it.

—ECCLESIASTES
The New International Version

# Contents

# A Brief History of the Vampires Blood Genesis

In the beginning were the spirits. They were invisible beings, heard and seen only by the most powerful sorcerers or witches. Some were thought to be malevolent; some were praised as good. They could find lost objects, spy upon enemies, and now and then affect the weather.

Two great witches, Mekare and Maharet, lived in a beautiful valley on the side of Mount Carmel, and they communed with the spirits. One of these spirits, the great and powerful Amel, could, in his mischief making, take blood from human beings. Tiny bits of blood entered the alchemical mystery of the spirit, though how no one knew. But Amel loved the witch Mekare and was ever eager to serve her. She saw him as no other witch ever had, and he loved her for it.

One day the troops of an enemy came—soldiers of the powerful Queen Akasha of Egypt. She wanted the witches; she wanted their knowledge, their secrets.

This wicked monarch destroyed the valley and the villages of Mekare and Maharet and brought the sisters by force to her own kingdom.

Amel, the furious familiar spirit of the witch Mekare, sought to punish the Queen.

When she lay dying, stabbed over and over by conspirators of her own court, this spirit Amel entered into her, fusing with her body and her blood and giving her a new and terrifying vitality.

This fusion caused a new entity to be born into the world: the vampire, the blood drinker.

From the blood of this great vampire queen, Akasha, all the other vampires of the whole world were born over the millennia. A blood exchange was the means of procreation.

To punish the twins who stood opposed to her and her new power, Akasha blinded Maharet and tore the tongue from Mekare. But before they could be executed, the steward of the Queen, Khayman, a newly made blood drinker himself, passed on to the twins the powerful Blood.

Khayman and the twins led a rebellion against Akasha, but they could not stop her cult of blood drinker gods. Eventually the twins were captured and separated—sent out as castaways—Maharet into the Red Sea and Mekare into the great ocean to the west.

Maharet soon found familiar shores and thrived, but Mekare, carried across the ocean to lands yet undiscovered and unnamed, vanished from history.

This was six thousand years ago.

The great Queen Akasha and her husband, King Enkil, went mute after two thousand years, maintained like statues in a shrine by elders and priests that believed Akasha contained the Sacred Core—and that if she should be destroyed, all the blood drinkers of the world would die with her.

But by the time of the Common Era, the story of the Blood Genesis was completely forgotten. Only a few elder immortals passed on the tale, though they did not believe it even as they told it. Yet blood gods, vampires dedicated to the old religion, still reigned in shrines throughout the world.

Imprisoned in hollowed-out trees or brick cells, these blood gods starved for blood until the holy feasts at which they were brought offerings: evildoers to judge and condemn and feast upon.


At the dawn of the Common Era, an elder, a keeper of the Divine Parents, abandoned Akasha and Enkil in the desert for the sun to destroy them. All over the world young blood drinkers perished, burnt to death in their coffins, their shrines, or in their tracks as the sun shone on the Mother and Father. But the Mother and Father themselves were too strong to perish. And many of the very old ones survived as well, though badly burned and in pain.

A newly made blood drinker, a wise Roman scholar by the name of Marius, went down to Egypt to find the King and Queen and protect them so that no holocaust would ever again ravage the world of the Undead. And thereafter Marius made them his sacred responsibility. The legend of Marius and Those Who Must Be Kept endured for almost two millennia.

In the year 1985, the story of this Blood Genesis was told to all the world's Undead. That the Queen lived, that she contained the Sacred Core, this was part of the story. It appeared in a book written by the Vampire Lestat, who also told the tale in song and dance in film and from the stage, where he performed as a rock singer—calling the world to know and destroy his own kind.

Lestat's voice waked the Queen from millennia of silence and slumber. She rose with a dream: that she would dominate the world of human beings through cruelty and slaughter and become for them the Queen of Heaven.

But the ancient twins came forward to stop Akasha. They too had heard Lestat's songs. Maharet appealed to the Queen to stop her superstitious blood tyranny. And the long-lost Mekare, rising from the earth after untold aeons, decapitated the great

Queen and took the Sacred Core into herself as she devoured the dying Queen's brain. Mekare, under the protection of her sister, became the new Queen of the Damned.

Lestat once again wrote the story. He had been there. He had seen the passing of the power with his own eyes. He gave his testimony to everyone. The mortal world took no notice of his "fictions," but his tales shocked the Undead.

And so the story of origins and ancient battles, of vampire powers and vampire weaknesses, and wars for control of the Dark Blood became the common knowledge of the Undead tribe the world over. It became the property of old ones who'd been comatose for centuries in caves or graves, of young ones misbegotten in jungles or swamps or urban slums who had never dreamed of their antecedents. It became the property of wise and secretive survivors who had lived in isolation through the ages.

It became the legacy of all blood drinkers the world over to know they shared a common bond, a common history, a common root.

**Prince Lestat** is the story of how that knowledge changed the tribe and its destiny forever. Brought together by a crisis, the tribe unites, begging Lestat to become its leader.

**Prince Lestat and the Realms of Atlantis** explores the history of the vampires ever more deeply as the tribe, governed by Lestat, confronts the worst challenges it has ever faced.

# Blood Argot

When the Vampire Lestat wrote his books, he used any number of terms taught to him by the vampires he had encountered in his life. And those vampires who added to his work, offering their memoirs and their experiences in written form, added terms of their own, some much more ancient than those ever revealed to Lestat.

This is a list of those terms, which are now common amongst the Undead throughout the world.

**The Blood**—When the word is capitalized it refers to vampiric blood, passed on from master to fledgling through a deep and often dangerous exchange. "In the Blood" means that one is a vampire. The Vampire Lestat had over two hundred years "in the Blood" when he wrote his books. The great vampire Marius has over two thousand years in the Blood. And so forth and so on.

**Blood Drinker**—The most ancient term for "vampire." This was Akasha's simple term, which she later sought to supplant with the term "blood god" for those who followed her spiritual path and her religion.

**Blood Wife or Blood Spouse**—One's vampire mate.

**Children of Satan**—Term for vampires of Late Antiquity and after who believed they were literally children of the Devil and serving God through serving Satan as they fed upon humankind. Their approach to life was penitential and puritanical. They denied themselves all pleasure except drinking blood and occasional Sabbats (large gatherings) at which they danced, and they lived underground, often in filthy and dismal catacombs and enclosures. The Children of Satan have not been seen or heard from since the eighteenth century, and in all likelihood the cult has died out.

**Children of the Millennia**—Term for immortals who have lived more than a thousand years and most specifically for those who have survived more than two.

**Children of the Night**—Common term for all vampires, or all those in the Blood.

**The Cloud Gift**—This is the ability of older vampires to defy gravity, to rise up and move in the upper atmosphere and to cover long distances easily, traveling the winds unseen by those below. Again, no one can say when a vampire might acquire this power. The will to have it may work wonders. All truly ancient ones possess it whether they know it or not. Some vampires despise the power and never use it unless forced.

**The Coven of the Articulate**—A modern slang term popular among the Undead for the vampires whose stories appear in the Vampire Chronicles—particularly Louis, Lestat, Pandora, Marius, and Armand.

**The Dark Gift**—A term for the vampiric power. When a master bestows the Blood on a fledgling, that master is offering the Dark Gift.

**The Dark Trick**—Refers to the act of actually making the new vampire. To draw out the fledgling's blood and to replace it with one's own powerful Blood is to work the Dark Trick.

**The Devil's Road**—Medieval term among the vampires for the road each vampire takes through this world; a popular term of the Children of Satan, who saw themselves as serving God through serving the Devil. To ride the Devil's Road was to live one's life as an immortal.

**The Fire Gift**—This is the ability of older vampires to use their telekinetic power to burn matter. They can, through the power of their minds, burn wood, paper, or any flammable substance. And they can burn other vampires as well, igniting the Blood in their bodies and reducing them to cinders. Only older vampires possess this power, but no one can say when and how a vampire acquires it. A very young vampire made by an ancient one may immediately possess the power. A vampire must be able to see that which he or she wants to burn. In sum, no vampire can burn another if he cannot see that vampire, if he is not close enough to direct the power.

**The First Brood**—These are the vampires descended from Khayman who were in rebellion against Queen Akasha.

**Fledgling**—A new vampire very young in the Blood. Also, one's own offspring in the Blood. For example, Louis is the fledgling of Lestat. Armand is the fledgling of Marius. The ancient twin Maharet is the fledgling of her twin, Mekare. Mekare is the fledgling of the ancient Khayman. Khayman is the fledgling of Akasha.

**The Little Drink**—Stealing blood from a mortal victim without the victim knowing it or feeling it, without the victim having to die.

**Maker**—Simple term for the vampire who brought one into the Blood. Being slowly replaced by the term "mentor." Sometimes the maker is also referred to as the "master." However, this has gone out of use. In many parts of the world it is considered a great sin to rise up against or seek to destroy one's maker. A maker can never hear the thoughts of a fledgling, and vice versa.

**The Mind Gift**—This is a loose and imprecise term which refers to the preternatural powers of the vampiric mind on many levels. Through the Mind Gift, a vampire might learn things from the world above even when he is sleeping in the earth below. And consciously using the Mind Gift, he might telepathically listen to the thoughts of mortals and immortals. He might use the Mind Gift to pick up images from others as well as words. He might use the Mind Gift to project images into the minds of others. And finally he might use the Mind Gift to telekinetically open a lock, push open a door, or stop the progress of an engine. Again, vampires develop the Mind Gift slowly over time, and only the most ancient can rape the minds of others for information they do not wish to give, or send a telekinetic blast to rupture the brain and blood cells of a human being or another vampire. A vampire can listen to many the world over, hearing and seeing what others hear. But to destroy telekinetically, he or she must be able to see the intended victim.

**The Queen of the Damned**—Term given to the Vampire Mekare by her sister Maharet once Mekare had taken the Sacred Core into herself. It was ironic. Akasha, the fallen Queen who had sought to dominate the world, had called herself the Queen of Heaven.

**The Queens Blood**—These are the vampires made by Queen Akasha to follow her path in the Blood and fight the rebels of the First Brood.

**The Sacred Core**—This refers to the residing brain or governing life force of the spirit Amel, which is inside the body of the Vampire Lestat. Before Lestat, it was in Mekare. Before it was in Mekare, it was in the Vampire Akasha. It is believed that every vampire on the planet is connected to the Sacred Core by some sort of invisible web or network of tentacles. If the vampire containing the Sacred Core were to be destroyed, all the vampires of the planet would die.

**The Savage Garden**—A term used by Lestat for the world, fitting with his belief that the only true laws of the universe are aesthetic laws, the laws that govern the natural beauty we see all around us on the planet.

**The Spell Gift**—This refers to the power of vampires to confuse, beguile, and spellbind mortals and sometimes other vampires. All vampires, even fledglings, have this power to some extent, though many don't know how to use it. It involves a conscious attempt to "persuade" the victim of the reality the vampire wants the victim to embrace. It doesn't enslave the victim. But it does confuse and mislead. It depends on eye contact. One can't spellbind anyone from a distance. In fact, it more often involves words as well as glances, and certainly involves the Mind Gift on some level.

**The Undead**—Common term for vampires of all ages.

# PRINCE LESTAT
## AND THE
# REALMS OF
# ATLANTIS

# Proem

I<small>N MY DREAMS</small>, I saw a city fall into the sea. I heard the cries of thousands. It was a chorus as mighty as the wind and the waves, all those voices of the dying. I saw flames that outshone the lamps of Heaven. And all the world was shaken.

I woke, in the dark, unable to leave the coffin in the vault in which I slept for fear that the setting sun would burn the young ones.

I held the root now of the great vampire vine on which I was once only another exotic blossom. And if I were cut, or bruised or burned, all the other vampires on the vine would know the pain.

Would the root itself suffer? The root thinks and feels and speaks when he wants to speak. And the root has always suffered. Only gradually had I come to realize it—how profound was the suffering of the root.

Without moving my lips, I asked him: "Amel, what was that city? Where did the dream come from?"

He gave me no answer. But I knew he was there. I could feel the warm pressure on the back of my neck that always meant he was there. He had not gone off along the many branches of the great vine to dream with another.

I saw the dying city again. I could have sworn I heard **his** voice crying out as the city was broken open.

"Amel, what does this mean? What is this city?"

We would lie together in the dark for an hour like this. Only then would it be safe for me to throw back the coffin lid and walk out of the crypt to see a sky beyond the windows full of safe and tiny stars. I have never taken much comfort from the stars, even though I've called us the children of the moon and the stars.

We are the vampires of the world, and I've called us many such names.

"Amel, answer me."

Scent of satin, old wood. I like seasoned and venerable things, coffins padded for the sleep of the dead. And the close warm air around me. Why shouldn't a vampire love such things? This is my marble vault, my place, my candles. This is the crypt beneath my castle, my home.

I thought I heard him sigh.

"Then you did see it, you did dream it too."

"I don't dream when you do!" he answered. He was cross. "I am not confined here while you sleep. I go where I want to go." Was this true?

But he had seen it, and now I saw the city flashing bright again in the very midst of its destruction. Suddenly it was more terrible than I could bear. It was as if I saw the myriad souls of the dead released from their bodies rising in a vapor.

He was seeing it. I knew he was. And he had seen it when I dreamed of it.

After a while, he gave me the truth. I'd come to know the tone of his secret voice when he admitted the truth.

"I don't know what it is," he said. "I don't know what it means." His sigh again. "I don't want to see it."

The next night and the night after he was to say the same thing.

And when I look back on those dreams I wonder how long we might have gone on without ever knowing any of it.

Would we have been better off if we had never discovered the meaning of what we saw?

Would it have mattered?

Everything has changed for us, and yet nothing has changed at all, and the stars beyond the windows of my castle on the hill confide nothing. But then the stars never do, do they? It's the doom of beings to read patterns in the stars, to give them names, to cherish their slowly shifting positions and clusters. But the stars never say a word.

He was telling the truth when he said he didn't know. But the dream had struck a chord of fear in his heart. And the more I dreamed of that city falling into the sea, the more I was certain I heard his weeping.

In dreams and waking hours he and I were bound as no two others. I loved him and he loved me. And I knew then as I know now that love is the only defense we ever have against the cold meaninglessness around us—the Savage Garden with its cries and songs, and the sea, the eternal sea, ready as ever to swallow all the towers ever created by human beings to reach Heaven. Love bears all things, believes all things, hopes for all things, endures all things, says the Apostle. "And the greatest of these is love . . ."

I believed it and I believe in the old commandment of the poet-saint who wrote hundreds of years after the Apostle: "Love and do what you will."

# Part I

# SPIES
## IN THE
# SAVAGE GARDEN

# 1

# Derek

THEY HAD BEEN talking up there for hours. If Derek lay very still he could hear them perfectly. At this hour, the Andrássy Út was noisy above him, with its cafés and bookstores, but this damp hidden mansion of cellar chambers was quiet. And what else did Derek have to do but listen?

Derek was a tall male with dark brown skin and large dark eyes that made him look forever young and vulnerable. His black wavy hair was parted in the middle and it had grown down just below his shoulders. An unmistakable broad blond streak grew from the center part on the left side, more golden than yellow. He wore a thin old shirt, filthy with dust, and the black dress pants he'd had on ten years ago when he'd been captured. He sat on his cot, in the corner of his prison dungeon cell, his back to the wall, his head bowed, and his arms folded as he listened.

Roland, the evil master of the house and its prison dungeons, talked and talked.

Roland's guest was an ancient one named Rhosha-mandes. And this Rhoshamandes spoke vehemently of one called "the Prince," whom he wanted to destroy. How many of these blood drinkers were there? Others came through this house from time to time, but they never remained. Others had talked of this Prince too. Derek listened, but without hope.

Rhoshamandes was a powerful one, Derek could hear this in his voice, and in the beating of the blood drinker's heart. Older than Roland most likely, much older, but he and Roland were friends.

This Rhoshamandes excited Roland. It was some sort of privilege for Roland that the fabled Rhoshamandes now sought his counsel.

Roland was the blood drinker who had taken Derek prisoner, luring him away from the opera house years ago, and locking him in this dungeon cell, beneath the city of Budapest. Roland was the one who came down the stairs at least once a week to drink Derek's blood and taunt him and laugh at him.

Roland was rawboned, tall, painfully gaunt, with long straight white hair bound with a bronze clip at the base of his neck to leave a white streak down his back. He had the most cruel eyes Derek had ever beheld, and he smiled when he spoke, which made his most casual unpleasant remarks completely sinister.

Derek had had years to study Roland, Roland who appeared to live in fashionable evening dress of fine-cut dark-tinted velvet dinner jackets with satin lapels, waistcoats of bright patterned silk, and boiled shirts with cuffs and collars as stiff as cardboard. His black patent-leather boots appeared as simple evening shoes beneath the cuffs of his pleated trousers, and a great evening scarf with fringed edges was forever wrapped around his neck. He drained the blood of Derek without ever spilling a drop. He wore kid gloves so sleek they showed the bony knots in his fingers, and his cadaverous face with its large gray eyes was the picture of sarcastic disdain.

Then there was Arion of the shining black skin, the wounded one, burnt and miserable, who had seen his home on the coast of Italy destroyed. He was much younger "in the Blood" than Roland, and for months he'd drunk from Derek nightly, and now he came several times a week. Arion had come to Roland in rags, and Roland had comforted him and restored him, and nursed his soul back to health as they spoke in the ancient Greek language of olden times when Rome had ruled the world and everything, it seems, had been better. Of course. Better. You could forgive human beings for such nonsense, but how forgive immortals who had lived then?

There was a gentleness to Arion, and a pity in his heart for Derek. Derek could sense this when Arion was drinking from him. Also Arion brought Derek gifts of fruit now and then and good wine. Derek could see the history and the pain of Arion in flashes— a great seaside villa burned, young blood drinkers immolated, a red-haired female blood drinker burnt to death, her red hair kindling and disappearing in flames. Only Arion had survived this rape of his home and massacre of his oldest companions. Arion sought shelter with Roland, and Roland sought to give Arion courage to "go on."

Arion's skin was quite truly as black as coal, and he had grave thoughtful eyes, eyes of a very pale green that appeared almost yellow. His hair was a cap of close-cropped silky black curls, and his face reminded Derek of a cherub. His skin had been blotched with white and pink scars when he had first come, and his neck and chest so badly burned that he could scarcely speak, but he was rapidly healing. And it seemed to Derek that Arion's skin was darkening though he did not understand why.

Earlier this evening, this powerful Rhoshamandes had given Arion his own ancient and healing blood. That was the way with these creatures, to offer their own blood to the host or his wounded guest, to exchange blood when they lodged under one another's roofs for some time, to offer blood as in the olden days humans had offered other humans food and drink and shelter as hospitality.

When they drank they opened their minds whether they wanted to or not.

But then so did Derek when they drank from him, and so they knew what they knew about him, though he sought desperately to hold back.

What would it do for them to have his innermost

secrets? Derek didn't know but he concealed everything from them and always would.

"You won't be here forever," he thought to himself quietly. "Someday when these night monsters are slumbering and helpless, you'll get out of here and you'll find the others. If you are alive, they must be alive." He closed his eyes and he looked at their faces as he remembered them. For most of the twentieth century, Derek had been searching for them. It was his third "life" wandering the earth, looking for the slightest trace of them. But this was a time like no other time and Derek had entered the twenty-first century with even-greater hope of finding the others, only to be snared by this blood-drinking monster.

He was weeping again now. No good. He couldn't hear what they were saying above.

He took a deep easy breath. And once again he listened.

"The Prince," whom Rhoshamandes hated, was a young undeserving maverick blood drinker named Lestat. Lestat had done an "unspeakable" thing to Rhoshamandes, cutting off his left hand and then his arm. They had been reattached, these limbs, as with blood drinkers that was possible, but Rhoshamandes could never forgive the injury, nor "the pardon." For in spite of the pardon, everywhere he went now he bore the mark of Cain.

Derek knew what that was, the mark of Cain.

When he had come awake in this time, it had been a poor priest in Peru who had educated him and taught him the ways of the world—in a farming village not unlike the one Derek had abandoned thousands of years before for the frozen caves of the mountain peaks. Derek had learned the man's religion inside and out, and read the biblical scriptures in Spanish many a time. Derek had not gone down into the cities of South America until the very middle of the century, and it had taken him decades to learn the great literature of the current period in Spanish, Portuguese, and in English. English had proved the most useful language as Derek traveled through North America and Europe.

Roland had brought books down into this prison—books that Derek had read over and over again. **Die Bibel nach Martin Luther;** the **Encyclopaedia Britannica;** a German-English copy of **Faust** by Goethe; the works of Shakespeare in many small ragged volumes, some in German, some in English, some in other tongues; novels by Tolstoy in Russian; a French novel entitled **Madame Bovary;** and English "spy" stories in modern times.

Books on opera. Roland loved opera. That's why he had made this refuge for himself blocks from the opera house. Books of opera stories, yes, he heaped them on the floor for Derek. But the music of these operas was all but forgotten by Derek, who had heard and seen only a handful of vivid and beautiful performances before Roland had lured him into this trap. Opera for Derek had been a late discovery, and one of the most exciting discoveries he had ever made.

Derek could learn any language within minutes, so he knew German and French better than ever from the books, but it bothered him that he did not know how Russian sounded. Roland for the most part spoke English even when not speaking to Derek, who had spoken English when he was captured. Arion's preferred tongue was English too. And so it was with this Rhoshamandes, who lived in England in a great house, apparently very much like this one, though in some lonely seaside place. English, the flexible language of the world.

It was plain that Rhoshamandes was despised amongst blood drinkers. He had slain an ancient one. He blamed this on Amel.

Amel.

There it was again, the name, Amel!

The first time the name had come to the surface of Roland's mind, Derek had scarcely believed it. **Amel.** Was this a reason for this captivity? Or was the mention of the name only a coincidence?

Derek's mind veered back, way back to the very beginning—to the Parents instructing him before he had ever come to this planet—"Now you have a mammalian mind and you will find yourself seeking for meaning where there is no meaning, for patterns where there are no patterns. This is what mammals do. This is only one of the many reasons we are sending you. . . ."

He closed his eyes. Stop this. Concentrate on what **they** are saying! Forget the Parents. You may never see the Parents . . . or any of the others, your beloved others, again.

Rhoshamandes was working himself into a rage. "New York, Paris, London, wherever I go, they are there judging me, cursing me. They spit at me, young and old. They don't dare try to harm me, but they taunt me knowing I won't dare to harm them!"

"Why don't you punish them?" asked Roland. "Why don't you teach a few of them a lesson? The word will go round and—."

"And I'll be visited by the great ones again, won't I? The great Gregory Duff Collingsworth and the Great Sevraine! I could easily vanquish any one of them, but not two or three of them. And what, would I be dragged again before the Prince? As long as he has Amel inside of him, he is untouchable. And I don't want war with them anymore. I want to be as I was before. I want to be left alone!"

The creature's voice broke when he said "alone." And now in that soft, slightly slurred broken voice he confessed to Roland that his longtime companion Benedict had left him, blamed him for everything, and disappeared.

"I think he's with them. I think he's with them at this court of theirs in France, or living in Paris—."

He broke off. "I know he is at the Court," he confessed. "It is agony to say it. He is living with them."

"Well, I'm not your enemy, I told you before," said Roland. "You're welcome in my domain anytime. You are welcome here as long as you care to stay." Roland paused for a minute and then continued. "I don't want any problems with this new regime, this Prince and his ministers. I want things to remain as they were."

"That's what I want too," said Rhoshamandes. "But I cannot go on as things are! I must have it out with them! They must exonerate me fully and completely so that I'm not hounded and harassed wherever I go."

"Is that really what you want?"

"I'm no warrior, Roland. I never was. If Amel hadn't seduced me, I'd never have struck down the great Maharet. I had no quarrel with her! I had no quarrel with her thousands of years ago when I was made a holy warrior of the Queen. I didn't care what we fought for. I broke loose as soon as I could. Amel seduced me, Roland. He convinced me we were all in danger, and then it all fell to pieces, what I attempted, and now the Prince sits in judgment on me, and Benedict has left me. And everywhere I go I am despised. There is no land of Nod for me, Roland."

"Go to them, and talk to them," said Roland. "If they wanted to destroy you, they would have done it already."

"I've been ordered to stay away," said Rhosha-mandes. "My fledglings for the most part are loyal to me. Allesandra is under my roof now. You never knew Allesandra. She's brought me their unequivo-cal warnings. Stay away! The others come and go and with the same warnings."

"They have to be uneasy about you, Rhosh," said Roland.

"Why? What can I do to them!"

"They fear you."

"They have no cause."

Another pause fell between them.

"I hate the Prince," said Rhoshamandes in a dark voice. "I hate him! I would destroy him if I could wrest Amel from him! I'd burn him until—."

"That's why they fear you," said Roland. "You're an enemy who cannot forgive them for winning. And they know this. So what do you really want?"

"I told you. A hearing. Complete exoneration. I want the pack, the rabble, and the trash ordered not to dog my steps and curse at me! I want an end to the fear that some rogue ancient one will blast me with fire for what I did!"

Silence.

Dim distant voices from the boulevard above. Derek could picture it, as he had a thousand times, the big brightly lighted cafés filled with crowded ta-bles, the cars streaming by.

"Tonight, when I came into the opera house, I knew you would be there," said Rhoshamandes.

"I've never once come to the opera here in Budapest that you were not somewhere near at hand. And Roland, I feared you!"

"No need," said Roland. "I don't bend the knee to this Prince. Why would I? You think I'm the only one who has never acknowledged any of these events? There are others like me all over the world. We don't despise him. We don't love him. We want to be left alone."

"Oh, I know that now, but do you realize what it is like to fear that at any turn you might meet some blood drinker who will not honor the Prince's order of restraint and it will be a battle? I detest battle, Roland! I detest it. I tell you, the great Maharet was ready to die. If she hadn't been, I would never have been able to strike her down. I don't have it in me to slay other blood drinkers. I never did! And without Benedict . . . without Benedict . . ."

"And you think if they gave you a hearing, heard you out, invited you to Court, brought you into the inner circle, that Benedict might come back."

Clearly this meant so very much to the one called Rhosh that he didn't even reply.

"Well, listen, Rhosh," said Roland. "I may have something that will help you. But it's a secret, a powerful secret, and I won't share it with you without your solemn oath. Give me that oath, never to reveal what I mean to share with you, and I will share it. And it may be something you and I can offer the Prince for whatever you want. I do think this Prince has it in his power to make things right for you. Seems they love him, the lately begotten. I hear they're flooding to his court from all of Europe. Seems the whole world of the Undead clamors for his love."

"Oh, true, of course, but it's Gregory and Sevraine and Seth who rule, and that spiteful Marius, that liar, that cheat, that secretive sanctimonious Roman, who . . ."

"I know. But all of them will want this secret. Especially Seth and his doctor fledgling Fareed; and Seth is older than you are, Rhosh, and older than the Great Sevraine."

"Seth's not older than Gregory," said Rhosh.

"What is he like?" asked Roland.

"No one really knows, not even Fareed. He's the son of the great Akasha, there is no doubt of it. And it is said he confides in no one as to his secret thoughts, claiming only to be a healer, claiming only to bring other healers into the Blood so that we might be studied, understood."

"I don't like this," said Roland. "No good can come of this studying of the Blood. But it's all the more reason why this Seth will want this secret."

"What are you talking about? What is this secret?"

"I have your oath, that we will ponder this secret together, and that if you have no interest you will not betray my trust?"

"Of course you have it, Roland," said the other

with obvious feeling. "Roland, in all the world . . . except for my Allesandra and my Eleni . . . you are the only one among us who has ever shown me love."

"I've always loved you, Rhosh. Always," said Roland. "It was you who sent me off long ago. I understood. I never held it against you. But others have loved you very much as well."

A bitter sound of derision came from Rhosh.

"Seriously, you know you've been loved," said Roland. "But do I have your vow?"

"You do."

"Come then, I'll show you the bargaining chip, as they say."

Chairs scraping on wooden flooring. Steps above, and, yes, yes, of course, **I am the bargaining chip, as they say!**

Derek heard the bolts thrown back, the creak of hinges, and their softer steps on the winding stone stairs.

Closer and closer.

"How old is this dungeon?" said Rhosh under his breath. "This is more ancient even than my house by the sea."

"Oh, there's a story to it, and to the centuries I lived here before the coming of the city above. Some night I'll tell you all of it."

They had reached Derek's door.

Derek turned his face to the wall. He pulled the blanket up over his shoulder and he started crying again and he couldn't stop it.

One bolt lifted and then another, and the grind of the hinges that were never oiled.

Roland snapped on the overhead light—a single small soiled bulb in a cage in the stone ceiling.

"Well, this is a cozy little dungeon cell, isn't it?" said Rhoshamandes.

"It would be a lot cozier if he would cooperate. I'd provide him with unlimited light, books, food, whatever he asks for. He could have the comforts of music, television, whatever he likes in this room. But he refuses to cooperate. He refuses to tell what he knows."

How Derek hated that tone, always so soft, so polite, as if it meant to say kind things, but it never said kind things. And even more he hated the mocking smile that went with it. He didn't want to see it. He kept his right hand clutched to his head.

Silence.

Derek knew they stood only a few feet from his bed.

"He's not human!" said Rhoshamandes in a whisper.

"That's correct. He is not."

Another silence in which the only sound was that of Derek crying.

"And don't be fooled by his seeming youth," said Roland, his voice growing hard now, hard with anger and frustration. "He looks so innocent, I know, and almost sweet. Just a boy. But he's no boy. And he's as stubborn as I am. I have the distinct impression that he's been on this earth far longer than you or I."

"And you think Seth and Fareed will want this."

"If they don't, they're fools."

"I've never seen anything remotely like this before."

"That's the whole idea. Neither have I. And neither have they. And if there are more of them, if there is a whole tribe of them somewhere, living in our world . . ."

"I see."

Derek took a deep breath, but he said nothing, and did nothing to acknowledge their presence. He shrank into his corner.

He had pushed the bed into the corner. Mammalian impulse, the Parents would have said. But he did feel safer, foolishly safer, in his corner, and with his blanket half covering him.

But the silence of the two was unnerving to Derek.

He wiped at his nose and looked up at Rhoshamandes and what he saw startled him.

Other blood drinkers had come and gone above, but the only two blood drinkers Derek had known were Roland and Arion, and this new one was vastly different, harder, smoother all over, with a face that looked like living marble and eyes that bored into Derek as if they could burn. His olive skin was dark as Roland's skin was dark, but this was superficial, accomplished through a calculated exposure to the sun so that they might more easily pass for human. The being's skin smelled as Roland's skin always smelled, of the sunshine of the day and burnt tissue, and a faint added perfume.

The blood drinker's hair was golden brown, short and wavy, and his clothing was like that of Roland—formal evening dress, with startlingly white linen and shimmering black lapels to his coat, and a long fur-lined cloak that fell to the floor. A ring that was a sapphire, and another that was a diamond, and yet another that was old gold. They all think of themselves as princes, princes of the night and they dress like princes. And they drink the blood of humans as if the humans were animals, as if they themselves had never been human, and surely they had been once. Something had changed them into what they were. No one would make such things as they. That was unthinkable.

"You have no right to keep me here," said Derek. He licked his lips. Finding his handkerchief under his pillow, he wiped at his face. "Whatever I am, whatever you are, you have no right!"

Roland smiled at Rhoshamandes, that vicious cold smile that Derek had come to loathe. His gray eyes were hard and cunning.

"There have to be more like him," said Roland. "But he won't admit it. He won't name them. He won't tell me who he is or what he is or where he came from. And when I drink from him, I see the faces of others . . . a woman and three men. But names, I don't hear names, no matter how deep I probe, and I don't get answers. I don't get words. He had an address in Madrid when I brought him here. I had it watched for a year through my lawyers. It yielded nothing. Why don't you drink from him?"

"Drink from him!" whispered Rhoshamandes. He continued to stare at Derek as if there was something horrible about Derek.

Well, what could that be? Derek was formed exactly like a human male of eighteen to twenty years in age. He had been made to look appealing to humans. He would have combed his hair if he'd been given a comb. He would have cut it had he been given scissors. He had no idea really how he looked now, however, because he had no mirror.

Indeed, there was nothing in this prison cell but the bed, a table beside it, the shelf of books, and a small refrigerator with bland and uninteresting packaged foods that comforted him only a little when he had the stomach to eat them.

"Why don't you try it?" asked Roland. "And drink as much as you like. Drink as you would from any mortal. Drink all that you care to drink."

"What are you saying?"

"That's how I discovered him," said Roland. "Drinking from him. I'd marked him for a victim and didn't realize what I had till he was in my arms.

Arion also drinks from him. Arion has drunk from him plenty. I want you to drink from him, Rhosh. I think you'll be very surprised when you do."

"Why? How?" The new vampire looked fastidious and almost fussy. What a pair! And I'm not fit to be this monster's victim? Derek smiled. He almost laughed.

For one moment Derek's eyes connected with those of Rhoshamandes, or Rhosh. And the compassion in this Rhosh's blue eyes amazed Derek. But then Rhosh looked away, down at the bed, at the walls, at the mean furnishings—anywhere but not back to Derek, who continued to stare at him in silence.

"You can't kill him, Rhosh," said Roland, "no matter how much you drink. Drink as much as you like, I mean this, as much as you ever drank from any victim. You'll never feel the death pass into you because he won't die. He will lie still, without a pulse, without a breath. But then the blood will begin to regenerate and, within an hour or two, he'll be as he is now. Healthy, whole."

"But you don't understand," said Rhoshamandes. He glared at Roland.

"What don't I understand?" The other shrugged.

"I've walked this earth since the early days of ancient Egypt," said Rhoshamandes. "I was born in Crete before the flood. I've traveled the world. I've never seen anything like him! I've never seen anything that looked this human and wasn't human."

"Are you sure?" asked Roland. "Maybe you saw them and you didn't realize what they were. Think back. Think hard. I have seen one other very like him. And so have you. Try to remember."

"When?" asked Rhoshamandes. He seemed slightly annoyed. "Where?"

"The ballet, Rhoshamandes, the theater, the place we always meet, the place we always go together. You and I. Don't you remember? Saint Petersburg, the debut of Tchaikovsky's **Sleeping Beauty** ballet. Think back."

Derek's breath caught in his throat, but he sat very still, disguising his excitement. He made his mind a blank as if these words had no import for him, when in fact they meant everything. **Go on, talk, explain.** His soul ached. He looked away as if he'd become bored.

These creatures could read human minds, this he knew, but they couldn't read his mind, though they constantly pretended that they could. Something in the circuitry of his brain blocked them.

Only when they drank from him could they sometimes access his thoughts, catch from him images he sought unsuccessfully to bury.

"We were there together, you and I," said Roland. "Don't you recall it? It was a wonderful night. And we saw the being together, you and I, across from us in the dress circle. Think back! I can't remember the name of the man who was with the being, but we knew, both of us, that the creature wasn't human."

"Ah, that one," said Rhoshamandes. "Yes. I do remember. The one in the box with Prince Brovotkin. And afterwards, we tried to find them, the Prince and the other one. We couldn't. And you said that the Prince had seen us staring at them, that he'd sensed something."

"We left Saint Petersburg immediately, but we should have stayed, investigated. . . ."

"Yes, of course, it's coming back. But all we had was a glimpse, and we weren't certain."

"Rhosh, remember the being's skin, smooth, dark brown skin, like this one's skin, and the being's hair. The hair was the same, thick like this and with loose curls and the very same golden streak in it, only broader and on the right side of the head."

**Was it possible?**

"I don't remember."

Go on, go on talking, go on, Derek thought desperately, staring off. . . . The tears came to his eyes again. Good, cry, and think about being hungry and wanting some red wine. Red wine, red wine, red wine . . . **Who was it they had seen—with the very same golden streak in his hair! On the right side of his head?** Bury the names as deeply as you can. Bury them, along with the faces, along with the story, along with the betrayal—.

"The thing was identical to this one in a number of ways," Roland insisted. "Taller, yes, with larger eyes, yes, but the hair was exactly the same. It was exceptionally long, unfashionably long, it gave the creature a savage look, unkempt, almost feral, but the creature was smooth shaven. This one has no need of a razor. And that one had no need either, I wager. Well, whether you remember or not, I remember. And this creature likely knows that creature and how many others like them there are and, more important, **what** they are, and how they came to be here."

Rhoshamandes was pondering, then very slowly he said, "I see what you mean." But he wasn't all that interested. He gave a dismissive shrug. He was frustrating Roland and Roland was revealing it.

Derek looked at them out of the corner of his eye. He couldn't conceal his excitement. He glared at Roland.

"Ah, and in all this time, you've kept this from me!" said Derek.

Roland glanced at Derek and gave him the usual maddeningly gentle smile.

"When you tell me what you know, Derek," he said, "I will tell you what I know. You are not friendly. You do not cooperate."

"You are a monster," said Derek, clenching his teeth. "You've kept me here for ten years, and this is wrong! By any law under the sun and the moon, this is wrong. I am not your property. I am not your slave."

But what did he really care! He had just been given the single most valuable bit of information he had ever received since he'd come awake in this time, since he'd awakened in the humble hut of the priest high in the Andes. Another one! Another one lives. Another one perhaps found in the frozen wastes of Siberia, another one found in the ice where Derek had slept for thousands of years, the ice to which he'd retreated in despair two times to freeze as he'd been frozen before.

And Amel. This Rhoshamandes had spoken more about Amel than Derek had ever glimpsed when Roland drank from him.

This Rhoshamandes creature glared at Derek again as if he were a little intrigued but repelled. "Can't read a thing from him."

"Not until you drink his blood," said Roland.

Rhoshamandes stepped back as if he couldn't stop himself.

"Rhoshamandes, listen to me," said Derek. "You're ancient. You come from times long past, before this one came into the world. I heard you speaking upstairs! Surely you have some morality. You remember something of human reverence for right and wrong. You spoke of a prince who injured you, affronted you. But it was about right and wrong, your quarrel, was it not? Listen to me. That I'm kept here, as a bottomless fount of blood for this monster, is wrong!"

He had begun to cry again. Oh, why had they made him the "most" human! Why did he have to be the one who felt things so deeply? He turned away. In a flash he pictured the others with him, comforting him the way they had always done. And he told himself as he had countless times, If you are alive, they are alive. If you are walking this earth once more, they could be walking this earth.

But something was changing in the room.

Rhoshamandes sat down beside him on the bed.

Slowly Derek turned and looked at him. Such pure skin, pure as liquid, as if it had been poured over the being, as if it had never been human! Yes, I look human, Derek thought, and these beings cease to be human apparently with every passing year.

"I understand you're here against your will," the blood drinker said leaning close to him. "I want to drink. I want you to yield to me, to allow it."

Derek laughed bitterly. "What, you insist on my permission?"

Roland laughed silently; his face was the picture of scorn.

But before Derek could say more he felt the loathsome creature's hand on his left shoulder and the being's face pressing close to the right side of his neck.

"Remember, you cannot kill him," said Roland. "Look deep, Rhosh. Drag the truth from him in the blood."

Why was the ancient one hesitating?

Derek gazed up at Roland, the white-haired Roland with the graven wrinkles of mortal old age inscribed forever perhaps in his long oval face. Roland of the cold indifferent eyes. Before Arion had come, this face was the only face that Derek had seen for nine years.

"Show him no pity, Rhosh," said Roland looking directly at Derek. "I have tried everything with him. Nothing works. He will not tell me anything."

Rhosh drew back, as if he'd bent to kiss and thought the better of it, and that probing right hand of his clasped Derek's head and smoothed Derek's hair.

In spite of himself Derek felt chills, the sweet high-pitched chills of being touched by another with seeming affection, even one as cold and inhuman as this being.

He closed his eyes and swallowed. The tears poured down his cheeks.

"Such a beautiful creature," whispered Rhosh. "And such a youthful voice. Such a pleasing voice."

"This Prince, does he believe in right and wrong?" asked Derek. "Take me to him, use me as your bargaining chip, as you call it. Maybe he's better than you and that one who keeps me here as if I were a bird in a cage, or a fish in a bowl of water! I have a heart, don't you understand it! I have a . . ."

"A soul?" asked Rhoshamandes.

"Everything that is conscious, aware of itself, has a soul," said Derek.

"Everything?" asked Roland. "How do you know?"

"I know," said Derek. But he didn't know. He really had no idea. He knew exactly how he'd been made, and by whom, and he had no idea whether or not a soul was included in the package. He couldn't bear to think that he didn't have a soul. He refused to even entertain the idea. But you can't really behave that way towards ideas, can you? With his whole being, he **knew** that he had a soul. He was a soul! And his soul was Derek, and Derek suffered and Derek wanted to live! And Derek wanted to be freed from this prison.

Rhoshamandes embraced him gently and brought Derek closer to him, and once again he bent to drink.

Derek closed his eyes, and felt the fang teeth touching his neck. He sought to empty his mind, to banish all words, all images, and to feel only the sharp prick of the teeth, the soft kiss of the creature's breath.

"Hmmm, warm, salty, warm as a human being," whispered Rhoshamandes, his voice now drunken even though he hadn't drunk. That was the way with them. Even before they feasted on him, the hunger made them drunken. Their eyes glazed over. Their hearts tripped. They became their thirst. That's how and why they could suck the life out of humans, and out of Derek. They turned into beasts. They looked like angels, but they were actually beasts.

"Drink, and find my soul," said Derek, "and know what you do is wrong. But then it's always wrong when you drink, isn't it? Everyone you kill has a soul."

"Open to me, tender one," said the stranger. "I mean you no harm."

Derek closed his eyes and turned away. Then came the sharp fine stinging pain and immediately behind it the rush of sweetness, of more of those rippling chills on his neck, his back, down his arms and legs. The world dissolved, and with it the fetid dust and soot of the dungeon cell. And he was floating as this thing drew the blood out of him in deep slow draughts.

In a mighty unexpected flash Derek saw a long table, blood drinkers on either side of it, and a blond-haired figure with an ax in his hand. The Prince! What a comely being, and with such a beguiling smile. Down came the ax and the Prince held up the severed left hand. They stared at each other in rage, Rhoshamandes and the Prince, and the blond Prince hacked off Rhoshamandes's arm! Derek saw the hand and the limb on the table. He felt the pain that Rhosh had felt, splintering, burning into his shoulder and then gone.

**Tell me where my son is. Or you will die.**

So that was it, was it? Derek was growing weaker. "You held his son captive, that's what you did, and you wonder that he hurt you? I would hurt you, if I could. I would hack you limb from limb and I've never hurt anyone. I am sworn never to hurt human beings on this planet, never, but your humanity long ago went dry inside you, and I would cheerfully torture you. . . ."

It was gone. He was gone. No more Derek the fighter who could look for anything in the blood drinker's mind. He was drifting without a body, without a place.

Dream.

Atalantaya, the splendid city of Atalantaya . . . no words, don't give them words. Look. But don't name. But then he was just there.

They were gone, the monsters of the present moment in Budapest.

Derek was in great Atalantaya with the others, his kindred, his own—Kapetria and Garekyn and Welf, all of them together, holding hands, his sister and his brothers—and they were watching as the Great One appeared. **Amel.** The Great One was unmistakable, a fine figure of a human male with a skin of unearthly paleness, and green eyes, and full reddish-golden hair. They'd made Amel to look like a god. But they'd made Derek and Kapetria and their brothers to look only human. Well, he did look like a god, if gods are pale and shining.

"Amel," said Kapetria.

Derek didn't want words, no, but he couldn't stop them, couldn't stop the words they were speaking. He was in the dream but not in control of it.

And for one moment the world was frozen. Nothing moved; nothing lived; the world was lifeless and meaningless and the voice of Rhoshamandes said: **"Amel?"**

Gone. No more Rhosh. No more voice. No more defenses. Just now . . . the warm sunlight pouring through the great clear luracastric dome of Atalantaya, beautiful Atalantaya . . .

Voice of the Parents. You must get inside the

dome. Remember, you must strike against him inside the dome.

All around them stood the populace of Atalantaya, dark eyed and dark haired as they were, Derek and Welf and Garekyn and Kapetria. But there came the Great One with the unearthly attributes of the god.

**"Our mistake, you see," said the Parents, "because he has come to believe that he is a god."**

In his hands the Great One held an oval object, shimmering in the sunlight, and all around the Great One the people were crying out, pointing, cheering, bowing to him, and calling out their praise. All around them in the windows of the high buildings and towers were faces turned to see the Great One. People stood way above on the rooftops looking down on the freshly turned field that lay ready for the object which the Great One now planted in the moist, fragrant soil.

Suddenly everyone was singing, singing in a rolling wordless melody. People put their arms around one another and began to sway as they sang. Kapetria put her arm around Derek, her familiar smile flashing warmly on him. And Derek held tight to Garekyn. And the fountains poured forth their water, raining down on the oval as the oval began to grow larger and larger and then to break open, its thin casing peeled back as if into a collection of petals out of which the great tall glistening shoots began to grow.

"But does the singing make it happen?" Derek asked Kapetria.

"No, beloved," she said. "It's entirely chemical. All of this is chemical. Everything you see here is chemical. But don't you see the genius of it? He is making the common people feel a part of it; he has given them a ritual so that they are united in it. Oh, he has been so clever, so very clever."

The Great One stood back with his thumbs hooked in his leather belt watching them all as they sang and danced, his eyes moving up the towers across from him to the thousands of beings clustered on all those terraces and in all those windows. How proud he was, how happy. Tears hovered in his eyes. He stood there, weight on his left foot, the other leg relaxed, his long blue tunic hanging loose around him, such richly colored wool, splendidly stitched with golden acorns at the hem, and so bright the buckle that sparkled on his belt and the buckles on his shoulders. How he gloried in it, and then his eyes fixed on Derek and even for Derek he smiled.

Amel.

The great clear shoots of luracastria were spreading out now, broadening, growing thicker, and then transforming themselves into great sheets of clear shimmering material rising higher and higher and growing wider and wider as the immense surrounding crowd began to cheer as well as sing.

Derek stood amazed watching the building grow out and upwards, watching walls and windows rising and forming in front of him, seeing the entire interior and exterior of the tower unleashed from the oval as if its birth into growth couldn't be stopped. It was like seeing a great tree grow from a seed in a matter of minutes, thrusting forth its mighty limbs, its tiniest leaves, its flowers, its seeds.

Everywhere the people laughed, shouted, and pointed, punctuating the waves of singing which never stopped. Up and up went the tower until it was now as tall as all the others, a splendid edifice of doorways and balconies and windows, grown out of the oval which was now lost beneath it, as its tentacles anchored themselves deep in the earth. Derek could hear them. Why, the thing had been growing downwards as surely as it had grown upwards.

"Behold the luracastria," said one of the people beside them. "I see you don't know what it is. Everything in the center of Atalantaya is built of luracastria, behold luracastria—in one form or another, even the great dome is luracastria."

Derek was so happy. So very happy. How could anyone want to destroy all this, destroy the Great One, destroy all these people, these happy multitudes, these souls whose songs rose Heavenward under the dome? It was unthinkable to him, as unthinkable to him as the idea of his own death. A fear took hold of him, so terrible that he began to tremble.

It was fading. No, I don't want to go. I want to

be with you, Kapetria. Hold tight to me! Kapetria, I'm alive, I exist still. Where are you! Find me. Welf, Garekyn, find me.

Darkness.

Blackness.

No sound from his own heart. Yes, a human would be dead now. He knew this, but it seemed to take forever for him to know it again, and know it was finished, and he would have his mind and his body back.

Surely Rhoshamandes had let him go. But Derek couldn't feel anything, neither up nor down, or right or left. But his brain was working. The cells in his bone marrow were working.

"But I have killed him!"

"No, believe me, you have not. He looks dead; he sounds dead; he feels dead. But he's not dead. Just be patient. The thing is not dead. It's what happens to him when he's assaulted; he loses consciousness; he stops breathing; but he's not dead."

Silence. Then the fragrance of the room again, damp stone, the soot from the little fireplace for which there was neither wood nor coal. The smell of the blood drinkers, of skin that had been in the sun to burn it by day as they slept so they could pass for human, and the scents of their clothes and their perfume. The smell of books, of old pages. **Thou know'st 'tis common; all that lives must die, passing through nature to eternity.** Well, not me.

"It tasted like human blood, the finest of human blood, only it was thicker, and a little sweeter. Just a little . . ."

"Yes."

"It has nutrients that human blood does not have."

"Perhaps. But I don't know what the Hell they are. It lasts longer."

"What **is** this creature?"

"It would be nice to have an entire stable of such creatures, wouldn't it?" Roland laughed. And laughed. How Derek hated that laugh. "And look at it, the blood's already being regenerated. Look at his hands, his fingers, his nails."

Something touched Derek but he couldn't locate the sensation. All through him he felt tingling and the tingling was Derek.

But they continued to talk. And his soul recorded every heartless word they spoke.

"He doesn't die, not from anything," said Roland, the cruel one, the one without feeling. "Not from starvation, not from thirst. I've left him a month without either food or drink. I haven't tried other means. But what did you see? What did you see that he couldn't conceal? Did he give you anything?"

Then came the warmer voice of Rhoshamandes. . . .

"I saw this place, this spectacular city, and this amazing phenomenon. It was as if a skyscraper, an intricate high-rise tower made of glass were growing from an egg!"

No. How did he see these things? Help me. Derek felt the tears slide down his cheeks. He tried to raise a hand to his face but he couldn't find his hand. It would be a while before he could feel his body again. But he could feel his tears. **Help me. Find me. Get me out of here—Garekyn. Garekyn, was it you that they saw in Saint Petersburg? Garekyn, your brother is alive.**

"But it was a great city, humming as if alive with electricity, running water, power, illimitable power—and the towers, I've never beheld anything like it, these giant spectacular towers . . . everything looked to be translucent as if made of glass . . . and beyond there were huge walls of glass . . . a great roof of glass. . . ."

"Could you identify the city!"

"No, I've never seen anything like it! And I saw his companions with him, creatures who looked like him as you said."

"I knew it. I knew you could go deeper than I've ever gone," said Roland. "What else, tell me!"

"They were like him, but one was a female, and they did all have the gold streaks in their black hair. They had these streaks to identify themselves to one another. Or identify them to someone else. And there were names, but I couldn't catch them, I couldn't catch the name of the city, the city had a name, though, I knew it—but I caught one name, one name and that name was Amel."

"Well, he's heard us talking of Amel for years. And now with the Prince and the Court, he's heard Arion and me speaking of Amel over and over. He's heard me speaking of Amel from time to time with others who pass through. He can hear keenly. He can hear the conversations we have in the rooms above."

"No, the name was coming from that time and that place, I'm sure of it, and he didn't want me to hear it, but he had no control over it. Roland, this Great One, this one who planted the seed that grew into a skyscraper, it was Amel!"

They were moving away. They were leaving him. The door shut, the key turned in the lock. The bolts slid into place. Soft footfalls on the staircase.

"Describe him."

"Reddish hair, golden. Tall. Finely dressed, dressed as if in my time. Roland, their clothes, their clothes were simple, wool but mostly silk, like the clothes of my time, but it wasn't my time. It wasn't any time or place I've ever seen. Roland, it could have been long before my time!"

Farther and farther away they moved.

Derek strained to hear them. **What have I done!**

Rhoshamandes talked excitedly. "This place, I don't know where it is, but don't you see, Roland, don't you understand what this means?"

They lapsed quite abruptly into another language. For a moment the words confused Derek, but he had only to wait, to concentrate before they became clear. He sensed, however, that this was an older and simpler language, a language they'd shared aeons ago. Soon the sense was clear.

"No, what does it mean?" asked Roland. He sounded sullen and cross, Roland. He had not the wit or passion of his friend, Rhoshamandes.

"Good Lord, Roland, if Amel was there in this place with this creature and his friends, don't you see, he's not a spirit, not a spirit at all, he's a ghost!"

"What does that matter? These spirits come from somewhere, don't they? Maybe they're all ghosts. What's the difference between a spirit and a ghost? I've never heard of any difference. What does that matter to us?"

"But Roland, if he's a ghost, if he lived before, if he had a personality and power, why this might change everything!"

"I don't see that it changes anything," said Roland. "But if Fareed and Seth are as interested as you are, they'll want this creature most certainly! They'll be willing to pay for him, Rhosh, pay a great deal. I could use that payment. I could use it for centuries to come. I need such a payment."

"I can give you all the gold you want, Roland. Think no more on any problem with gold. I'll pay you handsomely for the creature now. But you're not grasping the significance . . ."

Far away. Sounds of traffic. Vibrations moving down through the earth under the traffic.

Rhoshamandes was still speaking in a rush of excited words, Derek could no longer understand him.

"I still say . . ."

"No, you're wrong." And then it was a rumbling again like water in the pipes of this house, or cars on the boulevard above. And the monsters had left the house.

Derek sat up. He was nauseated, weak, thirsting. He grabbed for the pitcher on the table beside him. Empty. The monsters had left him without water. He lay back down again thirsting from every pore in his body. With all his will, he tried to feel vigor but his body was deadweight.

All he could hear now was the vibration of Rhoshamandes's voice and then he raised his voice in exasperation. "No, no, they mustn't know anything about this for now, Roland. Nothing. No one must know of this until I think this through."

Derek fell back on the pillow, hungry and cold. He stared at the distant lightbulb, this soiled ugly light shining in its rusted cage, and he cried with all his soul.

"Chop you up, rend you limb from limb," he whispered. "If only . . ." When had he, Derek, ever thought such vengeful thoughts? And to think he'd never understood this dimension of human beings, and now he was as poisoned with dreams of vengeance as any human could be.

He rolled over on his left side, and brought the blanket up over his shoulder. Was it safe now to remember that moment, when the tower had blossomed and grown from the egg? Was it all right to remember their being together, roaming Atalantaya together in those endless warm days and nights? He was walking again, with his arm around Garekyn under the great arching green banana leaves, and everywhere he looked there were flowers, pink and red and yellow and purple, flowers of such colors—petals caught swirling in the breeze.

Vines climbed the walls of luracastria, and clusters of petals shivered above him, clusters shaped like clusters of grapes.

Arion woke him. Arion had come in and sat on the bed beside him.

"I have something for you," he said.

"Water, please, I beg you."

"Oh, I brought that as well," said Arion.

Derek sat up. He opened the glistening plastic bottle of cold water and he drank and drank. "I love you for this," he whispered. "I've had no water in days and nights."

"I know. I've put water for you in the refrigerator. I've hidden several bottles under the bed. And I brought you this too."

It was an apple, a bright red apple. Derek took it without a word and devoured it down to the core and then swallowed the seeds and the stem. How fresh and sweet it tasted. He lay back staring at the ceiling. So sweet. He saw the endless fruit trees of Atalantaya, the yellow and orange fruit. You could pick the fruit anywhere at any time. But don't think about it lest this creature, good as he is, can read your mind.

Arion sat there staring off. He was dressed simply in a sweatshirt and jeans and an old leather jacket with shiny worn elbows. He had none of the elegance of Roland, none of the vanity, none of the preoccupation with subtle ornament. He looked sad, so terribly sad.

"Take what you want from me," said Derek. "I'd beg you to let me out of here but I know you can't."

Arion smiled, but not at Derek. Then he removed something small from his pocket. An iPod. It had to be, though Derek hadn't seen one in years. It had a thin white cord attached and an earpiece.

"Wait till morning," he said, "when you're sure all are sleeping, and then listen to this thing. It's stocked with music and archived radio broadcasts."

Oh, this was a treasure!

Derek accepted the device gratefully and tried to figure it out but unlike his last iPod, his iPod of ten long years ago, this one was a flat piece of glass.

With a few quick taps, Arion brought it to life. Derek followed his fingers, and heard a surge of music, a surge of mingled voices. He put the white earbud in his ear, and heard the throaty voice of the woman singing a song he'd known and loved, "Undercover Agent for the Blues."

"Tina!" he whispered. Oh, this was priceless. This

was too wondrous. This was like a magic portal out of his despicable prison.

He bent forward and put his arm around Arion and kissed his cold face. Like stone, it felt, so smooth, as if it were polished stone. They all felt that way, these blood drinkers.

"Now look here, pay attention," said Arion. "I'm going to show you how to find one particular radio archive."

"How will this radio archive help me?" Derek asked.

Arion sat there silent for a moment, pondering, his brows knitted and the iPod held idly in his hand.

"I don't know," Arion said. "But it's our radio, our broadcast. . . ."

"I've heard of this before. From the Court, the Court of the Prince."

"Yes, and no. I don't know. I think it comes from America. But it's something. There are two sound threads, one for humans and a lower one, one only for us. But you'll be able to hear it. Listen to it. Listen to it and maybe you'll come to understand us." He showed Derek the charger. He took it and plugged it in behind the little refrigerator. "Of course if or when he finds out you have it, he'll take it away."

"And you'll be in grave trouble for giving it to me."

"I don't care about that," said Arion. "I may be gone by then. I don't know. It is a canker in me that you're imprisoned here. But I cannot sin against my host." He stood by the refrigerator with his hands in his pockets. He was staring off again. He did not like eye contact. "I feel so sorry for you," he said. "It's full of music. Just listen to the music if you want to. I couldn't bear to think of you down here, all alone, and like this."

There were sounds above.

"Shut it off, and hide it," whispered Arion. "And make it work after we are asleep. I must go."

In less than an hour the great house had become a tomb. The mortal servants would not come till late afternoon, and they never ventured down the stairs. The city of Budapest roared with the world of daytime.

Derek played with the iPod. It was not so complicated at all. And in no time he'd found the broadcast archive and found himself fascinated to hear the unnatural voice of a blood drinker addressing the whole wide world under cover of music at a decibel level humans couldn't possibly hear. Now that was marvelously clever. He lay back on his bed listening.

"Benji Mahmoud here from New York this New Year's Eve, beloved brothers and sisters in the Blood—to report that all is well at the great Court in France, to which all are welcome. And to let you know that our beloved Prince has now officially turned the night-by-night governance of the tribe over to the Council of Elders, who will soon be drawing up for us our own constitution and laws.

In the meantime, those who wish to be in the good graces of the Court know how to conduct themselves. No more arguments, quarrels, pitched battles. No more feeding on the innocent. Brothers and Sisters, remember, as I say so often, we are no longer parentless!"

Derek wept again. He couldn't help it. He got up, clutching the little gadget as he listened and walked round and round the little room. He drank more of the water that Arion had brought him, all the while listening. He did not care that there was no purpose to which he could put this new knowledge of his captors. This was a voice speaking to him, and he was not alone.

# 2

# Lestat

IT WASN'T HARD to find them. The old monastery of Saint Alcarius was northeast of Paris, in a deep forest near the Belgian border. Gremt's secret headquarters for the ancient Order of the Talamasca.

Amel and I were both determined to pay Gremt a visit. We should have done this long before now, and I was ashamed that we hadn't.

Did I really want to be here just now? Well, no. I wanted to be across the sea, in New Orleans, because I'd persuaded my beloved fledgling Louis to meet me there. But this visit was important. And my mind was boiling with questions about and for Gremt and his spectral companions.

First things first, however. I had to apologize for not inviting them to Court and not coming here sooner.

In the village, a quaint and clean little place beneath which the past slept without a word, they told me the owners of Saint Alcarius were hermits of sorts, and that all their affairs were handled through a firm in Paris. They wouldn't let me in "up there." Don't bother to knock. In the summer months, the tourists and hikers were always welcome in the gardens, however. There were benches for them under the old trees.

The private road was unpaved and near impassable. Even in this light snow, we'd have a time with it.

But we'd come from Château de Lioncourt in a hefty four-wheel-drive vehicle, and we found our way easily over the potholes and the debris that hadn't been cleared in some months. I have been for decades enchanted with powerful motorcars. I loved driving them and feeling the surge of power when I stepped on the gas.

The moon was full, and the wintry night was bright and cold. I saw their lights through the ancient yew trees, and as we drew closer, I saw more and more lights go on in the old square tower and the high diamond-paned windows of the stone façade. A quick scan told me there were many beings inside, though what they were, I couldn't tell. Ghosts, spirits, blood drinkers.

I got out of the car and told Thorne and Cyril to wait for me. I couldn't go anywhere now without Thorne and Cyril. Those were the orders of Marius and Gregory, and Seth, and Fareed, and Notker, and any "elder" that happened to be hanging about "the Court." And the elders ran the Court, no doubt about it. I was the Prince, yes, but treated often like

a twelve-year-old under the thumb of a committee
of regents. They were the ones running things, and
the host could not venture out ever anywhere without his bodyguards.

Thorne, the big redheaded and hulking Viking,
would have given up his immortal life for me; and
for reasons I'd never fathomed, so would the obdu-
rate cynical Egyptian, Cyril, who pledged his loyalty the moment he walked through the door of the
Château. "I've always wanted to have someone to
whom I could pledge my all," he'd said with a shrug.
"And now you're it. No use arguing."

"You have the Core now," said Gregory whenever
I protested. "You fail to seek shelter well before sunrise, and the young ones burn!" As if I didn't know
this! Well, in truth, I hadn't even thought of it once
before devouring the Core, had I? But I knew it.
I knew it perfectly well. I didn't need Thorne and
Cyril dogging my every step.

Courtly life, endless demands for audiences, and
bodyguards who wouldn't leave my side. It was coming home to me every night just what it meant to be
the Prince and to have Amel inside me, in more ways
than they knew. And I had built up this secret fantasy that the one person in all the world who would
let me moan about it was Louis. Ah, Louis . . .

As for Amel, his infinitely mobile consciousness came and went, though the ethereal command
center remained rooted in my brain. He could talk

endlessly for nights on end, or vanish for as long as a week.

Amel was with me now, of course, since he'd nagged me incessantly for weeks to approach "the spirits."

I could always feel Amel's presence, or feel his absence, and sometimes I could feel his abrupt desertions, as if my whole body had been shaken. When he was here, it was the sensation of a warm hand on the back of my head, only inside of me, and I wondered if he had full control of how I experienced that telltale sign. I sensed he didn't.

How did he do his traveling? Was he like a giant spider skittering at lightning speed over the spokes of the visible web that united us all, or did he fly blind towards the heated or throbbing pulse of another consciousness? He wouldn't tell me. And every time I asked, I had the uncomfortable perception that he didn't understand the question. That's what disturbed me more than anything else—the things he didn't seem able to understand.

Most of his long silences were the result of his inability to understand my questions, and his need to think about all aspects of what I was asking him.

I was wondering so many things about Amel that I couldn't organize my thoughts. But of one thing I was certain. He wanted to see those spirits close at hand, and that's why he'd pushed me to come here. And he wanted me to go to New Orleans later on.

"I know you have some evil motive of your own," I said aloud as I stood there in the snow. "But just be quiet for once and let me do what I want to do."

I walked up the snowy drive. Lantern-style lights burned beside the ironbound double doors.

"Evil motive, evil motive, evil motive . . . ," he sang. "What nonsense, evil motive! You are a fool. If you neglect these monster spirits, they might turn on you."

"And then what?" I asked.

Gremt, Teskhamen, and Hesketh claimed to have founded the Talamasca over a thousand years ago. No one doubted their word on it, or that they still acted as guardians for the Talamasca today. But the human Talamasca knew nothing of its monstrous foundation, and the human Order carried on as it always had, studying the psychic phenomena of the world with scholarly respect.

I heard Amel laugh bitterly inside me, the voice no one else could hear. "Just remember. Spirits lie, and they lie, and they lie. And don't bother to knock. They 'heard' you thirty miles off. Teskhamen is in there. Teskhamen is a blood drinker, and if you don't think I've been inside Teskhamen of late surveying this place from stem to stern, you're an idiot."

"Okay, so now I'm an idiot and a fool in the same contentious breath," I said.

The doors opened. I was standing in a flood of warm light, and the air was warm too and fragrant with the scent of wax candles, old wood, old books.

Gremt stood there, looking as always as solid as a human being. Short neatly groomed black hair, smooth symmetrical face marvelously eloquent of human courtesy and apprehension. But there was none of the gracious generosity in his expression that I had seen in the past. His long priestly **thawb** or soutane was of dark heavy blue velvet, and he wore a dark gray cashmere scarf tucked inside the simple collar, as if he could feel the cold.

"Lestat," he said and made me an old-fashioned bow. "I'm glad you've come." But something was wrong, and I felt I knew what it was.

He stepped aside for me to enter. The bodyguards approached, and I put out my hand with a forbidding gesture. And just to bring it home, I sent a quick telepathic blast to force the Range Rover backwards some ten feet, crunching and crashing through the overgrown gravel. They hated it, but they stood stock-still.

"Never mind them," I said to Gremt. "They'll wait outside."

"They may come in if you wish," he said, but he was distracted, conflicted, ill at ease. He struggled to appear friendly, gesturing again for me to enter.

"I don't wish," I replied. "But thank you, just the same. I can't go anywhere without them, which I accept, but I don't want them breathing down my neck."

He shut the door behind me and led me through a hollow shadowy stone alcove into what might have been in ancient times a great hall. Now it was a great library, with a crude old fireplace on the long front wall, a giant gaping affair with carved lions' heads, and a blazing fire. Sweet the smell of the oak burning. But I could also detect the distinct scent of natural gas mingled with it.

The air was amazingly warm for a place populated with spirits and an ancient vampire. Maybe their bodies did feel it. I liked it. I don't need warmth, but I enjoy it. And I enjoyed this place a lot.

The bookshelves had been recently built, and smelled of fresh wood, turpentine, and wax. The books were orderly, and at opposite ends of the hall were large old Renaissance Revival–style desks, heaped with papers and old black telephones. There was a fancy harpsichord to the far left of the fireplace, obviously a new instrument but skillfully made to reproduce all the excellent engineering of the original instruments and carefully painted to resemble something from my time. I saw electric sconces on the walls, and a low-hanging iron chandelier with a tracery of electric wires stealthily following its chain from the arched ceiling, but nothing illuminated the room but the fire.

I'm a sucker for this sort of thing.

There were thick wool carpets everywhere on the stone floor, mostly Persian in design, worn, faded, but comfortable underfoot.

A grouping of large knobby Renaissance oak chairs was clustered before the hearth and there sat

Teskhamen and Magnus. No one else about. But I could hear beings moving in the rooms above. Someone up in the ancient square tower. Scents of modern plasterwork and paint, of copper plumbing and electrical equipment in distant rooms giving off the inevitable soft hum. A place of divine atmosphere and every modern comfort.

Teskhamen and Magnus rose from their chairs to greet me, and I braced myself for the encounter with Magnus, for looking into the eyes of this one who'd made me, and died on a pyre less than an hour after doing that, leaving me his powerful blood, his fortune, his home, and nothing else. Maybe our splendid vampire doctors, Seth and Fareed, could tell whether my blood had a discernible mixture that undeniably connected me to Magnus. Fareed was working on that. Fareed was working on everything.

I sensed a great unease on the part of all three of these creatures.

"Don't be their plaything," Amel said inside me. "Magnus is nothing as solid as he looks. He's a pathetic ghost. Notice that his monkly robes are part of the illusion. He isn't solid enough to risk real clothing or real shoes like Gremt."

I noted this. And I was certain that the last time I'd seen Magnus, he'd been the image of a living creature with real clothes. I wondered why the change.

"Can they hear you?" I asked Amel without moving my lips.

"How do I know?" he said. "Teskhamen can scour

your mind as well as any of the old blood drinkers if you let him. He can't shut me out any more than the others. But ghosts? Spirits? Who the Hell knows what they sense or hear? Get on with it. I don't like it." This was disingenuous. He was excited. I knew it.

"Patience," I responded telepathically. "I've waited too long in coming."

He made a soft disgusted fuming sound, but went still.

Magnus gestured for me to take the chair on the far left, closest to the fire. I saw none of that doting affection in his eyes that I'd seen last time we met in New York.

Nobody extended a hand. I didn't extend my hand.

I sat down and folded my hands over the wooden arms of the chair, liking the feel of the carving. It was a new piece of furniture but a splendid imitation of something fashioned in the time of Shakespeare. And above the fireplace I spied a great intricate tapestry that was also new, full of vibrant new dyes and chemical threads, but exquisitely rendered—with medieval saints clustered about the Virgin Mary and the Baby Jesus on a golden throne. I loved the thickets of trees surrounding them, and the birds in the branches, and the tiny creeping things amid leaves and flowers. I wondered if mortal hands had made this, or had it been done by manically focused blood drinker weavers with preternatural patience and eye for detail.

"I appreciate all these many refinements," I said,

my eyes sweeping the arched ceiling. "This was once a windowless croft, wasn't it? And you cut those big windows and made them beautiful with thick glass and iron lattices. You have kept this place well enough for the ghosts of old monks to be happy here, haven't you?"

"Yes, I think so," said Gremt, but he was forcing his smile.

"Well, this old ghost is happy here," said Magnus in a low rich voice. "I can tell you that much." I heard the past in the voice. I heard words spoken I hadn't remembered for decades. **There, my son, is the passageway to my treasure. . . .**

I tried not to recoil, but to meet his smile with my own.

Amel was right. His brown habit and soft brown leather slippers were part of the illusion. If he vanished, he'd leave nothing behind. And there was something else I observed about him immediately. His facial features, their proportions, and the details of his soft ashen-blond hair, they weren't fixed. They were not flickering like an image on a bad movie screen, but the entire illusion was fragile as if vulnerable to the slightest movement of the air. I don't think a mortal could have detected this. And I sensed it took a colossal amount of energy from him to remain solid-looking and stable. His intense gaze, his brilliant eyes fixed on mine, was the most vital thing about him.

Gremt, the ancient one, the pillar of the Talamasca, had no such difficulty. He appeared solid enough to be torn limb from limb. He looked no less real than he had at our earlier meetings, his obvious discomfort having no effect whatsoever on his visual anatomy. Spirit, powerful spirit.

Teskhamen was of course a blood drinker survivor of the millennia, old before he gave the Blood to Marius. He was his predictable elegant self, thick wavy white hair cut short, his skin darker than it had appeared when I'd first laid eyes on him some six months before.

They had resumed their places. Gremt closest to me, and Teskhamen beside him. Magnus at the far end just opposite. I looked at Teskhamen's skin, I could smell the sun when I looked at it.

A sudden jolt of pain passed through me. I'd never be able again to expose myself to the sun in any way, not to darken my skin, not to test my endurance, not to . . . Because if I did the young ones might burn up in seconds. There had to be some way around that. There had to be some way to test the old legend.

"I was a victim of the old legend," said Teskhamen. His face was bright, friendly. Whatever was bothering the other two, it was not affecting him. He was so lean and sharply contoured that his bones were part of his beauty.

He was also perfectly at ease with me—self-possessed and almost charming. He wore a dark gray wool suit of English tailoring and fine narrow hand-made high string shoes with wing tips, fashionable.

"I burned up in my cell within the oak here in this very country," he said, "when the Queen was exposed to the sun in Egypt." He spoke evenly, calmly. Only his many gold and jeweled rings looked ancient. "I felt the raging fire," he said. "I barely survived it. You know all this but let me verify it for you. Believe me, the old legend is quite true. All Marius ever told you of me is true. You hold my life in your hands as you hold the life of the entire tribe in your hands. Go forth into the sun, and we'll all feel it, some to survive, some to suffer agonies and wish they hadn't, and some to be immolated entirely."

"He's patronizing you," Amel hissed. "How can you stand him? Either you leave here or I will." But he didn't want to leave. I knew he didn't.

"Be still," I said silently. "I want to be here and I'm staying here, and there's nothing you can do about it." He was happy but wouldn't admit it.

Teskhamen laughed softly.

"Tell our blessed friend I can hear him well enough," said Teskhamen. "But be assured, Prince, we're glad to see you. I don't know that we are glad to receive **him**. But we are glad to see you. We didn't expect you. We'd more or less given up on hearing from you. We're very glad you've come."

The others said nothing. Gremt stared into the fire. He did not appear rude or hostile, but preoccupied, preoccupied enough to ignore me, preoccupied and anguished. His eyes moved uneasily over the burning logs, and there was a subtle gnawing quality to his lips, as if he truly was flesh and blood and unable to conceal his misery.

Magnus, who sat across from me, seemed supernaturally still. Then something came over him. I felt it as surely as I saw it, and in a flash, he was altered indescribably and completely. The made-up ghost was gone. There was the monster I knew from the night of my mortal death, the same hollow withered white cheeks and huge black eyes, and mop of long tangled black hair streaked with shining silver. A dark cold chill passed through me.

"Remember, any ghost is working with your brain, my beloved," said Amel, "to make you see what you are seeing."

What was I to do with that brilliant bit of intelligence?

Gremt was startled. He fixed his eyes intently on Magnus, and slowly the old image came back— the Magnus of now, the handsome ghost, the ghost dreamed up by the ancient mortal who'd endured badly formed limbs, a humped back, and a narrow hooked nose and now wanted none of it. Here were the even Grecian features and the beautiful forehead and the blond hair, the picture of a male in his prime, with the confidence of the fair.

Yet he looked away from me, humiliated, shattered. He stared into the fire, while Gremt stared at him with obvious concern. I was still shaken. In fact, I was beginning to feel a kind of panic.

Then a weariness took hold of Gremt and he settled back in the chair and looked up, perhaps at the figures of the tapestry, and he closed his eyes.

Amel was laughing softly and with a malicious delight. "What a crew they are," he said confidentially and with his low iron laughter. "Are you enjoying their company? Why don't you burn down their house and be done with it!"

"You're wasting your rage," I said to him. But I could see that Teskhamen had of course heard the threat and he didn't take it lightly. He was looking to me for some ratification that I had no such intention.

"I came here as your guest," I said. "I don't do what he wants."

"And how long before he can make you do what he wants?" asked Teskhamen. He didn't sound the least bit angry or impatient. Just smooth.

"He'll never be able to make me do anything," I said. I shrugged. "What makes you think otherwise?" There was no response. "Look, if he caused Akasha ever to do anything at his behest, it was because he deceived her, led her to believe that she was the author of the thoughts coming into her mind. He could never make Mekare do anything."

"What makes you certain?" asked Teskhamen. He was studying me intently. "Perhaps he coaxed Mekare into coming to you, offering herself to you, inviting you to take him out of her."

I shook my head.

"She came on her own," I said. "I was there. She

wanted to go on, to be with her sister." Flash flicker of those images, of the late gracious red-haired Maharet in a place of sunshine awaiting her surviving sister.

Teskhamen nodded, but it seemed no more than a courtesy. "You will be on the watch, however," he said gently. "You will be careful. You have inside you a powerful and evil spirit."

"Evil?" I asked. "Are we going to start arguing about the nature of good and evil?"

"No need," said Gremt under his breath. "We know what evil is. And you know what it is." He looked up at me. They were much alike in their demeanor, Teskhamen and Gremt, but then that made perfect sense—that all these years Gremt had been modeling his manner on that of Teskhamen.

Magnus was changing again, the flesh appearing to fade like an image in an old photograph, and in a silent shimmer I saw the old one, the narrow beak of a nose, the hunched shoulders and wrists of knobby bone, before he recollected himself and became the smooth handsome one again.

"Be what you like, monsieur!" I said to Magnus, leaning towards him. "Yea gods, don't hold on to any certain image for me." I meant to be helpful, kind. I wanted to thaw the ice.

But he turned and glared at me as if I'd made some unforgivable transgression. His eyes were narrow, and if he'd been a blood drinker still, he might have blasted me with his anger even without directing it. As it was, the anger made him all the more brilliant. I could see the faint tracery of blood swimming in the whites of his eyes. I could see his lips trembling. Does a ghost feel all of this?

Teskhamen rose to his feet.

"Prince, I'm going to leave you now with these two. Again, we are glad you've come."

"Don't go," I said. "I want to talk to all of you. Look, I know I've offended you and disappointed you." I didn't wait for them to respond. "It's been six months since you came to see me at Trinity Gate in New York," I said. "I promised you I would meet with you, invite you to Court. I promised, but then so much has happened. And I've been negligent, and I'm sorry. I came here myself to tell you this. And Amel wanted me to come, urged me not to put it off any longer. I couldn't bear the thought of sending some messenger or formal invitation. I came here because I am sorry for not coming to you sooner."

This clearly caught all of them off guard. I had definitely roused the interest of Gremt though he did not seem at all content. And a sadness came over Magnus's illusory features of which he did not seem to be in control.

What was wrong here? Something was wrong. There was a cloud over this group, a cloud that had thickened before I'd ever come to the door.

Only Teskhamen remained smooth. He was seated again.

"Thank you," he said. "I'm glad, very glad. I

want to know you," he said. "I want to know you
well enough that I can come and go at Court and
it will be nothing out of the ordinary. I've heard of
the Friday-night balls, the theater, your little performance of **Macbeth,** and the chapel wedding of Rose
and Viktor." He smiled. "All this speaks of vitality,"
he said, "vibrant communal life, something that's
never before united the Undead. Yea gods, are we
done forever with cults and ancient worship? And I
know you're exhausted. Others have told me. They
worry that it wears you out, and I don't blame you
for leaving the rules to a council. You can't make the
rules and be this powerful creative monarch."

"Then it's decided," I said. "You'll come and
often. You'll come tonight and tomorrow, whether
I'm there or not, and you'll come when you wish.
You'll walk through the front doors, just as blood
drinkers do who are coming from all over the world.
**Macbeth** is only the first of the plays I want to do, by
the way. I want to move on to **Othello.** The music
composed for the balls is being recorded and collected, and Marius is painting again, though how he
finds the time I don't know. He's covering new bedchambers and salons with his Italianesque murals."

I realized I was talking too fast. I was excited.
He'd spoken of exactly the aspects of the Court that
excited me, playing Macbeth myself on our little
stage for an audience of two hundred blood drinkers, young and old, and the Great Sevraine providing her enchanting Lady Macbeth with a deep

current of feeling that astonished her companions. Of course we had our critics—the cynical ones, the dark, deeply conservative ones who wanted to know why blood drinkers would bother with anything, presumably, but savaging humans for their blood.

**You can't build a culture with Devils out of Hell!**

"The Hell I can't" had been my answer. I went on for a moment, talking about Notker's musicians and how new musicians had appeared to make up our orchestras. I spoke of Antoine, my long-lost fledgling, writing concertos again for the violin. And then a sudden darkness came over me, because Antoine wanted to bring over into the Blood a musical secretary who could transcribe for him all he performed and recorded, and that had brought up the central question I couldn't yet face:

If this is all good, then why not bring people into it for our own purposes? Hadn't Fareed done it, making vampires out of brilliant doctors and scientists? Were we a thing that was good, or weren't we? And if I believed we were good, and believed the Dark Gift was just that, a gift, then I had to allow Antoine to find himself the musical scribes he wanted. And then what?

Teskhamen might have been reading my mind, but I wasn't sure of it. There are subtle rules about such things, matters of courtesy, matters of not stabbing into the mind of the other without permission to revert to the telepathic.

"Look, there's another matter," I said. "Some of

the others are afraid of you. That's the plain truth. They're afraid of you. You, a blood drinker, who claims a greater loyalty to the Talamasca than you do to us. And Gremt here, an incarnate spirit. I've always seen ghosts, but many a blood drinker has never seen ghosts, not at least that he or she was aware of."

I had their full attention as I continued. "This shouldn't have happened, this silence and neglect of you on my part. And please, please don't call me Prince. I'm Lestat, that's all. Lestat de Lioncourt on legal documents. And to all and sundry, simply Lestat."

"Oh, come on, you love being called Prince," said Amel. "You vain preening peacock of a monster. You love it. You coxcomb. Tell them about the crown jewels lavished on you by the vampires from Russia, all that Romanov booty soaked in blood."

"Shut up," I said aloud.

"And the crown expressly made for you by that old vampire from Oxford!"

"If you don't shut up—."

"What?" he asked. "What will you do if I don't shut up? What can you do? Are you looking at them, the way they're looking at you, the way they're studying you and listening to my voice inside you? Are you aware of their calculating evil minds!"

"Why did you want to come here?" I asked him without moving my lips.

Silence. It was like dealing with a child.

Then Teskhamen spoke. "He doesn't make life easy for you, does he?" he asked.

"No," I responded. "But he makes it very exciting. It's not so bad most of the time. Not at all." This was a magnificent understatement. I loved Amel. "And for long periods, he leaves," I said. "He goes running off to spy on others. But he can make life a perfect Hell if he wants to with all his noise, questions, demands, and denials. But that's **all** he can do."

**That's not true. If I want to, I can make your right hand jump right now.**

I made my right hand into a fist.

"A distinct personality?" asked Magnus. "Or a legion of hobgoblins wrapped into one?" It seemed a sincere question.

"Very much a distinct personality. Male. Curious. Loving."

**You're nauseating me; I'm going to make you vomit.**

"For now," said Teskhamen. He drew himself up. "But I have no choice but to warn you of certain things right in his presence, because there is no telling ever where he is, or in whom he might be hiding, including me. And I have to warn you. He wants more than to be trapped in you. He had a life as a spirit; a personality; we have fragmentary evidence of that, just what Maharet told you and the others when she told you the old stories. But in those stories he emerged as an evil spirit, a spirit who claimed blood and violence. . . ."

"Don't listen to this trash!" said Amel loudly. I was startled by the sheer volume of his voice and Teskhamen saw it. Maybe he heard it.

"Remember, Lestat," Teskhamen said, assuming the gentle tone again, "we are the Talamasca. We know spirits, and we know what we don't know about them. Never trust him. Never give him an inch to take over. Your body is powerful. He picked you on account of your body."

"Fool," said Amel. "Fool," he repeated. "He knows nothing about love; he knows nothing about the suffering of those whom he calls spirits. And what's your body compared to Marius's body or the body of Seth or Gregory or his body, for that matter!"

I looked at Gremt. "Can you hear him too? Can you hear him talking inside my head right now?"

Gremt shook his head. "In the beginning I could, centuries ago, when I was no more than an illusion; in those times I could see him superimposed over the figure of the comatose Queen. When I drew near her shrine, and I did come to her often, I heard a species of relentless singing from him that suggested madness. But no, I can't hear him now. I'm too solid, separate and individual." There was bitterness in his voice. I wondered if he had specifically shaped his voice, its deep timbre, as he had shaped his appearance. Maybe the voice had distinguished itself over time.

Amel started laughing again. A mean mocking laugh.

Another silence fell, and Gremt seemed lost in his thoughts, eyes on the fire. "I came here after him," he said as though speaking to the flames. "I came down into the flesh after Amel, enchanted by his example. And I wanted to be one of you, a human. It seemed so splendid."

"Burn down this house and see what they do," said Amel. "You never do anything to make me happy."

"Has it been splendid?" I asked Gremt.

He looked at me as if the question astonished him. To me, it seemed logical.

"Yes," he said. "It is splendid, but I am not human, am I? Seems I don't age, and can't die. The old story."

"Would it have been more splendid if you had become wholly human, grown old, and died?" I pushed.

No answer. Faint annoyance.

"And so for us you make good company, Gremt," I said. "You understand us."

Silence again and I hated it. Something unspoken in the air. And I thought suddenly of leaving, going ahead up into the sky and over the sea to find Louis. But it was far too soon to leave, just because I was uncomfortable.

"You have quite a sense of gravitas about being the Prince now, don't you?" asked Magnus. His smile was almost innocent, almost pleasant.

"Shouldn't I?" I asked. "Aren't you glad your fledgling and heir grew up to be the Prince of the Undead? Aren't you proud of me?"

"Yes, I am," he said sincerely. "I've always been proud of you, except when you retreat, and give in to your suffering. I haven't been so proud when you do that. But you always come back. Doesn't matter how dreadful the defeat, you come back."

"And does this mean you've been near me, watching me, all these years?"

"No, because I wasn't the ghost you see now all these years. I was another kind of ghost until Gremt rescued me and brought me here and showed me what I could be. After that, yes, I did spy on you. But that wasn't so very long ago."

"Will you tell me more about all this?"

"Some night, surely," he said. "All of it. At times, I write. I write pages and pages of my thoughts. I write poems. I write songs even. I write reflections. The autobiography of a vampire and a vampire ghost who was once an alchemist who sought to cure all the diseases of the world and make broken bones fuse perfectly, an alchemist who sought to comfort little children in pain—." He broke off, and his eyes left me for the flames. "I had written books for you, my heir. Then the night before I brought you to my tower, I burned them."

"Good God, why?" I asked. "I would have cherished every word!"

"I know," he said. "I know that now. I didn't know it then. We have much to say to one another, and you can have at me, you know." He glanced at me again and back to the blazing logs. "You can rail at me for snatching you out of mortal life, rail at me for abandoning you with hard cold jewels and coin when you might have gotten all that for yourself on your own. . . ." Again, he stopped, drifted, and the whole image flickered, but now the flickering couldn't conceivably diminish his seeming power.

"There should be no secrets with any of us," I said. "I mean the Talamasca's no more, right? You've let the human Order go into the world without your governance. And now you're free to come live with us for as long as you like! To be part of us, part of the Court, part of the company that we are."

He gave me a long loving smile. I was faintly humiliated.

Amel was silent but most assuredly present.

"You need never worry about the Talamasca anymore," said Teskhamen. "Surely you know that. And they'll never seek to harm you any more than they did in the past. They're off studying supernatural phenomena with the same dreary dedication for which they have always been famous."

"Hands off the Talamasca," I said with a shrug. "We agreed to that the first time we came together to agree on anything."

That didn't surprise them. Likely they knew. Likely they had some ghost in the very room spying on us. Where were the other ghosts? Hesketh? And that male ghost who'd come to Trinity Gate, bringing tears from Armand, the one called Riccardo?

"But you," I said, "you, the very heart of the

Talamasca, you must come and visit with us and share with us everything you ever discovered, ever learned. . . ."

"And what do you think we learned," asked Teskhamen, "that Maharet didn't long ago tell you? Ghosts exist. Spirits exist. Are all spirits ghosts? Nobody knows. It always ends with 'nobody knows.' And nothing changes the ascent of biological humans, humans of body and soul, to rule the planet and reach for the stars beyond it."

Suddenly in a silent flash I saw that city falling into the sea, that great city of glistening spires. . . . But the image vanished as if snatched away from me. A misery came over me, certainly originating with Amel. I knew because it was like nothing I ever felt in the regular course of things. The fire. The sea. A city melting? And then that too was gone, and the fire here on the hearth was crackling and the air filled anew with the sweet smoke of the burning wood, and I felt an icy draft moving along the floor that meant it was colder outside, and maybe it was snowing. I couldn't see out the windows from where I sat, but I could feel that it was snowing. I longed for the sweet balmy air of New Orleans, across the sea, for Louis.

Teskhamen started speaking again.

"The Order is stable now, quite harmless to you. But we've never stopped watching over them. The old traditions are still venerated, and the scholars are more than ever obedient to the old rules. We know everything. We watch them as they watch the supernatural phenomena of the world. And if there were to be any disturbance with the Order, if any of you were to be threatened, we would intervene. When it comes time for the Talamasca to die, we will dispatch it."

"In years past," I answered, "I made a lot of trouble for the Talamasca from time to time. But you know perfectly well, I thought the Order was made up entirely of mortals. I acknowledge that, and the trouble I made. I deliberately seduced and overcame David Talbot. I did other things. I offended the Order and now I know you were the Order, and though I can't say I regret any of it, I've never held any enmity for you."

"What happened with David Talbot and Jesse Reeves has been removed from the Order's records," said Teskhamen. "From all of the records in all forms. There isn't anything now in the archives to verify what actually took place. Also all Marius's paintings that were salvaged from his Venetian years have been returned to him. Surely he told you this. There are no blood drinker relics at all anymore in the vaults."

"I see," I said. "Well, that's probably for the best."

"It's for their protection as they continue, as they go on studying the paranormal phenomena of the world. Of course."

I sat considering all this, my elbow on the arm of the chair.

"So you trained them to watch us for over a thousand years," I ventured. "And now there is no need for the new Order to watch us, or report on us, or track us at all."

"That's exactly right," said Teskhamen. "The Order is concerned with reincarnation, with Near-Death Experiences, as they are called. And with ghosts, of course, always with ghosts, and sometimes sorcerers and witches. But the vampires have been withdrawn from the Charter, so to speak. And you have absolutely no reason to fear the Order. Do make a proclamation. I appreciate your self-deprecating tone, but you are the Prince and you can, and I do hope you'll do it. They are pitiful mortals, simple mortals, honest mortals, scholars and nothing more."

I nodded and made an open-handed gesture of complete acceptance. I wondered if it was really that easy, to command an Order of mortal scholars not to study vampires any longer, when in fact we were more visible in the world than ever. Had none of those proper British scholars heard Benji's radio broadcasts? Had none of them read newspaper accounts of the mysterious fires around the world that documented Benji's description of the Great Burning of vampires in far-flung capitals?

Memo to self: Have Marius, the Prime Minister, draw up a formal proclamation. And I meant "Prime Minister" in the sense that Mazarin and Richelieu had once been Prime Ministers for the French King, not in the sense of prime ministers today. Marius was my Prime Minister.

"It's easier than you think," Teskhamen explained, "to convince a group of scholars that some other secret department under their roof is working on the question of blood drinkers, when in fact there is no such secret department. We are guiding them. I told you."

I nodded. "I've never really feared the Talamasca," I said. "I don't fear you either. I don't say that to be difficult or unfriendly. But I don't. So we are agreed on all this."

Gremt was studying me. He'd come out of his deep thoughts and I could see his pupils moving in that subtle way which means mental calculation.

Why was Amel silent? I felt that prickling over my scalp, that interior grip on the back of my neck. "If you're so damned angry," I said silently, "why don't you race off down some branch of your immense vine and pester some other blood drinker and leave me alone?"

No response.

Even as I made a mental note of this, a pleasing warmth penetrated my spine. His doing, his physical doing. And then I heard his whispering voice: "Ghosts and spirits and shadowy shapes and things that go bump in the night. You're demeaning us both here. This is a tomb."

I realized that Magnus, or the thing that represented Magnus, was turned away from me and towards the fireplace, and the limbs beneath the brown robe had shriveled, and the one sandaled foot that showed beneath the hem was skeletal and white. The robe appeared threadbare and torn here and there, and I could all but smell dust coming from it. God, what went on in the mind of this creature as he experienced these transformations?

Hundreds of years dropped away. I saw that spindly white monster on all fours jumping up and down on his funeral pyre. I saw the jester's smile and the black hair flying in the swirling embers. . . . I heard my own screams as he went up in flames! I don't know that I remembered anything in all my life any more vividly than I remembered that. I felt myself trembling.

"Can we expect you at Court?" I asked. I looked from Teskhamen to Gremt. Then to Magnus.

"You're a person of surprises," said Teskhamen agreeably. "Of course we'll come. And soon. But there are things now that must be addressed. I have another warning to give you."

"Warning?"

"Rhoshamandes," said Gremt. "You're underestimating him."

"He's weak," I said. "His lover, Benedict, left him and came to us. Rhoshamandes is crushed."

Gremt shook his head. "He hates you, Lestat," he said. "He hates you and wants to destroy you."

"Lots of people do!" I laughed. "But he's the least of my worries. He can't destroy me."

"And there are other rumblings in the great world," said Teskhamen. "Small collectives of creatures of the night who resent that anyone has claimed a crown among the Undead."

"Of course," I said. "How could there not be? And then there are the blood drinkers flocking in every evening. And they want a prince and they want rules. And I never dreamed how much." I sat back and put my left ankle on my right knee. The fire felt good because the icy draft had made it burn brighter. I went on. "Two hours a night we hear grievances and disputes over territory, this one demanding that we punish that one, this coven insisting 'it was there first' and wanting the other banished. This one asking for permission to exterminate an enemy. It's like the time of Constantine with quarreling Christians coming to his court to demand he condemn this or that heretic, and nail down the core doctrines of a creed." None of this surprised them.

Teskhamen smiled and laughed under his breath. "You may be the perfect prince, Lestat," he said. "You really do hate having authority, don't you?"

"You bet I do," I said with an irresistible shudder. "Rhoshamandes told me before he was banished that there is only one reason really to want power and that's to keep others from having power over you, and he and I hold that much at least in common."

Gremt was still riveted to me and even Magnus looked more collected and at ease. But there was still something wrong here.

"Do you want to speak to the spirit himself?" I

asked. "Is that it? You want to speak to Amel?" I made an open gesture with my hands.

A low hiss came from Amel. He might have been a snake coiled at my neck and suddenly exerting a subtle pressure on my vocal cords and my breath.

I ignored him.

Suddenly he tried with all his power to make me rise out of the chair. He'd done plenty of this before, and I held fast without the slightest sign of what was happening. It was like holding still when one's limbs are cramped and crying in pain, but I outlasted him. And I hated him for doing this here, in front of this little group of merciless spectators.

"I can't make the spirit speak to you," I said, "but I can ask him to speak to you. I can surrender entirely to him and repeat only what he says. I've done this a lot of late for Fareed and Seth. I allow Amel to tell them anything he wishes."

"Traitor," said Amel. "Slut."

I tried to conceal my smile. I just love being called a slut. I don't know why. I just do. "Have at it, beloved numbskull," I mumbled without moving my lips.

"We can see how it is," said Gremt. His voice was gentle, and easy, but there was distrust in his pale eyes. "He's not at peace in you. Don't underestimate him. Indeed, I think your fault is that you underestimate others across the board."

I reflected for a moment. I wasn't going to talk about love to this group, but I wasn't above letting them know that now telepathically. **I love this being. Don't try to understand it. And don't try to undermine it.**

"Don't underestimate me," I whispered.

They didn't reply.

"Everything is about learning with Amel," I said calmly. "He told me that for aeons he could see and hear nothing distinct or separate from inside Akasha's body. He was flooded with sensations, echoes, vibrations, blazes of light and color. He had to learn to see, rather like a mortal blind from birth has to learn to see when sight is restored to him."

They were listening intently, and Amel was also listening.

"Well, now he can see and feel and taste," I said. "He can make these distinctions, and so what he's experiencing is wholly new. He speaks, but half the time he doesn't know what he's saying."

What, no response from my clever little friend?

There was no response from the three of them either. In fact their faces were concealing and almost hard.

"Please go on," said Teskhamen. "I want to hear more." He glanced at the others, but they remained fixed on me.

"What else can I tell you?" I said. "He isn't always inside me. But eighty percent of the time, he is. He wants me to take him places, inaugurate experiences for him, choose victims for him, flood my senses with music for him or visual stimuli—like films, for instance, or attendance at operas and symphony orchestras. The plays. He loved the plays. He loved me performing **Macbeth.** He loves the very concept of me, with him inside me, becoming another person on the stage. He will talk about things like that for weeks. He's fascinated with symphony orchestras. He'll ask absurdly simple questions, then offer the most sophisticated observations. He says things like the orchestra is generating a soul, a collective soul, an entity. I ask him what that means. He says consciousness generates soul. But most of the time, he can't explain such statements." I shrugged. My great overused gesture. I've been shrugging my shoulders at the world for one reason or another since I was born. "That's how it is with him. He isn't longing to go anywhere."

"And is he confiding in you as to where he came from?" asked Gremt.

"You should know perfectly well that he has no idea where he came from," I replied. "Do you have any idea where you came from?"

"What makes you assume that I don't?"

"I know you don't. If you knew where you came from and why you were a spirit, you would never have founded the Talamasca. You might never have incarnated. I think you and all your spirit entity brothers and sisters . . . assuming they have gender . . . are as confused as we are. So are ghosts. Everybody's confused. And yes, he has made some philosophical pronouncements if you must know."

"What were they?" asked Magnus intently.

"That in the realm of the invisible there is no right and wrong," I said. "He told me that. And he told me that ideas of right and wrong originate with biological beings and they seduce the spirit world, and the spirit world wants to know more of it. All quests, he says, come from us."

This totally surprised them, but it was absolutely the truth.

Amel was saying nothing, absolutely nothing. "Don't tell me you don't remember all this," I whispered to him.

Long pause, then in a low voice: "I remember."

Teskhamen looked calmly from Gremt to me and back again, in a manner which I found faintly disturbing. But he seemed to sense this and he lowered his gaze again to the fire, as if he'd been rude to me.

"Listen to me, Lestat," said Gremt. It was a tone I'd never heard from him before. His voice was low, markedly soft, but rather hard. "You don't know this spirit. You think you do. But you don't."

Silence inside me.

"Why do you say this?" I asked.

An ominous expression darkened Gremt's face.

"Because I remember in the airy Heavens a time when he was not there," he said.

"I don't understand."

"He's no simple spirit, Lestat," said Gremt. "I am a simple spirit, and indeed there are myriad simple spirits—there are simple spirits who 'possess' mortals, and there are even simple spirits who seek to make for themselves a secure citadel of flesh as I've done—and spirits without count—collected in the earth's thinner atmosphere whom humans cannot usually see or hear. But he—Amel—is no simple spirit. And I who can remember almost nothing of those airy aeons well remember when he came. There was a tumult in Heaven when he came. He was new. He had the name Amel when he came. Do you follow me?"

He broke off as if unsatisfied, and looked into the fire. No wonder we gather around fires because they give us something to look at when we can't look at one another.

Silence. Coldness. The serpent coiling inside of me had gone still.

"What did he say of himself?" I pressed. "Did he talk of where he'd come from?"

"No," said Gremt. "He was wounded, suffering, rather like an earthbound ghost, blundering through the invisible in agony. But he was no simple ghost. He has the immense power of a spirit."

"How so?"

"We are as different from ghosts as angels are from humans," Gremt said. "Don't think for a moment you know what he is. He has a cunning and an ambition which other spirits do not possess and never did. At least not as I have ever known them. I learned my cunning and ambition from watching him. And when he came into the flesh through Akasha, I came after him, but it took me thousands of years to achieve the concentration and strength sufficient for me to enter this physical world. Never for a moment think he is of the same ilk as me. Something different drives him and that something is rooted in experience and knowledge which I never possessed."

"So you're saying he is a ghost!"

"No." He shook his head. He was defeated.

Shimmer. Flash. The city falling into the sea. The huge cry of thousands. Gone.

I'd lost the thread. I put my hand to my forehead, massaging my temples. "You're saying he was flesh and blood before, that he's a ghost."

"He's no ghost," said Gremt. "I know ghosts." He gestured to Magnus. "This is a ghost, fired with the urgency and moral concerns he learned before he died. No. He's not a ghost."

"I think what my friend means," said Teskhamen, "is that you must not trust him, Lestat. Love him, yes, of course, and treat him with the immense concern you've always shown for him, but never trust him."

I nodded, to acknowledge that I was listening, of course, but I did not really respond.

"You've loved him from the start of all this," said Teskhamen. "You and you alone spoke up for him to the others who were seeking a way to dislocate him into some sort of secure trap where he might animate the vampire world for their sake. But you loved him. You saved him from that. You invited him into your own body."

Did they know how little I ever stopped to consider for one split second anything that I had ever done? Likely they did. Likely they knew how I lived my life, riding wave after wave of instinct and emotion, driven by immense greed as well as generosity.

But that was not the point here. They were driving at something crucial about Amel himself.

"So what you're saying," I asked finally, "is that the realm of spirits is populated by ambitionless beings, largely benign, drifting, flighty, whatever—the way Maharet had once described them to us . . . childlike things . . . but that this spirit, Amel, is something else?"

"Benign?" asked Gremt. "Childlike? Lestat, have you forgotten Memnoch?"

**Memnoch!**

"What do you know about Memnoch?" I asked. I could hardly contain my excitement. "If you know anything of Memnoch, anything at all, you must tell me! Tell me now. What do you know of him?"

Memnoch was a spirit that had once hunted me down, seduced me with visions and tales of Heaven and Hell, and begged for me to become his apprentice in a spirit realm. Memnoch had claimed to be one of the "sons of God" who had engendered the Nephilim. Memnoch had claimed to be the Jewish-Christian Devil. I'd escaped and repudiated Memnoch in utter horror. But I had never known whence he came or what he was—really.

"What did Maharet tell you about Memnoch?" asked Gremt.

"Nothing," I said. "Nothing other than what I told the whole world. She said she knew him. That's all. That's all she ever said. Maharet didn't tell people things. That's the whole point about Maharet. She sat down with us once, long ago, and told us her personal history, and how the blood drinkers had come into existence, and then after that, she retired from the world, refusing to be any sort of mentor or leader. When she brought young ones to her hideouts, she put them to studying old human documents, tablets, scrolls, or pondering mysteries dug up from the earth. She held court not as an instructor but as some sort of . . ."

"Some sort of mother," said Gremt.

"Well, yes, I guess so," I said. "She brought a letter to me from Memnoch, or so she claimed. And in the letter was wrapped my eye, this eye, which Memnoch's demons had torn out of the socket. The letter was mocking and vicious. The eye I restored to its place and the eye has healed. But the heart will never heal from an assault such as Memnoch made on me. But Maharet never told me anything. I think Maharet was constitutionally wary of all forms of ambition."

Magnus smiled at this, as if it delighted him.

"He played the Devil for you," said Magnus, "for

the little boy who had been frightened by stories of Hellfire and demons. He used your imagination, your mind, your heart, so to speak, to weave his airy realms about you."

"Yes, I know that now. I suspected it then. And I left. I fled. I fled even though they took my eye from me."

"You were braver and stronger than I was," said Magnus softly. "And you are right about Maharet. She was against all forms of ambition."

"She believed in passivity," said Gremt, "and sad to say, she believed in ignorance."

"I agree," I said.

"It comes to that after centuries and centuries of vain hope," said Teskhamen. "You can gaze on the struggling beings around you with a sad detachment. And you can thank Heaven for ignorance, for simple beings who don't long to know anything."

"Look, I don't want to talk about Maharet," I said. "There's time enough for that. I want to talk about Memnoch. If you keep from me what you know of Memnoch—."

I sat up in the chair. I planted both feet on the floor as if I were prepared to rise and attack somebody but this didn't mean anything. "Who was Memnoch?"

"Why use the past tense?" asked Gremt. "You don't think he's hovering near you, quite ready again to sweep you up into his imaginary worlds?"

"He can't," I said. "He's tried. He's tried for years."

They were skeptical.

"Every spellbinder has a signature," I said. "Once I learn to recognize that signature, I become immune. They can't make it happen to me after that." I studied them individually. "Centuries ago, Armand would seek to sweep me up in his spells. I learned to recognize them instantly." I waited but they volunteered nothing. "I want to know what you know of Memnoch," I said. "You said his name!" I said to Gremt. "I would not have asked, not now, not until much later on, when we had come to know one another, all of us, and love one another. I would not have presumed. But you said his name, and you know what this means to me. What do you know of him?"

Magnus roused himself, brightening and glancing at his companions.

"He's an evil spirit," said Magnus. "He believes all the things he said to you. He fed off your fear of God and the Devil. He is greedy. Long aeons ago he fell in love with the religions of human beings; he dwells now in great purgatorial realms of his own making, seducing the lost earthbound souls of dead believers, sustained by their faith in those systems. . . ."

"You do recall," I said, "that he claimed to teach love and forgiveness in his purgatorial Hell."

"Of course," said Magnus, "and he provides abundant images of those souls who have learned his lessons well ascending to Heaven. But nobody ascends from his domain. He is not of God. He is not of Hell. He's a spirit. And into his maw go the unwary, those longing to be judged and punished."

I sighed. I sat back in the chair. None of it was surprising, yet to hear it confirmed at last, that was something.

"Think of the great Catholic theologians of the twentieth century," said Magnus. "They are poets of their own intoxicating belief systems. They swim in an atmosphere of vintage theologies, and weave new and airy systems for themselves wholly detached from the real world, the flesh-and-blood world—."

"I know," I whispered.

"Well, think of Memnoch as being like that. Think of Memnoch as finding in religion a great creative milieu in which he could define himself!"

"He tapped into the lost devotions of your child-hood," said Gremt. "That is what he does. And now and then other souls go to his realm, wiser souls, and they seek out those who are trapped there and they bring them out and into freedom."

"How?" I asked.

"By alerting those trapped souls that they are prisoners of their own guilt and wretched disillu-sionment." Gremt looked at Magnus. "There are souls most skilled at such things, traveling the astral as they sometimes call it, and seeking to free the un-wary human ghosts who are lingering in labyrinths from which there is no exit."

"That is too horrible to think about," I said.

"That souls would be trapped in make-believe regions, when perhaps there is some other finer destiny awaiting them."

"And sometimes," said Magnus, "when those tormented souls are freed from such traps, they do ascend and vanish. And sometimes they do not ascend. They come back down, down to this earth, with their rescuers, and they linger earthbound, unfinished, restless. That is what you see in me, you see a ghost who has escaped Memnoch's Hell, and knows him well to be a fraud. You see one who would destroy every astral vestige of his kingdom, were it in my power to do so."

"You know all this, Lestat," said Gremt. "Your instincts told you. You fled from his purgatory, condemning him, rejecting him."

"Yes, exactly," I said. "How could I have shattered the place? How could I have freed them all?"

"Holy Saturday," whispered Magnus. "'And He descended into Hell.'"

I knew full well what he meant. He was speaking of the old idea that Jesus after His death on the cross had gone down into Sheol or Hell to free all the souls waiting for His redemption, so that they could ascend to Heaven. I don't know if even the most devout Christians believe such things anymore, in any literal sense, but I had been taught them, centuries ago, in a monastery school, and I remembered the priceless illuminated manuscripts with their tiny pictures of Jesus awakening the dead.

"Memnoch is a liar," said Magnus. "I suffered in his Hell."

"And now you're free," I said.

"Free to be dead forever?" he asked.

I realized what he was saying of course. He was earthbound. He was not one who'd gone into the Light, as they say. He was a haunt of the material world. He blazed bright and beautiful in my eyes. A serene expression smoothed his face.

"If I were ever in your presence, Prince," he said, "I would be the strongest of ghosts, I think! By day, I'd lie atop your sarcophagus and dream, waiting for you to wake, and your rising at sunset would be sunrise for me in terms of power."

"Forgive me, Master," I said, "but you seem to be doing very well on your own, and to have your tomes to write, your poems, your songs. What do you need me for?"

"To look on me," he said softly, his eyebrows rising. "To look on me and forgive."

Silence once more. He turned to the fire. They all did. I put my head back against the hardwood carving, and gazed off thinking of all this, and remembering other ghosts I'd known, and a dark fear gripped me, a fear of being dead and earthbound, and then it seemed not unlikely that all intelligent beings of the whole world were locked in some sort of dance with the physical. Maybe those who rose into the Light simply died, and the universe beyond this world was silent. I could drive myself mad contemplating a great nothingness filled with a billion pinpoints of light and millions of drifting planets generating their myriad biological kingdoms of insect, animal, sentient witness.

"This is the point," said Gremt. "Memnoch waits and watches and he might not make his move again for a hundred years. But don't forget ever that he is there. And don't forget Rhoshamandes. Best do away with Rhoshamandes."

"No," said Teskhamen as if he couldn't stop himself.

"Well, why not?" asked Gremt. He looked at me again. "And don't underestimate the rebels out there who want to topple you for the sheer sake of doing it. And don't, don't ever underestimate Amel!"

A low moan came from Magnus.

"How at times like this do I wish I were a musician, because music is the only fit vehicle for the emotions I feel. I died the night I made you, and what a fool I was to do it, to die in that fire of my own making, and not to have had the courage to embrace you, love you, travel the Devil's Road with you, my ancient body the eager pupil to your lordly newborn strength! Ah, the things we do. What are we that we can make such great blunders without the slightest realization of what we are doing? What is man that he is so mindful of himself and knows so little of the consequences of what he does!"

He rose to his feet and drew near to me, and in a flash I again felt as surely as I saw it that he ceased to be the blond-haired male of perfect proportions and became the very image of the monster I had known.

It took all my resolve not to get up and move away from him. He came close to me, the vivid embodiment of the gaunt, wraithlike being he'd been on the night of my making, except for his clothes which were dark and ragged and shapeless, with leggings like bandages and his eyes fiercely black, black as his hair.

**Scatter the ashes. Or else I might return, and in what shape that would be, I dare not contemplate. But mark my words, if you allow me to come back, more hideous than I am now . . .**

I found myself standing some feet away from him. Not a sound from Amel. Just this creature with its back to the fire, his wavering figure surrounded by a halo of flickering light.

Gremt came up silently beside me.

"This is my fault, all of this," he said. I felt his arm on mine.

"I did scatter the ashes," I whispered. It sounded so stupid, so childlike. "I scattered them just as you told me to do," I said to Magnus. "I scattered them."

The figure's face was in shadow against the blaze, but I could see the expression softening.

"Oh, I know you did, young one," he said in a frayed and broken voice. "I remember, and I remember your tears and your terror." He appeared to sigh with his whole spectral body, and then to cover his face with his long spidery fingers, his tangled

black-and-silver hair falling down over him like a
veil. "How stupid I was. I thought if you were born
in terror you'd be all the stronger for it. Child that
I was of a cruel age, I respected cruelty. And now I
deplore it more than any other thing under Heaven.
Cruelty. If I could strip the earth of any one thing,
it would be cruelty. I would give my soul to strip the
earth of cruelty. I look at you and I see the son of
my cruelty."

"What comfort can I give you, Magnus?" I said.

He threw back his head and lifted his hands. His
fingers fluttered, white and pleading, and he prayed
in Old French to God and the saints and the Virgin.
Then his dark eyes fixed on me again.

"Child, I wanted to beg your forgiveness for all of
it, casting you a vagabond on the Devil's Road without a word of instruction, making you the young
and vulnerable heir to what I myself couldn't endure."

He sighed and turned away and made his way to
his chair. He reached for the back of it. I could feel
that white hand that closed on the wood, feel it as it
had touched me all those long years ago:

**But you can't leave me! . . . Not the fire. You
can't go into the fire!**

That was my voice, the voice of the boy I'd been
at twenty, immortal for less than an hour.

**Oh, yes, I can. Yes, I can! . . . my brave Wolfkiller.**

I couldn't bear the sight of him, bent, shuddering,
seeming to lean for mortal support upon the chair. I

couldn't bear the groan that came from him, or the way he stood upright and rocked back and forth as though interrogating Heaven with his hands raised again.

Gremt slipped his arm around my waist, warmly, and placed his hand on my arm. But it was the ghost who needed comforting. My heart was breaking.

Teskhamen was gone. I'd barely realized it, but he had slipped out of the room, leaving us alone here. And some part of my mind registered that he, a living being, as I was a living being, who had never known incorporeal consciousness could not share the pain that these two specters shared in these moments.

"This will pass," Gremt said under his breath. "It is my doing, all of it. We are wanderers. We have no Fareed and no Seth for spirits and phantoms. Fate is merciless to the living who lack flesh and blood."

"Not so," said Magnus. He turned and as he did so his figure appeared to toughen, to lose something of its brilliant shimmer. "It is not your fault." He looked at me with the same gaunt white face he'd had when he made me.

Again the phantom wavered, turning its back to us, and becoming transparent, the sound of its voice vaporous as it wept.

I couldn't watch and do nothing. I moved towards Magnus, reaching out for him, trying to enfold him in my arms, and wrapping myself around what seemed a vibrant invisible force that was nothing now but light and voice.

"I have no regrets now, none," I said. "You can't be weeping for me. Weep for yourself, yes, that's your right, but not for me."

Someone else entered the room, as softly as Teskhamen had left it. Had he gone to summon this one, to send him in? I heard the step of the other, and picked up the scent of a blood drinker. But I didn't detach myself from the weeping spirit and I didn't want to be detached.

It seemed the spirit was wrapping itself around me. I could feel the subtle throbbing presence enclosing my arms, my face, my heart. A swoon bound us together. Images of long ago flooded my senses, the dim hollow cloister in which beneath the purpling dusky sky the mortal alchemist Magnus had bound the tender vampiric prisoner whom I now knew to be Benedict, the Benedict of Rhoshamandes, from whom he bent to steal the precious Blood. Denied this Blood, cruelly denied this Blood, no matter what his brilliance, his wisdom, his worthiness, because he was not young, was not beautiful, was not pleasing to the eyes of those who safeguarded it from all but their favorites, Magnus at last feloniously and greedily drinking the Blood even as his own blood poured from his torn wrists, drinking and drinking the pure nectar, not intermingled with his own but undiluted and supremely powerful. Weeping, weeping.

A voice filled the illusion, an ominous and punishing and angry voice, the voice of Rhoshamandes.

"Cursed are you among all blood drinkers for

what you've done. Abomination on the face of the earth! Blessed be the blood drinker who slays you."

I saw my old master rising in the air, rising as if to meet the stars tumbling in their purple mist, his eyes full of wonder. **It is mine. It is in my veins. I am among the immortals.**

And now he cried. He cried as miserably as I'd cried when as a boy blood drinker I'd seen him burned on the pyre. He swallowed and sought to muffle his cries, but the sound was all the worse for it.

Pain like this is unendurable.

Was that why Amel said nothing? Is that why he did not even seem to breathe inside me? Did he feel it because we felt it?

Somewhere near, a soft singing penetrated the swoon.

The blood drinker who had come in and was now, here in this great cavernous room, singing a hymn I knew with German words, the masterpiece of Bach, "Wake up . . . the voice summons . . . of the watchmen on the battlements, wake . . . you city of Jerusalem! This is the hour of midnight. . . ." And beneath the voice, the marching of the harpsichord. This tender-yet-piercing boy soprano voice of one of Notker's choristers.

The ghost who embraced me sighed, and slowly its limbs took form, its body solid once more and its head resting on my shoulder, the hair so fine to the touch, and the hands clasping my arms.

Love you, yes, always and forever. . . .

I'd be dead forever now beneath the earth were it not for you, or a ghost wandering without ever having glimpsed what you gave me. . . .

The music went on, the boy soprano blood drinker singing just above the volume of the keyboard, drifting into variations of his own on Bach's theme, as Bach himself might have done for pure amusement, taking the lyrics into uncharted places, "Wake, wake, the blood calls us from eternal sleep. . . ."

We stood together, and it was the music now that enfolded both of us.

Finally the music grew softer, and found its subtle finish.

A radiant silence gripped the room in which it seemed the walls gave back the ghostly echo of the cantata. Then the ghost turned and kissed me on the mouth. Magnus again, fully. Not the made-up ideal Magnus, but a strong powerful Magnus who'd brought me over, no longer the wraith, but robust, and clothed in simple black robes, his long dark glossy silver-streaked hair combed, and his gaunt face calm and etched with the fine lines that had become as pen strokes when he was made.

"You are my finest work, my finest miracle," he said to me. Once again he kissed me, and I opened my lips to receive the kiss and give it back. I bit into my lower lip, and offered the blood on my tongue. He took it, though how and what he felt, I couldn't know. He stroked my hair, my face.

"And now you are the Prince of the tribe, and old Rhoshamandes wanders with the mark of Cain on him, that winsome, capricious, heartless blood drinker, with the mark of Cain, so that no one will put him out of his anguish for what he did to the gentle witch, and you are the ruler."

He drew back, just as any living being might at this moment, and wiped the tears from his eyes, staring for a moment at his own hands. This was a creature I had never really seen—the true Magnus restored: the long thin nose and long mouth, the high domed forehead and white hands made of knots, and shoulders squared but misshapen—what he must have looked like in those early nights when the Blood had done all it could to make him near perfect. And who was to say this wasn't beauty?

"Aye, but I was never beautiful," he said with a sigh. "What is it that has made you see beauty here when others only ever saw ugliness and imperfection, and the ravages of disease?"

"My maker," I said. "Who gave me the power to see all things as beautiful."

Not one sound came from Amel inside me. Not one quiver. But he was there.

Magnus turned as if looking for the chair, reaching for it, in fact, yet unable to find it. I escorted him to the chair and held his hand as he sat down slowly, as though his phantom bones were actually aching.

Does a ghost become the full expression of the

mortal and the immortal? Does a ghost embrace the entire past of the being?

"Forgive me," he said looking up at me. He sat back, relaxing, putting his hands on the arms of the chair as we are wont to do with these old wooden chairs with their knobby carvings, and he looked at me calmly. "You came here seeking Gremt, and I've distracted you, caught you up in my griefs and madness. I was always mad, or so I was told, when I said things of the world that common men and women say today; I was thought mad, when I spoke of loving and how one had to learn to love; mad Magnus the thief of the Blood. I should leave you now to your talk with Gremt. But I am whole and firm again, and don't want to give it up."

"I understand."

I looked at Gremt. He was merely watching us. The slender vampire boy soprano had come up to stand beside him, eternal acolyte in a white lace surplice, and he held the boy around the waist as he'd held me moments ago.

I wanted to leave. It was time to leave. I knew that Magnus was weary to his heart, and he had had enough and so had I. And the silence of Amel was ominous and baffling. I found I was drained and sad and had nothing more to say just now to anyone.

I turned and took Magnus's right hand and kissed it. Flesh. Anyone would have thought so. I don't know that I'd ever kissed any being's hand before, but I kissed his.

"Anon, I come to you," he said under his breath. "Blessed heir."

"Yes, Master, whenever you wish," I said. I turned to Gremt and took Gremt's hand. "And I'll take my leave now and invite you to come whenever you wish to Court, you and all the household here."

"Thank you," Gremt said. "We'll come soon enough, but remember my words. Remember: he is not what you think he is. He is more and less. And don't be fooled by him."

I nodded. I looked at the boy singer and tried to remember if I'd seen him before with Notker's choir or musicians. Surely he had come from Notker's lair in the Alps.

He had been thirteen or fourteen when he was made, before the manly changes came over him, a boy of curly dark hair and dark glowing eyes and skin almost the color of honey by lamplight. His face brightened.

"Yes, Prince," he said. "I've sung for you and will sing for you again. It was Benedict who brought me to Notker, but your master who made me, and so I sing for him to bring him comfort."

"Ah, I see," I said. I repressed the simple urge to touch his hair affectionately. Against all evidence, he was hundreds of years old, a man in a boy's body, and no more the boy than Armand was a boy, or I a young man of twenty.

Gremt followed me as I headed to the front doors, hastening to open them for me.

The cold night air felt good, and I saw the snow was falling thinly. The ground was freshly blanketed in whiteness. And beyond, the trees glistened as they moved in the soft bitter wind. Two dim figures waited for me.

"Goodbye, my friend," I said. "Again, I came to break the silence between us. Come to me anytime, and I'll be back when I can, if you're willing."

"Always," he said. I saw the anguish in his face again, the strange grim unhappiness. "Oh, there's so much I want to confide, but I cannot confide without confiding in the one I fear."

I didn't know what to say.

We stood there, staring at one another, the snow swirling lightly and soundlessly around us, and then he took my hand. His fingers felt warm and human, and I felt the faint beat of his heart in them. What heart? The heart he'd made for himself to become one of us?

"Come to Fareed and Seth," I said. "They are physicians for us all. Come to me. Yes, Amel hears all but, hearing all, can't always hear any one. Come."

"Are they physicians for us all?" he asked.

"They have to be. If we aren't all one—ghosts, spirits, blood drinkers—then what are we? We're lost, and we can't be lost. We won't stand for it any-more to be lost."

He smiled. "Oh yes," he said. He seemed as im-pervious to the bracing air as I was. Yet his cheeks were slightly reddened and his eyes shining. "I've heard those words before on the lips of ghosts within this house."

"Well, then, go to them and come to me," I said. I was feeling the tears rise in my eyes. In fact, I felt such strong emotions I didn't quite know what to do or say. I felt desperation. "Listen to me, you must. The Court's too busy with being a court. But what is the point of the Court if not to unite all of us? Fareed and Seth are working in their new laboratories in Paris. And Armand's house in Saint-Germain-des-Prés is the Paris home of the Court. You know all this."

"Oh, yes, I know it," he said but he wasn't comforted or encouraged. What was holding him back? What was he not saying?

I couldn't bear this. I couldn't bear the thought of Thorne and Cyril only yards away waiting for me, overhearing all, and thinking what I would never know, and being there, always being there. I didn't know what I wanted, or what to do with the misery I felt, only that some raw feeling had been discovered in me that had been buried all this while in superficial concerns and random pleasures.

Inside the house, the boy was singing again, and the harpsichord notes seemed to be chasing at heated speed his sweet rushing syllables. How safe and strong the vast place seemed for a moment, against the random chaos of the drifting snow.

"Beware, Lestat," said Gremt. He pressed my

hand tightly. "Beware Amel. Beware Memnoch. Beware Rhoshamandes."

"I understand, Gremt," I said, assuring him.

I nodded. I found myself smiling. It was a sad smile, but a smile. I wished somehow I could convey to him, without pride, that all my life I'd been menaced by this and that adversary, all but murdered by those I'd loved, and even almost destroyed by my own despair. I always survived. I really didn't know what fear was, not as any permanent fixture in my heart. I just didn't "get" fear. I didn't "get" caution.

"All right, I'm going," I said and I took him by his shoulders and quickly kissed his cheeks.

"I'm glad you came, more than I can tell you," he replied. Then he turned and went back into the open door, and into the yellow light, and the door closed and the door appeared to vanish in the darkness of the wall.

I walked off through the silent snow, away from Thorne and Cyril and away from the warm yellow lights of the monastery windows. The boy was improvising those words he sang, to a concerto that never had words, and I realized in an exquisitely painful moment that he had likely spent his eternity doing such things, weaving such beauty, creating such magnificent songs, and marveled that Notker had given him this, or that he could give such things to Notker. All the world was filled with immortals who had no such purpose, no such thread to follow through the labyrinth of chance and mischance.

"Do you really not know what was bothering that spirit?" asked Amel in a low contemptuous voice. "Or are you simply pretending to be stupid in order to make me mad?"

"Well, he's obviously afraid for me," I said. "He fears you, he fears Rhoshamandes. . . ."

"No, no, no," said Amel. "Do you not know what is wrong with him, inside of him, what he's suffering?"

"So what is it?"

"He can't disperse the body anymore, you idiot," he said. "He's trapped in it. He can't vanish on cue. He can't disappear and reappear and dart from one place to another in the blink of an eye! He's caught in the solid body of his own devising and refining. He's flesh and blood now and he can't get out of it!"

I stood there motionless watching the snow. Far away, very far away, people laughed in a village tavern. The snow thickened. The cold was nothing to me.

"You mean this?"

"Yes, and he's confided it to Magnus," said Amel, "and he's shaken the ghost's confidence in his own material body. He's shaken them all. Hesketh is in fear now. Riccardo is in fear now. They are all in fear of the particle bodies they have created for themselves, that they may be imprisoned as he is now imprisoned. He wanted to ask you to drink his blood." Amel started laughing, his wild mad laugh. "Don't you see? The miserable spirit Gremt has gotten what he wanted: to be flesh and blood; and now there's no reversing it." He went on howling with laughter.

I wanted to protest, to say "How the Hell do you know?" but I had the strong sense that he did know and he was right. So what was this body in which Gremt talked and walked and slept? Could he ingest food? Did he sleep? Did he dream? Had he any telepathic power?

"Teskhamen knows," said Amel. "Teskhamen knows and did not mean for me to know, or you to know, and by way of trying to hide it, he revealed it to me." He laughed again. "Such geniuses!"

I said nothing for a moment. And then I looked back at the nearest window, at the light flickering beyond the snow in the leaded diamond panes of glass.

"That must be perfectly horrible," I whispered.

Amel answered me with more laughter. "Let's be off to find Louis," he said.

I didn't care about Amel. I thought of what this must mean for Gremt. I thought of what it had to mean. I weighed all aspects of it in light of what I knew of Gremt and ghosts and spirits. And I knew how this spirit had wanted to become flesh and blood.

"Well, he can die, then, and be a spirit once more, can't he?" I said.

"I don't know," said Amel. "Do you think he's willing to find out? No being on the earth wants to die, in case you haven't noticed."

Probably not. Most assuredly not.

"Come now, enough of these 'things,'" he said with a tone of remarkable weariness. "New Orleans waits. Louis waits. And if he hasn't come down to New Orleans as you asked, I say we go to New York and get him."

He had mentioned Louis countless times in the last six months, but the strange thing was, I didn't trust him with all these mentions of how I needed Louis, and ought to write to Louis, and ought to pick up one of the many telephones around me and call Louis. I had some deep fear that he was in fact jealous of Louis, but I was ashamed of that feeling. Now he was saying, Let's go, let's find Louis.

"Lestat, don't I always know what's best for you?" he asked. "Who was it told you decades ago to restore the Château? Who was it came to you in the mirror at Trinity Gate with the vision of what I was, so that you wouldn't fear me?"

"And who was it urged Rhoshamandes to take my son captive?" I asked angrily. "And urged Rhoshamandes to kill the great Maharet and would have driven him to kill her sister?"

He sighed. "You are merciless," he muttered.

Thorne came up close to me, with Cyril not far behind. Cyril was such a big hulk of a blood drinker that he made Thorne look a little small. Male beings like that know an insolent fearlessness that smaller men never quite know. But when I didn't move, when I just stood there in the snow, with the snow covering my head and my shoulders as if I were a statue in a park, the two of them said nothing.

"You need Louis," Amel said. "I always know what you need. Besides—."

"Besides what?"

"I like to look at him through your eyes."

"I don't want to think of you inside of Louis," I said.

"Oh, don't concern yourself. I don't go into Louis. Weak ones like Louis have never interested me. Consider those who heard 'the Voice.' Were any of them as human as Louis? No, they were not. If you must know, I can't find Louis. I can't go into Louis. Maybe in a century or two, yes, he'll be able to hear me, but for now, no. But I like to look at him through your eyes."

"Why?"

He sighed. "Something happens to your senses when you look on Louis. Behold Louis. I don't know. I see him more vividly than I sometimes see the others. I see a blood drinker. I think I see a whole life in Louis when I see Louis through your eyes. I want to know whole lives. I want to know big things, whole things, long things."

I smiled. Did he know when I was smiling? I was impressed by the continuity of what he was saying. Long things indeed. He spoke in brilliant bursts, but seldom did his thoughts hold to a continuity. Seldom was his train of thought long.

He was correct that most of those who heard his Voice last year had been the older ones. . . .

"You like the ones with power," I said. "You like to go into those who can make fire."

Long raw moan of misery.

"And your beloved Louis, if he has the power to make fire, would not discover it and not use it, unless of course someone threatens those he loves."

That was likely very true.

"Listen, I'm closer to you than any other being in creation," he said. "But I can't see you, can I, when I'm inside of you. I only see what you see. And something happens when you are with Louis, something happens when you reach out to touch him. I wish I could see you as he sees you. He has green eyes. I like green eyes. My Mekare had green eyes."

This troubled me, and I wasn't sure quite why. What if he suddenly wanted to hurt Louis? What if he became jealous of Louis—of my affection for Louis?

"Nonsense, go to him," he said. Calm voice. Manly voice. "Am I jealous of your son, Viktor? Am I jealous of your beloved daughter, Rose? You need Louis and you know it, and he's ready now to surrender. He's held back on principle long enough. I sense—." He broke off. I heard a sound like a hiss.

"You sense what?"

"I don't know. I want you to go to him. You waste

your time and my time! I want to go up! I want to be in the clouds."

I didn't move.

"Amel," I said. "The things Gremt said about you, were they true?"

Silence. Confusion in him. Agitation.

Again came that flash: a city of glistening buildings falling into the sea. Was it a real city, or was it some dream of a city?

A spasm in my throat, and in my temples. I looked up into the blinding swirl of snow. And then I closed my eyes. I saw the burning city etched on the darkness.

A beat. A moment. The soundlessness of snow is remarkably beautiful. I had a hand filled with snow. And my fingers suddenly curled around the snow though I hadn't told them to.

"Stop that," I said.

No answer from him. There was a faint pain in my fingers as I relaxed them against his will. This really alarmed me. What if he could take over my entire body like this, make me stand, make me sit, make me go up—?

"Gentlemen," I said beckoning to Cyril and Thorne. "I'm going up and over the sea. The sun's just setting on the city of New Orleans."

Thorne nodded. Cyril said nothing.

"I want to be in the only city I love more than I love Paris," I said as if I were speaking to people who cared.

"Where you go, we go," said Cyril with a shrug. "Long as I feed sometime or other in the next fortnight, what's it to me if you want to go to China?"

"Don't say that," Thorne muttered, rolling his eyes. "We're ready when you are, Prince."

I laughed. I think I liked Cyril a little better than Thorne, but then Thorne had his moments too. And Thorne had suffered agony when Maharet was killed. Maharet had been the maker and the goddess of Thorne. Thorne had begged for permission to lead a band of vengeful vampires to burn Rhoshamandes for the slaying of Maharet. So the real and true Thorne was only just emerging from that grief.

"All right, gentlemen, and now we make for the stars."

I shot upwards with all my strength, traveling above the clouds within seconds. I knew they were right behind me. Did they see the constellations as I saw them? Did they see the great white moon as I saw it? Or were they simply fixed on me as they struggled to keep up with me?

With all my strength I sent out my call.

**Armand, Benji—tell my beloved Louis I'm on my way.**

Over and over I sent out the call, as if my telepathic voice could strike the moon and be deflected with its light, shining down on the busy world of New York, on the many rooms and crypts of Trinity Gate, as I rose higher and higher and soared across the great dark void of the Atlantic.

# 3

# Garekyn

As the sun set in New York on this mild winter evening, Garekyn Zweck Brovotkin was walking briskly up Fifth Avenue, headed for a trio of Upper East Side townhouses called Trinity Gate. The air was fresh and clean, or clean as it could ever be in New York, and he had hope in his heart.

This might prove a colossal waste of his time, he realized, but then what did he have in this world but time, so why not check out the mysterious resident of Trinity Gate—a youngling radio star Garekyn had been listening to of late, an audacious character by the name of Benji Mahmoud, who claimed to be a "blood drinker"—a species of mutational immortal—and spoke in a heated whisper over the internet nightly to other mutated beings who referenced again and again the name of a controlling force in their lives called "Amel"?

**Amel.**

It was a name Garekyn had not heard spoken in

twelve thousand years, and he could not afford really to ignore it.

The broadcasts of the blood drinker had been going on for years. They lasted from one to two hours nightly; and thereafter the internet stream was made up of recordings of older broadcasts, and Garekyn had sifted carefully through all that material for the last six months until he had exhausted all broadcasts currently available in media of any form. He had learned all he could in this way about Benji Mahmoud and the beings who made up Benji's universe: blood drinkers all throughout the world, thought to be fictional by the New York journalists who wrote now and then on the "phenomenon" of Benji's "program," though human ears could not know the full extent of it.

Ah yes, Garekyn thought as he walked faster now, it might all be a waste of time. But he loved New York at twilight, with the traffic thickening, and lights coming on brilliantly all around him in towers and townhouses, and people taking to the streets as they left their places of employment to join in the vigorous nightlife that would go on unabated until the small hours of the following morning.

And so if I do not find literal immortals on this night, Garekyn thought, what have I lost?

Garekyn was a tall male, just over six feet in height, of a powerful and lean build with long black curling hair to his shoulders. There was a heavy gold streak in his hair, on the right side of the center part, and he had fierce engaging brownish-black eyes. His nose was long and narrow, and he had very dark brown skin. He was walking fast, wanting to reach his destination before darkness. The exalted tribe of Benji Mahmoud came alive only at darkness, according to their "mythology," and he was out to discover if the mythology had a bit of truth.

In 1889, Garekyn had come awake to a planetary culture viciously marred by deep ignorance and judgment of people based on race. But strong pejorative attitudes towards people of color had never penetrated to Garekyn's soul, because the long-ago ancient world into which he'd been born was so very different.

In those days, when Garekyn had been made and sent to Earth, most everybody on the planet was the color that he was. Most everyone had Garekyn's black hair and dark eyes. And newly awakened in 1889, in Siberia, by a loving Russian anthropologist, Garekyn had been treated not as an inferior black man but as a miracle for which science could not account—a being sleeping unconscious in the ice, desiccated and seemingly without feeling, who through simple warmth and hydration had been restored to vitality.

Prince Alexi Brovotkin, the man who rescued and educated Garekyn, was an amateur anthropologist and collector of fossils, son of a Russian father and an English mother—a committed scholar who eventually wrote a lengthy paper on the discovery of

Garekyn, only to have it rejected by every periodical to which he submitted it. Not a single scientist in Russia or Europe ever accepted Brovotkin's invitation to meet the twelve-thousand-year-old man he had delivered from the frozen wastes of Siberia. Of course, twelve thousand years was just an estimate of how long Garekyn might have been frozen. No one could actually know.

No matter. Prince Alexi Brovotkin loved Garekyn from the moment that Garekyn had opened his eyes and looked at him. Brovotkin had taken Garekyn from Siberia back to his palace in Saint Petersburg, and within less than a week, the shocked and dazzled Garekyn had been baptized into the modern world by an experience that surpassed anything he had ever imagined.

It was January 15 in the year 1890 and Prince Brovotkin had taken Garekyn to the premiere of **The Sleeping Beauty** ballet by Peter Ilyich Tchaikovsky at the lavish gilded Mariinsky Theatre.

Garekyn had never conceived of such music or a spectacle as ornate and lovely as he beheld on the stage that night. Never mind the splendors of Saint Petersburg, or the libraries and luxuries of Brovotkin's vast home. Never mind the glittering decor of the Mariinsky Theatre. It was the music and the dancing that enchanted Garekyn—the coordinated power of orchestral instruments to make an intoxicating stream of music to which highly disciplined humans performed rhythmic movements of near-impossible artifice and grace.

It took years for Garekyn to explain what he had felt when he watched **The Sleeping Beauty** ballet and why this immense affirmation of innate goodness was so important to him. But the pleasure he experienced that night had convinced him that he bore no horrible, irrevocable guilt from some former and half-remembered omission or commission.

"We made the right choice," he said haltingly and repeatedly to Prince Brovotkin that night and for many nights after. "My brothers and my sister and I. We were right. This world, this gracious world, exonerates us!"

Ever after, Garekyn was convinced that if his original companions were alive and well and living in that century, he would find them in palaces devoted to the performance of opera or ballet, for they would find this new music and these new performances as enchanting as he did. They too would see it as emblematic of the splendor of humanity, of an innate goodness that surfaced in innumerable and unforeseen ways.

Someone a long time ago, a very long time ago, had used those words, "the splendor of humanity." That was in a different language, a language Garekyn could hear in his head but not write, yet Garekyn had translated the sentiment easily into the Russian or English he'd been learning from Prince Brovotkin.

Garekyn's mind had been equipped for the quick understanding of language and the quick analysis of patterns and systems. He loved learning. And Prince Brovotkin loved him for it. But Garekyn's earliest memories were broken and fragmentary. They accosted him in unexpected and sometimes inexplicable flashes. His mind had been bruised and hurt in the catastrophe which had locked him in the ice. And who knew how the passage of time had affected Garekyn? He sought with all his might to recover every bit of vagrant memory that he could.

Three years after the premiere of **The Sleeping Beauty** ballet, when the great Tchaikovsky died, Garekyn wept bitterly. So did Prince Brovotkin. By that time, Garekyn had been thoroughly educated in the Prince's library and Prince Alexi had taken Garekyn to Paris twice and London once, to Rome and Florence and Palermo, and was planning to take him to America. Garekyn knew more about the late nineteenth century than he'd ever known or understood about his brief existence twelve thousand years earlier.

To Prince Brovotkin, Garekyn confided all that he knew of himself, of how he'd been sent with three other humanoid beings to Earth specifically to correct a grievous error. Bits and pieces came to Garekyn when he talked, when they traveled, when Garekyn read new books or saw new cities—when Garekyn encountered new wonders such as the Pyramids of Giza or the great Crystal Palace in London, or the great cathedral of Saint Mary of the Nativity in Milan.

People of the Purpose is what they had called themselves, Garekyn and his kindred, but not because they meant to fulfill what the Parents had sent them to do, but because they had conceived of another purpose far more important.

**Splendor of humanity.** A being who had spoken those words . . . but there Garekyn's faculties betrayed him. He could hear the voice, and see the eyes, pale eyes, not brownish black like his but remarkably pale greenish-blue eyes, so rare in that time on Earth, and golden-red hair—such lustrous golden-red hair.

Fleeting images, and broken questions obsessed Garekyn. He saw jungles in his dreams, jungles through which they'd walked together, he and his companions, struggling against insects and reptiles and the curious savages who had invited them into their villages and offered them abundant food and drink. He saw a vast glittering city beneath an immense transparent dome. **Everything depends on your getting into the city itself. Nothing can be achieved unless you do.** He recalled the faces and forms of the others, beloved Derek, the boyish one, and Welf, gentle, patient, and ever-smiling Welf, and the brilliant and commanding Kapetria, who never raised her voice in anger or enthusiasm.

The Parents had said to them all: You have been created for this one purpose and you will perish as you achieve your purpose, and without your perishing it cannot be done. Derek had cried when the Parents spoke those words. "But why do we have to die," Derek had asked. The Parents had been surprised by the question. Kapetria had taken Derek in her arms. "Is it necessary that this boy suffer so?"

Prince Brovotkin died in 1913 on the voyage to Brazil, leaving his entire estate to his adopted son, Garekyn. For a time, Garekyn had been lost. It was agony to see the Prince's body committed to the ocean deep, and he wept nightly for months afterwards, even as he traveled the length and breadth of the American continents. Even music did not comfort him. Garekyn had never experienced the death of a loved one, or grief. And he had to learn how to go on in spite of it. The search for his lost brothers and sister soon came to obsess him.

Even now as he walked up Fifth Avenue in the bracing cold air of mild winter, Garekyn wore an old military coat of fine black wool with brass buttons given to him by Prince Alexi. And in his vest, he carried the Prince's great pocket watch with the quotation from Shakespeare engraved inside the cover: LOVE ALL, TRUST A FEW, DO WRONG TO NONE.

Garekyn had never found any evidence anywhere of the others, his kin, as he called them. But he had never given up searching. If he was alive, they might still be alive. If he had been locked in the ice for thousands of years, so surely might they have been locked in the ice. And indeed, they might be locked in it still or only just released thanks to the strange phenomenon the world called "global warming."

And Garekyn's memories were increasing, bit by bit, and growing ever more detailed and disturbing.

The late twentieth century had given Garekyn new powerful instruments to fear, and also to help in his search for the others. Everywhere he traveled, he needed complex and carefully worded documents, and he lived in dread of an accident or illness that might put him in the hands of doctors who might discover in an emergency room that he was not human.

But the invention of the internet and the spread of social media had greatly emboldened Garekyn with regard to his search, providing opportunities for him that hadn't existed before. And it was through the internet that Garekyn had discovered the delightful and spirited Benji Mahmoud and the complex realm of Benji's blood drinkers, blood drinkers of all ages who called Benji's phone line for help from everywhere in the world, often enlisting the broadcast itself as a means of finding their lost ones.

What a striking idea, thought Garekyn. Might he not somehow through this broadcast find his lost ones? But how should he go about it, and how might he prevent an onslaught of responses from playful blood drinkers eager to pretend that they were Garekyn's companions and eager to play along with Garekyn's realm as humans sometimes did with the realm of Benji Mahmoud?

Benji Mahmoud thought he had a foolproof way of separating all others from his blood drinkers. He and his vampire kindred spoke in voices on the radio that only other vampires with their powerful preternatural hearing could hear. But Garekyn Brovotkin could also hear those voices effortlessly and detect a subtle difference in timbre in those voices from the voices of the humans who so badly wanted to play the imaginary game of the Children of the Night and the kingdom of the great Prince Lestat.

Almost immediately after his discovery of these enchanting broadcasts, Garekyn had heard mention of "Amel," and of the curious mythology of Amel, and Garekyn's mind had been disturbed as if by a whirling sandstorm. Amel. That very name, Amel.

This "Amel" according to the mythology of Benji Mahmoud was a spirit who had entered the world of human beings through the seduction of two powerful red-haired witches in ancient times, witches who had learned to communicate with the spirit and manipulate him. That these witches were red haired had also startled Garekyn. Garekyn had seen in a flash for the first time the being that he himself had known as Amel—with his pale white skin and red hair! And it had been this being who had said the words: the splendor of humanity.

Coincidences, probably. Coincidence and poetry. Fictive worlds. Likely Benji Mahmoud was an artist of fictive worlds of some sort, and made millions from his broadcast, though Garekyn could not turn up the slightest evidence of this or any money-making motivation. The program's websites offered nothing for sale. It did offer lots of exquisite pictures of beings who appeared to be human beings of unusually pale and radiant complexions, all of which might have been faked.

The more he listened, the more Garekyn had been intrigued that there had been disastrous consequences to this seduction of the spirit Amel, that he, in seeking to please the red-haired witches, had plunged into the physical body of an early Queen of the land of Kemet and created in so doing the very first "vampire." From this vampire came all other vampires, with Amel animating every single one in an unbroken chain to the present time.

Red hair. Amel. Ancient times. Immortals. It wasn't much to go on. But what about the distinct timbre of the voices? Was the spirit of Amel responsible for that as well? Amel gave great powers to his vampire children; they could spellbind "mortals," read minds, and develop over time the power to kinetically burn their opponents or break down doorways. They could even learn how to defy gravity and fly.

Now think on it.

How did Amel live and breathe in these creatures? Who was Amel?

All the vampires of the world, according to Benji Mahmoud, were animated by this Amel who had since those early times been moved from one primal host to another, and finally into a young blood drinker now known as Prince Lestat from whom the spirit kept the entire tribe of vampires animated and thriving. The "Amel Consciousness," as Benji sometimes called it, could travel from vampire to vampire through invisible weblike connections—and Amel himself had actually phoned the program more than once last year through the voices of random blood drinkers whom he had seduced.

But of course any blood drinker might boast that Amel spoke through him, and Benji had brushed off a number who made such claims as not credible.

Then the Prince had come, Prince Lestat, and Amel was safe inside him, Benji reminded the tribe.

Full darkness. It was just settling all around him, swallowed up and warmed by the rush of pedestrians on the pavements and the endless parade of motorcars, and the streetlamps snapping on silently all around him.

Garekyn had reached the proper street. A newspaper article had given the description of the three townhouses for which Garekyn was searching. As he turned right and made his way towards Madison Avenue, he saw them and their central iron gate. This much is real, he thought. The lights were on throughout the compound from the basement windows near the pavement to the high stories.

Garekyn stopped on the narrow pavement to adjust his silk tie as if this was his only concern. Scanning the people loitering about he saw at once that they were simply human beings. Young people, some with books or magazines under their arms, obviously eyeing Trinity Gate with awe and expectation. It was not a large crowd, and it appeared faintly restless. But it made it easier for Garekyn to loiter as well.

More humans passing by, simple humans coming and going. Garekyn played for time without causing attention. He took out his watch and marked the hour and promptly forgot it. He walked slowly from one end of the block to the other.

An hour passed during which most of the crowd had moved on.

Garekyn was prepared to wait. He could have waited until midnight or after. From time to time he had the feeling that someone was watching him from inside the house, though he saw nothing to indicate this. Again and again, he walked the block. Finally a great sinking sadness came over him. He might never find the others. He might be lost forever on this planet, concealing himself from its mortal inhabitants forever.

How could he love again and lose in death a cherished companion? How could he ever alleviate the loneliness and isolation he felt unless he defined himself a new purpose?

Purpose.

He came to the corner of Madison Avenue again in his little promenade and was just starting back down the block when he saw the shining lacquered front door of the central townhouse open. Out onto the small granite porch stepped a diminutive male figure dressed in a black three-piece suit of worsted wool, with a sharp Italian fedora on his head. Little Man! Benji Mahmoud himself! Garekyn recognized him at once from a thousand descriptions uttered over the airwaves in the past year, and from his pictures online, and he also knew in a flash that Benji Mahmoud was not human. This was beyond question. Benji Mahmoud might not be the heroic revenant he claimed to be, but human he was not.

How Garekyn's fine senses told him this, Garekyn couldn't know. But the skin had a luster, and the being's walk, though graceful, was unnatural.

"Little Man," as they called him, paused at the foot of the steps to sign autograph books for a couple of young humans. And to another he tipped his hat with a charming ease and then, with a tactful little hand gesture pleading for privacy, walked swiftly towards Madison Avenue and towards Garekyn.

Garekyn came to a halt as they passed one another, and then pivoting he discovered that Benji Mahmoud was gazing back at him.

**Not human.**

Benji Mahmoud had marked Garekyn for what he was, or what he wasn't, as well. But Benji Mahmoud had turned and continued walking on fearlessly and indifferently.

Garekyn could hardly contain himself. He wanted to approach the figure and confess all he knew of himself and beg Benji Mahmoud to help him. But something stronger than instinct kept him many paces behind as he tracked Little Man now, who turned right and started walking downtown.

Garekyn didn't know what to do! He realized how surprised he was, how positively amazed, and though he knew that nothing like this had happened to him in a hundred years, indeed that he had never seen a being like this Little Man anywhere in the world, nor a being like himself anywhere in the world, this was in fact happening, and this Benji Mahmoud was ignoring him! Indeed, it was worse than that. Little Man picked up his pace. In the thin leisurely crowds on Madison Avenue, Little Man appeared to be trying to lose him.

In fact, it was amazing how fast the little blood drinker could walk without attracting attention. Like many another New Yorker, he darted gracefully past people to the right and left, with his head slightly bowed, and vanished from moment to moment as Garekyn, half a block away, sped forward trying to catch sight of him again.

Garekyn's mind raced. It wasn't calculation to have one's thoughts race like this, and to have the inevitable mammalian emotions clashing wildly in one's body and brain. And suddenly, he began to repeat the name "Amel" under his breath, repeat it as if it were a prayer. "Amel, Amel, Amel . . . ," he whispered, as on and on he walked. "I must find out about Amel!" he whispered. "I must know about Amel!" Could the vampire be hearing what

Garekyn was saying? "Amel, tell me, I must know about Amel."

The figure he was following stiffened, and then came to a stop.

For a moment, Garekyn couldn't see Benji for the passersby, but then he did see him. Benji had turned around and was looking at him, and Garekyn felt the nearest thing to panic he'd felt in years. **Danger. Threat. Retreat.**

Now, Garekyn had no instinctive fear of humans. He was, by his own calculation with the help of Prince Alexi, about five times as strong as a human male. But every molecule in his body alerted him to overwhelming risk.

He couldn't retreat. He couldn't. He had to make contact with Benji, and Benji had to talk to him! Besides what could this "blood drinker" do to him? He walked on towards Benji and he kept repeating that word, "Amel, Amel."

A car appeared at the curb beside Benji.

Garekyn and Benji weren't thirty steps from one another.

Benji fixed Garekyn with his sharp black eyes, and then he climbed into the car and the car sped away, rushing northbound past Garekyn and on into the steady flow of cars that choked the avenue.

Garekyn cried out, begging Benji to wait.

But the car was gone, spurting away almost recklessly through the other cars, and turning off two blocks ahead.

Garekyn's heart sank. He ran his fingers back through his hair, and finding a handkerchief in one of his many pockets, he wiped angrily at his face.

He walked on, trying to think.

Perhaps this had happened for the best. Perhaps this thing, this Benji species of mutant, could have done him harm. If he were to go back now to Trinity Gate, perhaps a collection of these beings, alerted by the redoubtable Benji, could do him harm.

Only slowly did he come to realize this had been a great experience for him, a unique experience, and that he had now much to ponder, whereas he'd had almost nothing tangible at all to think about before.

But he was stung, stung to his soul. He'd encountered somebody, somebody vital in his search for the past, and that someone had fled from him, and so he would have to approach the entire matter in some new and more cautious way.

He found a café where he felt at home.

It was a restaurant actually, not open as yet for "dinner," as they called it, but it was fine with them if he took one of the smaller tables near the front window and drank a glass of the house wine.

The wine went to his head as it always did from the first mouthful, and he felt the relaxation move through him as if he'd sunk down in a warm bath.

He had never forgotten the warning of the Parents that during his mission on Earth, he must refrain from all spirits or fermented drinks, and all other intoxicants, that he would have little or no defense against them, that indeed human beings had little or no defense against them, but that they might cripple his cerebral circuits even more quickly than they worked on human beings.

But he liked wine. He liked being intoxicated. He liked having the pain and loneliness dulled by intoxication. He loved it, in fact, and he wept as he called for another glass and drank it down as if it were a shot of bourbon. Why not a bottle? The waitress nodded without a word, and filled the glass for him again when she returned, setting the corked bottle beside it.

Silently, Garekyn shed tears. People passed him on the other side of the glass. He wiped at his eyes crossly with his handkerchief, but it didn't make him feel better. He sat back in the comfortable little chair, and began to take a swift inventory of everything Benjamin Mahmoud had ever said about the "spirit Amel."

Then something utterly unforeseen happened.

Garekyn's eyes were closed. He had pressed two fingers of his right hand against the bridge of his nose as a mortal might who was experiencing a headache.

But he saw—. No, he **was** in another place. A vast room with walls of glass, but it wasn't glass, no, nothing like glass, a vast room and beyond were the towers of—. He had almost seized on the name of the city when the voice of Amel interrupted him, Amel rising from behind his desk, pale skinned, red haired, yes! Amel! Amel speaking in that rapid, emotional, classic mammalian voice with which they'd all been endowed: "Don't tell me you are the People of the Purpose when your purpose is to do just what they sent you to do! For the love of your souls, find for yourself a finer purpose! Just as I did."

In shock, Garekyn opened his eyes. It was gone, this fiery fragment from the past. And he felt both an overwhelming desire to recall it to himself, and a fear of doing so.

Suddenly the weight of his frustration crushed Garekyn, and the rejection of him by the silent Benji Mahmoud cut his heart. He could have spoken to me! What did he have to fear from me, this strange being, who was brave enough to hide in plain sight among humans in the busiest metropolis in the world?

Angrily, Garekyn rose from the chair and sought out the lavatory. He needed to slap water on his face, wake himself up, come to his senses. The waitress directed him to a small corridor behind the dining room that reeked of dust and disinfectant. He made his way to the "last door on the left."

Then he came to a halt. **Danger.**

There was no one in the little hallway but him. Beyond the kitchen wall to one side was the clatter and clang of pots and pans and the shrill cacophony of voices. He moved on, opened the door, and stepped into a large room containing a toilet and a fancy mirror and sink. As he turned to snap the lock, the door flew back, striking him on the forehead, and he found himself against the hard cold marble wall, stunned, as a blood drinker locked the door behind him.

**Danger. Full alert. Massive danger.**

Waxy, luminescent skin, a mass of dusty brown hair, and vicious eyes. A smile that was the baring of fangs and not a gesture of conciliation.

"You're coming with me, stranger," the male spoke in an ugly voice. "What do you mean stalkin' little Benji? I have friends who want to talk to you."

"And you are—?" asked Garekyn coldly. He did not move. He eyed the being as if he had all the time in the world to do so. Shorter than he; shorter arms; a massive head; old scars carved in the strange unnatural flesh as if painted on the face of a doll; and broken teeth between the glistering fangs; clothes that reeked of dust and mildew.

Laughter came from the other. "Killer's my name," he said. "And there's a reason for that. Now you're going to walk out of here with me, and back up to Trinity Gate, and don't attract the slightest attention. My friends have been alerted. I don't know who and what you are, but we'll get to all of that very soon."

As he spoke, the being's pale eyes appeared to narrow and glaze over. Something stirred in his battered face and it became as expressionless as the face of a giant cat. "Flesh and blood," he murmured. He took a deep breath and inhaled. He closed the gap between himself and Garekyn, driving his sharp vampiric teeth into Garekyn's neck before Garekyn could stop him.

A dizziness came over Garekyn. A great yawning darkness opened. He saw the immense circuitry of his own blood illuminated in a flash. **No, not like this, no.** He felt the pull on his veins and on centers of power within himself of which he knew nothing. A vision exploded in the darkness. Amel? Benji Mahmoud's face, the name Armand whispered. And then again Amel. Amel.

It was as if something invisible from within Garekyn was reaching into the other, the other who was sucking the blood so powerfully that Garekyn was shuddering and nauseated and suddenly terrified.

Garekyn fought it with all his strength, driving the creature back against the other wall so hard that the creature's head struck the marble with a dull sound. Now it was battle, the creature lunging for Garekyn again; and this time, applying all his might, Garekyn drove the creature back again and down, slamming his face hard against the porcelain of the sink. Something broke, but with a sound so soft Garekyn could barely hear it.

Blood flowed on the dirty white porcelain. The blood glittered! The darkness rose up to take hold of Garekyn again. The creature's hands closed on Garekyn's neck, but with his left hand, Garekyn grabbed a full hank of the creature's hair and swung his head down again and again on the edge of the sink.

The skull caved, the blood shot out of the creature's mouth like the jet of a fountain—glittering. Amel. Armand. Names called in a void that might replace the little lavatory room if Garekyn didn't hang on with every bit of stubbornness he could muster.

Again and again, he slammed the head down, this time on the chrome faucet and he felt the head close around the faucet as the faucet pierced the skull.

"Armand!" roared the creature as the blood bubbled from its lips.

Without hesitation, unsure of his strength, and determined to control all that would happen henceforth, Garekyn ripped the head forward and turned the head with all his might so as to break the creature's neck.

Done!

The creature dropped to the floor, his face appearing to slide from his skull like a mask, blood flooding from his eyes and his mouth and once again the blood glittered, glittered, as if with myriad tiny pulsing bits of living light, skittering, swirling in the blood.

The creature lay in a heap.

Garekyn put his fingers into the blood and lifted the blood to his lips. A zinging sensation swept through all his limbs. He licked and licked at the blood. **Amel.** Motion, voices, another realm breaking in.

He reached down and ripped with his fingers at the white flesh, scraping it loose from the gleaming white bones of the skull and there in a great fissure he saw what must have been the brain, sizzling and hissing with tiny pinpoints of light.

Images swam in his ken. The twins, the Mother, the devouring of the brain, Benji talking on and on about the old tales, the new tales . . . Amel in the brain.

He squatted down beside the battered heap of the creature, and he scooped up the brain and forced it into his own mouth, his throat locking in nausea even as he did it. But the nausea vanished. The world vanished.

An immense web, a web so intricate and beautiful and vast it appeared to compass the Heavens, and the stars pulsing in it like tiny beings, alive, calling, pleading. Dim echo rising as if it were a splash of blood on a wall: **Armand, help me, attacked, murdered, not human, not human!**

Retching, doubled over, Garekyn held the dissolving brain in his mouth, pressing against it with his tongue, the great web growing brighter and brighter.

He opened his eyes. He was sprawled against the cold white toilet. Blood all over his clothes. Blood all over his hands.

Unthinking, he shot to his feet, unlatched the

door, and fled, not back into the restaurant but out a back passage and into a dim alley. Smashing into large glistening black plastic sacks and stacks of cardboard boxes he blundered, nearly falling, slipping in puddles of grease and water, running as fast as he could, with no idea of what lay ahead of him.

He heard someone pursuing him. He knew he was meant to hear this, hear the boots striking the stones. On he ran only to see a wall rise up in front of him.

He pivoted just in time to recognize the white-faced being who closed in on him. Beatific face, auburn hair! Armand. The master of Trinity Gate. Upwards, they rose, higher and higher until the wind was roaring in his ears. And once again, fang teeth were in his neck, and this time a chorus of voices crying in the great empty darkness.

**All be warned. Something not human!**

"Don't kill me!" he pleaded without a voice. "Help me. I didn't want to kill him. He hurt me. I didn't want to kill him. I wanted to know—." He had no voice and no body. He was just this sweetness and this pain, this swoon, and the voices rising all around him speaking words of condemnation and menace but in tones so tender and melodious it was like singing. He saw the circuit of his blood again and felt pain throughout as the blood was drawn out of him, his heart beating faster and faster as if it would explode.

**Amel, it is you? Are you here? It is you after all these centuries, are you here? This is Garekyn.**

He was high above the city, and he was dying. No escape this time, no matter what the Parents had said. **And if the pain is too great to bear, you will lose consciousness, but you will not die. And you will slowly revive and restore, no matter what they have done to you.** Snow without end, snow and ice. Go into the ice and freeze. Mountains of ice. Snow without end.

"They sent you here to destroy me, didn't they?" said Amel, Amel of old in his great office in Atalantaya. Warm air. Windows filled with the spectacle of the city's towers, like a forest made of glass. "Well, didn't they?"

Darkness. **You will not die. . . .**

And how horrible that it should come finally like this, at the hands of monsters, this magnificent world, to see it no more, to lose it, to lose all of it, without my understanding anything!—

Before him suddenly, a sky of endless blue and the great translucent city of Atalantaya exploding with smoke and fire! Amel cried out against it. Or was it he, Garekyn, screaming in defiance as the towers melted, shattered, the great dome cracking, the whole city tilting and sliding into the boiling sea? My death, just my death. Because that was long ago and they are all dead.

# 4

# Lestat

SOMEWHERE OVER THE North Atlantic, when I was riding the winds, Amel left me.

When I entered the carriageway of my old townhouse in the Rue Royale in New Orleans I was apparently alone. Had Louis come as I'd asked him to do? Very likely not. But how was I to know? Masters can't hear the thoughts of fledglings. Masters are forever locked out of the minds of their children. And for all I knew I was locked out of Louis's heart.

The back courtyard was luxuriantly overgrown the way I loved it, the bright magenta bougainvillea heaped over the high brick walls. The little common flowers of Louisiana, the yellow and the purple lantana, were huge and fragrant and softly beautiful with their dusty dark little leaves, and the oleander magnificent with its pink blooms. The giant banana trees were rustling and swaying in the cool breeze off the nearby river, and the new fountain, the splendid new fountain with its moss-covered cherubs, was filled with water singing in the lights of the lanterns along the back porch.

Did I feel an immediate sense of well-being? Well, no. This was as painful as it was sweet; this was honey with a bitter taste. I'd had my heart broken here more than once, almost died upstairs in this flat, hadn't I, and I'd come out of a deep sleep once not so long ago to find Louis in this very courtyard, in an open coffin, nearly burnt to death by the sun. I'd brought him back with my blood then. And my beloved fledgling David Talbot had helped me. Louis had been more powerful since then—thanks to that new infusion of my blood—and though at first he'd been happy, happy for a while with the love of David and a strange unearthly blood drinker named Merrick, he had come to hate me for the increased strength that took him even further away from the human he could never be again.

I knew what I was up against with Louis. I had to convince him that this time was different from the earlier times when we'd tried to come together—different from the brief coven of the old Night Island, different from the brief connection after he'd tried to destroy himself, different even from his time at Trinity Gate which was forever changed now by recent events—different because we were all different now and I, in my heart and soul, was different. And I needed him to help me write a new page in the history of our entire tribe.

But what was the point of pondering it further? Words wouldn't carry the motion. One way or other, he'd make a decision of the heart.

I hurried up the iron stairs to the door of the flat, ready to kick in a wall if the place was truly empty, ground the doorknob nearly to rusted powder as I turned it, and went inside.

The old back parlor looked splendid with its fresh burgundy velvet wallpaper, and a new Victorian couch of lacquered fruitwood with artful pillows plumped with modern chemical foam. Ah, I didn't care. What matters to me is how things look, and it all looked fine, the machine-made blue-and-beige Aubusson carpet as lovely as any ever made by human fingers. Same old gilded Louis XV desk and chairs, but all was shining, restored, pretty. A Chinese vase filled with fragrant leafy eucalyptus, and a small undoubtedly genuine French Impressionist painting on the wall of a woman in profile, a woman with long russet hair.

I breathed in the scent of furniture wax, the eucalyptus, and stronger blooms, roses perhaps in another room. The place felt tight, smaller than I remembered, but that was always the case when I first arrived.

There was someone here. And it was not Cyril or Thorne, who were now in the courtyard below, exploring the old slaves' quarters building and the concrete crypts recently created beneath them which could shield at least six of the Undead from sunshine or catastrophe during the hours of the day.

I stood for a moment in the hallway, peering towards the front parlor where the lights of the Rue Royale shone yellow in the lace curtains, and I closed my eyes.

For fifty years we'd lived here, Louis, Claudia, and I; and Claudia had put a match to it for all the inevitable reasons that Adam and Eve turn their backs on paradise every night or day. These boards, these very boards, once carpeted and now hard and gleaming with lacquer! How she loved to run the length of this hall, ribbons streaming, and leap into my arms! A shiver ran through me as if I were feeling her cold white cheek against mine, and her confidential husky voice in my ear.

Well, the place wasn't really empty, was it; it was haunted, and always would be haunted, and no new Chinese patterned wallpaper would change it, nor electric chandeliers replete with glistening crystal illuminating the rooms to the right and the left.

I went into his bedroom—the chamber that has always been for Louis, Louis sitting up against the back of his massive four-poster, reading Dickens, Louis writing at the desk in a diary I never read, Louis dozing there with his head on a pillow staring at the flowers above in the tester as if the flowers were alive.

Empty. Of course. A museum chamber, down to

the old brass brackets of the gas lamps with their frosted globes, and the tall hulking armoire in which he'd once kept all of his simple black clothes. Well, what had I expected? Nothing personal marred the effect until I realized I was staring at a discarded pair of worn black shoes, shoes so thoroughly coated in dust they seemed made of it, and there on the chair beside the chest of drawers was a worn old shirt.

Could this possibly mean—?

I turned around.

Louis was standing in the door of the room opposite, across the hall.

I drew in my breath. I didn't say a word. **I like to look at him through your eyes.**

He was outfitted entirely in the new clothes I'd ordered for him, a long black riding jacket, sleek at the waist and flaring, and a pale pink European-linen handmade shirt. He wore a tie of green silk, almost exactly the color of his eyes, and there was an emerald ring on his finger of that very same green. Bit of handkerchief in his breast pocket to match the tie, and fine-cut trousers of black wool and sleek boots fitted to his calves like gloves.

I was unable to speak. He'd put on these clothes for me, and I knew it. Nothing else in this world would have prompted him to dress like this, or to have brushed all the dust out of his glistening black hair. And the hair he'd left long on rising so that it was full as it had been in the old days, wavy, a little unruly, curling just under his ears. Even his white skin looked polished. And a scent rose from him of a rare and expensive male cologne. That too, I had sent for. That too, servants had brought here along with my other gifts.

Silence. It was like when Gabrielle, my mother, undid her long braid and combed her free and luxuriant hair. I could scarcely breathe.

I sensed he understood. He crossed the hall and put his arms around me and kissed me on the lips.

"This is what you wanted, isn't it?" he asked. Nothing mocking or mean in the tone.

Shocked. Unable to respond.

"Well, I figured you could use some new clothes, that you always can." I was stammering, clinging to a shred of dignity, trivializing the moment with ridiculous words.

"A whole room full of clothes?" he asked. "Lestat, the century will be ended before I can wear all that."

"Come, let's hunt," I said. Which really meant, Let's get out of here, let's walk together and be quiet together and please let me see you drink. Let me see you draw the blood and the life out of a human being. Let me see you need it, and go for it, and have it, and be filled to the brim with it.

I slipped on my large violet-tinted sunglasses, so essential to helping me pass for human in crowded streets, and guided Louis to the door.

We made a swift exit like two normal human beings, and we were halfway down the block, and turning towards Chartres Street, before he noticed

Cyril and Thorne behind us, too close, and too con-
spicuous, and asked if they were going to follow us
wherever we went.

"Can't get rid of them," I said. "Price of having
the Core in me. Price of being the Prince."

"And you truly are the Prince now, aren't you?"
he asked. "You're really trying to make a go of it. You
don't want it to fall apart."

"It will **not** fall apart," I said. "Not this time, not
while I have breath in my body. It's more than another coven, more than a gathering of three or four
in a new city. It's more than anything that ever happened to any of us ever in the past." I sighed. I gave
up. "When you see the Court, you'll understand."

"I felt certain you'd already be sick of it," he said.
"The Brat Prince becoming the Prince? I would
never have predicted it."

"Me neither," I said. "But you know my motto,
what it's always been. I refuse to be bad at what I do,
and that includes being bad. I won't be bad at being
bad. I won't do **this** badly now either. Wait and see."

"I already see," he said.

"I can make the bodyguards take to the roofs, if
you want."

"They don't matter," he said. "You're the one who
matters."

We headed down Chartres towards Jackson
Square. There was a fancy restaurant café on a
nearby corner, and he seemed drawn to it, though
why I wasn't sure. It was too thrilling just being near

him, walking with him as if we'd been walking like this for a hundred years. The night was balmy and almost warm, the way winter nights can be in New Orleans, between colder weather, and the crowds were mostly well-dressed tourists on the prowl, innocent, exuberant the way people become when they are in New Orleans and looking for a good time.

Soon as he was seated at the café table, he had his eyes on a couple near the back. I could tell from the manner in which he fixed on the woman that he was listening to her thoughts. He'd gained telepathic power from his new blood, and with time. She was perhaps fifty, in a sleeveless black dress, exquisitely groomed with hair like white nylon, and firm well-molded arms. She wore very dark glasses, which looked a bit ridiculous, and so did the man opposite, who was, however, disguised. She didn't know that he was disguised. His mouth had been deliberately distorted by something artificial that he wore on his gums, and his short uninteresting brown hair had been dyed. She was paying the man to kill her husband and she wanted the man to understand why. The man didn't care at all why she wanted the deed done. He wanted the money and to be gone. He thought the woman was a complete fool.

I sized up the situation easily enough and obviously so did Louis.

When the woman started to cry, the man hastily took his leave, but not before receiving an envelope from the woman, which he slipped into his inner coat pocket without so much as a glance at it. He was gone, off fast, towards Jackson Square, and then she sat there brooding, crying, refused another drink from the waiter, insisting to herself that she had to get her husband out of her life, and this was the way to do it and that no one would ever understand the miserable life she'd lived. Then, leaving a bill on the table, she went out. It was done and couldn't be undone. She was hungry; she would have a good dinner and get drunk at her hotel.

Louis went after her.

I went ahead and drifted around to the Rue Royale entrance of Pirates Alley as she came walking towards me, weeping again, head bowed, shoulder bag clasped to her side, her handkerchief twisted in the other hand.

The huge silent cathedral rose to my right like a great shadow. Tourists trickled by, jostling one another; and she came on, with Louis behind her silently, his face like a pale flame in the half-light as he drew up to her and placed his hand, the hand with the emerald ring, on her left shoulder. He turned her as gently as a lover and tenderly pressed her head to the stone wall.

I stood watching as he drank from her, slipping into her mind now to find him and what he was feeling as all that sweet salty blood flooded his mouth and his senses, as the heart of the woman weakened and slowed. He paced himself, letting her recover ever so slightly—the inevitable images of childhood, fetched in desperation as the body realizes that it is losing its vitality, her head drowsing to her right and his fingers holding her chin firmly—and passersby thinking them lovers, and the voices of the city humming and rustling and the scent of rain coming on the breeze.

Suddenly he collected her in both arms and ascended, vanishing so quickly the tourists walking to and fro never saw it happen, only felt the faintest disturbance in the air. Wasn't there someone there a moment ago? Gone. Gone the scent of blood and death.

And so he was using all his faculties now, his new gifts, the gifts of the powerful blood, gifts he wouldn't have come by in the regular scheme of things for maybe another century or maybe never, ascending to the clouds or just up and up into the darkness until he could find a place to deposit her remains on some remote rooftop, tucked between a chimney and a parapet, perhaps, who knew.

Well, if someone did not dispose of the assassin in the subtle disguise, the murder of her husband would take place as usual though all the reasons for it were gone.

But a distant blast of intelligence let me know that Cyril had taken care of the rascal, feasting on him quickly, and then depositing him in the river, while Thorne had hung back to remain with me. Bodyguards have to feed.

Amel was still gone, after all that talk of wanting to see Louis through my eyes, and I'd closed my mind to telepathic voices, and Louis was gone, and I was hungry and tired from riding the wind, and sick at heart. Innocent blood. I wanted innocent blood, not minds and hearts like sewers, but innocent blood. Well, I wasn't going to drink innocent blood. Not while preaching to so many others that they couldn't drink innocent blood. No. I could not.

I walked down Pirates Alley in the direction of the river, and then along under the porches opposite Jackson Square. The shops were closed up. And it seemed a shame. There were crowds close to the river, and I heard the calliope of the tourist steamboat, and for a moment nothing in the whole world seemed changed from when I'd lived and loved here before.

The streets might as well have been mud, and the gas lamps dim and grimy, and the barrooms packed with deliciously filthy riverboat men and the sound of dice and billiard balls, and carriages might have been crowded in the Rue Saint Peter with people coming from the old French Opera on Bourbon at Toulouse. And it might as well have been the night, long after Louis and Claudia had left me after trying to kill me, that Antoine, my fledgling musician, and I had gone to see the premiere of a French opera called **Mignon**. I'd been scarred and broken and crushed in soul, led as if blind by Antoine, as people scurried out of our path to get away from the burnt one, yet I'd allowed him to bully me to sit there in the dark with him and hear that lustrous clarinet or oboe begin the overture. Music like that could make you feel that you were alive. It could even make you feel like all the pain in the world was headed some-place glorious that could be shared by the simplest of the beings around you.

Well, what did it matter now?

Rain, light rain.

Dampening the spirits of the line outside the Café du Monde. But I loved it, and loved the scent of the dust rising from the wet street.

I moved to the head of the line, and dazzled the waiter in charge to believe I had some special right to a table now, a simple little trick of words and charm and soon I was seated in the midst of the throng, and with my hand locked on a hot mug of café au lait. The place was packed and noisy with chatter, and waiters coming and going with trays of mugs and plates of sugar-covered beignets. And the open air moved sluggishly in the wet breeze. I looked up at the slowly churning overhead fans, descended on long rods from the dark wood-paneled ceiling, and I fastened on the blades of the nearest fan and felt myself drifting away from memory and reason and just thinking, I am alone, I am alone, I am alone. Amel is with me night and day, yet I am alone. I am a prince and live in a château with hundreds under my roof nightly, yet I am alone. I am in a crowded café filled with beating hearts and laughter and the sweetest most innocent merriment and I am alone.

I stared at the marble top of the table, at the white powdered sugar heaped on the hot doughnuts, and felt the coffee mug growing colder and colder by the second, and remembered from long ago, my father, my old blind father, sitting up in his wretched bed, hung with all the mended mosquito netting, being fed by a sweet lovely servant girl, and complaining, Nothing is hot enough, nothing is hot enough anymore.

King David dying in the Bible, begging for warmth . . . **and they covered him with clothes, but he gat no heat. . . .**

Terrible thing to be cold and alone. The cup was cold. The marble top of the table was cold, and the wind was cold now thanks to the rain, and the fans were churning the cold air so slowly. I thought of King David lying there, as they brought the damsel to him to keep him warm. **And the damsel was very fair, and cherished the king, and ministered to him; but the king knew her not.**

Why didn't I hunt for the one thing that could make me warm, the blood of a victim coursing through my veins, a soul breathing its last in my arms? Because it wouldn't have made me any more warm than the damsel made King David. And I could not claim to have killed a single Goliath in my life, or . . .

A shadow fell over the table, over the bright white sugar on the beignets, and the white marble. Louis was sitting there. Calm, and collected, as they say, arms folded on his chest, very much clear of the sticky marble table, and his mellow green eyes fixed on me.

"Now why the Hell do you want me, of all people," he asked, "to come with you to France?"

Vaguely, I was aware that Thorne wanted me, that moving about restlessly in the crowd beyond the café he was signaling to me, something important, something, please attend now. I shut him out.

I looked squarely at Louis, who looked as splendidly human as he ever had. A rage of jealousy exploded in me against the blood in his veins that wasn't mine.

"You know why," I said turning my head and looking at the nearby crowds. Street performers were out there, dancing, singing, bringing big soft explosions of approval from the crowds. "You know damned good and well why. Because you were there when I was just Born to Darkness. You were there when I stumbled onto these shores and sought to find a companion, and found you; and you were there when we lived all those decades together, you and me and Claudia, and you are the only one living who remembers the sound of her happy voice, her young voice, or the ring of her laugh. And you were there when I almost died at her hands, and when the pair of you fought me again and left me in the flames. And you were there when I was humiliated and ruined at the Théâtre des Vampires, and they murdered her due to my crimes, my weakness, my blunder, my ignorance, my failure to steer one fragile little bark in the right direction, and you were there when I rose from the dead and had my shabby little moment of triumph on the rock music stage, my cheap little hour as Freddie Mercury before the footlights, you were there. You came. You were there. And you were there when I took the spirit of Amel into me, and when all around me were telling me I had to be the Prince whether I wanted to be or not, you were there. You were there when all these streets ran with mud and river water, and when you and I went to see **Macbeth** onstage, and I couldn't stop dancing under the streetlamps afterwards reciting the words, 'Tomorrow and tomorrow and tomorrow,' and Claudia thought I was so handsome and so witty and so clever, and we would all of us always be safe, you were there."

Silence, or the inevitable silence one enjoys in a crowded noisy café where someone is screaming with laughter at a nearby table, and someone else is arguing with the man beside him over who should pay the check.

I didn't dare to look at Louis. I shut my eyes and tried to listen to the river itself, the great broad Mississippi River only a matter of yards from us, running past the city of New Orleans and so deep that no one would ever find all the bodies committed to its depths, the great broad river that might swallow the city one night for reasons no one would ever be able to explain, and carry every particle of the city south into the Gulf of Mexico and the great ocean beyond . . . all that wallpaper, all those gas lamps, all the laughter and the purple flagstones and the shimmering green banana leaves like blades of a knife.

I could hear the water, hear the earth itself shifting and softening, and the plants themselves growing, and Thorne, Thorne insisting that I come out, that I talk to him, that I was needed, always needed, and Cyril saying, "Ah, leave the son of a bitch alone."

Now that's my kind of bodyguard! Leave the son of a bitch alone indeed.

I turned to see Louis was looking at me. The old familiar green eyes and the faint smile. **Is Amel inside you? Is it you, Amel, looking through Louis's eyes?**

"Very well," Louis said.

"What do you mean?"

He shrugged and smiled.

"I'll come if you want me. I'll come and I'll stay and I'll be your companion if you want. I don't know why you want this or how long you'll want it, or what it's going to be like, being with you and watching all your antics up close, and trying to be of help and not knowing how to be of help, but I'll come. I'm tired of fighting it; I give up; I'll come."

I couldn't believe I'd heard right. I stared at him as helplessly as I had in the hallway of the townhouse when I'd first seen him, trying to grasp what he had said.

He leaned close to me, and he put his hand on my arm. " 'Wither thou goest, I will go, and where thou lodgest, I will lodge; thy people shall be my people'; and because I have no other god and never will, you shall be my god."

Was it Amel speaking these words through him? Was it Amel touching my arm through his hand? Had Amel lied about not being able to find Louis? When I looked into these green eyes, I saw only Louis, and the words echoing in my mind were Louis's words.

"I know what you need," he said. "You need one person who is always on your side. Well, I'm ready to be that one now. I don't know why I tormented you, made you pay for asking, made you come all this way. I always knew I was going to come. Maybe I thought you'd lose interest because I never really understood why you wanted me in the first place. But you're not losing interest, not even with the whole Court, and so I'll come. And when you tire of me and want me gone, I'll hate you, of course."

"Trust me," I whispered. He was cutting me to the heart and making me happy, and this was pain.

"I do," he said.

"It's you, you saying these things, isn't it?"

"And who else would it be?" he asked.

"I don't know," I said. I sat back and looked around the café. The lights were too bright here and people were staring at the strange men with the luminescent skin. The violet sunglasses always distracted people, and helped to cover a face that was too white and eyes that were too bright. But it was never enough. And Louis had no such glasses. Time to move on.

"You'll enjoy the Court," I said. "There are beautiful things to hear and see."

# 5

# Fareed

THEY WERE SEATED together in the "blue" salon of Armand's house in Saint-Germain-des-Prés, in the suite that Armand had given to Fareed for his private use. Fareed was at his desk, and Gregory sat opposite at a round table on which he had spread out a game of solitaire with gilt-edged playing cards.

Fareed was staring at the material on his computer screen.

"I understand what you're saying," he said to Gregory. "You don't hands-on manage Collingsworth Pharmaceuticals. But there's a reason I'm asking about this particular project."

"I'm happy to tell you anything I know," said Gregory. "It's just that I'm not likely to know the slightest thing." He sat back in the gilded armchair and looked at the unyielding cards. "There must be a more amusing game than this," he said under his breath.

"It's the doctor involved—a woman."

"I wouldn't know a thing about her," said Gregory absently. "Others vetted her, hired her, approved her projects, not me." He turned up another card and looked at it with disappointment. "Maybe I should start devising our own card games, card games for us."

"Sounds like a stroke of genius," said Fareed, his eyes still on the screen. "Solitaire for blood drinkers. Perhaps you could devise a new deck of cards."

"Now that's a thought, or possibly an exquisite deck with face cards that have special meaning for us. Would our beloved Prince be the jack of diamonds? If so, who would be the king?"

"It's too early to be talking treason," Fareed murmured, eyes on the central monitor before him. There were three monitors, all the same size, and a couple of small monitors, dedicated to specific purposes, off to each side.

It was near 4:30 a.m. and there was little noise coming from the narrow streets that surrounded the immense nineteenth-century townhouse. The restaurants and cafés of the famous district were far away.

"Bear with me," said Fareed. "This doctor's reports to her superiors have been brilliant; but she's not who or what she claims to be. And her projects all have to do with cloning. You know this, of course."

"Cloning?" asked Gregory as he dealt out a new table of cards. "I know nothing about it, but it doesn't surprise me that people in my company are working on human cloning. It's illegal, isn't it? But I have never believed for a minute that the mortal doctors of the world could resist something so exciting as human cloning. There are times when I've encountered mortals in Geneva whom I suspected of having been genetically engineered. But then I know so little about it."

Fareed sat quietly absorbing all this.

"Collingsworth Pharmaceuticals has nothing official to do with cloning," said Gregory. "We have a policy against it. We have a policy against fetal tissue research."

"That's amusing," said Fareed. "Because your laboratories are engaged in a great deal of research involving fetal tissue."

"Hmmm . . ." Gregory was studying the cards closely. "I would love to design cards specifically for the Court. I think Lestat would have to be the king, though he eschews that title, and I think Gabrielle might be a magnificent queen. The jack could be Benjamin Mahmoud."

Fareed smiled.

"But then perhaps each suit could be different. Marius might be the king of clubs, and I might be the king of diamonds, and Seth might be the king of spades."

Fareed laughed. He said, "Collingsworth Pharmaceuticals has been working on the cloning of human beings covertly for twenty years."

Gregory sat back again and looked at Fareed. "Very well. This offends you in some way? You think it's dangerous? You think I should stop it?"

"You could stop it in your own company but could never stop it worldwide."

"So what do you want of me here?"

"Just to listen to me for a little while," Fareed said.

Gregory smiled. "Of course." He went back to lining up the cards in suits.

What a charming, genial individual Gregory was, Fareed thought, and it was extremely difficult to realize that he was likely the oldest blood drinker now in existence. With Khayman and the twins gone, he was almost surely the oldest. He had been made before Akasha's son, Seth, Fareed's master, mentor, and lover, but not by much.

Everything about the tall, lean, and often silent person of Seth suggested great antiquity—including his eccentric mode of dress—a taste for sandals and custom-made floor-length robes of linen—and his slow and often unusual speech. That he now understood almost every current Indo-European language was plain enough, but he chose his words with extreme care and favored a stripped-down vocabulary which suggested a preference for concepts formed in his mind long before a plethora of adjectives and adverbs had been developed in any tongue to nuance them or sharpen them. And even the look in Seth's deep-set eyes was chilling and remote. Often his expression seemed to say: "Do not seek to understand me or the time from which I came. You cannot."

Seth had gone out hunting the dark corners of Paris tonight, a willowy white-clad wraith decked out in antique Egyptian bracelets and rings, likely to attract predatory mortals by his sheer peculiarity and seemingly defenseless reserve.

Gregory Duff Collingsworth on the other hand was thoroughly fortified by a modern demeanor in all respects. He moved with the easy grace of twenty-first-century men of power, comfortable on escalators and in elevators, in high-rise towers or cavernous shopping malls, and before television news cameras and human interrogators—an impeccably groomed and conservatively dressed "man of business," who spoke to one and all with an effortless courtesy that was both formal and warm.

Even here in this vast rococo drawing room, Gregory had the manicured gloss of a male of these times. He wore a "casual" belted gray suede jacket, with a pale-blue-checkered shirt under it and denim slacks. He wore his usual gold-banded wristwatch, and a pair of soft brown calf-leather pull-tab boots. All the immortals who took to the air wore boots.

Of course Gregory went to great lengths to "pass." He spent his comatose daylight hours in a glass rooftop chamber. Everybody knew this. At the Château he slept exposed atop the south tower. Here in Paris, he slept in a high-walled courtyard. This kept his skin always darkly tanned. And every evening on rising, he cut and trimmed his dark hair perfectly, so that few of his new immortal companions even guessed that it had been shoulder length when he'd been made.

This question of the hair afforded him great flexibility. With his long hair grown out and tied back, he could and did now and then wander through the corridors of his own company in Geneva as a "mailroom boy." And when hunting he could use the long hair to advantage, decking himself out in torn dungarees and neon shirts to roam alleyways and drug dens unnoticed until he chose to strike.

When Gregory met with human employees and reporters, he was skillfully painted with modern cosmetic compounds that disguised his preternatural skin even further, and he never lingered in the company of any human very long. Almost all of his business he conducted by phone or email, some by Skype when it was absolutely necessary, and much by long and often witty "Letters from the Desk of Gregory," which he circulated amongst his employees from the top to the bottom of the giant company of which he was the de facto owner and chairman of the board. The glossy publicity photos of him which the company distributed to news services were all taken by his beloved Blood Spouse, Chrysanthe.

Fareed understood that this company was a repository for and a generator of immense wealth, and he also knew that Gregory would soon retire from it altogether, Gregory had once explained this, sinking his fortune into some other enterprise that assured him similar security and opportunity. What that was, Fareed could not guess. "The times will tell me," Gregory had said. Gregory had at least ten more years to play out this mortal role, and he meant to make the best of them. It was all so easy for him that he couldn't quite grasp why it surprised or interested anyone else.

What interested Fareed about Collingsworth Pharmaceuticals was that it was a medical enterprise, a conglomerate of research laboratories, and a pioneer in perfecting antiviral drugs. And thanks to Gregory, Fareed had computer access to virtually everything about the company; and Fareed also had access now, through Gregory, to every bit of equipment or drug that Fareed himself might want for his own secret and special work. Gregory had given Fareed total cooperation in setting up his Paris laboratory, and Gregory understood that Fareed was a vampire doctor, wholeheartedly, who lived and breathed now to care for the blood drinkers of this world, and to them and them alone Fareed had transferred the devotion he had once felt for his mortal patients.

Fareed wanted to learn from Collingsworth Pharmaceuticals. He wanted to profit from this unfettered access to its research projects and its experimental drugs. He hoped to expand his own special research under the cloak of Collingsworth Pharmaceuticals. He wanted to exploit to the maximum the complete latitude given him by Gregory for such plans. Gregory had enlarged the Paris Collingsworth compound, specifically for Fareed, and he would shift any project to Paris from its original location on the say-so of Fareed.

But Gregory claimed again and again to know little or nothing of the many projects that now fascinated Fareed.

Fareed got it. Gregory himself had never been a scientist. Gregory was an immortal with a vague fascination for "money, investment, the complex realm of wealth and economic power in the modern world." Yet there was no doubt that his genius had shaped the success of this enterprise. Specialists in myriad research fields appealed to him for policy decisions that were unfailingly efficient, and creative and smart.

Again, this wasn't what interested Fareed, except tangentially. He wanted to survive amongst the Undead. So of course he took note that the great wise survivors of the millennia—Sevraine, Gregory, Marius, Teskhamen—never struggled as to questions of wealth. To them the vagabond pickpocket maverick vampires of the world were rabble too stupid to arouse pity. And though they took pains now, the elders, to teach the young ones coming to Court how to negotiate the human world with some efficiency, their patience was short.

The present world afforded rich prey for blood and wealth in the international drug dealers and the sex slavers that congregated in just about every major city east or west; and even the youngest fledgling could feed on this mortal underclass with some success. Even the youngest fledgling could befuddle, outsmart, and easily dispatch the more organized of mortal criminals, and pocket the stacks of cash lying around in gangster hideaways and drug depots, and if he or she could not, well, best to keep that secret from the elders of the tribe as well as from one's own companions, as far as immortals like Gregory were concerned.

"It's not the cloning that interests me here," said Fareed, "though it's an immensely interesting subject."

"Irresistible to many," Gregory answered. "I'm sure."

"It's this doctor. Something's wrong here, or perhaps I should say something's strange."

"I'm listening." Gregory sat back looking at the four long streams of cards. "Why are they just red or black?" he asked under his breath.

"First off, she's not who she claims to be at all."

"How can that be?" Gregory asked. He gathered up the cards and shuffled them, as expertly as a dealer in a gambling casino.

Fareed explained.

"She's created an identity and a record for herself using, as far as I can tell, the records of four deceased researchers in genetics. I've pretty much tracked all of this to its roots. She came to work for you ten years ago. And I understand, she never met you and you never laid eyes on her. And she's been publishing brilliant papers and reports ever since. All to do with genetics and genetic engineering, medicines genetically perfected for the individual user, that sort of thing. The cloning has gone on under the radar. I've cracked into her secret records. But she's too clever for matters to be transparent. She writes in German and English mostly, and I'm sensing the use of a highly sophisticated personal code."

"And all this strikes you as dangerous, as a justification for us to intervene? Or do you want to bring her over? Make her one of your own staff?"

"Well, that's how it started," said Fareed. "I thought just maybe she'd be a brilliant addition. But now I'm quite obsessed with something else."

"And that is?"

"Why did she create this fake identity? She's obviously brilliant. So why would she do that? I can't find a single shred of evidence as to who she was or might have been before she created this persona for Collingsworth Pharmaceuticals. It's as if she came into existence ten years ago."

Gregory was listening now intently. "Well, how could you find any evidence, I mean, if she doesn't want you to?"

"I've run facial recognition software, I've run records of missing persons, of doctors worldwide of the same physical description, living or dead. I find nothing. Yet she's a superbly talented researcher and research writer. I want to meet her."

Fareed enlarged the most recent available photograph of the woman until it filled the screen.

"Well, nothing's stopping you," said Gregory. "I suppose I could arrange it if you like. You're blessed, my friend. You look human. You're an entirely credible Anglo-Indian doctor. You're striking but not threatening. I'm sure you could sit down with her over coffee in Geneva and talk to her. What would be the risk in that?"

Fareed didn't answer. A strange frisson had come over him. He was staring into her face, looking into her eyes.

Gregory rose from the table and approached the desk. He stood behind Fareed and looked at the monitor.

"Lovely woman," he said. "Perhaps she'd like to spend eternity with us."

"That's all you see?" Fareed asked. He glanced up at Gregory. "You see nothing else?"

"What is there to see?"

Fareed stared at the image. Creamy brown skin, oval face, deep brown eyes, and dark brown hair parted in the middle, drawn back severely from the face yet in a flattering style. Prominent gold streak in the hair running back from the widow's peak and an expression of almost forbidding intelligence.

"Dr. Karen Rhinehart," Gregory read from beneath the photograph.

"The name's fake," said Fareed. What was it he was feeling? A vague but deep alarm. "It's somebody else's name, a doctor who died in a car accident in Germany. The name means nothing."

"I honestly don't know how she could have put this over on my company. Are you sure?"

"Completely sure."

"Meet her if you wish. Should I shoot her an email? Easy enough to do. She could be in Paris tomorrow to meet you."

"No. I don't think that is a good idea," said Fareed.

"Why?"

How could Fareed explain it? He opened his mind deliberately to Gregory, asking him silently to read the subtle feelings that he himself could not identify.

**Something not quite right about her. Something formidable. Something to suggest that she might be in her own way equal to us . . .**

Gregory nodded. He rested his hand on Fareed's shoulder with a familiarity that was unusual.

"Whatever you wish," he said. "She couldn't have fooled my personnel office. You don't understand the caliber of the checking they do on our scientists."

"Well, she has fooled them," said Fareed. "And I don't want to be close to her just yet, not until I have a few more answers."

Gregory shrugged. "I have to go back to Geneva," he said. "Perhaps I'll meet with her myself."

"No!" said Fareed. "Gregory, don't do that." He turned and looked up at Gregory. Gregory didn't understand this wariness. Gregory was fearless, and had been for so long he possessed no root understanding of Fareed's apprehension at all. "Don't let her get close to you," Fareed said. "Not until I know more about her. Will you agree?"

Gregory was staring at him in silence.

"Gregory, I don't want her to see any one of us up close."

Again, Gregory shrugged. "Very well," he said.

"And there's another aspect to it," said Fareed.

"I'm listening."

"She petitions to see you constantly. She's been turned down at least four or five times every year since she came to work for you. Yet she keeps petitioning, arguing she has a grant proposal for your eyes only."

"Well, that's not surprising. They all want to meet the captain of the ship. They all want to be invited for supper in the captain's cabin."

"No, it's more than that."

Fareed brought up a series of group photographs with a few clicks of the keys. "The woman's been stalking you for years. If you look here, she's in every single one of these pictures."

"But those were press conferences," said Gregory.

"Lots of the different staff attended, made remarks, reported on recent developments."

"No, you don't understand. She's in **every** picture, and not with the staff but with the press. She's trying to get close to you, to see you. I think she may well be trying to get some sample of your DNA."

"Fareed, I think your suspicions are running away with you. It would be quite impossible for her to do that."

"Not so sure."

Fareed enlarged the latest group shot of reporters gathered for a precious few minutes with the head of Collingsworth Pharmaceuticals. And there she was, in the front row of those holding microphones, recording equipment, steno pads, a tall woman in a dark jacket and long skirt, her wavy brown hair loose but carefully groomed as it hung behind her shoulders, the long gold streak in her hair quite prominent, her secretive and probing eyes fixed on Gregory, nothing visible in her hand but an iPhone.

"She's photographing you, of course."

"They all are," said Gregory. "Fareed, my company investigates every single person working anywhere, Paris, Zurich, Geneva, New York."

"But look at her eyes."

"I don't feel it," Gregory confessed. "She's beautiful, intriguing, and how nice for her, and for those who know her, and for me if she's doing good work."

Fareed went silent. But as he stared at the dark

focused expression on the woman's face, he shuddered.

"I don't think . . ."

"Don't think what?"

"I don't think she's human."

"What do you mean? She's one of us?"

"No, definitely not. She lives and works by day and night, obviously. I have footage of her coming and going during the day. She's certainly not one of us. No."

"A ghost then, is that what you're saying? Another one of these genius spirits—like Gremt or Magnus, or the others lodging with them?"

"No. She's flesh and blood all right. But I don't think it's human flesh and blood."

"Well, that's easy enough to verify. Her DNA should be on file. Nobody works in research for me who doesn't have his or her DNA on file. The woman took a physical when she was hired, gave blood, submitted to X rays. . . ."

"I know. I checked. But I don't believe the results. I think the whole package was fabricated. I'm running the DNA through every data bank in the world."

Gregory turned and walked back slowly to the table. He sat down rather heavily in the damask armchair and once again laid his right hand on the deck of cards.

"Fareed," he said in a more serious tone. "Never mind that a breach of security like that is almost impossible. It does concern me and I will check on it. But what you're saying is preposterous."

"Why?"

Gregory sighed. He sat back in the chair, eyes moving wearily over the room.

"Because I've roamed this earth for so long I can't count the years or think of them in succession," Gregory said, "or grasp how they've shaped me. . . . I have no sense of the continuity of my life except from the times of the Emperor Julian. But it has been thousands of years, years of hunting, years of roaming, years of loving, years of learning, and I tell you, in all this time I have **never** encountered any flesh-and-blood creature of intelligence on this planet that appeared human but was not human."

Fareed was unmoved.

"Are you listening to me?" asked Gregory. "Will you try to grasp what I'm saying?"

Fareed thought to himself that he'd been alive for less than fifty years, but he had seen so much in those fifty years, so much of vampires, spirits, ghosts, and other mysteries that it did not surprise him at all to encounter a human-looking thing that was not human, but he did not say this aloud.

He'd enlarged the picture of the woman in the dark suit jacket and long skirt, standing among the reporters. Perfectly almond-shaped eyes. And the skin, the lovely bronze skin. **Not human.**

"Fareed, are you listening to me? Spirits and ghosts, I've known. We all have, all the old ones.

But not biological humanoids who are not really human."

"Well, I'll know better if I can get close to her, won't I?" said Fareed gazing steadily at the woman's face. It was not a cruel face. It was not a mean face. But it wasn't generous and it wasn't curious and it lacked some spark, some definable spark—.

"What, you believe in the human soul?" asked Gregory.

"No," said Fareed, "but I do believe in the human spirit. How else would there be ghosts knocking on our doors now? I don't say it's a divine spark, I am thinking only that some human spark is not there."

"Is there a spark of something else?"

"Good question. I don't know."

"Do you have time for this?" asked Gregory. "You haven't completed your research on Mekare's remains or Maharet's remains. I thought this was of great importance to you and the remains were deteriorating. I thought you were inviting Gremt here so you could test the body he'd made for himself. I thought you wanted to expand the Paris laboratory—."

"No, the remains are not deteriorating exactly anymore," Fareed murmured. He couldn't take his eyes off the woman. "And I am busy, that's true, impossibly busy, and I need more help, but this can't wait." He brought up yet another photograph. Press conference to announce a new insulin pump for the treatment of diabetes, 2013. The usual dim lighting. Gregory in deep shadow, and the bank of reporters a little more fully illuminated. And there she was again, this time in softer more feminine attire. A silk blouse, a string of lustrous pearls, a loose cardigan jacket, and the iPhone with its visible photographic eye held close to her chest. Long tapering fingers, oval nails.

"Fareed, you aren't seriously suggesting that she herself is some sort of clone, planted in my company to clone others—."

"No, I have not used the word 'clone,'" said Fareed.

"I think you're mistaken if for no other reason than that she is singular."

"I don't follow."

"Have you ever seen another one like her?"

"No," Fareed conceded, "but that has no bearing. We might be observing the first to ever come to our attention. This does not mean she is the only one. In fact, I'd be willing to wager she's not the only one."

He brought up a third picture from another file. In this one Karen Rhinehart appeared in the laboratory with her colleagues. She wore a starched white coat like the white coat that Fareed wore now. Her hair was brushed back so severely in this photo that it might have been brutally unflattering, but it was not. She had a strong chin and a calm determined look, and for some reason, some indefinable reason, she stood out from the others glaringly to Fareed's eye as if she'd been cut from another picture entirely and pasted into place. Well, she had not. But she was not human. And that is what he saw and what he sensed.

"I do have too much to do now," Fareed said dully, eyes still studying her. "That's true. But I want to go to Geneva and have a look at her without her looking at me. I want to get into her living quarters. . . ."

"Fareed, my employees trust me not to violate their privacy or their dignity."

"Gregory, be serious! If I wanted to bring her over, you wouldn't have the slightest objection."

"Look, Fareed, the woman must work late hours. They all do. They're all there in the evening hours. You can watch her by video feed. Every laboratory and office is video monitored."

"Ah, I didn't think of that!"

"I'll give you access."

"You don't have to," Fareed confessed. "Why didn't I think of it? Of course."

His fingers were flying over the keyboard, the keyboard specially engineered to accommodate his preternatural speed.

"I'm in," he whispered, quickly entering the data to home in on the correct laboratory, and all files on record of that laboratory and none other.

"Well, enjoy it," said Gregory with a faint mocking laugh. "Have a wonderful morning watching her every move for the last ten years. As for me, I'm going out. These long winter nights exhaust me but it's worth it. I want to walk for a while on my own."

Gregory moved to the tall fruitwood secrétaire

à abattant against the wall, and tucked the deck of cards in its middle drawer. He turned to the door but then doubled back, and bending over Fareed he planted a kiss on his head.

"I love you, you know. I love your brilliance and your single-mindedness. I love that you're so patient with all of us."

Fareed smiled and offered a small nod. He reached up, found the hand he hoped would be there, and clasped it. But his eyes were on the task in front of him. He barely heard Gregory's footsteps as he left the room.

The great three-storied house was silent and seemingly empty around Fareed. The mortal servants were asleep in their wing. The pavements were deserted. Mortals in their surrounding apartments slept. There were faint threads of music in the air.

Fareed heard Gregory Duff Collingsworth climbing the stairs to the roof. In a moment the faint low thrumming beat of Gregory's heart was no longer audible.

The hair stood up on Fareed's neck. A rodent worked in the walls somewhere near him, behind the lacquered paneling. A small car passed in the street.

He was suddenly aware of how very excited he was, how very excited by the mystery of this woman, and how much he enjoyed it, no matter how disturbing it was.

He went at the keyboard again, fingers moving

too fast even for his eyes, trusting to the feel of the keys and his unerring knowledge of them, the codes racing down the monitor, as he scanned the video surveillance system of Collingsworth Pharmaceuticals and digested all of its systems and limits.

He identified the live feed now from Dr. Karen Rhinehart's laboratories and found them empty. No surprise. It was early morning in Geneva as well, of course, only three hours away from Paris by train. Now he brought up the archive of dated tapes and soon found strong, clear footage from two nights prior that revealed the subject, Dr. Rhinehart, seated on a stool before a laboratory counter, making notes with what seemed an old-fashioned black fountain pen on a white pad. A mug of steaming coffee or tea sat beside her. She wrote in brief bursts, paused as if to think, then continued writing. Now and then her left hand moved through her long loose hair.

A preternatural stillness gripped her. Her few gestures were startlingly deliberate, and her long periods of immobility strange. When she moved her hand to write, nothing else about her moved, not the angle of her head, or the fingers of her idle hand. He was powerfully fascinated. Clone, droid, cyborg, replicant—the common vernacular words for human duplicates ran through his mind, detached from the various fictions that had engendered them.

A half hour of this footage passed and then he recognized an exact repeat of an earlier gesture, an earlier lifting of the coffee cup, an earlier rake of the left hand through the hair. The woman had blocked the camera with a digital loop. Of course. He fast-forwarded to confirm: the loop ran for the rest of that evening and night.

Well, they might be geniuses, the mortal employees scanning or storing this material, but likely the value of this system depended solely on someone seeking to retrieve a particular moment for a particular use. And likely nobody had.

A little annoyed, Fareed fast-forwarded swiftly through hours of footage, most of it of group sessions, group discussions, and work by young doctors who were not Dr. Rhinehart, and only now and then did she flash before the camera on her way across the screen.

"So she avoids the cameras," he whispered, "and skillfully, and when she does work alone in the lab, she throws up tape loops, and she's good at it, and nobody guesses." He went on scanning, and was just about to give up when he came across footage of the mysterious woman at that same laboratory counter, again with pen in hand. In this footage she was talking on her iPhone and of course there was no audial feed, or was there? He slowed down, searched, picked up the audial feed, amplified it, and now he could hear her voice distinctly, speaking in soft slow Swiss French.

It was nothing consequential, a plan to meet someone for a meal later, remarks about weather—a rich, pretty voice, distinctly feminine, with an easy subtle laugh now and then.

And he was furious suddenly that he would have to put all this aside for now and go to the crypts beneath the house. But he was growing cold as he always did near sunrise, as they all did, and it was maddening to leave this. . . .

Because it was not—he was certain of it—not a human voice.

What could this possibly mean? No matter what Gregory said, he had to get to Geneva tomorrow night and see this thing, this creature, this artificial human, up close.

He rose from the chair and was turning to go when an alert stopped him. It was from Dr. Flannery Gilman, his blood drinker assistant and confidante, mother of Lestat's son, Viktor. It had to do with the woman's DNA.

"I found a match all right," wrote Flannery. "It's for a woman living in Bolinas, California, manager of a bed-and-breakfast famous on the California coast. All the material is from this woman's medical files in the Kaiser Permanente data banks. And the blood is definitely this Bolinas woman's blood. Signing off for the night, obviously, and will look immediately for your reply when I wake. But do you want Collingsworth Pharmaceuticals alerted? This is serious fraud."

"Get everything you can on this woman in Bolinas," wrote Fareed. "And forget the corporation. The security breach is the least of our worries. I'm heading to Geneva at sunset to have a look at this woman for myself."

The plain concrete-and-iron crypts beneath Armand's Paris house were like all the crypts in which Fareed and his brothers and sisters slept. They were unimportant to Fareed, who had been Born to Darkness in the late twentieth century when the blood drinkers of the world no longer valued coffins and heavily carved sarcophagi, and legends had no meaning anymore. He cared only that in his own private place deep in the earth, he was safe.

He had lain down on the narrow padded bed in the clean dry windowless cell and was about to close his eyes when a message jarred him, a telepathic message faint but garbled, stabbing at him, as if someone were tapping his temple with the tip of an ice pick but could not penetrate his skull. **Danger. New York.**

Well, those across the sea would have to deal with it, he concluded, his mind slowly clouding and losing all sense of urgency about anything in the whole world. Some night, Fareed would figure some way to free the entire vampire tribe from this daytime unconsciousness, this living death that came over them when the sun rose.

But for now, Lestat would have to deal with that alarm. Or Armand. Lestat was in America. Lestat had gone there tonight to meet his beloved Louis in

New Orleans, or so it was being said. Lestat needed his old companion, Louis, all agreed. "He's our King James, needing a George, Duke of Buckingham," Marius had said. And Armand was in New York and had been for a month, making certain all was well at Trinity Gate. Well, they would take care of all this, Lestat or Armand. Or Gregory perhaps having a few moments left of consciousness. Or maybe Seth. They'd have to. Fareed's mind closed as securely as his eyes had closed. And he was gone. A dream had him, vivid, beautiful, filled with riotous sunshine, sunshine the way he remembered it from his home in India, and in this riotous sunshine Fareed saw a city, a great sparkling city of glass towers—**Oh, this dream again**—erupting in flames and falling into the sea. . . .

# 6

# Lestat

"A NON-HUMAN THING?" I asked. "A non-human thing that has killed a vampire and eaten its brain? You disturb me for this?"

"Well, yes," said Thorne, "when the message comes from Armand in New York. He wants to take this inhuman thing to Fareed and Seth in Paris."

"Well, that sounds like an excellent idea to me," I said.

Louis and I were walking uptown towards the old Lafayette Cemetery. We'd been talking for hours, talking about Amel and what it was like for me with Amel inside of me, and I was doing most of the talking and Louis doing most of the listening. I didn't want to be disturbed. I wanted to talk to Louis forever, share with Louis what had been happening to me, and Louis was attentive, appreciative. This meant the world to me. But I knew Thorne and Cyril would never have approached if there hadn't been a good reason.

I took the glass cell phone from Thorne, and put it

to my ear which always felt absurd and never would feel natural, but there was no getting out of it.

"What sort of non-human thing?" I asked.

Armand's voice came through soft, yet clear.

"Looks, smells, and feels just like a human being," he said. "But it isn't a human being. It's tremendously strong, I'd say perhaps eight to ten times as strong as a human. And it should be dead right now considering the blood I drew from it, but it is not dead. In fact, the blood is regenerating rapidly. It's in some sort of deep sleep, what Fareed might call a coma. It has a name, papers, and an address in England." He went through it with me. Garekyn Zweck Brovotkin. Fancy address on Redington Road, Hampstead. Keys to a Rolls. Passport, British driver's license, British and American money, and some sort of paper ticket for a flight to London at midday.

"And you're holding this thing as a prisoner?"

"Yes! Wouldn't you hold it prisoner?"

"I wasn't challenging you, just asking."

"I'm bringing it to Paris tomorrow for Fareed. What else can I do with it? I've sent out warnings. If there are others like this, we should all be on alert."

"I'll be there, tomorrow, in Paris, myself," I said. "I'll see you then and I'll see it."

"Louis is going with you?"

There was a great deal more to the question than any casual listener might have supposed. Louis and Armand were the pillars of the New York household at Trinity Gate. Louis and Armand had been together for almost a century long before that.

"Yes," I said. "I'm taking him back with me as soon as we wake." I waited.

I stood on the flagstone sidewalk looking at the distant white wall of the old cemetery. It was quiet and beautiful on this Garden District street with its giant black-barked oaks, and the dark silent multistory houses on either side. "I need Louis," I said.

Oh, the old entanglements, the old jealousies and defeats. But what creature in the world doesn't want to be loved for itself? Even a non-human thing that looked human might want to be loved.

"I'm happy for you," Armand said. Then, "This is serious. This being, whatever it is, it smashed the skull of a blood drinker and devoured the brain."

"But did you actually see this happen yourself?"

"Yes, I saw it all from the point of view of the victim. I couldn't get there fast enough. Remains have been confirmed. The brain's gone."

"And who is the dead blood drinker?"

"Killer, the old friend of Davis and Antoine. Killer, the one who traveled with the Fang Gang."

"I remember," I said. I sighed. I hadn't despised Killer. In fact, I'd liked him. But there had been something blundering and petty and "small time" about Killer. I hadn't liked the idea of his hanging about Trinity Gate. "What is this non-human thing made of?"

"Flesh and blood, Lestat, just like any human,"

Armand replied. He was becoming annoyed. "Cut the thing, it bleeds. But it's not human." He went on explaining. The blood was thick, good tasting, but it had a flavoring that wasn't in human blood. A flavoring. He couldn't do better than that. Benji had spotted the creature hovering around Trinity Gate. It had followed Benji. The creature had been muttering things about Amel, like a crazed human follower of the radio station, only he wasn't human. Benji called at once for a car and headed home, sending Killer to approach the creature and try to find out what it wanted.

"Well, that was likely very stupid," I said.

"Benji protected himself," said Armand crossly. "And Killer was the oldest blood drinker under the roof. No one else was here, except Killer and a couple of fledglings who'd recently arrived. Antoine had gone home to France when the sun set. Eleni had been with me in Midtown. I came as soon as I could. But I wasn't fast enough. And Killer was eager to go, certain he could manage the thing."

"Eleni," I said. "My old friend Eleni? Everard's Eleni?"

"Yes. Is there another Eleni? She's weary of Rhoshamandes and his fledglings sitting around gnashing their teeth. Or so she says. Look, we can talk about all this later. Holding this thing throughout the day will be a problem, but we're doing the best we can."

I didn't like the idea of Eleni being there. I didn't

trust Eleni. I loved Eleni, true, from the old Théâtre des Vampires. She'd been a veteran of Armand's Satanic coven under Les Innocents, who had come to join me at the theater, to be free. She'd become my correspondent during the years I wandered in search of Marius. But she'd been made by Everard de Landen under the authority of Rhoshamandes, and she'd been spending most of her time with this bitter enemy of mine and his other fledglings. But to whom was she truly loyal? Armand, who'd once made her a ragged and tormented slave of Satan, or the powerful vampire who'd ruled the household in which she'd been made? I knew Everard's heart. He never tried to disguise it. He loathed and detested the great Rhoshamandes. But what about Eleni? Rhoshamandes had been master of the coven in which she was Born to Darkness and learned her first indelible lessons of the night. Didn't like it. Didn't like it at all.

Louis stood a few feet away watching me. Undoubtedly he heard every word, but his face revealed nothing. He had a remote dreamy expression on his face as he so often did, but I sensed he'd been absorbing everything.

What have I to do with all this, I thought with irritation, but I knew perfectly well what I had to do with it. This was my life now, by choice, to be involved in all things, to be the one whom Armand called to report a comatose non-human imprisoned at Trinity Gate.

"Do you need any assistance from me now?" I asked Armand. "This is all fascinating, of course, but there isn't time for me to come to you."

"I know that. I'm letting you know for obvious reasons. Why do you behave as if I'm deliberately harassing you? Are you the Prince, Lestat, or not?"

"Of course, yes, you did the right thing. I'm sorry."

I saw Louis's faint smile.

"I'll see you tomorrow in the City of Light," said Armand. A beat. "And I am happy for you, that you're with Louis."

I sighed. I wanted to say we all love one another. We all have to love one another. If you and I and Louis don't love one another after all we've been through, well, then all our powers mean nothing, and our dreams mean nothing, and so we have to love one another. And maybe I did say this silently and he heard it, but I doubted it.

"I know," I said. "I'm eager to see you too."

I gave the phone back to Thorne. Where was Amel? Was Amel in New York? Did Amel know what this thing was?

Thorne jarred me out of my thoughts.

"If you gentlemen are determined to proceed on foot," he said, "it's time to head on back downtown."

# 7

# Garekyn

H E'D BEEN LISTENING to them for about an hour. They'd tied him to a table, with some sort of steel cable. And they were anxious as to how to hold him through the daylight hours when they, obviously, had to sleep.

He was no longer astonished to be alive. It had been all too like his coming out of the ice in Siberia so long ago, the sense of waking from a long sleep. The Parents had promised that there was almost nothing in this world that could kill him, and he felt disloyal somehow to the Parents that he'd feared it was the end. The Parents . . . oh, if only he could remember.

The strongest blood drinker, the one who'd overtaken him and drained the blood out of him, was speaking. This was Armand.

"And if I put him in my crypt and he does manage to break out of it, then he will find me in one of the other crypts."

"Well, then, what shall we do?"

Steel cables. Strong all right, but was this vampire correct in saying that Garekyn had the strength of ten men? That's what Garekyn had heard him say in his phone call to the Prince. The strength of eight to ten men.

If Garekyn did have that much strength, he'd escape from these cables as soon as they had gone to their rest. And he wouldn't waste any time breaking open their crypts. He had discovered exactly what he had come here to discover. He had seen it as Armand drew the blood out of him. Amel, the Core, Amel the spirit that did in fact animate them all. Amel was in this being Armand who had attacked him, and in the midst of the struggle, as Garekyn fought the blood drinker who was killing him, he had seen the city, unmistakably the city of Atalantaya, and not as he could ever have envisioned it, but from another perspective, a distant perspective, a godlike perspective as the city erupted in flames and slowly fell into the sea.

He locked these thoughts deep in his mind now, fearing their telepathic gifts, of which they bragged over the airwaves night and day.

What a brazen bunch they were to tell their innermost secrets to the whole world and trade on the credulity of human beings to see them as fantasy makers, role-players in an elaborate game, dedicated and fractured fans of vampire lore. But it made sense. Who would believe Garekyn if he told "the world" these pale fiends were living and breathing vampires? Who believed the ancient tale of Atlantis as told by Plato, which Garekyn had first read in Alexi's library in Saint Petersburg a century ago?

Even the Prince had not believed the one called Armand when he'd explained that Garekyn wasn't human.

"All right, listen to me," said Armand. "The thing's coming round. There's only one crypt in the house that can safely hold him, the one made for Marius. Now I'm going to see whether or not I can open it and close it unassisted and somehow secure the door from the outside. You stand watch, Eleni, and you, Benji, come with me."

Sounds of their retreat, down a passage, up a stairway, the quick steps of the young one, Benji, trying to catch up with the barely perceptible steps of Armand. Up out of this cellar into the house above and on across a wooden floor.

Silence. Only the sound of the female blood drinker breathing. Sounds of traffic, sounds of trucks on Madison Avenue, those big noisy trucks that make their deliveries to the restaurants and bars of the metropolis before daybreak.

Cautiously he opened his eyes. She stood with her back to him, intent on some task. Then he heard it, a tiny electronic voice emanating from her cell phone.

"You know who this is." A male voice. A blood

drinker voice too soft for human hearing. But Garekyn could certainly hear it. "Leave a message of any length."

Garekyn lifted his head, trying to see exactly how he was bound here and to what. Steel cables all right, heavy and strong. And the table itself was stone, likely marble. The obvious point of weakness would be the table itself, the brittle quality of the stone. If he were to buck, kick, apply all his strength, the marble tabletop would shatter. But what if it was granite? Well, if it was granite or any stone too dense and strong for him to crack, it might nevertheless break loose from its base, and then the cables might slide off of it. But when was the right time?

"Rhosh, listen to me," said the female blood drinker into the phone. "There's a creature here, a non-human. Armand's going to try and secure it at Trinity Gate for the day. At sunset he'll take it to Paris. This might be an occasion for all to come together, for you to go to Court and ask about this discovery, to find some way to be welcomed back in." On and on she talked. The thing was dangerous to vampires. The thing fed on vampire brains! "If the Prince calls all to come together, you must come, Rhosh. We must have peace." Silence.

Well, that was interesting, wasn't it? As she turned around, Garekyn slowed his respiration, closing his eyes again.

The female came close to the table. She was anxious, fidgety. He could hear her agitated breathing, her heels clicking on the concrete floor as she paced. She drew closer. He could hear her heart. Her heart was strong but not as strong as the heart of Armand. He listened for Armand. Only barely could he hear the voices of those two, not in this cellar but in another cellar, likely under another one of the three houses that made up Trinity Gate, houses that had been built separately a century ago.

Slowly, he opened his eyes, to see that she was staring down at him, and when she realized he was looking at her she jumped. Backing away, she caught herself, ashamed of her fear, her eyes fixed to his. Long banks of fluorescent lights glared from the ceiling, clearly illuminating her slender frame, her pale ivory skin, and her eyes as dark as his own. Her long glossy black hair was parted in the middle, hanging to her shoulders, and around her graceful neck she wore strands of cream-colored pearls. He could hear the black silk of her long dress rustling in the moving air. Some machine somewhere forced the air into this cellar chamber. She studied him as intently as he was studying her.

"Who are you?" he asked in his gentlest voice. He spoke English to her because they had all been speaking English before. His eyes inspected the room about him, but so quickly she wasn't likely to realize what he was doing. A great concrete chamber with an iron door of immense thickness, standing open before a dimly lighted passage. The door was like the doors one saw on large walk-in freezers or refrigerators with the big handle and lock on this side.

"Who are **you,** that's the question," she answered, but her tone was as gentle as his tone had been. "Where do you come from? What is it you want?" She appeared powerfully fascinated by him. "Listen, you mustn't be afraid of us."

He lay back gazing at her calmly. He realized that his wrists weren't fettered, and that he could flex his fingers now, that all the sluggishness of his sleep had worn away. He strained imperceptibly against the steel cables. There were perhaps four of these cables binding him to the table.

"What is this, marble on which you've bound me?" he asked her. "Why, why am I a prisoner here?"

"Because you destroyed one of us," she said. She sounded simple, sincere.

"Ah, but I thought that he was trying to destroy me," said Garekyn. "I came here to speak with you, ask you questions. I made no menacing move towards your friend Benji." He spoke slowly, almost whispering. "Then your emissary tried to kill me. What could I have done, but what I did?"

She was obviously enthralled. She came closer and closer until the silk of her dress brushed the side of his arm.

"Is this marble? Is this an altar?"

"No, it's not an altar. Please be still until Armand comes back. It's a table, that's all."

"Marble," he repeated. "I think it's an altar. You're primitive, savage beings. You hunt the city like wolves. This is some sort of place of worship. You mean to kill me on this altar."

"Utter nonsense," she said. Her face was beautifully animated, her cheeks rounded as she smiled. "Don't excite yourself over nothing." She appeared to mean it. "No one here will harm you. We want to know about you, we want to know what sort of a creature you are."

He smiled. "I would like to trust you," he confided. "But how can I? You have me bound and helpless."

Her eyes appeared to be misting suddenly. Such large dark eyes, with thick lashes, such a fringe of lashes, lashes as lustrous as her hair. Her face was almost blank.

Was she charmed by him, as he was by her?

"Can't you set me free? Can we talk to one another plainly without all this?" He glanced down again at the cable binding his chest and upper arms to the table. "This marble altar is cold."

She bent closer as if she couldn't stop herself. Her eyes were now positively glazed, vacant, as the eyes of the other one, Killer, had appeared just before he'd sunk his teeth into Garekyn's neck.

"It's marble, tell me the truth," he prodded.

"All right it's marble," she murmured but her voice was sleepy, a monotone. "But it's not an altar, I told you. . . ." She was bending down as if to kiss him, and with her right fingers she touched his lips. "We're taking you to the scientists among us. We're not wild beasts." He could hear her heart tripping. Somewhere far off Armand was arguing with Benji. But they were too far away for Garekyn to hear what they said. How far away? How long would it take them to get back here if this woman were to sound an alarm?

She was so pretty, so very pretty. Her hair fell down around him. He could feel it against his forehead and his cheek, feel it falling on his neck. It was now or never.

With all his might he bucked, pulling up with his arms, pounding down with his heels, convulsing his whole body. The marble cracked and he found himself sitting upright, the cables falling loose around him, and the whole stone platform of sorts crashing to the floor in three giant fragments as the woman screamed.

Freeing his arms instantly, he reached for her and clapped his hand over her mouth. Dragging her with him as he stepped out of the coils of cable and the debris of the broken marble, he moved to the door. She struggled mightily, almost managing to free herself.

He slammed the door shut tight in its huge metal frame.

She fought him with all she had, scratching at him, biting at him, even stabbing his left leg with the sharp heel of her shoe. He tried to throw her off but he couldn't, and finally grabbing her by the hair, he waltzed awkwardly to the side with her, pulling her off-balance, and slammed her head against the concrete wall as he had done with Killer.

She screamed so loudly it was like a dagger going right into his ears. But the impact had stunned her body, and the scream was all she could control.

He flung her head at the wall again, and then again.

The bones broke, but her screams did not stop. She slid down the wall to the floor, the blood pouring out of her mouth and out of her ears and down the front of her black silk dress. He could see the pearls being covered in blood, thick, sparkling blood, blood alive with something he could see in the light.

He knew he should flee, get down the passage and up the stairs before Armand and Benji could intercept him. But he stood paralyzed gazing at the blood, the unnatural glittering blood. And her dark eyes gazed up at him as her screams continued, ripping through his thoughts, ripping through his will, her eyes pleading with him though she could not move her arms or legs.

He found himself embracing her and lifting her. He held her as if he meant to kiss her, her breasts against his chest and her head fallen back as if her neck had been broken. Dipping his fingers into her open mouth, he brought the blood to his lips! Sweet sizzling sensations just as he'd felt them with Killer. He brought more to his lips. Rippling chills all through his body. He bent to suck the blood out of her mouth with his own.

**Let her alone. Do not harm her!**

Who was this speaking to him?

**Let her go. Do not harm her. It is Amel who is speaking to you. Let my child go.**

"Amel?" he whispered aloud.

It seemed an age ago that her screams had stopped, and that a great pounding on the metal door had commenced.

He drank more and more of the blood.

**She is my child, Garekyn.**

"It is you?" he said, the words lost in the blood flowing into his mouth and down his throat. But he caught no image to confirm it, no flash of the Great One of long ago. Only a great web came alive in intricate detail against a sea of fathomless blackness, and all through this great web myriad tiny points glittered and brightened.

The door flew back off its heavy hinges and clattered to the concrete floor.

Armand stood there facing him. Benji was right behind him.

Garekyn held Eleni against him, drinking from her open mouth as though it were a fountain, his eyes fixed on Armand.

"Give her to me," said Armand. "Give her to me or I burn you alive."

**Garekyn, do as he tells you to do. He can restore her. I will make him let you go.**

Garekyn wanted to do it, to surrender her, let her go. But he couldn't let go of this blood, this sizzling blood that was so rich and so beautiful and the telepathic voice that was speaking to him almost tenderly, the voice he was certain he knew, coming through this blood. He saw the web growing in all directions, ever more elaborate, and strangely beautiful to him with its myriad pinpoints of twinkling light but even more beautiful was the sense of meaning, the sense of understanding everything utterly and completely, and yet losing his grip on it as soon as he had grasped it. And then he would have the sense again.

He saw the towers of Atalantaya melting. Millions of voices screamed in panic, in agony.

**Garekyn, let her go.**

Armand stood right before him. Garekyn held Eleni's helpless body by the waist. And slowly, lapping the blood from his cupped right hand, Garekyn let Armand take her away. Gently, Armand laid her body on the floor.

"Get out of here," Armand whispered. He appeared unable to move, staring at Garekyn even as his eyelids descended, even as his eyes appeared to close. Then the creature appeared to shake himself all over, and his eyes fixed on Garekyn again.

Garekyn couldn't reason. He had no will. Sluggishly he backed up and gazed on the ruin of the room—the shattered marble, the stupid steel cable coils tangled in the weak iron table frame that had supported the marble. And then he spied something that quickened his pulse. His leather wallet lying there on a wooden table against the back wall opposite the door. His keys. His passport, his phone, his things.

He cleaned all the blood clumsily from his hand with his tongue and, in an instant, he'd scooped up these personal items of his, these indispensable personal things, and he was moving out the door.

Benji Mahmoud cowered against the wall, speaking a stream of frantic words into his little phone. It was Garekyn's full name he was saying over and over, Garekyn's description he was repeating, Garekyn's address in London!

Every instinct told Garekyn to get away as fast as he could. But he turned back once.

Armand held the broken, helpless Eleni to his chest, his left wrist pressed to her mouth. She was moving her mouth. She was sucking his blood. The creature was doing all he could to restore the damaged Eleni, the poor broken Eleni, and he made no move to stop Garekyn.

And neither did the helpless Benji, who sat asleep against the wall now, his head bowed, his cell phone beside his right hand on the concrete floor.

Garekyn rushed towards the staircase.

As he came up into the empty house above he understood why the monsters hadn't tried to stop him. The pale white morning light filled the first floor of the townhouse. It made the glass in the front door look like ice. The sun was rising over the city of Manhattan.

The creatures couldn't come after him. It was true, their vampire lore. They were powerless when the sun rose, and that's why Benji had dropped down unconscious against the wall and Armand had used his last few precious moments to heal Eleni.

He could go back now. He would have them at his mercy! He could examine them ever more closely! He might batter them to pulp with the fragments of the broken marble slab.

But a sudden banging noise sent a shudder through the building. The great heavy door below had been slammed back into its metal frame sealing the basement chamber off from the outside world.

Garekyn fled.

In the taxi, on the way to his hotel, he almost lost consciousness. He was physically sick. However well the restorative properties of his body functioned they could not restore the equilibrium of his soul. He had almost killed that thing, and Amel had spoken to him, his Amel! His Amel!

Like a stunned and drunken creature he blundered into his room, stripped off his bloodstained clothes, and headed for the steady blast of the shower.

Pray they had no human protectors, no human task force that could overtake him here or stop him from escaping New York. Ah, but they were such clever beings! Clever enough to track his credit cards, clever enough to find him here or anywhere else he went.

At the airport, the first flight he was able to confirm would have released him at London's Heathrow Airport after dark. Impossible. He couldn't chance it. They knew where he lived. He had to throw them off his trail. In his desperation, he had to make something resembling a plan. For surely if the wounded Eleni had not been restored to herself by nightfall, they'd be after him with two murders charged to his account.

Where could he go? What could he do?

"Amel," he whispered as if he were praying to a god for help, a god who had no earthly reason to help him except that the god might love him as he, alone in the whole world, loved the god. "I would never have harmed you. You know this. You remember the vow we took, all of us, we, the People of the Purpose."

Slowly, he was able to collect his thoughts.

"Los Angeles," he said. "Earliest through flight."

For five solid hours as the plane flew west, he listened to Benji Mahmoud's archived broadcasts on his iPhone, examining all that these creatures revealed of themselves in a new light. But at the same time, he was thinking, dozing, and remembering, remembering more than ever before. It seemed at times it was all coming back to him, all of those splendid months, but then he would lose the thread, and every time he tried to sleep he would see the city again sinking under the waves.

He'd wake gasping with the passengers and the steward asking after him, if he needed anything, if there was anything they could do.

It was early afternoon when he checked into the Four Seasons in Beverly Hills, using cash and requesting an alias be observed by the staff. They thought him an actor and a performer. No problem, once they'd verified his passport.

After leaving a lengthy message for his solicitor in London, he at last lay down to sleep in a clean fresh bed. He had a few hours until sunset, and then he might have to start running again.

# 8

# Lestat

## Château de Lioncourt

"VERY WELL," I said. "We're all here, or at least most of us are here. Let's go over it again. What do we know?"

We were gathered in the Council Chamber of the northern tower, a reconstructed part of the Château that had not existed in my day. It was a vast room at the very top, with a solitary coil of iron stairs leading to the battlements, and richly decorated, plastered, and painted, as was every single room of my ancestral home. Marius had only recently painted the murals depicting the battle of Troy on the surrounding walls and on the ceiling, a spirited depiction of the tragic journey of Phaeton, vainly struggling with his father's steeds as they drew him across the sky. The murals had the eerie perfection of a vampire painter, which made them look both magnificent and contrived at the same time, as if someone had blasted the walls with photographic images and then a team had painted them in.

I liked this room, and I liked that it was remote from the public rooms below. There were many young ones in the house and older ones not all that well known to us.

Now, there was no fixed membership in the Council. Attendance varied. But seated about the round table here were those I knew best and trusted best and mostly truly loved. Gregory, Marius, Sevraine who had only just arrived with my mother, Gabrielle, and Pandora, Armand, and Louis, and Gremt along with Magnus and another incarnate ghost, Raymond Gallant. This Raymond—a very impressive figure with dark gray hair and a narrow somewhat angular face—had once been a confidant and helper of Marius, and I had glimpsed this being a number of times with Marius in Paris, but we had not spoken, and he had not been with Gremt and Magnus when I'd visited them last night. Cyril and Thorne clung to the walls, of their own will, not choosing to sit amongst us as equals. Seth and Fareed were in Geneva and would report in as soon as they could.

Benji, who had crossed with Armand, had absented himself to be broadcasting from a chamber below, warning the Undead worldwide against Garekyn Zweck Brovotkin, who could destroy vampires who had been over five hundred years in the Blood.

Armand spoke first. He appeared drawn and hungry, and his voice did not have its usual silken strength.

"Well, Eleni will recover," he said. "She's in Fareed's laboratories in Paris now, in the hands of several of the medical apprentices." He addressed Sevraine and Gabrielle as he spoke, his eyes moving on to Pandora. "They say she will be whole again soon."

This compound of laboratories was the only hospital in the world ever created strictly for the Undead. It was skillfully and securely hidden in one of Gregory's many high-rise office buildings in the small industrial compound known as Collingsworth Pharmaceuticals on the outskirts of the city.

"We're all relieved that Eleni is well," I said, "but explain to me what you saw when you drank from this creature. We know the facts of how it happened. But what did you actually see?"

Armand sighed. "Something about an ancient city," he said, "falling into the sea. A metropolis of distinctly modern-looking buildings, futuristic buildings, suggestive of some long-forgotten utopia, I don't know how to describe it, and this being having been there with others like him, and these beings having been sent to the city for a special purpose. I couldn't see his companions clearly. And somehow it was all about Amel."

"Is Amel with us?" asked Gregory looking at me.

"No," I said. "That doesn't mean he isn't in any

one of us at this table," I added. "But he's not inside me now. He left me last night before I crossed the Atlantic. I don't think he's been back since."

"That's highly unusual, isn't it?" asked Marius.

"I would say so," I replied. "But there's nothing to be done about it, so why bother to talk about it?"

"Armand, explain what you mean," said Sevraine. "That this was all about Amel."

Sevraine was certainly one of the most impressive of the ancients. She and Gregory and Seth were clearly the eldest amongst us. And her soft golden skin, though often darkened by sun, had an unmistakable gleam to it that marked her age and power. I knew very little of her really, though she'd opened her house to me and her heart.

"The thing was looking for Amel," said Armand. "The name Amel means something to the creature. The non-human thing had been listening to Benji's broadcasts. I don't think the thing meant to harm anyone. It came to find out if we and our Amel were real."

"And you say that the blood you took from him was completely replenished in a matter of hours?" asked Marius.

"Absolutely," said Armand. "And when the blood was replenished the thing came back to life. He overpowered Eleni and that took some doing. Eleni was made by Everard de Landen. She has the blood of Rhoshamandes in her. I don't know how this creature managed to spellbind her or overpower her but he did. We had no real way of containing such a powerful creature at Trinity Gate."

"Well, no one can blame you for what took place," said Gregory. "This ancient city you saw, did it have a name?"

"I heard it but the syllables didn't make sense to me."

"The lost city of Atlantis," said Marius. He was making notes on a pad in front of him. "Did you hear a name that sounded like Atlantis?"

"Perhaps," said Armand. "I thought that was a legend."

"It is a legend," said Gregory. "Nobody ever believed that legend in my time. But it was repeated now and then." Though he was the eldest at the table, born some thousand years before he'd brought Sevraine over, he never assumed an air of authority or command. He saved that for his vast enterprises in the mortal world. Here he wanted to be an equal among equals. He went on. "A great empire, thriving in the Atlantic Ocean, that perished in the space of a day and night."

"And where is this being now," asked Pandora, "this being that can destroy vampires? Crack their skulls as if they were eggs?" Pandora was usually quiet during these council meetings, but she spoke up with obvious concern.

"We've traced it to the West Coast of the United States," said Gregory. "It's a male human for all the world knows, with substantial private holdings, and several residences, the main one of which is in London. And it is most certainly an immortal, having arranged to inherit its own fortune at least twice. The account of how this being was discovered in Siberia in the ice by an amateur Russian anthropologist named Prince Alexi Brovotkin is all available in several obscure sites online. Brovotkin died a hundred years ago. The story goes that Brovotkin's team came upon the starved and frozen body of the individual in a cave in Siberia, and managed to resuscitate it with simple ordinary fresh water and warmth.

"Of course nobody believed the preposterous paper Brovotkin wrote on the subject. But the 'story' was popular in Saint Petersburg at the end of the nineteenth century, and the Prince and his protégé were extremely popular in society until Brovotkin died at sea and Garekyn never returned to Russia."

It was Gremt who spoke up now.

"So this being," said Gremt, "we are to presume, has been frozen since the fall of the legendary Atlantis, and only came to light due to the explorations of this adventuresome Russian explorer?"

"Perhaps," said Marius. "Brovotkin never refers to the legend of Atlantis. He offers no speculation as to the origins of the creature. And the trail we've uncovered—of Garekyn, and his fictitious son Garekyn, and the next fictitious Garekyn—is a simple one of men of means traveling the world."

"I saw a group of such creatures when I drank from him," said Armand. "I received the impression that this creature had been searching desperately to find anyone connected to the fallen city, anyone who might have also been there."

"And how did Amel figure in the story of the city?" asked Gremt. He glanced at Marius and then back to Armand.

Armand thought for a long moment. "Unclear. But it was the name Amel spoken so often by Benji and others on the radio broadcast that brought the creature to our door."

With a small subtle gesture of his right hand, Teskhamen spoke up. "The Talamasca has accumulated materials on the legend of Atlantis for centuries," he said. "There are two lines of research."

I nodded for him to go on. "There are the legends beginning really with Plato's account written in four hundred B.C. And then there are the recent speculations of modern New Age scholars that some sort of catastrophe did affect this planet around eleven to twelve thousand years ago, at which time a great civilization was destroyed, leaving underwater ruins all over the world."

The comely ghost of Raymond Gallant was studying him, hanging on his every word. When Teskhamen didn't say anything more, Raymond spoke up. "There's a lot of evidence apparently that there was indeed an ancient civilization before this cataclysm, and possibly more than one civilization. Yet scientists are resistant. The climatologists argue constantly. The sea levels did change drastically, but why precisely we don't know. Biblical scholars claim it was Noah's flood. Others go about examining underwater ruins, attempting to relate them to the catastrophe. The British writer Graham Hancock writes elegantly and persuasively on the topic. But again, there is no consensus."

"Fareed says it's all bunk," I volunteered. "But beautiful bunk."

"I'm no longer inclined to agree," said Marius. "Certainly I thought so centuries ago, yes, that Plato gave birth to a splendid idea with the story of Atlantis, but he was writing a moral tale."

"And where are Fareed and Seth?" asked my mother.

"Off on a mission to investigate what just may be another of these creatures," I explained. "The minute word reached Fareed as to this creature, Garekyn, he went off to have a look at a mysterious female employee of Gregory's whom he'd come to suspect wasn't a human being."

I could see that some at the table knew this and some didn't. It was always the way with the blood drinkers. Some knew all that was happening everywhere as if they received every telepathic emission generated anywhere by anyone, and others were startled, like my mother, who looked up and at me with narrow scornful gray eyes.

My mother's hair was in her usual long solitary ashen-blond braid, but she was dressed like Sevraine for this meeting, or because it was the way she dressed now in Sevraine's underground Cappadocian compound—in a long simple gown of gray wool trimmed in thick silver embroidery obviously made by vampiric hands. She looked no softer or more feminine than usual, and in fact slightly disdainful of the entire meeting and even annoyed.

Gregory explained about the mysterious woman, how she'd been working for him for ten years. Brilliant, imaginative, a scientist engaged in longevity and life enhancement research and possibly human cloning. It was Fareed who had insisted she wasn't a human being.

"I suspect Fareed will come up with nothing," Gregory offered now in his usual low-key polite manner. "Except perhaps a good candidate to come over into the Blood. I could see nothing in the photographs or tapes of the woman to indicate she wasn't a simple flesh-and-blood mortal like all the rest."

Only the scientists among us boldly brought creatures into the ranks of the Undead to do important work. Well, one couldn't discount Notker of Prum, who had brought over many a fine singer or musician during the last millennium. But in general the rest of us had not caught up with the idea of "turning" a mortal simply because we had a job for him here or there. I found myself pondering all this again. The matter had huge implications, implications we'd have to deal with at some point. Who qualifies for the Blood? And how do we give it? Or does it simply go unregulated and ungoverned as it has for centuries, with every vampire determining for himself when it was time to select a companion or an heir?

"I don't know what's taking them so long," said Gregory. "They must be in Geneva by now. In fact, they should be back here."

"Now, let's get to the matter of where other blood drinkers are just now," said Marius, "and whether or not all know about this Garekyn, and how important it is not to harm him but to bring him back here alive, to speak to us, and tell us what he is and what he wants."

"Well, Avicus and Zenobia are in the California desert at Fareed's old compound," said Marius. "Rose and Viktor of course are in San Francisco. Rose is revisiting the places that meant so much to her when she was alive. And they did receive the general alert and called in last night."

"I want them back here now," I said. "I told them. And I don't like that this creature Garekyn has gone to Los Angeles. That's too close to where they are."

"I think we may be disturbing ourselves over nothing," said Gregory. And then he repeated what he had said several times earlier that evening, that in all his life in this world, he'd never seen a creature that looked human but was not human. He had seen some strange beings all right, and certainly ghosts and spirits, but never anything biologically human that wasn't human. "I think we'll find some puerile and disappointing explanation for all this," he said.

"You didn't see it," said Armand sharply. His tone was low but hostile. "You didn't drink its blood. You didn't see that city falling into the ocean, those towers melting."

A chill passed over me.

"I've seen the city," I said turning to him. "I've seen it in my dreams."

Silence all around.

"I've seen it too," said Sevraine.

I waited, looking from one to the other of them around the table.

"Well, this is clearly like the old telepathic images of the red-haired twins that were fired round the world when the Queen rose," said Marius. "Some have seen this, some haven't. That's the way it was then."

"Seems so," said Teskhamen. "But I too have seen it. I didn't think it important. I saw it perhaps twice." When no one spoke up he went on. "A great beautiful capital, replete with glassy towers sparkling in the sun; it was like a great forest of glass towers, yet they were all translucent or reflective and then quite suddenly it is night and then comes the fire; it's as if the city exploded from within."

"I too have seen it," said Louis in a small voice. He looked at me. "But I saw it only once, the night before I met you in New Orleans. I was still in New York. I thought I picked it up from others at Trinity Gate. A dreadful horror accompanied it, the cries of countless people perishing."

"Yes," I said. "You can hear people crying out to Heaven for help."

"And a wailing sound," said Armand. "As if of horrific grief."

Quite suddenly, I felt the telltale warmth at the base of my skull. I said nothing about it. I wasn't about to raise my hand and volunteer that Amel was back and breathing down my neck. It seemed too clumsy to do that, too mundane. I simply let it be known telepathically and the information was absorbed around the table within seconds.

Teskhamen whispered to Gremt that the spirit had returned, and I looked up to see Gremt staring intently at me.

"He doesn't know what the images of the falling city mean," I said defensively, as though I were defending Amel's honor. "I've asked him. He knows nothing of it. He sees the same images when I see them. He feels them. But he knows nothing."

Then without moving my lips I spoke to Amel. I knew when I did this that the others could hear me, except for Louis whom I'd made.

"You have to tell me if you understand all this," I said.

In a strong clear masculine tone, audible telepathically to the others, Amel answered: "I do not know." Then he went on.

"Fareed and Seth found nothing in Geneva. The woman's laboratories were empty, and her apartment vacated. The non-human female has fled."

"He's probably lying to you," said Teskhamen in a gentle voice. "He knows what it means." Gremt nodded to this. And so did Raymond Gallant. But Marius said nothing. Gregory said nothing.

"We can't jump to that conclusion," I replied. I tried not to become angry. "Why would Amel lie?"

I felt a great dejected gloom in Amel, a dark oppressive feeling radiating through my limbs.

"If only I did know," Amel whispered. "If I had a heart that wasn't your heart or some other blood drinker's heart, if I had a heart that was my very own heart, I think it would tell me never **never** to find out."

# 9

# Derek

DEMONS, THERE WAS no other name for them. Demons, all of them, his captors, wrapping him in suffocating wool blankets and carrying him out of that dismal horrid room in Budapest, only to take him riding into the clouds on the freezing wind and down now into this, yet another dungeon, deeper, more spacious, more remote from all the world.

"There's no one on this island to hear you scream," said Rhoshamandes standing over him, a monk from Hell in his long gray habit. "You are in the Outer Hebrides in the North Sea, and in a castle built for me a thousand years ago so that I might be forever safe! And you are in my power." He pounded his chest as he said those words, "my power."

How proud and haughty the being looked, striding back and forth, his leather sandals slapping the stone floor, his white face grimacing with feeling like that of a nightmare haunt one minute and curiously blank and cold the next, as if it were made of alabaster.

Even Arion and Roland, in their pedestrian street garments, standing well behind him, gazed on Rhoshamandes with something akin to fear. And the deep-voiced female, Allesandra, in the long red gown, a figure as otherworldly as Rhoshamandes, sought again and again to quiet his fury.

Derek sat in the farthest corner of the vast room, his knees drawn up to his chest and his arms holding tight to his legs. He struggled to keep his bitter joy locked in his heart. **Garekyn lives! Garekyn has survived! Garekyn is alive and he will come for me! Garekyn will find me.**

The demons had revealed this to him as soon as they'd come to bring him to this new prison. Garekyn was alive.

He was shivering violently, oh, so cold from the icy wind whipping through the high naked window. The fire blazing in the blackened hollow cavern of a fireplace was too far away from him to provide anything but light. Uneven light. Lurid light. Light that played on the long dark gray robes of this striding giant as he issued his threats.

A solitary candle burned on the crude mantelshelf that was no more than a long horizontal slot in the plastered wall. Sooner or later the wet wind from the high small open window would extinguish it.

"You can rot in this cell forever, if you refuse to talk," said Rhoshamandes. "I have no compunction about starving you till you dry up like a husk, like this being was dried up, this Garekyn Zweck Brovotkin when they found him in the Siberian ice."

Derek shut his eyes tight. And if Garekyn had survived in the ice, then Welf and Kapetria had surely survived in the ice. But bury the thought deep inside you, in that chamber they cannot reach with their conniving, larcenous powers.

Rhoshamandes slapped the computer-printed picture with the back of his hand and then let the paper float to the floor.

"You know what this is, you stubborn little miscreant! You've discovered Benji Mahmoud's broadcasts! This is a printout from his website. You know what that is, too."

Derek tried not to look at it, tried not to look at the bold and handsome face of his beloved brother Garekyn, staring out from the computer-generated portrait with the very same expression Derek had seen on his face countless times. Patience, curiosity, love. A smiling man with skin as dark as Derek's and as Rhoshamandes had thundered: "The very same black hair with the same telltale gold streak! Do you deny it? Look at it. This is another one of you! How many of you are there out there, and **what** are you!"

Earlier that evening, when they had first come for him, Roland had discovered the iPod on its charger behind the refrigerator and ground it to fragments and dust in his hand. But not before tapping its

screen for all sorts of intelligence as to what Derek
had been listening to, and berating the humiliated
Arion as a traitor under his roof.

"Old programs," Arion had pleaded in his defense. "Just old archived programs. I gave it to him
as a diversion, that's all."

And all had been forgiven, it seemed, before
they'd spirited Derek away and to this horrid place
on the edge of the European world.

"Rhosh, please, be gentle with the boy," said the
woman Allesandra. What a commanding manner
she had for one so obsequious to this monster. She
was as tall as Rhoshamandes was, and her face a portrait of compassion carved in stone. Her long thick
hair seemed the perfect color of dust, and her skin
was the color of waxen lilies. Demons, all of you.

**Garekyn, Kapetria, help me. Give me the
strength to hold out for your coming. Give me the
strength to betray nothing.**

"He is no boy!" roared Rhoshamandes. "And he's
going to tell me what he knows, and he's going to
give me something to take to them so that they will
have to recognize me and what they've done to me!
He's going to talk or I will chop him to pieces!"

The creature stopped in his tracks. It was as if
his own words had given him an idea. Oh, brilliant!
Derek held his breath. Had the monster taken those
words from Derek's own thoughts? Chop him to
pieces, it had been the very thing Derek dreamed of
doing to these monsters. Rhoshamandes turned and

marched out of the dungeon chamber leaving the others puzzled.

Allesandra took this moment to plead with Derek. "Derek, poor Derek, give him the intelligence he demands," she said earnestly. Her demeanor was almost regal. "Why do you hold out? To what purpose? All he asks is for your knowledge so that he might take it to the Prince, bargain with the Prince for a place at the table!" She stood over Derek reproving him as if he were a child. "This Garekyn. You know him. We all saw your reaction to this news. You know the man in the picture. Now he is loose and a threat to our kind. And you can explain to us what he is, and what you are. What do you have to gain by keeping this back?"

Rhoshamandes had returned and in his hands he held a large ax with a long thick wooden handle.

Derek was terrified. It was the kind of ax Derek had seen in hotels and other public buildings, usually residing in a glass case against a wall, an ax to be used in case of fire, an ax that could chop through plaster and wood with its mighty head and its cunning sharp edge.

"Yea gods, you can't be serious!" said Arion. "Rhosh, put the thing away, I beg you." He was the smallest of the evil tribe, and looked so wholly human as he stood there, in his simple leather coat and jeans. "Rhosh, I cannot be a party to such cruelty!"

"And who are you to question Rhoshamandes?"

asked the cold unmoving Roland. "And to think I sheltered you, gave you comfort."

"Don't fight with one another," said Allesandra. She turned to Derek again.

"Derek, give us the simple answers to the obvious questions. If you have listened to Benjamin's broadcasts, you know we are many, and you know what power we have. Now confide in us, and give us all that you know so that we might present it to the Prince."

"Stay out of this," said the king of demons to all of them, as he held his treasured ax.

Derek turned his head to the side. "I'll tell you nothing," he cried suddenly. "You hold me here against any law in this world." His words came out in sobs. "You keep me your prisoner year on end and you drink my blood as if it belongs to you! I loathe you and detest you. And you, cruel one, the whole tribe despises you and is it any wonder? And you think you can make me an ally?" He tried to stop himself, but he couldn't. "Some night, I'll get even with you for all this, some night, I will have you as a prisoner and you will be at my mercy! Some night you will pay for all you have done to me! Some night I'll get to your Prince and tell him all that you did to me! Some night I'll tell your whole world!"

Rhoshamandes laughed.

"You're doing yourself no good at all, Derek," said Roland with his usual icy condescension. "Simply tell us what you know of this Garekyn."

"This ax is sharp," said Rhoshamandes. Derek was too frightened suddenly to make a sound. He went over the promise of the Parents again in his mind, that if pain was too much for him to bear, he would lose consciousness. And then what? Awake to a world in which he was a butchered fragment of his former self? And would he live on if this demon did hack him limb from limb, even severing his head from his trunk? He gasped and wiped frantically at his eyes.

"Someone cut off my left arm not very long ago," said Rhoshamandes, "and the effect of that blow was amazing. There is nothing quite like seeing your own limb hacked off."

"Yes, it drove you mad!" said Allesandra. "It robbed you of all hope and optimism! Now put that tool aside. You will not harm this boy. What would you gain by doing that? You've gone about this all in the wrong way."

"Don't harm him any further," said Arion. "Can't you bargain with the Prince by offering to bring the boy himself?"

"No, I need more than that! As soon as they know about the boy, they'll come in such numbers that we can't defeat them, and they'll take the boy!"

"Why not try it, Rhosh?" asked Roland. "I've given him to you for whatever you wish. Tell them what you have here, a living specimen of the same ilk as the one that escaped. And that we will bring this creature to them at the Château if they will guarantee your complete exoneration, if they will welcome you into the Court on terms of full equality."

"The Prince will keep his word if he gives it," said Allesandra, "just as he did before."

"I need more than that, much more," said Rhoshamandes. But he was pondering, obviously.

Derek sat as quiet and still as possible, not daring to hope, not daring to say, Yes, take me to them, to the Prince, and I will tell all, for certainly they could not treat him as horribly as this fiend. For hours he'd listened to Benji's old broadcasts, and realized the great camaraderie that existed within the tribe. They were not all lawless fiends. The Prince was no lawless fiend. But then again, how did Derek know what they would do with him? Could he expect the mercy they'd shown Rhoshamandes when Rhoshamandes had fallen into their hands? Rhoshamandes had been one of them, after all.

Allesandra made a soft exasperated noise. She stood between Derek and Rhoshamandes, and turned her full attention once more to Derek. She spoke again of "the bulletin" which had gone out over Benji's "live" broadcast this evening, of Garekyn in New York, of Garekyn slaying one of their kind and devouring the brain, of Garekyn wounding a cherished blood drinker by the name of Eleni and escaping the powerful blood drinker Armand. She spoke again of what Armand had seen in the creature's blood. The city. Amel. Derek put his arms over his head and buried his face in his left arm like a bird burying its head beneath its wing.

**Glad he killed one of you, glad he escaped, glad he is free! And blast the intelligence to the whole world on your radio programs! Do it! Blast it to those of you who are not wicked, and not spiteful and not full of evil! Blast it to those who have hearts still in their breasts.**

Rhoshamandes moved Allesandra to the side so that he loomed over his prisoner once more.

"I saw a city in your blood," Rhoshamandes said, "and now the others are calling this city by a name, they're calling it Atalantaya. Is that the name of this city? Are you the survivors of Atalantaya? This is Atlantis, isn't it, Plato's Atlantis?"

"Oh, don't give him any ideas," said Roland. "And certainly not anything as grand as the lost kingdom of Atlantis! The little fool. Don't you realize that this creature is likely nothing but some form of mutant, who knows no more about himself than humans know about themselves?"

Arion interrupted. "They're broadcasting more on this," he said. "There is a woman now under investigation."

"A woman?"

Derek kept his eyes tight, listening.

"Dark skin and the same black hair with the golden streak in it. Well, this is certainly beyond coincidence."

"What, gold streaks in dark hair?" asked Roland. "What does that mean?"

"There's more to it."

Through the web of his fingers, Derek peered out to see Rhoshamandes holding the ax in his left hand while with his right he gazed at the screen of his cell phone. Arion too had his phone in his right hand. Their phones were talking, but the words had no meaning for Derek, something about a great drug company, laboratories, a doctor, a suspicious doctor with a common name.

"It's one of them," Rhosh said. He was powerfully excited.

He glared at Derek with narrow eyes. He strode forward and pushed the cell phone at Derek. Derek tried to turn away but another pair of hands had hold of his head and was making him turn to look at the cell phone. A lovely perfume rose from the silk robes rubbing against him.

"Child, just look at the picture on the phone," said the female blood drinker. "Tell us if you know this woman."

Fearfully, Derek looked through his tears.

And there she was all right, most certainly, there she was, without doubt, his magnificent Kapetria!

He struggled to turn around, to crawl through the very wall to get away from them, to conceal his thoughts and his heart from them. She too lives! He broke into frantic sobs again, sobs of relief and excitement and happiness, let them parse his sobs as they would, he didn't care. They are both alive, Garekyn and Kapetria. He had only to hold out until they found him, he had only to hold out until he could somehow be free.

"I say call them now," said Arion. "This woman too is on the run. And they are beside themselves. They're calling all to the Château. Call the Prince and speak to the Prince. Tell him about this boy. Tell him you want peace and to be accepted again and you'll bring the boy to Court now."

"I loathe the Prince with my whole soul," muttered Rhoshamandes. "I will not call him nor will I go to his court."

"That's it, isn't it?" asked Allesandra.

"Which means what?" demanded Rhoshamandes.

They moved away back closer to the fire, and Derek peered at them again secretly through his fingers. In the very depths of his soul, he sang the word "Kapetria" over and over again. Kapetria. **And at all times it will be Kapetria who will determine the time and the place, and it will be Kapetria to whom you are to defer. . . .**

"You want a great deal more than you've ever admitted," said Allesandra, her voice rising in her anger. She reached out for Rhoshamandes and took him by the shoulders. "Rhosh, you cannot destroy the Prince," she said in an imploring whisper. "You are powerless against them. Don't dream of vengeance now. Take the possibility of truce and acceptance."

"For now, yes, I will and I do, but for always?"

Rhosh pulled away from her. "There will come a time when I will destroy the Prince and take that lying demon spirit Amel out of him! And this boy is far too valuable to hand to them on a silver platter. That I will not do."

"Well, I'm with you in your opposition," said Roland, his voice colder and nastier than the voices of the others. He gazed mockingly at Derek and gave Derek one of his usual vicious smiles. "And if you want to hold on to this valuable hostage, I understand it. But don't go cutting him to pieces."

"To pieces, no," said Rhosh. "But the removal of one piece might do wonders."

He lunged forward. Allesandra screamed. There was no escape for Derek. Rhoshamandes brought him up to his feet, turned him around, and flung him at the wall. "You don't have the strength of your friend Garekyn, do you?" Rhoshamandes whispered in his ear, his hand against Derek's back. "Or is it confidence you lack?"

Derek clawed helplessly at the stone.

The blow came without warning. The pain exploded in Derek's shoulder, and once again Allesandra screamed and this time she didn't stop screaming. For one instant Derek prayed to die, to perish so that it was all over. He heard his own scream mingled with that of Allesandra, and the world went dark, but only for an instant.

He woke to find himself slumped on the floor

and the pain in his shoulder throbbing unbearably and, with utter horror, he saw his own left arm lying on the floor, the fingers of his left hand curled inward, a piece of lifeless meat wrapped in the filthy white shirtsleeve.

His eyes rolled up into his head. Their voices were so much babble, and he slid into darkness.

Far away, he heard a woman pleading. "Now Benedict will never come back to you, don't you see? Oh, when did you ever become so cruel! And this cannot be undone and for all time now this being will exist maimed and robbed of his arm and you have done this, you, my master, my maker." She was crying. Far away, she cried.

Then they were all speaking at once.

"No . . . no, look, the wound's healed, he's not bleeding."

Derek was dreaming. Jungles. With the others, laughing together, talking, stopping to pick the fruit from the trees, large yellow fruit. So luscious and sweet. No, here in this horrid place, and their voices . . .

Derek's eyes opened before he could will them to do so.

The firelight. The candle flickering on its shelf. The sound of the wind beyond the window, and perhaps rain in the wind, sweet rain cooling his face. Oh, the miracle of rain after all those years beneath the ground in Budapest. The sweet smell and taste of rain. His left shoulder was warm but the pain had gone. He stared forward hearing their mingled voices.

". . . completely healing."

**Don't touch me. Get away from me.**

". . . skin growing back, sealing it up."

Warmth in his shoulder, warmth in his chest.

"What's done is done . . ."

"You should never . . ."

And then they were all singing the same song to him to talk, to tell what he knew, where he came from, to tell the names of the others, to tell what the visions of the city meant. And Amel. What did the name Amel mean to him? And it was like so much noise. He felt sleepy all over and crushed inside and he realized that if he listened very carefully he could hear the sound of the sea beyond this prison, the sound of waves crashing on rocks perhaps or on sand or even on the walls of this citadel. Sleepily he began to visualize the sea. He opened his eyes and stared up at the distant window and he could see rain swirling in the darkness like tiny needles in a whirlwind.

"All right, let's leave him now. Nothing more can be done tonight. Let's leave him here to reflect on what his obstinacy has cost him. And we will see if you are right."

Staring at the swirling rain made him feel colder. Listening to the sea made him feel colder. The warmth in his shoulder and chest felt good.

He turned so that he lay with his left shoulder against the wall, the warmth intensifying to heat again, staring dully at the distant window, wondering if stars would ever become visible there when perhaps the rain stopped and the heavy pregnant clouds were gone. Only slowly did he realize that when the night died, he would see blue sky through that window! He would see actual light! Now that was something to hope for, to cling to, even if the fire were allowed to die, and the room grew as cold as the sea.

And would that severed arm now live forever just as he, Derek, had lived forever, all these long years since then, since Atalantaya fell into the sea, the cold sea?

"No." The woman screamed again.

"Let it burn!" said Rhosh.

"I will not!" screamed the woman.

Derek turned his head. Arion reached into the fire and grabbed the severed arm and threw it down on the stones as if it were horrible to him, this severed part of Derek. And it was smoking, the torn sleeve smoking! Overcome with horror, Derek felt himself losing consciousness again.

Roland came close. "No, not bleeding, it's all sealed. Ah, what an amazing creature you are. But I'm not surprised. I've beaten you before, haven't I, and you've always healed. I broke your arm once, didn't I? Was it your left arm? And it healed, didn't it? I wonder how much of you might be divided away before you lose your capacity to reason. Any gift can be used as its opposite. Immortality can be a terrible thing."

His face was dark because the fire was behind him. But Derek could just make out the glitter of his eyes, and see his gleaming white teeth as he smiled.

"I suppose if your chest is divided from your head, you'll die, but perhaps not."

"Roland," said Arion, "I beg you. Don't torture him. This is all so wrong."

Allesandra was weeping.

"Think on it now," said Roland to Derek, "and when we return, have something to offer us in exchange for your right arm, or perhaps for your right eye, or for your right leg."

Derek closed his eyes. I want to die, he thought. I am finished. It is over. Kapetria lives, but she will never find me. It is too late for me. He was sobbing, but his sobs made no sound, and the tears slid down his face and it didn't matter. He tried to feel his missing left arm and hand as if they were invisibly still connected to him, but they weren't there, and the dull heat throbbed in his left shoulder stronger than before.

"That's enough, I can't bear anymore!" cried Allesandra. "I say we leave him alone now. We have work to do. Rhosh, you have solicitors, men who can use the information about this Garekyn creature . . ."

". . . So does the Court!" said Rhosh. "You don't think they're using a battery of human cohorts to track down these missing beings!"

"And that should stop us from searching for him as well?"

"Let's go now, Rhosh," Arion pleaded. "I need to hunt. I want to hunt. I've had enough of this. This Garekyn has an address in London. Rhosh, your solicitors are in London. You might find out far more about this Garekyn being than you'll ever get from this poor battered boy."

And they were going. He could hear them. He lay, knees to one side, wounded shoulder against the wall still, and his right hand on his leg, and he waited for the sound of the door being closed and bolted. But no sound of the door came.

He turned his head and looked up. Only Rhoshamandes remained in the doorway. And the creature had never looked more calculating and menacing—a mighty angel of Hell with his serene face and soft curling hair. He stepped forward with a quick furtive glance behind him, and then snatched up the arm and once again hurled it into the fire.

Then he was gone and the door was slammed shut and the bolt thrown, and Derek sat frozen in terror.

The sobs poured out of him like blood.

He had to get to the fireplace, take his arm from it, he had to, but he could not bear the thought of touching it himself. And he could hear a crackling, a noise as if of logs shifting. Move, Derek. Go, that's your arm burning on the fire!

The demons were gone. All sound of them gone.

Move, Derek, before your own flesh and blood burns! But what does it matter? Despair paralyzed him. What good would it do?

He opened his eyes and attempted to crawl on all fours until the horror of his missing arm struck him full force, and then he sat back on his heels staring forward.

But his arm had rolled out of the fire. It had rolled out of the fire and onto the stone floor again. It lay on the floor, the torn shirtsleeve blackened and smoking as before.

No left hand with which to cover his eyes, only his right hand. No left arm to wrap around his middle, only his right arm.

Demons, some night I will have my revenge. Kapetria is alive. Garekyn is alive. And they will find me. Try keeping your secrets from your wary tribe, your talented tribe of blood drinkers who can read your minds, just try! And they will come to find me here just as Garekyn found you in New York.

He stretched out on the floor full length, and resting his face on his right hand he cried as if he really were a child. And it seemed he'd never been anything else. Why had the Parents given this innocence to him, this capacity for suffering to him, why had the Parents fashioned him as such a tenderhearted being? And he wondered now, as he had any number of times since that long-ago time, had he and Kapetria and Garekyn and Welf been wrong to disobey the Parents—to put the purpose aside?

**. . . to destroy all sentient life, to destroy all life-forms . . . until the primal chemical innocence is restored and this world may begin its ascent all over again as it would have originally, had not circumstances favored the ascendancy of the mammalian species . . .**

No voice or sound from anywhere in the castle.

Perhaps they'd taken to the air again, spread their invisible wings and flown high towards the stars. If only the hand of God would pluck them out of the sky and rub them to powder between its thumb and forefinger.

A scratching noise distracted him. A low scratching sound. Something alive and moving in this cell. No, not a rat, that he couldn't bear, not a rat come to gloat and mock him and somehow escape beneath a door that rendered his own escape absolutely impossible, a rat that might seek to bite him as they'd done in the past.

But if a rat had come, he would chase it from this place, that much he would do for himself.

He opened his eyes, praying for the strength to do it, and gazed forward.

In the light of the fire he saw a long black shape hunching and moving on the stone floor, propelled, it seemed, by a collection of curling legs at one end, hunching and lurching and coming right towards him!

His mind was wiped clean of words. What he was seeing could not be. Yet he knew what he was seeing.

The arm, his own severed left arm, was crawling away from the fire and straight towards him, by means of the fingers of the left hand, which reached out to gain an inch and pull the arm behind them over and over again. This was impossible. He was hallucinating. Mortals hallucinate. Why couldn't he?

He'd had little food for days and nights. Unspeakable things had been done to him.

He rolled over on his back and stared at the ceiling. How the shadows danced from the licking flames of the fire. And the scratching noise continued.

Sharply, defiantly, he turned his head. The advancing hand was now only a yard from him. The fingers reached out, curled, lifting the hand, the thumb tucked underneath, and dragged the arm forward. Then once more the fingers reached, then curled and lifted, and the arm dropped down again on the stones, and again they reached.

Losing my mind, losing my soul, mad. Mad before they ever find me or free me. He couldn't take his eyes off it. He couldn't **not** look at it making its way towards him. Is it going to connect again? It is going to attach to my shoulder!

His horror slowly turned to hope. But as it drew closer, he caught sight of something on the palm of the hand, something glittering, indeed a pair of small glittering particles and something that resembled a mouth.

He gasped. He couldn't move. It was a face that had formed on the palm of the hand, and the small gleaming eyes were fixed on him, and the small mouth was making soft sucking noises, gaping, smacking its lips, its tiny thin lips, and the eyes met his eyes.

His mind sank beneath all that he knew. Yet some prayer was voicing itself, some prayer to the Parents to help and to guide, the Parents who had given him not the slightest word of what such a horror could mean as it came closer and closer.

The hand was almost touching him. The arm lay on the stones full length behind it and the fingers were raised and spread apart and waving in the air, and then with a lurch the fingers grasped Derek's shirt, grasped it and ripped it, tearing the buttons loose from the long placket.

Derek struggled to reason, struggled to think, I must help it, if it means to reconnect, I must help it, but he could not bring himself to move.

The heat had never left his wounded shoulder, and now it spread through all of his left side, even to his pounding heart. It was as if his heart were beating all through the left side of his body.

The arm was against him. He could feel its weight, its living weight, and with his head lifted, he stared at it, stared as the fingers touched his naked flesh, the flesh of his chest, and slowly moved upwards. It wanted to be on his naked flesh.

His eyes rolled back into his head once more. He expected to go under. He reached for the blackness, the emptiness.

He felt the fingers touching the left nipple of his chest, felt them pulling on the nipple, pulling and pulling, and the warmth collected into heat beneath his nipple.

A soft wet mouth, a tiny mouth, closed over the nipple.

And then the blackness came. And he was sliding into oblivion.

It was a dream of Atalantaya, but he was not walking her polished streets or feeling her soft warm breezes. No, he was far away from her and Atalantaya was on fire and all her people cried out to the Heavens. Smoke billowed from the melting dome, and the sea rose up to drown Derek. Kapetria and Welf were locked in each other's arms, crying for Derek as the waves carried him away, Kapetria screaming for Derek, and Garekyn was gone into the deep.

He opened his eyes.

He rubbed his face with his hands. Oh, this, the dungeon of Rhoshamandes. And the fire still burned, but it was now little more than tiny flames on one thick black log and piles of glimmering embers. The night had paled behind the high window.

And no sound came to him from the castle around him of monsters plotting to torture him.

He rubbed his eyes hard with both hands again. His face was sticky from his tears.

His hands!

He had both his hands. He sat up in one swift motion staring at his hands, and down at his left arm fully restored! It had been true, the arm and the hand, but how he couldn't divine. And what would that monster Rhoshamandes do when he saw him restored? Would this be his warrant to torture Derek with the ax forever? But oh, it was glorious to have his arm restored! He flexed his fingers, opening and closing his fist, scarce believing it, that he was whole once more.

He sat there still and quiet, so relieved at the restoration of his arm that he could think of nothing else for the moment, and even the terror of Rhoshamandes was nothing to him. This was his arm, all right, strong and normal to him as it had ever been since the Parents had made him, and his left hand carried no tiny face in it.

"Father."

He looked up. What he saw so shocked him he let out a loud hoarse cry.

But the naked dark-skinned figure standing against the wall put out its hands.

"Father, be quiet!" said the figure.

It approached on bare feet and stood looking

down at him. The very duplicate of Derek himself, to his dark skin and his own hair except that the long black waves that hung down around his shoulders were shot through and through with the golden-blond streaks, so that the massive head of hair was more blond than black. Otherwise it was Derek. And it was Derek's voice that had spoken.

Slowly the truth dawned on him! He knew it complete and entire without words. This being, this duplicate of himself, had formed from the severed arm, and he was staring at his own offspring! He looked down at his restored left arm and up again at the creature that was his son.

The son dropped on his knees in front of Derek. He was indeed naked, and perfect all over, dark skin without blemish, sharp eyes fixed on Derek.

"Father," he said as if he were the parent addressing the child. "You have to lift me up to that window now so that I can climb down and then when the monsters have gone to their rest, I will find my way back into the castle, to this room, and get you out of here."

Derek reached out and clasped his son's face with both hands. He sat up and kissed his son on the lips and then broke down again as he always did, always, into tears.

And the new one, the new Derek, Derek's son, cried with him.

# 10

# Lestat

I climbed swiftly up the mountain until I was in the thick of the old forest that extended to the very end of my ancestral land, moving effortlessly through the snow that had so exhausted me when I was a boy and a young man. Many of the old trees I recalled were gone, and I was in a dense thicket of spruce and other fir trees when I came to the cement bench I had hauled to this high and deserted place when I'd first returned in the twentieth century.

It was a common kind of garden bench, curved about the bark of an immense tree, and deep enough for me to sit comfortably with my back against the tree to look down on the distant Château with her glorious lighted windows.

Oh, the cold winters I had spent under that roof, I thought, but only in passing. I was almost used to it now, the splendid palace that the old castle had become, and this sense of ownership, of being the lord of this land, the lord who could walk out to the very boundaries, and gaze on all that he ruled. I shut out the sound of distant music, voices, laughter.

"We are alone now, you and I," I said, speaking aloud to Amel. "At least it seems so."

"We are," he said. His usual tone, distinct and clear.

"You have to tell me all you know of this now."

"That's just it, I have so little to tell you," he responded. "I know that this Garekyn knows me and speaks to me as if he knows me and spoke to me through Eleni when I was in her, and I saw him up close, and I tell you, he is the positive replica of a human male."

"And in the blood, what did you see?"

"I wasn't there when Armand drained him. I was there when he fought with Eleni. I gave her every assistance I could, but it came to nothing. I can't move limbs or stop them from moving. I can't increase or decrease the power of a blood drinker. I gave her courage, but it wasn't enough."

"That doesn't stop you from trying to move my limbs," I said.

"I admit that. Wouldn't you want to move limbs if you were me? Wouldn't you want to pilot the ship? Look, I don't know what the city is or what it means. But I do know this. I did once know all about it."

"How do you mean?"

"It has to do with me. I knew that the first night we dreamed of it. I thought the dream was coming from someone in the Blood, of course. But now I'm not so sure. I think the images came from deep inside me, and the images are from my past, and the images want me to remember that past."

"Then what Gremt said was true. You have lived before. You weren't always a spirit."

"I know that I lived before. I've always known! I told all those addlebrained spirits that I'd lived before, on Earth. Oh, you can't know how stupid and bumbling and hopeless spirits are! They are made of nothing and they are nothing!"

"That isn't entirely true," I said, "but you have a way of immediately revising your past to support whatever you've come to know in the present. Try to think when you first dreamed of the city."

"It was when you dreamed of it. What? A month ago? I think maybe I do know why I started to dream of it."

"Well, then?"

"It was when Fareed first happened on the face of that doctor in Gregory's company, the black woman who has vanished."

And indeed, Dr. Karen Rhinehart had vanished.

Gregory and Fareed had returned from Geneva to report that she'd hastily taken her exit not only from the company laboratories, but from her apartment on Lake Geneva as well—at about 2:00 p.m. in the afternoon, or scarcely an hour after a crack-of-dawn radio alert had gone out from New York as to the escaped Garekyn. Indeed, Benji had been frantically broadcasting in his low secret voice until sunup that the creature was escaping, issuing pictures of the creature to the website along with all the details he knew of the creature, including his London address.

Rental records and surveillance tape from Geneva had revealed Dr. Karen Rhinehart had been with a companion, another of the mysterious dark-skinned black-haired tribe with the telltale golden streak in his thick curly or wavy black hair.

Felix Welf was the official name of the male. Six feet or slightly less in height, strong heavy build, decidedly square face, and full beautifully shaped African mouth, a small somewhat delicate nose, and large dark curious eyes with prominent supraorbital ridges and thick well-defined eyebrows.

"That's the only moment I can pinpoint," said Amel. "I pass in and out of Fareed when I choose, of course. I've never trusted him, any more than I trust any of the others. You're the only one I love and trust. And at one point he was looking at pictures of that woman. He was trying to make up his mind to tell Seth and Gregory about her, or whether he was just being foolish. And perhaps something in that woman's face triggered for me the dream of the city falling into the sea, and I felt it the way you might feel a kick to your gut, and I hated it."

This was an amazingly coherent and straightforward confession for Amel, and I knew that he was leveling with me. I held back, hoping he would go on, which he did.

"I dreamed about it more. I homed to Fareed and did my best to get him to focus on that woman again, but Fareed is good at ignoring me, or turning on me, seizing on my presence and demanding to know all manner of things so that I leave because his questions are deafening. That's when I think it started. I saw her, and I remembered something. I think I remembered her voice—the actual sound of her voice. And yes, I know damned good and well that I was once living, walking around this earth just like you, and those spirit friends of yours don't know anything. Anyone who believes a spirit is an idiot."

"And that goes for a ghost too?" I asked.

My right hand jerked suddenly and then fell back down on my thigh.

"You didn't like that, did you?" he asked.

"Try to do it again," I said. But in truth it alarmed me. It had been no more than a spasm, but I didn't like it. He who can cause a spasm can cause a fall, or perhaps . . . Didn't want to be thinking about it.

"Why don't you trust me!" he demanded. "I love you!"

"I know," I said. "I love you too. And I want to trust you."

"You're all so emotional!" he said.

"And you're not? Okay. So that might be the reason you saw the city—that he had stumbled on that woman, and was considering bringing her over."

"He thinks he can make other blood drinkers

without asking anyone. He is a god unto himself, that doctor. He thinks his maker, Seth, protects him against your authority."

"Likely that's true," I said. "Who is he supposed to ask for permission to make others anyway? Me? Or the Council?"

"Well, whom do you think, genius!" he replied. "Who is it that animates the entire Corpus Amel, may I ask? Your Frankensteinian friend would have put me in a jar if he could have done it."

"I'll never let him do anything like that to you ever," I said.

"And I'll never let anyone hurt you. Remember that!"

"Is somebody trying?"

Silence.

"These creatures, these non-humans. They would hurt you, wouldn't they? This Garekyn thing ate the brain of Killer and ruptured the skull of Eleni."

"Blunders," I said. "Why are they looking for **you?**"

"I don't know!" he said.

"So why did you feel a blow to the gut when you saw the vision of that city?"

"Because I loved it and all those people perished and they were crying. It was a horrible thing what happened to them. Aren't you cold out here? The snow is getting thicker. We are covered in snow."

"I'm not cold," I said. "Are you cold?"

"Of course not, I don't feel hot and cold," he said.

"Yes, you do," I said.

"No, I don't!"

"Yes, you do. You feel cold when I feel cold and it takes more than this."

"You just don't understand how or what I feel," he said dejectedly. "You don't understand how the world looks to me through your eyes, or feels to me through your hands. Or why I want innocent blood."

"So you're the one who wants innocent blood," I replied. "And that's why I'm thinking of it all the time, night and day, the boss man who's telling the Children of the Night all over the world that they can't drink innocent blood."

"I loathe and detest you."

"How big was the city?"

"How should I know? You saw it. It was big like the city of Manhattan and packed with towers, overgrown with towers, towers of pale azure and pink and gold, the most intricate and delicate of towers. You couldn't see all of it in those flashes. You couldn't see the flowers and the trees that lined the streets—."

Silence.

I didn't dare to say a word. But he was not continuing. . . .

"Yes?" I asked. "What kinds of flowers?"

I felt a small convulsion in my neck.

Did that mean he was feeling pain?

"Yes, that's what it means, you imbecile," he said. I remained quiet, waiting. Far down the hill, more and more of the tribe were arriving. I would not rest until Viktor and Rose had returned. And they could not possibly reach the Château before sunrise. It was night in San Francisco, but five in the morning here. I prayed they had gone to New York as they'd promised. I couldn't bear to think of Rose and Viktor most of the time, out there, newly Born to Darkness, determined to roam the planet free of all guardians, Rose gone back to explore her old home and her school and find that devoted mortal bodyguard who'd once saved her life, and bring him over into the Blood if she and Viktor could manage it.

That had been Rose's only request: to offer the Dark Gift to her beloved Murray. And I had acquiesced though I gave all the predictable stodgy warnings of my generation in the Blood that it could spell disaster. Rose had vanished into our world leaving the mortal Murray bewildered and hurt that his precious charge, the college girl he'd guarded with such love, had simply abandoned him.

Of course I'd investigated Murray. He was a complex man, of deep feeling, a lover of things of the mind to which he'd made his way only through comic books, fantasy novels, and television, but a lover of the spiritual, and moral to the core of his being. He had been in awe of Rose's education and refinement; in awe of her ambition. Maybe it would work, this invitation to Murray.

How curious and human to be thinking of all of this at the same time.

"What is it you see right now, Amel?" I asked.

"That city," he answered. "Would you think me a boastful fool if I told you I—?" Silence again.

"If you only knew," I said, "how much I cherish every single word that comes from you, you wouldn't ask. Boast to me. You're allowed for all eternity to do that."

"I know that city," he said in a small wounded voice. "That city was—."

"Your home?"

Silence. Then:

"It's time," he said. "The Egyptian idiot and the Viking thug are making their way up the mountain."

"I know," I said. An idea was forming in my mind, of how I might draw him out further on the city, but the sun waits for no vampire. I wondered if Louis had gone into his crypt, the special crypt I'd prepared for him, a monkly chamber of essential things with an antique black coffin that I'd chosen specially, with its lining of thick white silk padding. Pretty much like mine.

"He sleeps," said Amel.

I smiled. "And did you look at me through his eyes when I was with him?"

"No, I can't go into him," he said. "I told you that. But I love looking at him through your eyes and I know what I see. He loves you so much more than he lets on. And others know that Louis loves you, and they see his love, and they're glad he's finally here."

That was more reassuring than I cared to admit.

And true, it was time, and there were my guardians off in the falling snow, sturdy as trees, waiting for me.

I rose slowly as if my bones ached when they did not, and walked towards them. And for some reason, unbeknownst to me in my present frame of mind, I put my arms out to receive Cyril and Thorne, embracing them, and we walked down the mountain together.

As I entered my crypt, I saw, in a flash, the city tumbling into the sea. I saw the smoke billowing up and up into the clouds and then making black clouds spreading out to block the sun.

"Doesn't seem possible," Amel whispered, "a city like that, to have died within an hour."

"And you died there," I said.

But he didn't answer me. A hideous wailing filled my ears, but so faint I had to hold my breath to hear it. A wailing in dreams, not from him or me. A wailing that speaks of grief without the need of language.

# 11

# Fareed

FAREED WAS BACK at the Château working on the computer in his private quarters. Gregory stood by his side. And in a far-off corner of the great carpeted chamber, seemingly lost among the gilded furnishings, sat the solitary figure of Seth, black haired and golden skinned as Fareed was, dressed simply in a collarless black Chinese jacket and soft pants as Fareed was, yet occupying a stillness which the more animated and agitated Fareed never knew.

Fareed was tapping rapidly on the computer keyboard, reviewing screen after screen of information as the great Château entered its quietest hour before the rising of the sun. A full snowstorm was closing in on the Château and the little village beneath it, and the forests that surrounded them both.

Lestat had already gone to his crypt in the bowels of the mountain, as had most of those under the roof. And Fareed, fascinated as he was by what he was discovering, would soon have to retreat to the crypts as well.

Only an hour before, Fareed and Seth had returned from Geneva, to begin the search for the story of two dark-skinned fugitives, Dr. Karen Rhinehart and her male companion, online. These two weren't human, no one any longer was disputing that, and Fareed was more fascinated by the mystery of what they might be than the question of any threat they might pose. Fareed was a powerful blood drinker, having been made by Seth, who was one of the eldest survivors of the tribe. And through a series of blood exchanges over the years, Fareed had imbibed the blood of young and old vampires, seeking to enhance his own mental and physical gifts. Fareed had a multitude of theories about the biological nature of vampires. His life offered him countless magnificent discoveries, no matter where he turned. But he had to focus on Dr. Karen Rhinehart now, no doubt about it.

He was convinced there had been some sort of complex laboratory in Dr. Rhinehart's private apartment in Geneva. That was the only explanation he could find for the innumerable electrical and gas outlets he'd discovered there, and the long tables, one of which had been fitted with restraints that might have been applied to a body.

Surveillance video revealed Dr. Rhinehart and her companion taking extra precautions with two of the crates removed from the building, both of which were at least seven feet long and might have contained bodies.

Fareed was furious with himself that he had not closed in on her sooner before she'd had a chance to flee. He was absolutely certain now that Dr. Rhinehart was onto the nature of Gregory Duff Collingsworth, the founder of Collingsworth Pharmaceuticals, and that listening to Benji Mahmoud's nightly broadcasts had alerted her to the existence of another non-human entity like her, Garekyn Zweck Brovotkin, who was still evading capture on the West Coast.

Why else would she have begun her move at the very moment the news of Garekyn's capture and escape had been broadcast?

Fareed had returned from Geneva anxious to use the powerful human resources of the Court to trace the two non-humans.

But in the meantime, the DNA material in the records of Collingsworth Pharmaceuticals for Dr. Karen Rhinehart—her faked health records—had led Fareed to a remarkable story, which he shared now with the others in bursts of reading aloud and wild verbalized speculation. He never forgot for a moment that Seth couldn't read his thoughts, or that Gregory seemed unreasonably skeptical with regard to the missing doctor, and really had to be convinced of how extraordinary was all this talk of non-humans.

As Dr. Flannery Gilman had discovered, the

DNA match for the blood samples had proved to be a woman in Bolinas, California, owner of a famous bed-and-breakfast hotel. Her name was Matilde Green. Old newspapers, now available online, recounted how Matilde Green had found two people unconscious on the beach one night near her hotel in 1975. It had been in the aftermath of a great storm.

The woman and the man, severely emaciated, naked, and unconscious, had been locked in each other's arms as if they'd been "sculpted out of stone together," until revived by Green, who had built a fire of driftwood to warm them while rushing up to her hotel for brandy and blankets to aid in the salvation of the pair.

In the dark ages of 1975, the only telephone connection at the bed-and-breakfast hotel had gone down during the worst of the gale.

For twelve years the woman and the man, known as Kapetria and Welf, lived with Matilde Green in her large ramshackle hotel, providing invaluable aid to her in the restoration of the old building and its management. They had also been Matilde's devoted caretakers during several severe bouts of illness that landed Matilde in the hospital for extended periods. The bed-and-breakfast became a legend on that part of the coast, and so did Kapetria and Welf, and Matilde Green.

Cheerful stories in small regional newspapers, and a couple in the **San Francisco Examiner,** told how Welf and Kapetria were experts in homeopathic medicines, and medicinal teas, of how they gave as good a therapeutic massage as any to be found anywhere, and painted and roofed and repaired the old hotel with boundless gratitude and zeal. Matilde who has suffered all her life with juvenile diabetes credited her two friends with keeping her alive when doctors had pretty much given up on her. Indeed, she was alive now, against all odds, at the age of one hundred and three, and was still visited by the mysterious pair on a regular basis.

However, the couple had taken their leave in 1987 "to go forth into the world," as Matilde put it tearfully, when she had hosted "a huge bash" to say farewell to her "children of the sea." After that came a number of brief mentions of the hotel's continuing prosperity, and finally full newspaper and YouTube video coverage of Matilde's last birthday party, with Welf and Kapetria helping to feed over two hundred guests on a bright sunny afternoon last spring.

These careless home videos maddened Fareed somewhat for what they did not reveal, nevertheless he got his closest glimpse of the faces of Kapetria and Welf and his best taste of their voices. Both spoke perfect accentless English, fielding questions about their mysterious appearance on the California beach years before with polite admissions that they loved being a mystery, and part of local lore and the tales of the amazing health benefits of the area for those who sought out the "B&B" for restorative retreats.

"Well, that's it, there isn't anything else," said Fareed finally. "But it's obvious, the comparisons to the stories of Garekyn found in a Siberian cave."

"But how did this woman become part of my company?" said Gregory. "She's been working for me for years. My security should have caught all this. My security isn't what . . ."

"Your company's security is not the issue at hand," said Seth in a low voice. "It's imperative we discover what these beings are because they know about us."

"I'm not convinced on any of this," Gregory responded, using his most agreeable tone of voice. "I told you, I have traveled this world," he insisted politely. "I have been everywhere. I have never seen anything like these beings before, and I trust that there will be some very disappointing explanation for all this, and we'll soon go back to facing the true important issues that challenge the Court now."

"And what are those issues, if not our own safety?" asked Seth wearily. "This woman's been studying you at close hand for years; and using your money for her occult enterprises."

There seemed some deep gulf between these two that Fareed could sense but not fathom. But it was clear that in some way, Gregory looked down on Seth as the resurrected relic of a primitive age, while considering himself the full expression of what an immortal could be. And Seth regarded Gregory as compromised by the immense energy he put into his identity in the mortal world as the resolute chairman of his chemical empire. At times Seth let slip that he was weary of Gregory's vanity, and preoccupation with worldly power. Seth had no need to be known or loved by mortals. Far from it. But Gregory seemed very much dependent on the adulation of thousands.

"I have the lawyers in Paris on her credit cards," said Fareed, "but the woman may have multiple identities, in which case there is likely no clue to where she and the man have gone. We can call this woman Matilde, of course, and send people to watch the B and B, but Kapetria and Welf would be fools to go there."

Seth rose from the chair. He appeared stiff and cold as he often did right before morning, and this was his mute signal that it was time for him and Fareed to retire to the crypts.

Fareed rose from his desk. The three moved towards the door.

"Well, it's all over for us for the moment," said Gregory. "I should have the analysis of all her research projects on my desk at the Paris office when we wake. We'll find out what she was actually doing at the company."

"No," said Fareed as they left the apartment together and made their way down the dimly lighted corridor. "We'll find out what she wanted others to think she was doing in your laboratories, no more and no less."

Gregory didn't want to admit that. And Seth walked on ahead impatiently.

Moments later Fareed and Seth were alone in the large crypt beneath the Château that they shared.

Neither had a taste for coffins or other Western romantic trappings of the grave, and this room was a simple though elegant bedchamber. It had a dark carpeted floor, a broad bed in the ancient Egyptian style with gilded lions supporting it, and a solitary standing lamp that gave a warm light through a parchment shade. The walls were painted with the golden sand and green palm trees of ancient Egypt.

Fareed slipped off his boots and lay down among the silk-covered pillows. For the first time in many months, he was actually tired, tired in his bones, and wanted to sleep for a while.

But Seth stood with his arms folded staring off as if he were not in this tiny windowless chamber, but gazing out at the snow falling all around them on the mountainside.

"There were always stories in those ancient days," he said, "of wise men and healers who came out of the sea. I spoke to many a teller of tales in this or that city of such legends. And there were tales of a great kingdom that had been swallowed by the ocean in more places than one. These wise men and women were survivors of that great kingdom, or so some thought. I used to put hope in such legends. I used to think I could one day find one of these wise men or women and discover from that person some great and salvific truth."

Fareed had never heard the word "salvific" spoken by anyone. He said nothing. He had never had any such idealistic or romantic beliefs. Reared by two entirely modern parents, Fareed had been protected as much from mythology as he had been from religion. His had been the world of science and scientific obsessions all of his life. The great gift of immortality meant that Fareed would live on and on discovering one scientific truth after another, witnessing the world of science make discoveries in the future that would so dwarf the present time that it would seem primitive and superstitious to later generations. And Fareed would share this future. Fareed would be there.

But he could feel a great sadness in Seth. He wanted to say that it was all fascinating, that there was nothing to be sad about, but he knew better than to question any mood or emotion from Seth, who in his heart of hearts was unreachable when it came to speculations as to what this world was, or what he himself was, and why he was alive six thousand years after he'd been born.

"Remember the description of the two intertwined in each other's arms," Fareed murmured sleepily. "Why don't you come and lie here beside me and let us make that picture now and sleep? Two in one another's arms as if carved from stone?"

Seth obeyed. He kicked off his boots and lay down beside Fareed, his right arm over Fareed's chest.

Fareed breathed deeper, pushing away the slight panic he always felt at losing consciousness with the rise of the sun. He moved closer to Seth, and closed his eyes, and began almost immediately to dream. Fire, smoke rising in a great dark column to the Heavens . . .

He barely heard the dull throb of the cell phone in Seth's pocket, or Seth's voice as he answered. Seth was so much stronger than Fareed. Seth had an hour yet of wakefulness before the paralysis would come over him. And Fareed barely heard Seth's suddenly angry voice, but he tried very hard to hear it, to follow what Seth was saying.

"But how? Why did they move to take him prisoner on their own?"

Fareed could hear the voice of Avicus on the phone. Avicus, who months ago had gone to California to guard the old medical compound there as it was thoroughly evacuated. Avicus, who had been gracious to do that. But then Avicus would have done anything for Fareed and Seth and for the tribe.

"But they shouldn't have gone alone," Seth was saying, "just the two of them! How perfectly stupid. They should have waited."

He felt Seth beside him again, and the arm catching hold of him and bringing him closer to Seth.

"Another blood drinker destroyed by the one called Garekyn," Seth said. "A maverick in California, name of Garrick. Two of them caught the intelligence that the being had used his passport at a local hotel. Avicus hadn't meant for them to act on it. They thought they could take the creature prisoner easily, and bring him back as far as New York. They wanted to be heroes. The creature decapitated Garrick and got away with his head."

Fareed felt the pain, though he couldn't move or speak. Ah, foolish young ones. And this fiasco would inflame the wanderers throughout the area, increasing the danger that the thing called Garekyn would be destroyed on sight by the next band of assailants. It was not even midnight in Los Angeles.

Seth was voicing the grief and frustration for both of them. But Fareed could no longer hear what he was saying. In fact, he was dreaming. He was seeing that city again, that city tumbling into the sea in flames, and smoke so black it turned day into night as it spread out across the sky in greasy rolling clouds, that city winking out below, collapsing in on itself as the ocean swallowed it. Thunder. Lightning, rain falling from Heaven. All the world trembling.

# 12

# Derek

WHAT IF HE had fallen? What if someone had seen him? Perhaps the fiendish Rhoshamandes had lied about the island being deserted. What if there were human guards who had taken him prisoner, and even now he was being put into some cell in this very dungeon, too far away for Derek to hear him crying for help?

It was morning, cold and bleak, and the fiends had not, as far as Derek could tell, returned to this citadel to sleep. He had not heard their voices, or their little cell-phone radios, nor any sound to indicate anyone was in the castle except for him. But the castle was vast. He'd seen it from the air. How could he know what the fortress contained?

For hours he had sat here alone, hunched over, shivering in his torn shirt and thin pants, barefoot, and desperate for the approach of his son on the outside of the door.

His new left arm seemed no different from the old limb, the fingers flexing easily as always, the skin the same dark tone as all the rest of his skin. It seemed like a dream that he had ever felt that ax coming down on his shoulder. He regretted that he'd not been conscious to see the new arm growing out of him, forming, developing a hand, achieving completion. He regretted that he hadn't seen the severed limb formed into a man. But maybe he had to be unconscious for these prodigious accomplishments to take place.

The fire still burned, but the great charred log in the middle was cooling now, and all that was left of the brush and leaves that had once filled the fireplace were embers. Soon there would be no heat in this abysmal room at all.

Derek's greatest armor against his fear, however, had been new ancient memories, the flood of new memories awakened in him by the formation of his son.

He was quite certain that the Parents had never breathed a word to him and his companions to indicate that they could multiply in this way or any way. Had Kapetria known of this and kept it secret? It was to Kapetria that they had given the superior knowledge, which the Parents had said is all they needed to survive and complete their mission. How vividly he saw the Parents now explaining that they were to fulfill their mission, how vividly he heard their soft voices as they explained that it was for "this purpose and this purpose alone" that they had been made.

**And remember, you must all be together inside**

the dome, and you must assemble to do this before him if at all possible, explaining to him how he has failed us and why this is to be done.

Of course the Parents hadn't told them how they should multiply. It wasn't necessary, was it? And how the Parents had stressed that they would never send to the planet another as educated as Amel. That had been their terrible error, they'd said, equipping Amel with immense knowledge and intelligence to loose the plague on the planet and study its effects over the centuries in all the many ways that the Parents required.

**Almost never do mammals on a planet gain ascendancy. Had it not been for the asteroid striking the planet this would never have happened and we know the fruits. . . .**

They had made Amel to be received as a god on the planet by the crude mammalian primates so that Amel could rule them and force their cooperation as he prepared to loose the plague.

Had Derek ever reviewed in his mind these specific things before? In a flash he saw the Parents, saw their immense round eyes, and their magnificent faces, saw them when they lifted their wings.

There was a phrase in these times on Earth for what had become of Amel. He had "gone native" on the planet. He had abandoned obedience to the Parents. He had used all of the fine knowledge they'd given him to gain power among the primitive primate mammals whom he discovered. He had adopted their ways.

So the four born to punish Amel had not been made with the immense knowledge of Amel. They had been equipped only with the knowledge they needed to complete the mission that Amel had never completed. And Kapetria, the leader, would be their authority in all things that they did not understand.

The vast spacious abode of the Parents had never been so vivid to him before in his memories, those many chambers lined with walls that lived and breathed with living visuals of Earth, and the great lofty enclosures in which the Parents would ascend to the topmost branches of the great trees. The chamber walls had been monitors with the resolution of today's motion-picture screens. Had they received images from everywhere on Earth or only the great wild lands around Atalantaya?

"You are equipped," said the Parent of the luminous round eyes who spoke to them with such gentleness, "with all you need to know to fulfill this mission, and this gentle one, this sweet and gentle Derek, will alert you to danger, as he is the one most attuned to the emotions of the inhabitants, so mark when he is agitated; mark when he weeps; mark what arouses his fear. Observe what is happening around you. And do what you can to comfort him because he suffers as you do not."

Oh, what a bitter thought—that they'd deliberately endowed him to suffer. And if so, why had they been so surprised when he wept at the idea that they would all die? He could not stop thinking of that moment. "But I don't want to die."

Oh, but it was still fragmentary, this remembering. He couldn't put the pieces together. He could feel the gaps. He had a sense of great time spent with the Parents now lost. Welf and Kapetria had merely watched as Derek wept. It was Kapetria who had ventured the question: why had the Parents made them such complex and powerful units if their mission was to terminate in their own death?

"It's simple for us," said the greatest of the Parents, "to make creatures such as you. And you will need the power and resilience with which you're gifted to survive in the savage lands, and to safely gain access to Atalantaya, without arousing the suspicions of Amel. We will be watching you always. Your bodies contain the means by which we can track you and see you and hear you. That is, until you enter Atalantaya, where the dome will make it impossible to monitor you or give you aid." There was so much more.

Ah, would Kapetria be angry with him when she discovered that he had managed to birth a duplicate of himself through the severing of his arm? Kapetria lived, she lived and breathed, and he must stop thinking of her anger. When had Kapetria ever been anything but loving to him? And surely she would understand he didn't know what was happening, and he couldn't have prevented it. And then what if Kapetria did not know . . . ?

Slowly the pale milky daylight of the North Sea filled the dungeon. Derek pushed at the dying embers again, but it was no use. He thought of removing his shirt and burning it but that was not enough to reignite the log. Derek's teeth were chattering.

A sound. He had heard a distinct sound. He rose to his feet, and moved away from the door. Someone was outside the door. Someone was lifting the simple bolt out of its slots. And now the door was opened outwards and Derek saw the marvelous figure of his son standing there.

His son was dressed in heavy black jeans and a thick white sweater and he had on socks and shoes. His gold and black hair had been tamed and combed. He wore a handsome heavy tweed coat that hung to his knees.

"Come, Father, hurry," said the boy. "I know where we are and how to get out of here. There are humans on this island, and I don't know how long we'll be alone."

Derek rushed into the young one's arms.

"Father, there's no time for tears now," said the boy. "We can weep and rejoice later. I've found bedrooms and wardrobes of garments, garments that fit me, and you. I've packed suitcases with clothes, money, lots of it, and passports and credit cards, every conceivable thing we'll need. Now you have to come and dress. You are shivering. And there's more work on the computer that I must do. These creatures will pay for having imprisoned you for so many years. They will pay with everything we can take from this place."

The boy took Derek's hand and led him fast up a coiling flight of stone steps and into an upper hallway of stone as severe and barren as the dungeon chamber had been.

But within minutes they had reached another floor, with doors open to many well-furnished bedchambers. Ah, the wealth of these demons, Derek thought. His hatred wasn't strong enough to overcome his fear.

They entered a large oak-paneled room with an upholstered bed, thick blue carpets, and pale salmon-colored draperies over the high-arched windows. The weak northern sun was burning through a gray sky beyond. There were large modern paintings in heavy gilt frames on the walls, and velvet reclining chairs and a thin flat-screen television much larger than Derek had ever seen before.

Desk, computers, chests of drawers, closets overflowing. And the computer on the desk was on with a screen filled with pictures of the sea. It had been years since Derek had seen a computer, and he had never seen one with such a large monitor.

"I suspect the monster's acolyte, Benedict, was the owner of these closets," said the boy as he opened a pair of double doors. There were jackets and entire suits of clothing on hangers, shelves of folded shirts and sweaters, rows of shining boots and dress shoes.

The floors were strewn with paper money, English, French, what appeared to be Russian, and euros, and American dollars, passports, and bundles of credit cards bound with rubber bands.

"Father, come alive!" said the boy. He began to pull jackets and sweaters and pants from the hangers and the shelves, which smelled vaguely of cedar. "Here, Father, dress as quickly and as comfortably as you can. Choose what you like, but hurry. And the suitcases on the bed are packed."

"I don't understand how you know all of these things," said Derek.

"I know all that you know, Father," said the boy. "We can talk about that later. This blood drinker creature, Benedict, had a collection of watches. Here, put on this watch. It is brand-new. "

Derek struggled to pull himself together.

"Now I need to get back on the computer," said the boy. He seated himself at the desk and starting tapping the keyboard with two fingers just as Derek always did it. "We're north of the island of Saint Kilda. There are three boats in the harbor and I have to find more information on how to pilot the larger cabin cruiser. The speedboat is too complicated, and the smaller boat will not go fast enough."

Derek struggled with the watch but managed to buckle the leather band. It was an old watch, but it was ticking. So this would now tell him the minutes and the hours of his new freedom. He felt suddenly hungry and exhausted and overwhelmed. He wanted to be excited, efficient, and helpful to the boy.

He drew close to see the computer monitor over his son's shoulder.

At once pictures of a giant yacht filled the screen, a Cheoy Lee 58 Sportfish. The boy was fast-forwarding through interiors of sumptuous cabins and what looked like a control room or cockpit of sorts. Derek knew nothing of modern boats.

"Father, get dressed," said the boy. "Let me take care of this. Hurry."

Derek found a pair of dark wool pants, put them on, and unwrapped a new white shirt from its plastic. As he balled up his old mutilated shirt, a surge of bitterness and anger moved through him.

"For ten years, they kept me prisoner," he said under his breath. "Ten years, if you can imagine it, ten years, in a dreary locked room in a cellar in Budapest . . ." The words were bubbling up out of him uncontrollably.

"I know," said his son. "There is time for vengeance. I can manage this boat easily. Everything I need to know is here. No problem. Channel sixteen is the universal Coast Guard channel. If the boat has full tanks . . ."

Derek found a brush and comb. He caught sight of himself in the long mirror on the open closet door.

He hadn't seen his own reflection in so many years. It felt unbelievably good to rip the brush through his thick hair. But he knew his son had a confidence and demeanor he didn't possess. He looked like his son's younger brother.

Suddenly the computer began to talk. But the talk was entirely mixed with the sound of a piano playing. Ah, it was Benji Mahmoud talking on the vampire radio station.

"And all the Children of the Night throughout the world must be on the lookout for these three, Felix Welf, Dr. Karen Rhinehart who might also use the middle name Kapetria, and Garekyn on the West Coast of the United States, who has murdered another blood drinker."

"Welf! Did you hear that?" Derek cried. "Welf is with Kapetria. We are all alive, all of us! That is all of us!"

"Yes, I know," said the boy indifferently. He was tapping the buttons relentlessly as the voice continued. Suddenly Derek saw three faces on the screen: Garekyn unconscious lying on some sort of table; and official frontal portraits of Kapetria and Welf.

Welf was smiling in his photograph, Welf the calm one, the one who had always smiled so easily, my big brother! His curly hair was massive and handsome, and his dark eyes brimmed with spirit.

And we will be together once again! Derek was struggling to keep back tears. "We have to escape, we have to survive, we have to!" he said childishly. And then, "You will never in a million years know what all this means."

He buttoned his new clean shirt and tucked it into his pants.

The voice went on, words running steadily under the soft sweet current of the music, like a dark unfurling ribbon.

"I do know what it means, Father," said his son, "because I know everything you know, I told you, but I don't have so much emotion attached to the information." The boy looked at him. "Now I want you to give me a name."

The computer voice was saying something about murder, blood, decapitation. He was describing the trio of black-skinned black-haired non-humans as murderous, and a danger to the Undead. Worldwide alert. All blood drinkers were to hunt the trio.

"Listen to him, he's lying!" said Derek. He was going through the socks and boots laid out on the bed. "Listen! This is all wrong. We are not the enemies of anything. What did you say about a name?"

"I suggest my name be Derek Two pronounced as one word and spelt as such, Derektwo, and I'll take your modern last name, Alcazar, which you took after your rescuer."

"No," said Derek, but he was focused on the radio voice. "You're not as clever as you think you are. Roland knows the name Alcazar. Roland went back to my apartment in Madrid after he'd taken me prisoner, and sacked it for information. Roland reported me dead."

He sat down on a leather ottoman with the black socks and brown shoes he'd chosen from the bed.

"Of course, you are right. All you know is inside me, but I'm not perfect at summoning the information. Give me a name."

"Derektwo sounds absurd and will look absurd," said Derek.

Black skin, said Benji Mahmoud, black curly hair, highly visible gold streaks in their hair. Strength of ten human beings. A desire for the vampiric blood, the vampiric brain.

"That has to be a lie!" said Derek. "We have no craving for vampiric blood or brains. That is a filthy lie."

"My name, Father. You are to give me my name."

"What is this, a baptism?" demanded Derek. "Shorten your name to D-e-r-t-u," Derek said. "That's plenty good enough. And it sounds fairly normal. And if there is to be a Derek three and a Derek four, we'll figure some way to sound it out properly. Dertu will do. You don't need a last name now."

"Very well," said the boy, "Dertu it is. I never thought of that. The last name can wait. We can't risk anything with new names from this computer, anyway. We'll worry about last names when we reach Scotland or Ireland."

Derek pulled on the black socks, loving the silky feel of them. The brown shoes were fine, smooth, without buckles or zippers, but it was a chore to pull them on.

". . . extremely dangerous," said the low barely audible computer voice. "All elders are asked to come to Court. The Prince has asked this. All elders should come to Court if they possibly can, to confer on the matter of these menacing non-humans."

"This is all wrong, what he's saying. They must have done something to Garekyn."

Dertu knelt before him, helping him with the shoes.

"Now put on a sweater, maybe two sweaters," said the boy. "The gloves and scarves are on the bed."

Dertu turned up the volume on the computer.

"Anyone sighting any of these strange non-humans must call us at this number," said Benji Mahmoud. "Remember, a machine will answer you and take the information night or day. To go directly on the air in my absence, press the numeral two on your keypad. Provide your information at the usual level. Be clear and succinct as to where you've seen the non-humans and at what time. It is very important that you include the time. When I come back on the air, I will return your call as soon as I can."

Dertu at once picked up a ballpoint pen from the desk and wrote something on his wrist.

"What are you writing?" asked Derek.

"Never mind."

Derek was in a daze. There was an abrupt crackling sound from the computer. A female voice was speaking: "This is Selena calling in from Hong Kong, Benji. We are all on the alert here but we cannot make it to the Court at this time. Benji, please update us as soon as you can."

Dertu was offering Derek a good thick cashmere sweater. Red. Derek hated the color red, but there was no time. Derek pulled it over his head.

"If you knew how hard it is to craft identities," muttered Derek. "And Roland went back and destroyed my identity. He used to say to me, No one will ever come looking for you. No one will ever seek to find out what happened to you."

Dertu handed him a black coat, a coat as soft as the sweater. This was a man's formal overcoat, exquisitely lined, German made.

"Well, maybe it's not so hard anymore," said the boy. "Maybe it just takes money, and we have plenty of money."

"These things may be even more physically powerful than we realize," Benji Mahmoud was saying. "Garekyn Zweck Brovotkin may have left Los Angeles and we have no clues as of now to his destination."

Dertu put a scarf around his father's neck.

"Clean clothes," said Derek under his breath. He saw himself again in the mirror, restored. He couldn't move. "Clean clothes," he said. "Being warm."

"And we know that the monsters are aware of this broadcast," said Benji Mahmoud through the computer, "and that they are listening to it. Only hours

after we broadcast the alert on Garekyn Zweck Brovotkin, Dr. Karen Rhinehart and her companion
Welf disappeared from their Geneva apartment.
We suspect that Dr. Rhinehart and her companion
had been spying on us for some time, and regularly
listening to this program was undoubtedly part of
it. . . ."

Dertu appeared transfixed staring at the computer.

". . . you must be circumspect when you go on
the air with your reports. You want to alert your
brothers and sisters. You do not want to aid these
monsters in any way."

"My God," said Derek. "They are our avowed
enemies. They will seek to destroy us on sight! We
have become fiends to them as they are to us."

"No, not on sight," murmured Dertu. "They
want us to come in."

He put up his finger for quiet.

"I don't believe that," said Derek. "I want to get
as far away from them and their kind as I can."

But someone had entered the great stone castle.
Again Dertu motioned for quiet. They could hear
a heavy uneven tread echoing as in a wooden stair-
well, and a faint sound as if the person were singing.

Dertu turned off the volume on the computer.
He motioned for Derek to shut the closet door.

"There's no time to do any more work here now,"
Dertu whispered. "Put on the coat, Father."

Yes, a human male voice singing, singing some

pleasant little ditty as the footsteps made their way closer. Dertu gathered up the two leather suitcases, handing one off to Derek.

"Shall we meet the human being as two proper guests of the house?" he asked.

They discovered the old gray-haired human caretaker in a large parlor where the man sang to himself as he dusted the furniture with a rag that reeked of pungent oil, completely oblivious to their presence until Dertu spoke to him.

"Our host has suggested we take the smaller of the two big boats," said Dertu to the old man. "He said he thought it would be easier to manage. Did he remember to have the gas tank filled?"

"Oh, the **Benedicta**," said the old man. "She's always fueled and ready to go." He was peering at Dertu and Derek through watery gray eyes. He smiled cordially. He looked utterly harmless in his sagging green cardigan with its brown patched elbows and old pants stained near the cuffs. "The master didn't tell me anyone was here. Why, I would have brought up your breakfast."

"I am starving," whispered Derek. "I cannot remember not being hungry."

"Well, you know our beloved host," said Dertu cheerfully to the old man. "Would he be insulted to be called an eccentric? Is there any food on the boat?"

The old man laughed. He slipped a pair of glasses out of his shirt pocket and peered at Dertu through thick lenses. "I think the master loves to be called eccentric," he said. "And yes, the refrigerator on the **Benedicta** is always stocked with the basics. That's the boat my wife and I use. The master drives the new one. The keys are in the boathouse office. You can't miss the boathouse. But I'll go down with you if you like."

"Not necessary," said Dertu. "How long will it take me to reach Oban?"

"Oban? Good Lord, young man, it will take you three hours in that boat just to reach Harris. You'll be at sea all day. Listen, why don't you go down and make yourselves at home on the boat? It has a fireplace, you know. And I'll pack up lunch and dinner for you. And whatever else you might need. You really should take a flight from Harris if you're determined to reach Oban. Unless you're in love with the sea."

"Thank you so much," said Dertu. "Now our gracious host said there was a laptop computer somewhere that I might take, and a cell phone."

"Well, he must have meant those he stored after Mr. Benedict left. There were a couple unopened. Now you go down and become acquainted with the boat, and I'll see what I can rustle up. You'll find wine and cheese in the refrigerator. Fruit juice, vitamin water. The bread's in the freezer. You just toast it, you see. And the Brie defrosts perfectly as well."

"You are very kind, indeed," said Dertu, grasping the man's hand, "and you must tell our gracious host we had the most splendid time, that we found his castle simply amazing, and not a single aspect of it was lost on our appreciation, to be sure. Come, Derek. Let's go."

The wind was whipping wildly around the great castle, as they made their way down the steep steps to the path. The path circled the caretaker's cottage and fields, and went down to the harbor. All around them the trees of the island were gray and twisted from the fierce wind, and the earth was wet from the recent rains.

"I'm free," Derek whispered to himself. But he couldn't feel the joy. He stopped, turning, and leaning into the wind, he looked up at the bleak hulk of the gray stone castle one last time. It filled him with fear as did the great churning gray sea all around him.

"I might have been imprisoned there forever," Derek whispered, and he could not feel it that he had escaped and he was free and that Dertu was with him.

"Come on, Father," said Dertu.

There were actually four different boats in the small port, three of which were cabin cruisers, and all being rocked violently against their moorings. The largest of the boats looked sinister to Derek, but the giant cabin cruiser, the **Benedicta**, looked substantial and heavy, and safe perhaps for the freezing sea.

Dertu marched down the pier to the boathouse, emerging a moment later with the keys held high in his hand.

He led the way onto the boat, and then helped Derek, relieving him of his suitcase and carrying both suitcases to the large salon. The salon resembled the images Derek had seen on the computer. Built-in furniture, striped couches, gleaming wood floor. The galley was as large as the salon, and there stood the giant refrigerator with its precious wine and food.

Dertu inspected everything, then took a bottle of brandy out of the bar, uncorked it, and offered it to his father.

"Not too much, just enough to make you warm."

"We cannot drink," said Derek.

"Yes, I know all about that and that you did and you have. All of you. You loved wine and beer and spirits when you came here to Earth. Now just a swallow. Go ahead."

Derek's hands were shaking. The boy had to steady the bottle for him.

"When we're at sea, when we're safe, I will become the man you want me to be, I promise you," Derek said.

"Just leave it all to me," said Dertu.

The brandy was liquid fire. But he loved it, loved the warmth in his throat and his chest. His eyes began to water. He took another swallow, some of the brandy spilling down his face.

Dertu climbed a short flight of narrow wooden steps and entered the upper control room, or bridge, or cockpit, or whatever they called it.

Derek followed, attempting to show support, but the whole venture terrified him. Dertu was excited. He sat down in one of two large white leather chairs and examined the wheel, the dials and gadgets and levers.

"And what if we drown at sea," Derek said. It was as if the words came out on their own. "Defeated again, both of us this time, and it's years before we come to the surface?" He took another gulp of the brandy. He felt elated suddenly. It was so good that the fear was almost entirely and instantly gone.

"Father, stop worrying," said Dertu. "I can get this ship to Northern Ireland. That's where our problems begin, because without picture identification we can't travel in this world."

"I thought you said Oban," said Derek.

"To throw the old man off, of course."

Derek thought again of how time consuming and difficult it had been for him to create his earlier identities, the identities that had taken him through three-quarters of the twentieth century. He thought of friends he'd made in the modern world, friends who'd never known a particle of truth about him, if they had missed him or ever searched for him. There had been a woman. . . . He hadn't thought of these things in years. He was weeping again. Oh, this was so awful, this crying. Other memories came back to him of those earlier times when he'd opened his eyes on a more primitive world. He took another deep drink of the brandy. Kapetria would be angry if she knew he'd been drinking this brandy.

"Well, maybe we can reach the others from Derry," said Dertu. He appeared to be calculating. "We'll manage. It's getting to the mainland from here that is our first problem."

They heard the call of the old man.

He and his white-haired wife had come on board and were loading bags full of fresh food into the refrigerator. The wife set a brand-new packaged laptop computer on the built-in table. And several new cell phones still in their wrapping.

Dertu hit the man with questions.

"Oh, no, no tracking system on this boat," said the old man. "No Wi-Fi. The master would never stand for that. He is leery of all GPS trackers. Very old-fashioned ideas on all that. Not even the big boat has any sort of tracking device built into it. As you said, the master is an eccentric man."

Derek helped the woman with the groceries. The sight of the roast fowl in the plastic wrap was so delicious to his starved belly that it put him in pain. And the bananas and the fresh fruit, how did they manage all of this out here? He couldn't wait for them to be gone so that he could devour something, anything, and feel his old companion starvation go away.

How sweet and considerate they were, both of them, Derek thought, and how angry the great Rhoshamandes would be with them this evening when he discovered how they'd been duped. Derek felt fear for both of them. But then the monster had his reputation to keep, did he not?

Dertu embraced them both and proffered his thanks.

Impulsively Derek put his arms around the old man. "You tell our gracious host we had to leave," he said mimicking Dertu's manner, "and we thank him for all your kindnesses, and that you never complained of a thing, that you and your wife were so good to us." He realized this might not have the effect he wanted. But what other message could he send to that ruthless monster? Pray the fiend had no time to abuse his caretakers.

The old couple hurried ashore and started to untie the ropes to free the boat.

The great engines of the boat were thrumming; Dertu was on the bridge speaking through some sort of microphone, perhaps to a coastal agent. Derek couldn't hear him.

It was happening. They were escaping. They would move away from the island of the prison.

Derek found blankets under the leather couches of the salon, and carried them up to the bridge.

"The weather isn't as bad as it looks," said Dertu. "We've plotted a course to Harris, though that's not where we're going. But there is something I want to do first. I want to follow my instinct." He looked searchingly at Derek.

"You're asking me?" Derek shrugged. "Do it, whatever it is, your instincts are far better than mine."

Dertu quickly disembarked. He said a few words to the old couple, and then as they waited, he ran towards the boathouse, the wind blasting his long golden and black hair.

Derek stood there shivering, hands stuffed into the pockets of his coat, wondering, was it possible the boy knew everything, everything of his long life, of the times he'd awakened on a primitive world and gone back up in the ice caves of the mountains to freeze again, of those sad times amongst the primitive humans of the continent the world knew now as South America?

Was it all on the surface for the boy or did he have to reach to retrieve this information? Whatever was the case, they were together, he and Dertu, and Dertu seemed a brand-new and improved version of Derek himself, unhampered by fear or sorrow, and able to do things Derek had simply never learned to do. Was that the intention of the method of propagation? Would all of his progeny, assuming he could develop more, would all of them be better than him?

Hurry, Dertu. Hurry. These monsters have humans working for them in this world, solicitors, lawyers, whatever. Hurry.

At last he saw his son running down the pier towards him. He cut a splendid figure in the finest of garments. "And were I to sever a leg, would such a being spring from that limb," Derek wondered. "And what if I were to sever the very same left arm?"

There was so much to discover together.

Dertu shook hands with the old man, hopped aboard, and the last rope was loosed. He rushed up into the cockpit and flopped down in his leather chair at the wheel. At once the boat moved forward, pulling away from the pier. The old couple was waving them off.

"But what did you do back there?" asked Derek.

Dertu's eyes were on the wheel and great front window now bespattered with spray from the sea.

"I called Benji Mahmoud's program from the phone in the boathouse. I went right on the air. I spoke as softly as they speak. I said, 'Derek is alive, and wants Kapetria and Welf and Garekyn to know that he is alive. And Derek is not alone. Blood drinkers have cruelly held Derek prisoner. A blood drinker of Budapest named Roland has done this for ten years and deserves our vengeance. And Rhoshamandes, his confederate, has visited unspeakable cruelty on Derek. They have concealed all this from the great Prince and the great Court. Derek and I would never harm any blood drinker intentionally; do not hunt us down. Let us come together, we beg you. We have never meant any harm to human beings or to you.'"

"You didn't!" Derek was in shock. "You should never have done this!"

Dertu was smiling as he guided the boat towards the open sea. The waves seemed large enough to swamp the boat but they did not. The sea spray thickened on the glass.

"Dertu, are you mad?"

"Father, it was the perfect thing to do," said Dertu. "I didn't tell them we were at sea. I didn't tell them where we were going. They will trace the call to the landline on this island but only hours from now when it is no longer daylight here, and when we are far away."

The heavy cruiser picked up speed pushing against the huge waves. Sky and sea were steel gray.

"They'll come after us!" said Derek. "There are blood drinkers awake now somewhere in the world. Dertu, these creatures can fly."

"Well, they can't fly here now, can they?" said Dertu. "It will be daylight for eight more hours. And all those blood drinkers now know that the despised Rhoshamandes has kept secrets from the Prince and the Court. The Court will know in a matter of hours what Rhoshamandes has done."

This was true.

"But where are we going?" asked Derek. "Where can we hide?"

"Not a worry," said the boy. "We'll be with Kapetria sooner than you think. Go down, get something to eat for yourself. Light the fireplace in the salon. You're starved and unable to think."

In a daze Derek stumbled down the steps and moved through the salon to the galley. Out of the refrigerator he took a bottle of orange juice and, cringing at the cold against his gloved hand, he drank half of it. Heaven. Nectar of the gods. So delicious. There were other bottles of vitamin water, vegetable juice, and milk and more orange juice, and there were all those paper plates of food covered in plastic, the chicken, roast beef, ham.

He stood there shivering. Then he forced himself back up the steps into the cockpit and gave the bottle of orange juice to Dertu.

"If Kapetria is listening to that broadcast," said Dertu, "and they think that she is, we will connect with her this very night, in Derry in Northern Ireland. That is my plan."

"But how can that be?" asked Derek.

Dertu swallowed the remaining orange juice down. "I confess, Father," said the boy, "I consumed a good deal of food earlier, in the castle's kitchens. I was ravenous. I devoured food like a wild animal. You are the one who must eat now. I should have brought food to you. I am not a good son."

"Oh, nonsense," Derek whispered. "You were a newborn being. You must have been famished. I'm a dreadful father. And how can we connect with Kapetria tonight?"

"I left a further message on the phone line, Father. And pray that no one removes it or shuts off the line. I do not think that they will."

"Another message saying what?"

Dertu was obviously excited by what he'd done. He piloted the boat without looking at his father, but he couldn't keep from smiling.

"Speaking in the ancient tongue of Atalantaya," he said, "I told Kapetria to alphabetize the language according to English transliteration and litter the internet, if she had to, with websites or postings as to how we might find her. I told her to offer email addresses for us in the ancient tongue. And in the ancient tongue, I told her of our true destination. I told her the name of the land and the city. Oh, if only I'd used my time at the computer better. If only I'd thought of all this sooner. I could have given her the very name of a hotel. No matter. They'll never crack the ancient language, the blood drinkers, no matter how supernaturally clever they are. It is too foreign and they have no key."

Derek was astonished. "I would never have thought to do all this."

"Well, I didn't think fast enough to plan it out well myself," said Dertu.

"And what if Benji Mahmoud kills the broadcast, deletes the message, prevents it from being archived?"

"Father, the message must stay up only long enough for Kapetria and Garekyn to hear it, don't you see? And when we reach land, I'll search for Kapetria's messages. I have phones already with which to do that immediately."

"They want to kill us, the vampires," said Derek.

"Somewhere in the world Kapetria is listening to that message in the ancient tongue," said Dertu. "She will come to Derry to find us, if she possibly can. I remember her as vividly as you ever do, Father. Kapetria is wise. It was Kapetria who conceived of the new purpose. She will come. And the blood drinkers can't gather their resources fast enough to prevent it, because they don't have the information I gave Kapetria in the ancient tongue."

Derek was speechless. He stood there holding on to the empty orange juice bottle and then he licked the neck of it with his tongue. A wunderkind, this boy, he thought. No one could ever have kept him for ten years in a Budapest basement.

"Go on down," said Dertu. "Light the fire. Eat and sleep."

"And if you give one of your arms for an off-spring, Dertu," Derek asked, "will that offspring be more clever than you are, as you are so much more clever than me?"

"I don't know, Father. But I bet we will soon be able to find out. In the meantime, please stop being afraid. Please trust in me."

Derek went down into the salon. He was stunned. He stood stranded for a long moment, and then remembered what he meant to do. The sea had quieted somewhat, and the boat was obviously traveling very fast.

The fireplace was electric with porcelain logs and it was simple to turn on, and it provided prettier more natural-looking flames than he had ever thought possible. He sat still, on the striped couch, looking at the flames as the cabin slowly filled with warmth, blessed warmth.

It seemed he had never felt anything as wondrous as this warmth. He had never walked the warm jungles of the savage lands long aeons ago with Welf, and Kapetria and Garekyn, as Kapetria spoke of the danger of capture, and that they must all remember they had been made to survive.

And then die in Atalantaya, Derek had thought, when it goes up in flames and smoke. But he had not said it aloud. He knew that he was not to complain. He was born for one thing and one thing only. And he had not yet seen the glories of Atalantaya. None of them had. They had known only the chambers of the Parents with the motion-picture walls and their great garden enclosures.

Now on the gently rolling little ship, he lay down on the striped couch and covered himself with one of the blankets. It was soft as his overcoat. A lovely warmth filled the room, lovely as the light from the fireplace. In a half sleep he was walking through the jungles again, with those he loved. Maybe we will not have to rush there, he thought, and that was before the natives had found them and been so kind to them, and they had sat down to their first feast. He remembered the drums and the dancing, and the eerie music of the wooden flutes, and the headman saying to Kapetria, "Our Lord, Amel, will welcome you to Atalantaya. You are the very kind he welcomes. We'll send word to the port in the morning. He will welcome you with open arms."

He closed his eyes. He was dozing. He saw Amel, Amel of the pale skin and red hair, Amel with his godlike green eyes. Amel said, "They are liars and they are evil. They are the origin of all evil!" Kapetria was trying to reason with him. "Even if what you say is true . . ."

He opened his eyes with a start. Rain thundered down on the boat all around him. The panes of the windows ran with water. The cabin was wondrously warm and filled with the sweet flickering light of the fire. He was not in that horrid room in Budapest, and he would never be there again. He was free.

Music came from the cockpit. Dertu had found some way to play music. A magnificent tenor voice was singing in Italian. **Amor ti vieta di non amar.** It was so beautiful, this music, so poignant. Derek's heart broke, and as always his eyes filled with tears.

The boat rocked him like a child in a cradle. Or so he imagined, because he had never been a child. Just like a child in a cradle, riding the whale path! Derek drifted. Was Kapetria on her way this very minute to meet them in Derry?

# 13

# Lestat

THE ENTIRE WORLD of the Undead was in the Château or so it seemed, all the public rooms filled with blood drinkers talking in whispers to one another and turning to bow to me or salute me in some subtle way as Louis and I appeared. Every beeswax candle in the old castle was lighted; every electric sconce or chandelier was aglow. I could hear the orchestra playing in the ballroom.

Rose and Viktor had returned and came at once to greet me as I entered the main hall. I was relieved to see they were here. Avicus also came to embrace me, and so did Zenobia, his eternal companion. They were sorry for the blunder of the young ones in California.

"They've convened a Council of the Elders only," said Thorne, pressing me to move through the crowd. "They don't want the younger ones at the table. And they are waiting for you."

"Yes," I said. "I know."

But in every doorway stood some curious friend

or stranger glancing to me expectantly as I made the march through one vast salon after another to the north tower and its great curving stairs. Ah, the splendor of it in this decidedly feudal moment when all the lesser lords of the world had come to seek shelter under the roof of the great lord who would defend them all against the invaders as long as these great walls would hold.

I was painfully thirsting. Innocent blood. I kept thinking about it, and I blamed Amel for it, but Amel might not have been behind it after all. But there was no putting off the meeting.

Amel had started murmuring to me in a strange language as soon as I opened my eyes. At first I'd tried to penetrate it and translate it, but that proved impossible. But the sound of it was like the sound of Sanskrit which I had not heard spoken very much in my life at all. Well, it wasn't Sanskrit, I knew that because I can understand Sanskrit.

Whatever the language, it became clear that Amel was repeating the same bits and pieces of material over and over again. A song? A poem? A speech?

Within no time, the telepathic intelligence of the world around me came piercing through to let me know that messages left on Benji's radio broadcast provided the songs that Amel was singing, messages from the non-humans, and no one had achieved a translation. For the moment the radio phone line was still open, because no one had made the decision to shut it down. The non-humans were using our greatest mode of communication to communicate amongst themselves.

I hurried up the staircase to the Council Chamber, ignoring Louis's protests that he should hang back. "Nonsense," I whispered. "I need you at my side."

I brought Louis into the Council Chamber with me, but I could see that it was indeed a gathering of the elders and Louis was surely the youngest in the room. Cyril and Thorne took their usual places against the wall.

I sat down at the head of the table and gestured for Louis to take the empty chair to my right.

Opposite, on my left, sat my mother, Gabrielle, and her beloved Sevraine, both in casual modern male attire, handsome dark wool suits with linen shirts open at the collar, Sevraine's long hair the usual veil over her shoulders and my mother's hair in her usual single long braid.

Marius was at the far end of the oval table, directly opposite me, which was his usual place, and maybe the only fixed place at the table other than mine. And this was the Roman Marius, responsible for the present Pax Romana of the blood drinkers, Marius who more often than not resolved all issues of authority on which I refused to take a stand. He wore his long-sleeved red velvet tunic as he almost always did at the Château, and he had not bothered to trim his hair as he so often did. It hung long and free, curling just above his shoulders. And he had a writing pad before him and a golden fountain pen.

"You should have destroyed that Rhoshamandes," he said immediately, to which Gregory and Seth both nodded. Gregory sat to his right, and Seth was to the right of Gregory.

"What is this, the Marius Party, assembled against me?" I demanded. "I've told you more than once. I'll never give an order for the destruction of Rhoshamandes."

Marius sighed. "There has to be an authority here," he said, in a reasonable tone, "and that has never been more obvious than now."

I studied the faces at the table.

Teskhamen sat to Marius's left and he nodded to this last remark, and so did Gremt, who was at Teskhamen's left hand. The Marius Party indeed, I thought. No ghosts were present, which meant that these two alone represented the Talamasca. And it also meant that they had in some way finally and officially come over to us, with Marius's approval, otherwise they wouldn't be here at this time of crisis.

David, my beloved David Talbot, was to the left of Gremt, and he sat with his head bowed and his arms folded over his chest. He looked spent, if nothing else, his khaki jacket and blue cotton shirt badly rumpled, as though he'd only just wandered into the Château.

Armand sat close by Louis on my right, and was

his usual self in a dark burgundy velvet coat with layers of lace at the collar, very much the stylish master of Trinity Gate, his pale boyish face as unreadable as ever.

Next to Armand was Allesandra, Allesandra my old queen from the Satanic coven under Les Innocents, who had not been at Court since the beginning of the New Year. She had continued to grow in beauty and presence since her resurrection, and her ash-blond hair was tied back with a bone clip on the top of her head, spilling loosely down her back and over her shoulders. She wore a simple velvet gown of dark blue, without ornamentation.

I sensed an immense sadness in Allesandra.

Next to her—between her and David Talbot— was a stunningly beautiful black vampire whom I'd never seen before, though I knew who he was and he silently gave me his name, Arion, as our eyes met. He was so black that his skin was almost bluish, and his eyes appeared yellow, though I think they must have been more truly pale green. His jacket and shirt were almost rags. He wore an incongruous watch on his left wrist, one of those devices that tells the time all over the world. And his curly black hair was clipped short.

I felt a sudden pain in my heart at the sight of him. It was with this powerful vampire, somewhere on the coast of Italy, that two young ones, two young ones very dear to me, might have been lodging when the tragic conflagrations of last year had begun. No one had seen or heard of those two vampires since the Burnings. And I had a desperate feeling that this Arion knew their fate. I also had the sense he was withholding this information from me now because it was not the time to reveal it, and his quick furtive glance to Marius let me know he thought other things might take precedence here.

Pandora was directly opposite Arion, in her usual embroidered gown, her long tightly waving brown hair shining clean, and at her left was Arjun, Arjun of India, her fledgling and companion, dressed as usual for him in a fine black sherwani.

To the left of Arjun sat Fareed, who was always at the right of his maker, Seth. Both wore the simple white cotton coats of doctors, with nondescript shirts and ties.

No Benji, though I knew he was in the building, and had expected him here due to the importance of the radio broadcast.

And no Chrysanthe, Gregory's wife. In other words only those who were assuming power and wanted power.

Marius began at once.

"This is what has happened," he said. "During the daylight hours, the non-humans used the radio broadcast to communicate with us and with one another. We have to decide immediately whether or not to shut the radio broadcast down."

"I say leave it up," said Teskhamen, which surprised me, and I think it surprised Marius a little to be interrupted. Teskhamen was fashionably dressed in a fine suit and linen much like Gregory. "Let them communicate and let them come together," Teskhamen said. "Especially now that we know Rhoshamandes is hunting them down. We hear that Rhoshamandes is in a rage, and plotting against us with a vampire from Hungary named Roland. Both have powerful resources. And you—we—need to make contact with those creatures, and we need to find out what they know of Amel."

"Yes, that is the name of the emergency," said Marius. "The name of the emergency is Amel."

"Well, Amel's inside me now," I said. "But he's gone silent."

"Let me summarize what we know," said Marius. "This morning at about nine a.m. a non-human without a name called the radio broadcast and explained that he and someone named Derek were escaping Rhoshamandes's castle on the island of Saint Rayne. The creature explained that Derek had been held captive by a blood drinker named Roland of Budapest who'd had the being imprisoned in that city for ten years." Marius's voice gave a subtle indication of his anger over this. "Rhoshamandes only lately came in possession of this Derek and subjected him, according to the caller, to great cruelty. Immediately after this, the unidentified caller gave a long message in an unknown tongue."

I nodded. "I've heard it, sounds most like Sanskrit to me," I said, "but perhaps Arjun knows this language."

"I don't know it," said Arjun a little apologetically. "I can't crack it. It does sound like Sanskrit but it is not related to Sanskrit."

Marius continued: "Now what the being said about Rhoshamandes holding this creature Derek and treating him cruelly is true," he said. "Allesandra joined us just before sunrise this morning and is here to verify that she saw firsthand Rhoshamandes's treatment of Derek. Rhoshamandes hacked off Derek's left arm and actually tried to burn the severed arm in the fireplace. This Derek creature healed at once from the injury. And he is most certainly a creature exactly like Garekyn Brovotkin **and** Kapetria and Welf, whose stories you know. Indeed, Allesandra has left Rhoshamandes on account of his treatment of Derek and his refusal to make Derek's presence known to us or to bring Derek here to the Court. Arion has also left Rhoshamandes on account of this. Now Rhoshamandes knows full well of Garekyn's attack on Killer and Eleni. And yet he withheld knowledge of this Derek from us."

"Was it a human being who made this call?"

"It was not a human," said Marius. "We can only assume it's another of the non-human group, presumably one who managed to rescue Derek, though how he'd known where to find Derek—that we can't know at this point." He motioned for patience.

"About two hours after that call went on the air," he said, "Garekyn himself called on a throwaway cell phone from somewhere in England and he too left a message, obviously, for the others who share this strange language. But before he signed off he also left a detailed message for us, that he meant us no harm, and had never meant us harm, but wanted only to make contact with us for reasons having to do with the identity and history of Amel. He said it was not his intention to kill anyone, indeed that he had only been defending himself when Killer was taken down, and that wounding Eleni he did only in order to escape Trinity Gate."

"Does that sound reasonable?" I turned to Armand.

He seemed unprepared for this, and glanced at Marius as if for permission to speak. Marius nodded.

"Yes," said Armand. "I do believe Killer took the wrong tack with this powerful creature. But there's more." He gestured to Marius.

"This Garekyn sounded entirely reasonable, and even persuasive," said Marius. "Less than an hour after that, another call came on the line. This time it was Dr. Karen Rhinehart who identified herself as Kapetria and she too left a long message in the strange language, before telling us that she and her kindred, as she called them, meant no harm to us whatsoever, and were deeply distressed to discover that we had now chosen to make enemies of her and Welf and Derek and Garekyn, who would never have sought to harm us."

"Eventually, I want to hear these messages, but for now go on."

"About an hour after sunset," said Marius. "While you were still kept safe away from the sun's rays, there was yet another call and this time it was from Derek himself. Of course he issued a long and obviously emotional message in the ancient tongue, before telling us in no uncertain terms of the wickedness of Roland and Rhoshamandes, and that he feared they would try to destroy him before he could ever reach his kin. Now if you want to hear the messages, I'll play them for you, but frankly, I don't think we have the time. We have to decide now whether to keep the broadcast phone lines open and what answer, if any, we are to make to these creatures about our interest in them."

"I say leave it open," said Teskhamen again. "It is imperative we make contact through the line ourselves with these creatures."

"Yes, absolutely," said Gregory, "especially if Rhoshamandes is hunting for them and plans to use them as hostages."

"Well, Amel knows of the obscure messages," I said, "because he began repeating them or I should say chanting phrases or sentences from them to me as soon as I opened my eyes. But I can't tell whether he understands the language or what it means to him."

Gremt gestured to speak. "If Amel doesn't understand the language now," he said, "he will soon." His face was sad, and he seemed to have none of the energy of the others around him. "Amel is a learning creature. All along he has been a learning creature."

Still Amel was not responding, and I gave them to know this without speaking a word.

"We must decide how to bring the creatures here," said Marius.

Allesandra had said nothing all this time, but she had begun to weep during the description of Rhoshamandes's cruelty. Armand had slipped his arm around her and was holding her as she rocked back and forth, apparently in deep grief. "If you had seen that poor creature, Derek," said Allesandra, "if you had seen what he suffered. It is possible that Fareed can help him. Restore the arm if the poor being did remove it from the fireplace."

"Perhaps I can," said Fareed. "You might use this as an inducement to Derek to come here for shelter immediately."

"He'd never make it if Rhoshamandes is about," I said. "Rhosh would see him approach and move to take him prisoner again."

"So they need to come here by day," said David, "to remain in the village until close to nightfall and then to be brought up to the castle before sunset."

"Yes, exactly," said Marius. "This is what must happen."

Now, the village beneath the Château was not a real village at all, but a community of the humans who had restored the Château and were still in the process of refining it, and improving it, and the technicians who worked on its electricity and computer connections, and the gardeners who tended the vast grounds which were now twice the size of what they'd been in my father's time. The restored church was for these people. So was the town hall. The inn was for their occasional visitors or new workers who did not have housing as yet. The shops were for their necessities, including DVDs, CDs, and books as well as groceries and the like. They had a chocolate shop. They had clothing stores as well. It was a pretty place, meticulously created in period architecture. But all of these people were paid handsomely to ask no questions about us whatsoever and would indeed greet these beings and put them up in the restored inn until nightfall.

"And what if they're hostile to us?" I said. "You want us to bring them into the house, so to speak?"

"We have to do that," said Teskhamen.

"Look, what threat do they pose?" asked David. "This poor Derek was a prisoner for ten years under the abode of a solitary vampire. So there are five of them now, assuming we can bring them together. What could they possibly do? Clearly they want to know us."

"And why is this so urgent?" I asked. "Because they know about us? The whole world knows about us. So they know we're real and the whole world thinks we're not real. You think they can persuade the whole world to take another view of us without revealing themselves? And why should these creatures reveal themselves to the world? And why ever would they put themselves in our hands if they are indeed a species whose blood is naturally replenished within a few hours? Why, we could keep them here forever as prisoners."

Armand whispered under his breath that that might not be a bad idea at all.

"That's just what Roland did to Derek," said Allesandra. "And Arion here has drunk from the creature's blood many times, and indeed the blood does come back over and over and over again. And Roland kept him as just such a fount of blood." She was plainly outraged at it. "You cannot do such a thing, Prince. You wouldn't."

Marius shook his head in disgust and folded his arms. He muttered to himself under his breath. I realized something which perhaps I should have seen before. The Court had given Marius immense new life and purpose. It had taken him out of the limbo in which he'd been existing since Those Who Must Be Kept were destroyed. He had been gaining in vitality for six months, and I wondered now why he put up with me at all. Wouldn't he have made the better monarch? I found myself strangely indifferent on the matter of a power struggle.

I turned to Arion:

"And what did you see in the blood of the creature?" I asked.

"Bits and pieces, nothing of great value, but it

was Rhoshamandes who saw a strange vision of the great city before it fell into the sea. He explained it to me and to Roland. He saw the city teeming with people, filled with flowers and fruit trees, and giant translucent buildings beyond count. He said there was a 'great one' in the city and the Great One was . . . Amel."

"We have to invite them now, before Rhoshamandes finds them!" said Marius impatiently. "We can't let them fall into his hands."

"Well, how in the Hell can Rhoshamandes find them?" my mother asked. She spoke up in her usual cranky voice. "But I have to say, if you'd executed Rhoshamandes last year you would have saved everyone a lot of trouble."

"I agree with that," said Seth in a low voice. He turned to me for the first time. "He should die for what he did and what he has done now."

"Rhoshamandes has his own human lawyers," said Allesandra. The tears stood in her eyes, but she went on, in a carefully controlled voice. "He has teams of them who work for him, and he has sent them to search for Garekyn Brovotkin, using the same sort of intelligence your lawyers and solicitors use." She turned to me. "Rhoshamandes despises you, Prince," she said. "And his hatred and bitterness have grown. If he knows you want these beings, he will most assuredly try to capture them before they can come here."

"We're wasting time," said Marius. "Please send for Benji and go on the broadcast and talk to the non-humans."

"I understand all that," I said. "But I'm trying to think this thing through. I don't see that we have to be hasty. These creatures are a total unknown. Are you assuming that Amel was somehow once one of them?"

"Amel has brought them out," said Teskhamen. "Amel, the mention of Amel in Benji's broadcasts. Amel. They are seeking Amel. And the doctor and her companion, it was no coincidence that that Dr. Rhinehart was working in Gregory's company, spying on Gregory, studying Gregory. They'd been around for years, these beings, perhaps since the time you first wrote of Amel in your books, Lestat."

I nodded. "There's something here I'm not understanding. So they want to know about Amel. But we don't know for sure that our Amel is their Amel. We don't . . ." But I stopped. What was I thinking? "Our Amel doesn't have true coherent memories of this city. He gives no indication he knows who these individuals are, only that he might have seen them once."

"Lestat," said Fareed. "Look at the history of Amel. What do we know about Amel? Think of the centuries when the blood drinkers of the world thought he was a mindless spirit, when even the great Maharet and Mekare thought he was a mindless spirit. And look what happened when this mindless spirit gained a consciousness of its own, and a point of view."

"Yes, of course."

"But don't you see," said Teskhamen, "even when Amel gained a purpose and started to incite the Burnings, and even when he incited Rhoshamandes to kill Maharet, you still assumed he was a spirit who had never lived on the earth before in any bodily form, a spirit evolving towards some sort of purposeful activity."

"Do you really not understand what's involved here?" asked Gremt. "Lestat, Amel has lived before. He is not a spirit evolving, he is a spirit with an identity, a personality, nourished in flesh and blood that can be restored to him."

"Amel was the leader in that city," said Arion. "Rhoshamandes saw evidence of this, and that he controlled a technology which is beyond our present dreams."

"I see," I said. And I was beginning to see. "If Amel could do what he did when he did not know who he was, think what he might do if he remembered his entire history."

"That's it, exactly," said Fareed. "And Amel is in you and in all of us and we are inextricably dependent upon him."

"Gremt, what do you know of this ancient city?" I asked.

Gremt was quiet for a long moment, and then he spoke. "I have no knowledge of it," he answered.

"But as I told you, there was a time in the airy Heavens in which I lived when Amel was not there. Then there was the coming of Amel and wars in Heaven, so to speak, with his tempestuous challenges to other spirits and his wild courtship of the red-haired human witches Mekare and Maharet."

"Red hair," said Armand, "and red hair is what I saw in the blood of Garekyn Brovotkin. A red-haired male, a male with pale skin, and red hair and green eyes."

"Was it that simple," I mused, "that he warmed to the witches for their red hair? And not their power?"

"It was both!" said Teskhamen. "The Talamasca has studied for centuries the link between red hair and psychic power. We have files and files on witches with red hair from our earliest days."

The room went silent. It seemed they were all watching me, but I couldn't help but believe they were searching for some outward sign of **him**, and there never was any outward sign. There was only the pressure on the back of my neck, the pressure that I could feel and something else like a chill passing through me.

"Lestat, listen to me," said Marius. "There is no stopping Amel from finding out anything he wants to know from these creatures. Let it be through us and not through Rhoshamandes."

A terrible foreboding gripped me. It had nothing to do with executing Rhosh. It was all-powerful, this foreboding. " '**Out, out, brief candle,**' " I whispered.

I heard my mother laugh. But no one else laughed.

"So," she said, laughing still, "these otherworldly scientists have come for Amel, have they? And was it a body they were making in their laboratories at Collingsworth Pharmaceuticals? A body for Amel? Tell him, Fareed, about the crates. Was there a body in one of those crates, prepared for Amel, should he want to escape the vampires once and for all?"

No one answered.

I bowed my head. I stared at the glossy surface of the mahogany table. "Amel, why don't you speak?" I asked aloud. "You're listening. You are hearing everything. Why don't you speak? Are these your friends from a former time and do you know their language?"

I heard his answer loud and clear and I was certain the others heard it too. If Louis and my mother could not hear it from me, they heard it from all the others who had heard it in my mind.

**I would never do harm to you. You love me. You loved me when no one else did.**

"That's true," I said. "I gave you my body willingly. But who are these people? Are they your people?"

**I don't know. I don't know who they are. And I don't know what I am, but they know what I am, don't they? Let them come.**

Silence once more.

"Well, then," I said. "Go on the radio and give them a number by which they can reach us now."

Armand rose at once and went off, presumably to find Benji in his studio.

"There is one thing more that must be done immediately," said Marius.

"And what's that?" I asked.

Allesandra began to weep again. But Marius ignored her.

"Rhoshamandes cannot be allowed to live," said Marius. "We all know this and we knew it last year after he slew Maharet. You must proscribe him now! And let those who wish destroy him."

"Become a virtual Sulla is what you mean! Proscribe! Is that what I'm to be in the time I have left, a dictator who proscribes! I won't. The voice of Amel misled Rhoshamandes! The voice of Amel drove him to kill Maharet. And I will not go back on my word to him. Listen, we can get these creatures to come to us. It's simple. I don't care how many human elves or apprentices Rhosh has in this world, he doesn't control the radio phone line."

"Gregory, Seth, Teskhamen, and I can do it," Marius said. "We can overpower him and destroy him."

"No," I said. I sat back. I shook my head. "No! It's wrong. Rhoshamandes is thousands of years old. He's seen things, he knows things. . . . You don't do it with my blessing, and if you do it, you don't want a prince in me, you want a figurehead. And frankly, I think that's what you've always wanted. And you would be the ruler here, Marius, not me. You do this and you become the Prince. You begin your reign when he dies."

Spasm in my neck. Spasm in my temples. My right hand cramped suddenly. Amel was trying to make it jump. I looked down as if I were in my thoughts but I wasn't. I was trying to defeat his move to control my hand. And when I looked up again, I saw the eyes of all at the table were fixed on me. But only Gregory, Fareed, Seth, and Marius seemed aware of what was going on. Seth was staring at my hand. Add Gremt to that. Gremt was staring at my hand as well.

"Rhoshamandes's people have already searched Garekyn Brovotkin's house in London," said Teskhamen. "They frightened off his staff. They are no doubt tracking any and all banking connections they can find for this woman Kapetria."

Enough. I looked at Arion.

"I'm going to go on the air and invite them here," I said. I rose. "But before I do, I must talk to Arion here. It's about a personal matter. And then I need to go down to the village and make sure everything is done to protect the village and the Château, that the sprinkling systems are functioning in case Rhoshamandes does attack."

"That's all done, taken care of," said Marius. He too was on his feet. "But think what he could do if he sought to burn us out."

Thorne spoke up for the first time. "If Rhoshamandes attacks, we have to be able to attack back," he said. I knew how thoroughly he hated Rhoshamandes for killing Maharet.

There was a murmur of assent from those at the table.

"Of course," I said. "If he attacks, if he attempts to burn the Château, or the village, yes, of course, but he likely knows full well this will bring down the wrath of everyone on him. Yes, if he dares do any of this, burn him. Burn him with everything you've got. But he won't be so stupid."

"He can attack and withdraw very fast," said Gregory. "All of us, we must be on alert from the time you go on the air until morning." They were rising to their feet, pushing back their chairs. "We must make a plan for guarding the grounds."

A long miserable sigh came from Sevraine. She'd risen to her feet. "I'll stand guard with you," she said.

This was what they wanted, obviously, and they were right and there was no stopping them anyway. I hoped and prayed Rhoshamandes would stay away, but then if he were foolish enough to attack, well, he would get what he deserved.

I looked to Arion again. He was already moving towards me. And we went out of the Council Chamber together.

# 14

# Rhoshamandes

HE HAD NEVER been in such a rage, not
ever in his entire existence. Not even the
night Benedict had left him did he know
a rage such as this. His beloved **Benedicta** had just
been found drifting off the coast of Northern Ireland with one life raft missing, and his poor feeble
mortal caretakers had been in tears for having been
duped by the supposed "guests" right after daybreak.
Who had rescued that miserable Derek? How had
the rescuer found him!

And what was the meaning of the strange description of the pair on the part of the old people,
that they looked like twins except for the hair of one
being filled with rampant streaks of gold? Otherwise
they'd been identical!

"It's inconceivable, what you're thinking," said
Roland.

They stood together in the huge drawing room of
the Tudor-style house on Redington Road in Lon-

don that belonged to the non-human Garekyn Brovotkin. It was silent and empty around them, just as
it had been when they arrived.

"What do you mean 'inconceivable'?" said Rhoshamandes. He was growing weary of Roland,
dim-witted Roland who'd kept the secret of the otherworldly Derek for a decade. "If I can conceive of
it, it is conceivable, my friend. The arm grew into a
duplicate being!"

"But if the creature could multiply in that way,
surely he would have done it a long time ago."

"Not if he hadn't known how to do it," said
Rhoshamandes. "Did you think he was a genius of
his kind? He was a child, a pawn, a foot soldier at his
best. He would have cracked easily if I hadn't had so
much interference."

"You have to tell the Court," said Roland. "You
have to tell them to turn off the radio broadcast. You
have to go to them now."

"The Hell I do," said Rhoshamandes. He was
humiliated, angry. The words of his frightened old
caretaker echoed in his ears. "We thought they were
guests. We provided them with food, wine. . . ."

When he thought of the sight of Benedict's old
room, in chaos with clothing and money and documents strewn all over the floor, he knew a rage he
couldn't contain any longer.

"The creature is not coming back to this house,"
said Roland. "Whatever these things are, they're too
smart to do that."

When Rhosh didn't answer him, Roland pressed again:

"Tell the Court you want to come in," he said. "I'll go with you. They won't dare to harm you at a time like this. They'll need you, want your cooperation and assistance."

For a brief second, only a second, it seemed possible—a future in which Rhosh would be welcomed, in which Benedict would be there, pleading perhaps for his acceptance, and then he would confer with the Prince, and he would see Sevraine again, Sevraine who had refused to receive him in her own compound, and he would be with Gregory, Gregory who'd been brought into this realm of darkness six thousand years ago. But it vanished, this brief flash of possibility, as if it were the flare from the guttering of a dying candle.

Before he'd even decided, the heat had gone out of him, blasting the heavy draperies that flanked the windows of this room, causing them to explode in flame.

Roland was startled, Roland who would do well to stop talking altogether, Roland turning around and around as all the draperies of this great room went up in flames, as the dark oak paneling began to blister and smoke.

Oh, it was a most convenient power, and in some ways the most delicious of powers, though in truth, Rhosh had discovered it only very late in his long journey through time, and seldom if ever used it as he was using it now, reserving it for the most mundane things—the lighting of fires on hearths, the lighting of tapers in chandeliers. But it felt wondrous all right, the invisible muscle tightening and releasing behind his forehead and the sudden spectacle of smoke roaring towards the ceiling from the synthetic fabrics all round him.

With an intake of breath, he blew out the double doors, and walked over the broken glass into the stillness of the night, ignoring the electronic wail of a fire alarm. Roland was right beside him like a faithful dog, and how he detested him suddenly. But remember, this is your only ally in all the world! All the world! Allesandra has deserted you. And Arion, that duplicitous and worthless soul, had gone with her as well, straight to the Prince.

The telepathic voices of the vampiric world were laughing at him, laughing at Rhoshamandes as his fledglings deserted him. Only Roland remained, Roland who had welcomed Rhosh into the house, Roland who had given him the gift of Derek, the non-human with the thick, delicious blood.

Rhosh turned and sent the fire blast against the upstairs windows, one after another from left to right, blowing the shattered glass in all directions, incinerating the rooms that lay within. And now the air was filled with the sound of sirens. The lowering clouds were the color of blood.

Oh, if only Rhosh had known of this power centuries ago. He would have destroyed that Satanic coven under Les Innocents, destroyed Armand, and taken back the fledglings the Children of Satan had stolen from him. But he hadn't known. No, it was the great Lestat in his books who had become the first real schoolteacher of the Undead, and Marius their professor. How he loathed them all.

He turned his back on the house, seeing his own long shadow thrown out across the wet grass in front of him, and the shadow of Roland like a hovering angel beside him.

"Let's go back to Northern Ireland," said Roland. "Let's keep searching, searching minds until someone throws up the image of the pair of them."

"They're gone from there by now," Rhoshamandes said. "It's been too long since that sniveling little boy-thing called the radio station and told them where he was."

"But they have no identification, and they can't travel in this world without it."

Oh, ye of little faith and little knowledge!

They moved fast through the dark and with all the speed at their command until they found a quiet street far away from the inferno of Garekyn's house, and the fire engines gathering around it.

Roland was talking again. Roland almost never stopped talking. Roland was saying something about the broadcast, and Rhosh was thinking how good it had felt to burn that house, how good it had felt to melt to cinders anything that belonged to the comrade of that despicable weak little Derek, who had so reminded him of Benedict at times, an eternal boy, an immortal boy, a miserable combination of a man's rage and a child's helplessness.

Yes, put that little earbud in your ear and listen to the program. What do I care about the program? What do I care about anything?

It seemed a great void had opened beneath him the night Benedict had left; it seemed he had seen to the depths of that void, and he'd confronted the most awful truth of his existence, that without Benedict, nothing really meant anything to him, that it had been Benedict, poor sweet Benedict, who kept him alive, not human blood and the power of Amel forever changing his cells from human to immortal—just Benedict, Benedict's need and Benedict's love, and all the other passions of Rhoshamandes had gone up in flames, just as surely as if Benedict had used the Fire Gift as he left Rhoshamandes's life forever.

He thought of the Prince. He saw his smiling face; he saw his brilliant, flashing eyes; he heard the timbre of his voice. Had Rhoshamandes ever had such passion for living as the Prince had, the Prince who had already died and risen again in his short pampered vampiric life, the Prince who fed off the love around him as surely as he fed off blood, the Prince who declared love for that demon thing Amel that had brought Rhoshamandes to this ruin!—the Prince who was untouchable as long as Amel remained inside of him.

He could have turned the Fire Gift on the whole world! He could have burned these houses all around him, these trees. He could have blasted the very clouds above and brought down a storm of rain on fires that nothing could quench. He could have burned the city of London! The growing sense of his power vaguely thrilled him, warming his hard cold heart as if it might truly feel again.

Roland came striding towards him.

"The Prince is broadcasting now," said Roland. "The Prince is inviting them to call in. The Prince says he will invite them all to come to the Château. The Prince will arrange everything."

Roland held out the little cell phone for him to listen. How Rhosh was tempted to grind the little phone into sand, sand twinkling with tiny particles of glass. Or to turn the Fire Gift, so new, so deliciously powerful, on this one, Roland, to see just how long it took for one so old and so powerful to burn.

Something in Roland changed. His eyes fixed on those of Rhosh as if Rhosh's thoughts had leapt out of his mind and pinched at Roland's heart though Rhosh had never intended such a thing.

Rhosh smiled. He reached out and laid his hand on Roland's shoulder.

"'Get thee behind me, Satan,'" said Rhosh. "Follow or go away." And turning, Rhosh went up fast towards the broken clouds and the faint stars above them.

# 15

# Lestat

THE LITTLE CHURCH was dark and empty. Only ten years ago, my beloved architect had rebuilt it from the ground up, according to what historical records he could find, and my own remembrances. And it looked very like the old church of my times, when it had seemed vast to me as a child, and the Masses said on the distant altar had held the only connection with the Divine ever offered me.

I sat in the first pew, gazing at that altar, at the polished silver tabernacle and the crucifix above it, and beyond the great oval portrait of Saint Louis of France, in all his royal splendor riding off to fight the Crusades on his white charger.

My beloved architect and chief of staff had just left me, after assuring me that all firefighting systems in the village and in the castle on the hill were as they should be. And yes, the inn was prepared for the guests who would arrive sometime after sunrise, and yes, they'd be brought up to the castle right before nightfall.

Only Arion remained with me.

I stared at the altar and Arion looked at me, Arion who had his own sorrow to impart, his own story of those under the spell of the Voice who'd burnt his villa to the ground, and left his orchards and gardens in a blackened ruin.

"I saw her die," he had said. He had told the whole tale to me and now the chapel no longer echoed with the sound of his soft voice.

"I am certain it was Mona. I saw her red hair. I saw her die but it seemed she went in an instant, that she didn't suffer. And as for Quinn, I don't know if he was there, but if he was not there, then where is Quinn and why did he never come back? For three nights I waited in those miserable ruins, burnt and in agony, waiting for him. I never heard from him again. If he were alive, surely, he would have come back, or he would have gone to you. Or he would have gone to the Talamasca."

"She's dead," I said quietly. " 'Would she had died hereafter . . . when there might have been time to mourn for her.' " My voice was no fair reflection of what I really felt, this pain for which there is no remedy, not even the passage of time. This ache that will never go away. This grief for all the mistakes I'd made and all those I'd lost.

"I knew they were dead last year," I said in a small

voice, "when we gathered at Trinity Gate and they hadn't come, because they would have come, had they been living. I knew. I thought it was in Maharet's compound that they died, when Khayman was first driven by the Voice to burn the archive in which they'd been studying. I had letters from them. They had loved studying with Maharet. They wondered that I wasn't there, studying with them, talking to Maharet. . . ."

What was I saying? What did it matter? Maharet and Mona and Quinn gone.

"I am so sorry," said Arion.

He spoke so low no mortal spying on us could have heard him. He talked of his grief, his pain, of those he'd loved, loved for so long, now gone, of his paradisal palace being destroyed, and of all the things within those walls he'd collected over the years, destroyed, and how he'd gone off to Roland, Roland who had been his old friend from times when Pompeii had been a thriving city, and of how Roland had taken pity on him and how, thanks to Roland, the blood of the strange non-human Derek had restored him.

"Very well," I said. "You're here with us now."

"Yes, and I mean to stay," he said. "That is, if you will have me."

"This is your Court and I am your Prince, and of course you may stay," I said.

I closed my eyes. I was remembering Mona's voice, Mona's laugh, Mona the witch who had be-

come Mona the blood drinker, naïve, brash, coura-
geous, and in love with the Dark Gift and with all
the gifts of the world of day and the world of night.

"Come," said Arion. "Let's go back up the hill.
Your friend Louis is outside, and he's waiting for you."

I followed him down the aisle. Before we left I
looked up at the narrow stained-glass windows. The
five joyful mysteries of the Rosary were depicted
down one side of the nave; and the five sorrowful
mysteries of the Rosary depicted down the other
side. Very much more beautiful than in my time.
But strange, wasn't it, that the scent of wax was the
same, and the scent of wood. And the flicker of the
vigil lights before the Virgin's statue exactly the same
as it had been over two centuries ago.

I stopped to light two candles, one for each
of them.

The little phone suddenly vibrated in my pocket
as if it were a tiny rodent come awake to plead for
mercy. And I could hear Benji shouting as he ran
towards the church.

"She is on the line," cried Benji. "It is Kapetria."

# 16

# Derek

## Aix-en-Provence

He wasn't frightened anymore. Not now. Not with Kapetria holding him in her arms. He wasn't frightened. Oh, how beautiful she was, his Kapetria, with her hair swept back into a braid pinned to her head, in her fine saffron silk blouse and sleek black skirt, legs sheathed in translucent black nylon, and feet so dainty in her high-heeled shoes, Kapetria here, the real Kapetria sprung to life in a cloud of French scent, her mouth rouged, and eyes as dark as the night sky above them. No, no longer afraid.

She kissed his tears, kissed his eyelids, made the others stop questioning him. "Quiet now, both of you! And to think, this is your brother, and after all this time, what do you do, but interrogate him?"

And indeed they had, as to how in the world he'd ever been held captive for all those precious years, and why hadn't he done this to escape, and that to escape, and finally she had said,

"Welf and Garekyn, if I had a riding crop, I'd whip both of you."

Dertu sat there on the long low modern couch with the most placid expression on his face, studying the others intently, never saying a word himself, just studying them as if he were learning marvelous things from their gestures, their expressions, their horrid questions.

No more fear. No more tears. Kapetria had her arms around him.

He'd been terrified when he'd called the radio phone line, speaking as fast as he could in the old tongue, giving the number of the throwaway cell to his kindred along with the actual address of the old farmhouse outside Derry in which he and Dertu had found temporary lodgings, and terrified when the smiling gentlemen came to take them to the private airport on the other side of town, and terrified when the little plane had taken off right into the bloodred sunset sky—certain they would crash into the North Sea and never reach France. He'd been terrified when they landed in the early winter dark, and the big black car took them racing over the dimly lighted roads and into the quaint city of Arles and to a small hotel where the keys to a private car had been waiting at the desk for them. He'd been terrified as they walked two miles on narrow, crooked little streets to find the car to which the keys belonged and terrified as Dertu drove this roaring little monster down more dimly lighted roads to the pretty city of Aix and finally up into the hills to a lovely whitewashed house with white shutters where Kapetria and Garekyn and Welf had been waiting for them.

He had seen demons in the sky, monsters ready to swoop down and snatch them all up and carry them back to that hideous dungeon cell, demons coming forth from the dark trees that encircled the house, demons hovering at the top of the stairs in the shadows. Cloud Gift, Fire Gift, Mind Gift, he'd repeated the old lore in whispers to Dertu who had only nodded and held Derek's hand all the way, trying to calm him. Brave Dertu who had pumped the pilot and attendants of the little plane for all manner of knowledge, and chatted away with the chauffeur of the black car about tourism this time of year in the South of France, Dertu who drove the car with amazing ease and dexterity commenting on the speed and the handling!

But he wasn't frightened now.

Not now that she was holding him in her arms and she was saying all will be well, all will surely be well, and there was no reason ever to fear again, and no matter how many questions he asked, repeating the same entreaties and frantic what-ifs over and over again, she held him and comforted him and told him that all would be well. Fire Gift, Mind Gift, Cloud Gift notwithstanding. She, Kapetria, would take care of it and them and him, Derek. No one would ever do to him what Roland and Rhoshamandes had done. And she would, in her own time, see that these monsters were punished.

Suddenly Dertu gave her the phone. "The Prince is on the direct line," he said. "He's off the air. This is private."

She hit the button for them all to hear.

"I want to come to you," she said. "We have enemies as you know who are searching for us."

"I know," answered the Prince in the same French. "I want you to come."

Without a single condition, and in an even, confident voice, he gave her all the relevant information, the location of the Château, the distances from the closest towns, the electric codes for the different sets of gates, assuring her that his staff would welcome her and bring her to the village inn and then escort them all up the mountain to the Château itself. "But you can't attempt to come here until well after the sun rises," he said. "And you must be inside the Château itself before sunset. We are here. And you will be safe. And we will be with you."

"My brother Garekyn cannot be harmed over what happened in New York," Kapetria said.

"No, under no circumstances," said the Prince. "I can assure you of this." Such a pleasant voice, the

French so crisp yet melodic. "We want to know what you know about us and about Amel and why you've been watching us. We want to know everything."

"Yes, everything," she said.

"I give you my word," said the Prince.

"And what about these bad ones among you," asked Kapetria, "who imprisoned my brother Derek?"

"They're not part of us," the Prince said quickly. "But can we not agree for the moment that the death of our fellow blood drinker in New York, and the wounding of the other . . . can we not agree that this cancels out for the moment, just for the moment, the matter of Rhoshamandes and Roland?"

"Yes, for the moment, we can agree to this," she said. "Of course, this is reasonable."

"I promise you, no harm will come to you under my roof," said the Prince. "If I could compass your old language I would say it in those words. But I can't. I give you my solemn word."

"No one there knows our old language?" Kapetria asked. "No one?"

"No. No one here," said the Prince, "as far as I know." Once more he said, "No one."

Did he realize what he was saying, that the spirit Amel inside him, this spirit which supposedly spoke to him all night long if he chose, did not know the language?

Derek could see her disappointment, and see the disappointment in the others.

The Prince went on speaking politely. "You will

come here and inevitably you will leave here without being molested by any one of us, I assure you, unless you yourself or one of your kindred tries to harm one of us."

"Thank you," said Kapetria. "And you have my word that we will not do anything under your roof that would be a sin against your house. If you only knew how much we want to come to you."

"Is it possible we could come for you now, you and your friends?" asked the Prince. "If you allow that, we can protect you completely."

"No, it would be too soon," said Kapetria.

But why? Derek wondered. He had told her how he'd been carried through the skies by Rhoshamandes. But then, she knew all the lore and powers of these beings. The Prince and his companions could come now through the air.

"Very well," said the Prince. "But you do understand the quality of the danger?"

"Yes, I do," said Kapetria. "We'll be there well before sunset tomorrow."

"Excellent. And I make one final request. Say nothing whatsoever of our private concerns to my village people, my workers."

"You don't have to worry in this regard at all."

"Glad to hear it," said the Prince. "Then tomorrow night we can discover what it is that we have in common, and what it is that concerns us in common."

"Exactly," she said.

It was over, done, finished. Dertu collected the little throwaway phone.

Now they only had to survive for the next eight to nine hours of darkness in this nest of human dwellings, with the car safely hidden in the garage, without being discovered by Rhoshamandes.

None of the others had spoken a word during this exchange, but Garekyn had been called away for a call of his own, and when he came back into the room, he looked deeply disturbed.

"The monster burned my house in London," he said. "That was less than an hour ago."

"Contemptible," said Kapetria. "But it does mean the monster has no idea where we are. Or he wouldn't be wasting his time with such gestures."

It will be fine, thought Derek. It will all work. We will be safe, thought Derek, because she is here now to think of everything.

Welf was the first to dispel the gloom.

"It's time for us to feast," he announced. He had cooked a roast for them earlier, and he was ready to serve it up with cold beer, which should not affect their senses too badly. Welf and Garekyn set the table in the dining room. Dertu went about checking the locks of the house, though what good that would ever do Derek did not know.

At last they sat down, and clasped hands and bowed their heads, and they were together again, breaking bread, for the first time since those ancient days and nights, and Derek found himself weeping.

He was ashamed and wanted to leave the table, but Welf sat beside him, and comforted him, saying how sorry he was for all his early questions.

Kapetria was cutting Derek's food into small pieces as if he were a child, and Dertu was devouring everything in sight, carrots, potatoes, bright red slices of tomato in olive oil with garlic, hot bread dripping with butter, and slabs of pink meat.

They began to talk, asking about how Dertu had been born, wanting to know all the details, even the smallest, and soon they were going over the whole story in the ancient language. Dertu was struggling to describe what he didn't know—how he had developed from the severed arm and precisely how he had come to consciousness. Derek tried to describe the little face on the palm of the hand and the mouth sucking at his nipple, and the heat in his chest, but he remembered mostly the shock and the pain, and then opening his eyes eventually to see Dertu standing there.

Memories swept over Derek as the others talked, of that first night on Earth when they had feasted with the savages. The drums, the reed pipes, and the gentle face of the headman.

And another memory came to him unbidden and fresh, of the Festival of Meats in Atalantaya, when the whole city was allowed to feast on lamb and fowl before returning to its regular diet of fruit and fish and vegetables. Six times a year came the Festival of Meats.

He remembered standing in their apartment gazing down on the streets, at all those lighted tables in courtyards and little parks and rear gardens, on all those balconies, with so many happy people gathered in the candlelight to enjoy the Pleasure of Meat, and how much he had enjoyed it when they had gathered over their meal on the rooftop, where they could see out over countless other rooftops.

Atalantaya had seemed too beautiful to be described in words that night, and through the crystal-clear dome he had seen the stars spread out over the sky in their eternal patterns, and the bright burning light of Bravenna up there, Bravenna, the satellite or the planet of the Parents.

"I feel they are looking at us right now," Derek had said.

"But they can't see us here because of the dome," Kapetria had reminded him. "And surely they are becoming anxious. We've been in Atalantaya a month."

All had fallen silent. Derek remembered the taste of the ice-cold beer. He remembered the juices of the lamb from the slices on the plate, such a pretty plate, translucent as was so much else. He had put his finger in the juices from the lamb and licked his finger. He could no longer remember the name of the red fruit on his plate, the fruit with all the tiny seeds.

Welf and Kapetria had spoken often of Bravenna, of the Parents in their rooms with the talking walls,

walls filled with moving pictures of the jungles of Earth and the savages, the savages making love, the savages hunting, the savages feasting. . . .

"Are you sure they can't see us?" he'd asked then as he'd gazed up into the sky as if the dome weren't even there.

"Yes, I'm sure," said Kapetria. "The Parents told us they cannot see through the dome."

The shadow of their purpose had fallen over them. They had continued to eat, to feast, to drink the delicious cold beer that was brewed in Atalantaya, and they had been slightly drunk when the moon was at its highest. And all of them, look at them, the mammalian humans, how innocent they are, thought Derek, all of them all around us in these mighty towers and in the old Mud City and the old Wooden City, dining together, happy together with no thought of what it meant, that bright star in the sky!

"Oh, I wish," he'd said. "I so wish we had another purpose."

No one had answered, but Kapetria had been smiling at him in her loving way.

And now he was in a country called France on a continent called Europe again, and they were all together and he wondered did they still have the power—? **You must lock arms! You must stand together, with arms locked.** . . . And what about Dertu? Bright new Dertu? And they were still talking about how it had happened, the slice of the ax, the fallen arm, the fingers crawling. . . .

Finally Kapetria said, "I want Derek to sleep, to be restored. He's hollow eyed and weak from his ordeals."

She rose from the table and took Derek by the hand. "You come into the bedroom and sleep now," she said. "The rest of you, wait here for me. You wait as well, Dertu. You remain here."

He welcomed it, the quiet of the bedroom. Such a pretty house, but the French windows everywhere made him anxious; the black night pressing on the glass made him anxious. The sound of wind moving in the black trees made him anxious. He wanted to walk outside, see the stars, see the stars he hadn't seen in all those long years in that basement tomb under Budapest, but he was too sleepy, and when Kapetria helped him to remove his boots and lie down, he plumped the pillow under his head and fell asleep.

How many hours passed?

When he awoke, it was from a happy dream but the dream was gone, like a gossamer scarf of bright colors ripped away from him. Like a flag blowing in the wind.

A woman was standing in the room, a woman with golden hair. He couldn't see her face because the light of the hallway was behind her. Then Kapetria switched on the light and he saw that the woman looked just like her.

"It's almost morning," said Kapetria. "This is Katu," she said. She spelled it out for him. "And in the living room there is Welftu waiting to meet you.

We are now seven in number. And by midmorning when we leave there will be two more. Garetu and Dertu's child, though we don't know what to call him. They are being born now."

Derek was in shock. "How did you have the courage to try it?" He'd been so afraid that it would not work for each and every one of them. He had been so afraid of so many unknowns about it.

"We had to try it," said Kapetria. "We had to try it before we met the Prince. We had to know. And what better time than before going to see the vampires with their astonishing powers. My left foot was sufficient to make this child," said Kapetria, "and Welftu was made from Welf's left hand. And had those appendages failed to develop into new beings, had our own appendages not regenerated, we could have taken the severed hand and foot to Fareed, the blood drinker's healer, and asked for his help in restoring them."

"And you think he would have done it?" asked Derek.

"Oh, yes. I think he's ruthless for knowledge," said Kapetria, "just as I am. I think he regards us as a treasure, a resource beyond imagining, just as I regard them as a treasure and a resource beyond imagining, a resource that has kept Amel living and breathing and now speaking."

The smiling Katu came towards Derek. She was clothed in a smooth, tight dress of printed silk and wore those same fashionable black stockings that

Kapetria wore, and the same delicate high-heeled shoes. She was Kapetria's duplicate, of course, he thought, and only the hair, mingled gold and black, was different, the hair that had been brushed free.

But when she sat down beside him, Derek saw that her expression and demeanor were wholly unlike those of Kapetria. There was that same resolution and cleverness in her eyes that he'd seen in Dertu's eyes. What was it? Emotional innocence?

"Uncle," Katu said. "It's not a beautiful word in English or French, but I think in Italian it is pretty."

"Call him brother," said Kapetria. "That's how it should be. Call me Mother, yes, but we are all brothers and sisters really."

They led Derek into the living room. There was an electric fire there, as pretty as the fire on the **Benedicta,** and Welftu was standing by the fireplace peering down into it as if its myriad programmed flames were fascinating to him. He came to greet Derek, to kiss him on both cheeks and to clasp hands. Then he went back to his fire, as if he were counting patterns in the flames.

"But Kapetria," Derek said. He had settled into a comfortable chair near the couch. "Don't you see? The Prince will realize at once how we've multiplied. The vampires will know that we can increase our numbers almost as easily as they can."

"And why does that matter, darling?" asked Kapetria, as she stood on the other side of the fireplace. "We are not at war with the Prince."

"But what do we want of him? Why are we going there? What sort of alliance are we forming?" So many questions tortured him. **You must all be inside the dome and together, with arms locked. You must all at the same time . . .**

"You know I will speak for us," said Kapetria. "You know I will decide what is best to tell and what is best not to tell, and for now, it seems that it's best to tell all that we know and all that we don't know."

"Don't worry," said Welftu. He came and sat on the couch close to Derek. So sure of himself. So bright and clear eyed. He wore a smart jacket of gray worsted wool, and a white-collared shirt of yellow cotton. Welf's clothes. What had Welf been all these years on the planet? Oh, there was so much for them to share with one another. Had they had other "lives" as Derek had had?

Derek's heart was pounding.

Welftu was studying Derek. And Welftu did have Welf's pretty eyes, his thick black eyelashes. But there was something fierce and eager in him that hadn't been in Welf ever. Even when Welf had been asking Derek mean questions.

"They will protect us and we will protect them," Welftu said. "That is the only course that will make sense to them. After all, think what might happen if they did try to destroy us."

# 17

# Rhoshamandes

THE SMALL HOURS, as they call them. He was on the bluff high above the Château, looking down on its four towers, and on the curve in the road that ran below it to the center of the village, with its carefully reconstructed inn, church, and townhouses with their shops.

In the great ballroom of the Prince's castle, the vampires danced. Antoine conducted the orchestra, now and then playing his violin, and Sybelle's delicate white fingers sped over the harpsichord's double keyboard. Blood drinkers conversed in pairs or small groups. Some roamed alone through the many salons. Others were making their way down to the crypts.

But the village slept. The chief architect whom Lestat loved so much slept. The team of designers who worked for him slept, their street-level offices shuttered for the night, their tables strewn with ambitious plans for better stables, better electrical systems, better underground utility lines, and new and fine manor houses to be built in the little valley. What a strange tribe they were, these quiet men and women gathered from all over the globe who had been laboring in well-paid obscurity here for over twenty years, creating masterpieces of reproductive genius and technological innovation that the world beyond the electrical fences never saw.

Was it really enough, all that gold paid out to them, all those benefits, all those vacations on charter planes and yachts which the Prince lavished on them, enough for all they'd done and all they would do? Were they happy?

The answer was obviously yes, though when the ale and wine had been flowing in the great room of the inn tonight, there had been the usual raucous complaints that no one would ever know the real extent of their unique achievements. But no one wanted to leave. No one was ready to give up.

Alain Abelard, the chief architect who had grown up on this mountain as his late father oversaw the very first restoration of the old castle, was convinced that someday justice would come to them. Someday their reclusive Count de Lioncourt, called the Prince by his ever-increasing "family" of associates, would open the property to the hungering eyes of those who loved nothing more than to see great palaces sprung from hopeless ruins. Someday the tourist buses would roll through the many sets of gates that stood between them and the highway to Clermont-Ferrand, bringing eager men and women to marvel at all those painted rooms, all those vintage marble fireplaces gathered from near and far, all that exquisite fruitwood furniture so carefully chosen for the smallest rooms as well as the largest. Someday students of agriculture and hydroponics, of solar power and recycled waste, of electrical or fiber-optic systems, would come to study this little self-sustained world.

It was all right, thought Alain Abelard. At any rate he had thought so tonight over his wine. So what if his wife had left him, and his father was dead, and his sons had gone to work in Paris or Berlin or São Paulo? He was happy enough, with the Prince's weekly walks through the snow in the dark, with the Prince praising him for all his work, and offering new suggestions and new challenges. Alain would stay here forever. And he had no need, it seemed, to confide his suspicions that the Prince was no ordinary person, that some devastating secret was concealed by his placid and never-changing youthful face.

The Prince loved Alain Abelard. There was talk in the Château ballroom nightly as to when the Prince would bring him over. And what about some of the others, would Lestat ever make blood drinkers of the more promising craftsmen who excelled at painting and gilding and upholstering and woodwork and restoring the fine paintings which were always turning up in crates for newly developed bedchambers or stairway walls? Would the Court grow in the Blood the way the Court of Notker the Wise had grown over the centuries with new musicians chosen from the human herd?

The human community of the Prince was certainly growing, the project ever expanding. Take the de Lenfent manor house, for instance. How the Prince wanted it perfect, though the house itself had been burnt to the ground in the Great Fear when the last Count de Lioncourt of the **ancien régime** had just managed to escape to Louisiana with his life and a small band of devoted servants.

Now this manor house was to become the residence of Alain himself, the Prince had already explained to him. But it must be done according to the Prince's private research and dreams, and the little **cul-de-sac** leading to its front gates was already paved with the appropriate stones.

One had to marvel at what had been achieved here through imagination, ambition, and faith.

And Rhoshamandes did marvel at it. He marveled at all of it.

And in his heart of hearts he did not really want to destroy it, or harm it in any way.

Yet he had come for just that purpose. And they, the blood drinkers of the Château, certainly knew he was here. They had to know. As he eavesdropped on their thoughts and fears, he caught indistinct but certain indications that Marius knew he was here, and Seth knew he was here, and that his old loved ones Nebamun, now known as Gregory, and Sevraine knew he was here, though they could not hear Rhoshamandes any more than the young ones who flashed him the intelligence unconsciously and irrepressibly as they paused at the great open windows of the ballroom to look out over the snowy fields.

**Where is he? What does he want?**

Ah, that was the question. What **did** he want?

He could burn that intricate and marvelous little village to the ground now, couldn't he? He could start so many fires so fast that the flames would bring down every structure within an hour, no matter what precautions against fire had been taken. And he could blast the Château itself with such bolts of heat that its plaster ceilings and murals would be blackened and ruined before any flood of saving waters poured forth from all the hidden pipes. Indeed, he could melt wires, cables, computer systems, and motion-picture screens, sconces, the chandeliers. He could spend all of his energy blasting every nook and cranny, every outbuilding and vehicle, until the horses were running wild in the snowy night and mortals were racing to find their automobiles and drive off in terror, while immortals—did what? Fled through the portals to the sky? Or rushed down into the dungeons knowing that the sunlight would eventually drive away the enemy?

And what if he decided to die in this effort, to give it all the destructive power of his body and soul as they, the ancient ones, surrounded him and sought with their bolts to make the blood catch fire in his veins, to make his bones explode?

How much did Rhoshamandes want to eradicate everything and everyone the Prince loved? How much was he willing to suffer to make the Prince regret ever lifting that ax to sever Rhosh's hand and Rhosh's arm? How much did he want to punish the blond blue-eyed anointed one of that fickle and infantile spirit that had sent him rampaging into Maharet's compound to complete the annihilation of herself of which she'd been dreaming? How much did he want to punish Allesandra and Arion and Everard de Landen and Eleni for leaving him? And how much did he want to hurt Benedict, sweet Benedict who'd pulled the rug out from under Rhosh's past, present, and future?

He honestly didn't know. He only knew that the anger was eating away at him as if it were a fire, and that he was just on the verge, the verge of sending that first fatal bolt through the ballroom window before soaring above the castle to throw his powerful blasts of heat at the village roofs and those who slept beneath them.

Just on the verge? And why? Because a miserable mutant with a brain as empty as a helium balloon had somehow eluded all his efforts to gain information that he, Rhosh, had wanted to use against the Prince? It was as if the voices of the Dark World were taunting him, jeering at him, telling him, "You are nothing and you have nothing and all your yesterdays mean nothing and never did."

Was that enough to bring his journey to a close? Was that enough when he might not even touch the Prince himself, or the Core inside him?

And who knew what lay beyond in that undiscovered country? What if it was the Hell of the Greeks and the Romans and the Christians where demons exulted as they burned you with unquenchable fire? Or what if it was nothing, nothing but floating in the thin atmosphere above the earth along with mindless spirits such as Gremt had once been, and Amel had once been, and Memnoch had once been? What if he found himself there, bodiless, neither thirsty nor full, neither warm nor cold, neither sleepy nor wide awake, drifting forever as he peered down on the lights of the earth as his memories slowly dimmed and finally left him completely alone with all his suffering, a thing that might witness without understanding, or haunt out of a need for which he no longer had a name?

Was the air itself made of dead souls?

And what if some night, floating up there beyond the reach of love or hatred, of pity or fear, he heard the music again coming from the ballroom of a mountain château below, heard music which he had all his life so loved, music down there, music once more organizing his thoughts and his emotions and calling him back to himself to discover that he was as dead as anything in this strange world could be?

To die or not to die, that is the question; it is nobler to live in torment and rage than not to live at all? And to recall almost nothing of the slings and arrows that drove one over the brink?

Someone was coming towards him. Someone was walking rapidly up an old path through boulders and trees, towards the spot where Rhosh sat, like an angel perched upon a small cliff.

And who would that be? Well, who did it have to be—the Prince himself, of course, the one being that Rhosh could not blast into infinity unless he chose to destroy himself?

He watched and listened. The figure was hurrying. The figure had a time of it in the deep snow, and jumped uneasily from this outcropping to that. No, that couldn't be the Prince. The Prince was too strong and likely knew the woods too well.

Suddenly, as the figure drew closer and came up the rise directly below him, Rhoshamandes knew for certain who it was, and turned away, burying his head in the crook of his right arm.

Oh, that this too, too certain pain would not come.

It was Benedict standing only a few yards below him, his own beloved Benedict, who had left him six months ago in a rage of recriminations and condemnations and sought the shelter of those who'd forgiven Benedict for the slaughter of Maharet but not Rhosh.

Benedict waited, as if for a signal. And when no signal came, he drew closer, climbing up the steep cliff until he stood beside Rhosh. Rhosh could smell the scent of the hearth on his clothes, the scent of his old regular perfume, the scent of his clothes. Rhosh could hear the regular and powerful beating of Benedict's heart.

"Rhosh, please, I beg you, don't do it," said Benedict. The everlasting boy was sitting beside him, and wonder of wonders, he had put his arm around Rhosh.

"Rhosh, they know you burned Garekyn Brovotkin's house in London. They know everything. And if you do what you are thinking of, if you so much as burn any part of this place, they'll take it as an act of war."

Rhosh didn't answer. He listened to this familiar voice, this voice he hadn't heard for half a year, and he wondered that it could produce such pain in him, pain that was worse than the most searing rage.

"Rhosh, the elders want you dead." He said the last word the way mortals sometimes say it, with mingled horror and a fear of even speaking the word aloud. "Rhosh, they haven't settled all their questions of authority. Marius and the older ones, the very oldest of the older ones, want you destroyed, and it's only Lestat who is holding them back."

"Am I supposed to be grateful for this?" Rhosh asked. He turned and looked at his old companion.

"Rhosh, please don't tempt them to overrule the Prince. Even the Prince has said that if you strike at the Château or the village, that will be an act of war."

"And what do you care, my beloved old friend?" Rhosh asked. "You who said you'd never lodge with me again?"

"I'll go with you now," said Benedict. "Please. Let's go, the both of us, let's go home."

"And why would you do that?"

Benedict didn't answer right away. Rhosh turned and studied Benedict's profile as the boy looked out over the valley below.

"Because I don't want to be without you," Benedict said. "And if you are going to die, if you are going to bring upon yourself the judgment of those strong enough to destroy you, well, I want to die with you."

Tears. Plaintive youthful expression. Eternally innocent. Something sweet surviving through centuries of Amel's alchemy, something trusting.

"I hope and I pray with all my soul that you can come back to them, be rejoined with them, be part of them—."

Rhosh put up his hand for silence.

More tears. Tears so like the tears of that immortal child, Derek. Except that these tears were red with blood.

Rhosh couldn't bear it. He reached out and pulled Benedict towards him and kissed the tears.

Benedict put his arms around Rhosh.

Yea gods, what are we, that this means so much above all?

"Rhosh, these non-humans, they're coming tomorrow. And now let us go, let us leave here together, and let us take the time we have because of this, to think of some plan. Rhosh, if we don't think of something, sooner or later the elders will overrule the Prince. I know it. I—."

"Stop," said Rhosh. "Don't be afraid. I understand."

"They're bound and determined and—."

"I know, I know. Let it be."

He picked up the boy as he had so many times and gently ascended until the roar of wind in his ears was the only sound, and riding higher, through the banks of cloud, he turned and moved towards home.

# 18

# Lestat

THEY HAD ARRIVED in the village three hours before dark, and been given the best rooms at the inn. There were eight of them. And they were waiting in the grand ballroom when I came upstairs. The entire Court was curious, but the young ones were told to keep away from the main rooms, and that included of course not only fledglings but the many drawn to the Court who had no interest in power. Louis had steadfastly refused to join me. He was downstairs, reading, alone in his own crypt.

Marius, Gregory, Sevraine, and Seth were with the visitors, and had been during the forty-five minutes or more that I was confined to the shelter of my crypt.

Fareed met me in the salon adjacent to the ballroom. He explained telepathically and in a hushed voice that the visitors had admitted some of their group had not come with them. They'd been candid. They couldn't see entrusting themselves entirely to this meeting with us.

"We know Derek was locked up for ten years," said Fareed. "Yet there's a perfect clone of Derek in this group, except for the hair. And there's a clone of the female Kapetria with the same distinct difference, more gold in the hair. Same with Welf; same with Garekyn Brovotkin."

"What does this tell you?" I asked.

**That they are the most dangerous threat to this planet that I have ever known. And they are certainly a huge threat to us. We must make the most of this visit in every conceivable way. They want us to know we are at a grave disadvantage.**

"Well, then. Let's go to it," I said aloud. "Amel is inside me, and has been since I woke. But he's not speaking. I expected as much."

Fareed smiled, but his manner was grave.

"This is it!" he whispered. "I want to record everything. The hidden cameras are on in the Council Chamber. And don't worry, I've already told them this."

The ballroom was fully lighted such as I'd seldom if ever seen it, with the electrical chandeliers and the candelabra on every mantel burning away.

The spectacular visitors were gathered in an area of damask couches and armchairs to the left of the harpsichord and in front of where the orchestra usually assembled, ranged comfortably about and in hushed conversation with Seth and Gregory, or so it appeared. Sevraine and Marius stood to one side, eyes following me as I entered. And from the far door, in came David Talbot with Gremt, Teskhamen, and Armand.

Armand came up to me, and put his hand on my arm. He sent his message telepathically but decisively. **I am telling you, be prepared to destroy them one and all.** Then he moved away as if he'd said nothing to me, and given me no sign.

It seemed all the Children of the Night had dressed for the occasion in the usual assortment of gowns, **thawbs,** and three-piece suits. I was in my usual red velvet and lace, and Armand wore the same extravagant style in shades of blue. Only our tall riding boots looked out of place, but these boots had become the common wear of all those who regularly took to the air, and it was not at all strange to see a blood drinker dressed to the nines, save for muddy boots, and so it was the case now.

I wondered how all this calculated and lavish eighteenth-century atmosphere appeared to our guests—decadent or beautiful, offensive or tasteful.

The eight visitors were in fashionable sports attire, the males in tweed or leather jackets, and clean pressed jeans, while the two women wore long sleek form-fitting black dresses, with spectacular and very bright twenty-four-karat gold jewelry and strappy gleaming high-heeled shoes. All appeared to be slightly cold, and trying to politely conceal it. I ordered the heat in the room to be increased immediately.

All rose when I approached—and as I made my way across the polished parquet floor slowly, I ascertained two things at once: their minds were impenetrable by telepathy, which Arion had already indicated, and they seemed in no way instinctively frightened of us as mortals usually are and they did not exude either distrust or menace. In sum, all the tiny indications of aggression in humans were absent from them. No human being can feel the texture of our skin, or look on it closely in bright light, without experiencing some sort of frisson. Sometimes the instinctive fear is so great the human panics and backs away whether intending to or not. But this distinguished party was surrounded by us, and they appeared to be experiencing absolutely nothing hormonal or instinctual or visceral.

They certainly weren't humans. I didn't even think they were mammals, though that is what they appeared to be—two women and six men.

They were all brown skinned but in varying tones from the darkest, Welf and Welftu, to the bronze-skinned women. All had black hair streaked with gold, or black hair heavily streaked with gold. In other words, they appeared to be what the world calls black people, regardless of the differing tones of their skin. And all wore their hair parted in the middle and long to the shoulders which gave them a sort of consecrated look as if they were members of some special sect.

"Our Prince," said Fareed, adding, "He's eager to welcome you."

I nodded and I was smiling because I always

smiled at moments like this, but I was registering everything.

Fareed was absolutely right about the group including clones. It was easy to see this due to the skin tone and the hair if nothing else.

Overall, I could find no recognizable ethnic traits in their features, nothing that resembled any known African or Indian or Australian tribe. Welf had a full African mouth, but did not look African otherwise. They didn't look Polynesian or Sentinelese particularly. But of course Seth or Arion or any of the elders might be seeing something I couldn't see. In sum, they might have come from a time before the ethnic traits we see today in various parts of the world had started to develop.

"I want you to feel comfortable and safe in my house," I said in English. "I'm relieved you made it here without mishap."

There were immediate nods and murmurs of thanks. Each in turn took my hand as I offered it. Silky skin, flawless skin, like a fabric of superb manufacture. And they had the special beauty of dark-skinned people, a near polished and sculpted look.

All possessed similar expressions of high intelligence and inveterate curiosity, and they were truly all completely without fear.

They were slightly smaller than I expected. Even the taller of the males—Garekyn and Garetu, who were about my height—were thin with delicate bones. They were impeccably groomed and shining clean the way affluent mortals are in these times. And I picked up the scent of expensive perfumes, of the inevitable soaps and shower gels. And blood, yes, blood, abundant blood, blood being pumped strongly through their bodies, blood infusing them as blood infuses the bodies of mortals, creating a wave of desire in me, and once again in my mind that stubborn desire for innocent blood.

I welcomed each one of them individually, repeating the name that was offered. Garekyn, the accused murderer, looked no different from the others. He made no apology, but he showed no arrogance either. And when the woman Kapetria received my handshake last, she smiled and said:

"You live up to your legend, Prince." There was no accent to her English. "You're as handsome now as you ever looked in your music videos. I know all your old songs by heart."

That meant she knew everything. She'd read the memoirs, listened to Benji's broadcasts, of course, and she knew the story and mythology of our entire tribe.

"Ah, my rock music adventures," I said. "You're too kind, but thank you."

"I'm very glad you've agreed to receive us," she said. "I'm eager to tell you all about us—why we were sent here, and when and what happened."

This struck me as a remarkable statement.

"I'm impressed," I said frankly. "Very impressed. This is a great opportunity."

"Yes," she replied. "An opportunity."

"And you've been well treated, had a meal and time to rest?" I asked. This was a verbal gesture because I knew the answer, but they eagerly replied with nods and murmurs that it was a reception beyond their expectations, with Kapetria again speaking to me on behalf of the group.

"We found the entire village charming," she said with an easy and radiant smile. "We hadn't expected to be able to use our computers and cell phones here. We hadn't expected such interesting shops, and all this so far off the beaten path."

"Yes, it's a small self-contained world, the village," I replied. "Requires a certain retiring type to enjoy this kind of exile."

"But the rewards are considerable," she said, "or so your devoted staff has told me."

"I find myself marveling," I said, "that they ask so few questions about the people who live in this castle."

"Maybe they know more than they ever admit," she suggested, "and they aren't curious so much as cautious."

"Ah, could be," I replied. "Come, we'll go up to the Council Chamber in the north tower. The walls are lined with soundproof insulation. It cannot keep out all the telepathic eavesdroppers but it works surprisingly well against most."

And did these creatures have telepathic powers of their own?

I sensed that they did not.

"We will record all of this," said Fareed. "I want to remind you of cameras and speakers in the walls."

"We'll be recording it as well," said Kapetria. She held up a tiny black digital recording device with a small screen which would likely outlast the battery of any cell phone if the meeting went on into the night, which, frankly, I was hoping it would.

I smiled. Our coming out into the modern world had begun over forty years ago with a human radio interviewer in a rented room in San Francisco inviting Louis to tell his story to a tape recorder. And now here we were, all of us, storing every word and gesture of this historic meeting on the modern offspring of that old recorder.

I led the procession through the many large and small rooms to the northern stairs, with Kapetria walking beside me, her heels making that erotic click on the hardwood floors that women's high-heeled shoes so often make. Odd that it made the hair on my neck and arms rise, and that I felt again the intense desire for blood and for her blood. Were the others feeling this?

Pandora and Arion were there when we entered the Council Chamber, and so was my mother, hanging back with hard eyes, in her usual dusty khaki attire making a sharp contrast to the gowns of Pandora and Sevraine or the casual glamour of the two visiting women. Armand was the last to enter behind me. Again, I caught that signal to me as he passed by. **Be prepared to do what must be done.**

The room had been lovingly prepared, no doubt about that.

Additional chairs had been placed around the great central oval table, and the greenhouses had been raided for every perfect bloom imaginable, and the chandelier threw a warm glow over all. I felt a rather foolish pride suddenly at the spectacle of it with the potted rose trees in the corners, and vases of white lilies on the mantelpieces and on the side tables bouquets or pots of random flowers, and the twin fires vigorously at work on their oak logs. Mirrors, mirrors, everywhere, everywhere, that is, where there were not murals, with all the happy rosy-cheeked putti staring down from the ceiling corners, and other gods and goddesses gazing on from the plaster borders that surrounded the windows and the doors.

Our guests did appear to appreciate this. There was a flurry of new introductions, nods, and hand-shakes. Derek, the former prisoner of Roland and Rhoshamandes, seemed visibly delighted in some way by the scent and the colors of the flowers, breathing deeply and reaching out to touch a pot of exquisite fuchsias before examining the mahogany shield-back chairs as if they were treasures. His hand was trembling as he touched the carving.

Marius invited our guests to gather on the side of

the table to my left and Kapetria gestured for four of the party to take the chairs back along the wall.

It was plain the elder generation was at the table, with the clones behind them, though Derek took some coaxing before giving up and sitting to Kapetria's right. He'd wanted to have Dertu take his place, but Kapetria was firm on her wishes.

These four were the ones who had but one gold streak in their hair. Derek was the only one among them who appeared somewhat fragile, a bit thinner than the others, and perhaps tired. No wonder, but there was no fear in him of us either, and in fact, he was staring at me with the license of a little child, just the way he'd stared at the fuchsias or the furnishings. Marvelously innocent face.

But they all had highly expressive faces, mobile and flexible faces. And again that finely polished sculpted look that so enhanced their allure.

I took my usual chair at the head of the table, with Marius opposite me at the far end. My mother sat to my left with Sevraine beside her, and Pandora beside Sevraine, with Derek, Kapetria, Welf, and Garekyn filling out the remaining places. On Marius's left and coming towards me up the length of the table were Teskhamen, Gremt, Arion, Gregory, Seth, Fareed, and Armand.

Seth was about in the middle, directly opposite Kapetria. Then came David, the youngest blood drinker in the room. And Armand was close to my right hand.

Cyril and Thorne shut the doors and came round to where I could see them, and then took their positions as Marius directed, flanking the row of seated guests along the far-left wall. But they remained standing.

I sat forward and folded my hands, my eyes finding the tiny camera lenses in the walls, and my ears picking up the very low throb of the audio and video devices.

"Amel is with us," I said, addressing Kapetria. "He's inside me, but then you know all about that. You know the whole story. Well, he's present, so to speak, but whether he'll say anything remains to be seen. He may speak up. He may not. But he is here. And he can see and listen through any one of us, but not through more than one at a time."

"Thank you for explaining this," said Kapetria. She smiled. Her white teeth were perfect. They all had perfect teeth. But her face, expressive as it was, was transformed when she smiled. "And if I want to address a question directly to Amel?" I wondered if she was a true female in any sense.

"Address the question to me." I sat back and folded my arms, remembering vaguely some inane nonsense about what this gesture means in such a group, but ignoring it, and I continued to speak. "That's the best that I can offer. He is here, as I said. He is listening. I can feel it."

"How?" she asked, with an innocent curiosity. Her huge eyes suggested Middle Eastern women to me. Her eyebrows were high placed and long, rising at the outer ends.

"A pressure," I said, "at the back of my neck, the pressure of something living inside me, something that can flex when it wants to. When he's not here, well, the pressure's just gone."

She appeared to be thinking this over.

"Before we go on," I said, "let me say that we're prepared to restore the house of Garekyn Brovotkin in London. But there is no way our brother, Killer, can be restored to us or the blood drinker killed on the West Coast."

"This is unfortunate," said Garekyn immediately, "but I didn't mean to kill them. How is Eleni? You do understand why I tried to escape Trinity Gate, don't you, why I injured Eleni?" He alone of the group had an accent to his English, which was Russian. His eyes were smaller than those of Kapetria and he had a rather long thin nose. Too long, too thin, perhaps, but it complicated his beauty, made his eyes seem all the more vibrant, and his mouth all the more sensual, as if it were a very carefully designed flaw.

"I do understand," I said. "I would have done in both cases what you did," I volunteered. "And it's clear you could have killed Eleni had you chosen to do so."

"That's absolutely true," said Garekyn. He was obviously surprised to hear me say it. "I have no mad appetite for devouring vampiric brains," he assured me. "I am truly sorry for the death of the vampire in California, but that one had weapons and broke into my room. There was another with him. I could have killed both, but I killed only one."

"And what did you find so interesting about the brain of Killer?" I asked. "And why did you take the head of the one you killed in California?" I realized my voice was a bit too harsh and I was sorry for it. I was sorry that we had begun in this way.

But Garekyn appeared unfazed. "I saw something in the exposed brain of Killer," he said, "something obviously different from the other organic material, something alive in a unique way, and this some-thing, when I put it into my mouth, created visions in me, visions which intensified as I swallowed it. The visions had begun with a taste of the creature's blood." He paused, studying me intently. "I don't expect you to enjoy hearing such things, as these vic-tims were your brothers," he said, "but again, I was in each instance under attack, and these visions had a crucial value to me." He touched his chest with his fist as he said these words. "These visions revealed something potentially precious to me. I had come in search of you, all of you, for a specific reason, and these visions had to do with this reason." He glanced around the table for the first time, his eyes settling on Marius for a long moment before return-ing to me. "I tasted visions in the blood of Eleni, and I did not kill her. Of course I took the head of the vampire who attacked me in California. I took it to a safe place and I broke open the head and I drank the fluid of the brain and again I saw things."

I nodded.

"I understand," I said.

"What can I do to make up for this," he asked, "to put us now on even and secure footing?"

Marius spoke up.

"I think that we can put these things aside for now," he said. "After all, you were defending yourself." I knew he was very impatient with all this but I don't think they realized it.

"Yes, defending myself, and from death, I thought," Garekyn flashed back.

Welf, who had said nothing all the while, glanced directly at Garekyn when he said the word "death." Welf's eyes were heavy lidded, which gave him a drowsy and contented look, and his eyes and nose were more classically symmetrical. He had the fuller, more sensuous mouth.

Clearly these creatures were not automatons without emotion. And their faces reflected a multitude of tiny changes with every passing second. Even Derek who stared forward now as if he were in shock had a face that reflected his inner struggle, his black pupils dancing almost frenetically.

Marius went on speaking in his capable, gentle, and authoritative voice.

"And we ask you to be aware," he said, "that we had no knowledge whatsoever of Derek here being held prisoner by Roland of Hungary. We scarcely

know that blood drinker. He's never come to Court."
Marius looked intently at me. He was plainly frustrated. "We are engaged in a process here that's new
to us. Whatever is to be achieved here, it's not yet
complete."

"I know," said Kapetria under her breath. "I understand this. I've prepared myself with as much
knowledge of you as I could obtain."

"And we have no real control," said Marius, "over
Rhoshamandes who was so cruel to Derek. We're
relieved to see that Derek's arm has been restored."

"Derek's left arm regenerated," said Kapetria
without the slightest indication that what she was
saying was striking. "And Rhoshamandes's rash action led us to a remarkable discovery. We have Dertu
as the result of what happened." She gestured with
her left hand to the obvious duplicate of Derek who
sat against the wall, Dertu of the golden and black
hair. Not one distinctive streak, but many streaks,
Dertu who was so calm compared to Derek.

A low mirthless laugh came out of Fareed, who I
knew at once had figured this out long before. "You
came into this world," Fareed said, "without knowing that you might propagate in this way—by simple fragmentation?"

"We came into this world, my friend, without
knowing many things," said Kapetria. "We were
sent here for a specific purpose. Indeed, our makers called us 'the People of the Purpose.'" Her eyes
moved easily over us as she spoke, but came back to

Fareed. "And we were given only the information deemed necessary for the fulfillment of that purpose. It was for this purpose that we were made."

"And what was the purpose?" asked Marius. I feared his question had a sharp edge, but I saw no indication that anyone else did.

"We will come to that," said Kapetria. She narrowed her eyes as she looked at Marius, and then at Seth. "Believe me, I want to tell you. But first let me make this observation." She again addressed me. "It is that your method of propagation through the blood and through the brain has many things in common with ours. I suspect that Amel is no more in control of this propagation and its limitations than we are of ours." She paused as if to allow us to ponder this. "In fact, I have a working hypothesis that you are all connected to Amel because his method of propagation has failed. The method wanted each of you to be an independent unit; but the method couldn't achieve its end, and so you are somehow one enormous organism."

"I don't think so," said Seth. "I've considered this, but you see, it was Amel who pushed from the beginning for propagation—for more blood drinkers so that he might taste more blood—and for a group of connected entities to satisfy his thirst."

"He pressed for this, yes," Kapetria said, "but did he know what he was asking for? Was he an articulate mind at that stage or something lost and struggling? Yes, he begged to enlarge himself or to satisfy an immense thirst, but would it not have been more nearly perfect if each new unit in which he implanted himself through the blood might have eventually become autonomous?" She shook her head. "Tentative conclusion only: you are an organism that involves a failed attempt at propagation. You are an immense organism with a fragile core."

"Are you suggesting that some of us could be disconnected from Amel?" asked Fareed.

"Well, yes, I suspect that's entirely possible," she said. "Clearly he suffers agonies when your numbers are increased beyond a certain point, when the thin elusive material of which he is made has become stretched to its maximum length."

"Thin, elusive material," said Seth. "That is a fine way of putting it."

"Is it actually material?" I asked.

"Oh, he's made of material all right," she said. "Ghosts, spirits, whatever they are, they are all made of material." She looked at Gremt, Gremt who sat there impassively studying her with his perfect replica of a classical Greek face and body. "Are you not made of material?" she asked. "I'm not speaking of your physical body, I'm speaking of the core of your being, where your consciousness resides."

"Yes, it is made of a subtle material," Gremt said in a soft voice. "I came to realize this a long time ago. But what is that subtle material? What are its properties? Why did I come into being? These things we don't know, because we can't see or measure or test the subtle material."

"I have my theories," she said. "But Amel is made of subtle material for certain, a subtle material that implants and develops in every new host offered to him, and ideally, he would have disconnected his mind from this host in time, diminishing eventually in size until he became comfortable in one small group of hosts, or even in one alone. But it didn't happen. It's like all the spectacular mutations of this planet—infinitely complex, involving accident and will, and blunder and discovery."

"I see what you're saying," said Fareed.

"What surprises me is that you haven't been focused on this from the beginning," said Kapetria. "I don't say this as a criticism. I offer it as an observation. Why haven't you and your team of doctors been seeking to break the link of each individual vampire with Amel?"

"I can't see a way to do it," said Fareed. He appeared slightly defensive. "Of course I realize the importance of this, that we could free each individual from the host."

"Seems to me," said Kapetria, "that that might be one of the crucial areas for your research."

"Do you realize how many areas of research we're facing?" asked Gregory. "Do you realize what a revolution is involved here for us—that we now have doctors and scientists studying our own physicality?"

"Yes, Herr Collingsworth, but these strange invisible connections to Amel are so obviously vulnerable," said Kapetria, "and so obviously a mistake, a failure—." She addressed Fareed. "And another thing, why have you not been focused on some way to take the Amel neural circuitry out of one host and transfer it to another without injuring either one?"

"Because I don't know how!" Fareed said. "What do you think I'm doing in my laboratories, simply playing around with—."

"No, no, no, forgive me," said Kapetria. "I'm not saying what I mean to say. What I mean to say is . . ." She hesitated and then fell into her thoughts, her right hand curled under her chin.

"How would you do this?" asked Seth in a soft voice. "How would you propose moving the neural circuitry of Amel from one brain to another, when we can't even see this neural circuitry, not even in the most sensitive scans?"

"Stop," said Derek. "Just stop!" He glared at Kapetria angrily. His lower lip was trembling and a glassy film had come down over his eyes. "Stop right now!" he said.

She was clearly taken aback. She turned to him and asked in a small solicitous voice, "What's the matter?"

"Tell them," said Derek. He glared at me, at Fareed, and at Marius. "Tell them!"

Kapetria laid her right hand gently on his left hand. "Tell them what, Derek?" she asked tenderly.

"Tell them what may happen if they seek to harm us," said Derek. He stared directly at Seth, then at Gremt. His right hand was shaking as if palsied. His eyes flashed over all those across from him and then at me. "Tell them what might happen if they try to destroy us. They think they have us at their mercy here. I know they do. Well, they don't."

"You're in no danger of us trying to hurt you!" Marius said. "No one here wants to hurt you. No one here wants to be hurt by you, either."

"No, no danger at all here," I said. "We would never attempt to destroy you. That's the last thing we want. We felt that inviting you here like this would convince you of our trust."

"No, there isn't the slightest danger," said Seth.

"We can't be destroyed," said Derek. His voice was uneven. He was clearly struggling in ways that hadn't been easy to see before. "We can't be destroyed unless you want to destroy everything in this world that is of value to you." He clutched at Kapetria's hand and held it tight. "You tell them."

Kapetria was obviously unprepared for all of this but she seemed neither angry nor offended. She studied Derek for a long moment. Her eyelashes were thick and beautifully black and her beauty overall was distracting me as beauty so often does. If her beauty was incidental, if it wasn't rooted in something profound inside of her, well, it could be mighty misleading, I thought.

"What Derek says is probably true," Kapetria

said. "If you hurt us, you risk hurting countless others. You risk hurting the world. I'm not trying to sound dramatically apocalyptic. Our bodies may contain elements that, once released, might destroy the whole world. Derek is not exaggerating. But why don't I tell you the whole story?"

Every being present registered this, but the hard expression on Armand's face did not change. He looked at me. Faint telepathic whisper: **Containment, from which they can't escape.**

"Yes, please," said Seth to Kapetria. "The whole story. We're getting ahead of ourselves here. We need to know—."

Welf, the silent one, nodded, those big drowsy eyes of his flashing for a moment, and his full sensuous mouth yielding to a small agreeable smile.

"It's only seven o'clock now," Kapetria said. "I can tell you everything before sunrise, if you're ready to listen, and by the end you'll understand what Derek means. We cannot be physically destroyed without considerable harm being done to everyone here and people who are not here. And by the end we will be prepared to go forward together."

"I think this would be splendid," said Marius. "This is what we want. I'm moved by your trust, that you want to tell us everything."

I noted a quick glance from Gregory and Teskhamen responding in a subtle way as well. They weren't as sure as Marius about all this. But I was.

Gremt looked quietly and unobtrusively stricken

as if he were lost. I wished I could say something to him to comfort him—to tell him that he was as much a part of us here as anyone else was—but I wanted to hear Kapetria's story now as well.

"Let's get to it," I said. "You talk, Kapetria. We listen. We won't interrupt unless we feel strongly that we should."

"Excellent," said Kapetria. She removed her small digital recorder and set it on the table. I could see a tiny light pulsing from the device. "You have your cameras," she said. "We have these."

Marius nodded with an open-handed gesture of acceptance.

"Trust us," Marius said, "to understand."

"I do," Kapetria said.

She was still holding Derek's hand and she reached up and stroked his hair now, comfortingly. Then she looked at me again. And then she looked at David.

Perhaps she hadn't noticed David before. But she did now. Did she sense that David hadn't been the original occupant of his body? It seemed almost certain that she did sense this. Finally she smiled and nodded to him and he returned her smile with his usual graciousness.

Kapetria went on. "We've been sharing what we remember with one another. And I believe I have put the entire story together as best I can."

Nods from one and all.

"Now I will be speaking to you in English," she said, "because that is the one language we all share. I'll be using innumerable words and phrases and expressions in English which have no equivalent in our ancient tongue, but which are superbly effective—after thousands of years of linguistic development—for describing everything we experienced and everything we saw. I refer now to words like 'skyscraper' or 'polymer' or 'metropolis' or 'plastic.' Words like 'transmit' and 'magnificence' and 'empathy' and 'programmed.' Do you follow me?"

"I think we understand very well," said Seth. "There was no language in my home country of Kemet at the time of my birth thousands of years ago to describe automobiles, or airplanes, or parachutes, or the subconscious, or psychopathology, or force fields, or binary systems."

"Yes, exactly," she said with a delighted laugh. "That is what I am saying. And I will use the full power of the English language now to communicate rather than relive what happened. But there is another aspect of this too. I didn't always understand what I was seeing twelve thousand years ago. The world today has helped me to interpret much of what I saw, but whether those interpretations are accurate I don't know."

We were nodding, expressing in soft murmurs that we understood.

Gabrielle lifted her hand and pointed her finger at Kapetria. "There's one thing I want to know," said Gabrielle, "before you begin."

Kapetria turned to her attentively, and nodded.

I wondered how she saw my mother, whose face always looked cold and disdainful to me.

"Do you value us?" asked Gabrielle. She leaned forward and towards Kapetria, narrowing her eyes. "Or do you see us as something inherently undesirable and even abominable?"

"Oh, that's a very good question," said Kapetria. "We value you beyond measure. You are most certainly not an abomination to us. What? Because you feed on blood? Everything living must feed on something. You have no idea how we value you. You are our hope."

Welf gave a small laugh under his breath. "We've been studying you for years," he said.

"You are the only other biological immortals of which we know anything," said Garekyn.

"We would be alone if it were not for you," said Derek. But no sooner had he spoken than he began to shake all over. Kapetria put her right arm around him seeking to steady him. She kissed him, stroked his hair, tightened her grip on him. But it wasn't doing any good.

Dertu rose from the back row and came forward, putting his hands on Derek's shoulders. "Father, be still," he whispered. **Father.** So the clone calls this one Father.

"We should love one another!" said Derek. He was looking at me. He was cracking, obviously.

"Derek, listen to me!" I said. I leaned towards him. I couldn't reach far enough to touch his hand.

"I am sorry for what happened to you!" I said. "I am **sorry.** We are all sorry. We had no knowledge of your being held captive. We would have freed you if we had known. None of us would have done what Roland did!"

"He had no right!" said Derek, as he continued to look at me. "There is wrong and right and he had no right!"

"Yes, I know and I agree, and you are correct," I said. I looked to Marius.

Marius said, "There has been no authority in our world for centuries. We're trying now to come together, to make an authority, an authority under which such a thing couldn't happen."

"Oh, but you'd do terrible things to mortals, wouldn't you, any of you?" said Derek. "Haven't you imprisoned them so you could feed off them as if they were cattle?"

My mother laughed. She sat back and shook her head. She was making me perfectly furious.

"Maybe some of us have done such things," I said to Derek. "And some of us have never done such things! But we try to do what is right. We try. We believe in right. We believe in defining ourselves in terms of right. We try to feed only on the evildoer."

"**Some** of us feed only on the evildoer," said Gabrielle.

"Will you stop it, please?" I whispered to her. "You are exasperating."

Marius motioned to me to quiet down.

"Derek," said Marius. "We can flourish without gratuitous cruelty," he said. "There have always been ways."

"Yes, gratuitous cruelty," said Derek, his eyes watering. "Make a rule against it in your new government. Make a rule for the whole world against gratuitous cruelty. Amel knows. Amel knows what gratuitous cruelty is. And Amel knew a world where such a thing was condemned, Amel knows right and wrong, Amel knew a world of right and wrong. And there can be such a world again."

I saw Arion lean forward and reach for Derek, but he was too far away across the table from him just as I was. And so Arion laid his open hand on the table in the gesture of reaching.

"We all condemn what happened," said Arion. "Even I, who took from you what I had no right to take."

Derek nodded and even smiled as he looked at Arion. It was as if he trusted Arion and no one else here. I knew that Arion had showed Derek kindness and mercy, and it was Arion who had prompted Allesandra to abandon Rhoshamandes and come to us.

Dertu leaned down and kissed Derek on the cheek as lovingly as any mortal might have done it.

"It's over, Father," said Dertu. "It will never happen again."

"This is true," said Kapetria. "This will never happen again." She looked at me and then to Marius, and at Arion. "We all value one another too much for this to ever happen again."

"Yes," said Marius.

"I assure you of this, too," I said.

Once more there were murmurs of agreement—even from Gremt, who had a haunted, harrowed look in his eyes.

"We will bring this Roland of Hungary to justice," said Marius. "We are forming our means of government now. And I assure you, he will be brought to justice for what he did, and for what he withheld, and what he promoted."

"It was more than cruelty," said Derek in a raw excited voice. He was battling full-scale tears. "It was a missed opportunity, for we could have come together before, and helped one another."

"Yes," said Marius. "We do completely understand that. That is one of the worst aspects of evil, that it always involves the death of possible good, always proceeds from the destruction of something that might have been so much better."

"We need one another," I said.

"Yes, we do," said Kapetria. "Listen, we came to Earth as 'the People of the Purpose' and we abandoned that purpose for a finer one, and we are driven now by that finer purpose, and it is never, never to harm life. And you are alive just as we are alive, and we are all part of life."

"Well, I have the answer I wanted," Gabrielle said, as if absolutely nothing less mattered. "So proceed."

"Why don't you begin?" said Marius to Kapetria.

Kapetria nodded to Marius but she fastened her eyes again on Fareed. "Let me offer you one last observation on the matter of severing the individuals from the root. Remember that the nanothermoplastic of the web of connections is the only part of you not directly feeding on the folic acid in blood."

What that could possibly mean to Fareed and Seth I hadn't the slightest idea.

"Tell the tale," said Marius. "This is the moment to tell the tale."

Kapetria clasped her hands together on the table. "I will pour this out as it comes to me."

# Part II

# BORN
## FOR
# ATLANTIS

# 19

# Kapetria's Tale

## I

I CAME TO CONSCIOUSNESS about twelve thousand years ago. I could not see or move. I was listening to music, music that involved singing and the myriad sounds of complex musical instruments. Not till this modern age have I ever heard anything like this music, this blending of plaintive voices and rich chords and harmony. This music aroused in me a deep pleasure and also a deep longing. I felt something like sadness when I listened to it, a kind of emptiness, and I found myself searching for something, maybe some resolution of my longing as I followed the melodic threads. I think I cried. But it is hard to know whether I did.

All of us were nourished on this music. And to this day, we're hypersensitive to music.

The first thing I really knew was that I was finished, full grown, done, and a great success and the Parents were pleased. They opened the translucent cover of my bed, and helped me to my feet as other Parents did the very same thing for Welf, Garekyn, and Derek.

We found ourselves in a vast space that appeared to be in the treetops of an immense forest. But even as we looked, we saw the dark branches and green leaves dissolve to reveal walls alive with motion pictures, or portals to even greater forests outside with innumerable lighted dwellings or nests everywhere, high and low.

This was beautiful to us. Simply beautiful. And so were the Parents. And all of them were the Parents.

They appeared entirely normal, lovable, even charming, though they were quite different from us: very tall and thin, with large white faces and round glossy black eyes, and lipless mouths that smiled when they spoke. Their hands were lean and white and dry and perhaps twice the size of our hands. Whereas my hand here is six inches from the tip of the longest finger to the wrist, their hands were twelve inches there and their nails were pearlescent and sharp. They had five fingers on each hand.

Their legs were very long and lean and always slightly bent at the knee, and their feet were remarkably similar to their hands. They appeared to be wearing hooded mantles which were richly colored in layers, and similar bands of bright color covered their rounded torsos. Their backs were humped. And they moved gracefully and spoke softly in an Earth language, the language of the city of Atalantaya.

None of us realized at the outset that the Parents were covered with very tiny feathers, and wore no other clothing. We didn't realize that the humps on their backs were indeed folded wings. Or that their noses and mouths were in fact beaks, or that they were another species from us. This just didn't occur to us. They were the Parents. And the language of Atalantaya was the language we needed to know for our purpose.

The Parents had made us. We belonged to them and we made them happy. We were the People of the Purpose, they told us. And though their color patterns varied, they were otherwise interchangeable and numerous as they spoke to us and interacted with us on Bravenna. If they had individual names, they never revealed this to us. One might start speaking and another take up the thread and yet another after that, all rather seamlessly, so that no one individual ever stood out to us.

Now Bravenna was the world into which we'd awakened, a world that seemed vast, a world that was "Home," said the Parents, and the world where we would be prepared for our purpose.

As they helped us to dress in silken trousers and shirts, they praised us, stroked us, embraced us, and told us we were perfect for our purpose and that they loved us.

We were all then as you see us now. And they had a word for us which translates best as Replimoid. They would tell us over time that it was very easy

for them to make Replimoids but some turned out
better than others, and we were their finest work
so far. We were given to understand that we were
grown, just the way a human being is grown in the
womb of its mother, only we were organically developed from a blending of all the cells in the life
chain of the planet Earth, including those of plants,
sea creatures, insects, reptiles, birds, and mammals.
We were the result of blending and not the result of
evolution. We had been made to resemble human
beings in and out but we did not have the same neural circuitry.

For that reason we were unkillable in the normal ways that mammals could be killed and we were
constantly renewable. Of course, they said nothing
about propagation. Quite the opposite. They told
us to enjoy coupling with the mammals of Earth
as much as we wanted because we were sterile and
would never engender any offspring. This turned
out to be true. And we did enjoy coupling with humans, both men and women. And we enjoyed coupling with each other. Every factual thing told to us
by the Parents might have been true. They warned
us that different villages and groups of Earth had
different rules about coupling. We must be careful
and not run afoul of those rules. This too proved to
be true.

I could go on with this matter of coupling—
how we enjoyed orgiastic pleasure, how seductive
it was for us, but this is only a minor point in the

story I am telling. I will conclude by saying that Welf and I—for the most part—paired off early on, and Derek and Garekyn also paired off, most of the time. And for us, love and loyalty always enhanced the pleasure. We never developed much of a taste for coupling with complete strangers. And there is no doubt that erotic coupling strengthened our sense of belonging to one another.

Before I continue, let me try to give you some idea of the language of Atalantaya. It was highly repetitive, and could be very precise, and was usually spoken in a sort of rapid chanting. For example, when they lifted me out of my bed and pointed to the portals opening on the forest realm, the Parents said things like "Behold the world, our world, the beautiful world of Bravenna, the perfect world of Bravenna. Behold it. Behold this beauty. Behold the world of Bravenna in which you have been created. You are children of Bravenna. Behold the trees, behold the leaves, the light of the sun, behold your Parents. Love and obey your Parents. You are People of the Purpose, born for Atalantaya and one purpose."

It was like that continuously and we knew it was the language of Atalantaya before we knew what Atalantaya was. Their name for Earth was something on the order of "the blue-and-green planet with the mammals in ascendency," with that entire packet of information contained in the word every time they spoke it. But "Earth" is just fine as a translation. And I think there was a number attached to their name for

Earth, perhaps signifying one among many planets similar to Earth. Not certain. And no way to know their numbering system and they did not teach us arithmetic or mathematics. And they did not teach us any form of writing or reading at all.

We had vast stores of knowledge in us, they told us, which would enable us to understand any sort of language quickly, and we would recognize the useful or medicinal properties of animals and plants in the world to which we were going. And we understood the stars when we came to see them, and how vast was the universe, and how vast the "Realm of Worlds," to which they referred. It was for the "Realm of Worlds" that we would execute our purpose. The "Realm of Worlds" was horrified by the ascent of mammals on Earth, and was sending us to correct what had happened there.

Throughout the "Realm of Worlds," evolution had almost always favored other species, not mammals, and on Earth a dreadful thing had happened in that mammals had gained self-awareness and intelligence and now ruled the planet with tribes and packs and the great city of Atalantaya. To use Gabrielle's word, it was an abomination to the Parents, and to the "Realm of Worlds," and we were to go to Earth to infiltrate the mammals, and gain access to the domed city of Atalantaya.

How much of what we understood was already known to us, as opposed to being told us—this is all confusing to me now. But there was never a time when I didn't know how much the Parents abhorred mammals, and the emotions of mammals.

A great physical catastrophe had occurred on Earth and that was the only reason mammals had gained an advantage in the evolutionary process. This catastrophe was the result of several small worlds or asteroids colliding with Earth and poisoning the atmosphere so that reptiles and birds had died in great numbers while mammals survived, and grew to enormous and unwieldy size in the absence of reptiles and birds to prey on them. We, the People of the Purpose, as they called us, would work another catastrophe which would reduce the planet to an early stage where once again reptiles and birds would have a chance to overtake mammals in development.

I don't think the Parents ever spoke of mammals or mammalian nature without expressing outrage and distaste. They warned us that mammals were aggressive, vicious, and dangerous. Male mammals abused female mammals. But we would be able to fool them easily into believing we were mammals. If we did find ourselves at their mercy, if they tortured us or sought to kill us, we would survive. Indeed, it was our solemn purpose to survive. Intense pain would produce unconsciousness in us over and over again; and this unconsciousness would aid in the healing we would experience from any injury or wound.

We were not to be afraid of the pain that mammals could inflict. We were not to be afraid of them, loathsome and unpredictable and hateful as mammals were. And we were to remember in all our dealings with mammals that we ourselves were not really mammals and had this vastly different neural circuitry.

However, we had been grown to be warm blooded and to have mammalian emotions. We had been grown to think and feel and experience the sensual world and the visible world as mammals do, through a filter of emotions.

It had to be this way, the Parents explained, or we could not pass for mammals ourselves. Mammals were quick to recognize robots or mechanical beings who did not share their emotions. So we must understand that that is why we had been given human emotions.

Now as all this was imparted to us or awakened from our stores of memory, we were shown a great wall with a living picture of the city of Atalantaya, a magnificent metropolis of towers of varying heights beneath an immense dome, the whole city anchored securely in the sparkling blue waters of an endless sea in brilliant sunlight. We saw countless small white craft journeying to and from this city of Atalantaya, and we saw vibrant evidence of life inside the city itself, with myriad tiny beings living in these splendid towers, and myriad tiny beings alighting from craft to enter the domed city.

I remember thinking how beautiful Atalantaya

was. But then everything I saw was beautiful to me. Derek also spoke out as to the beauty of Atalantaya.

The Parents said, "It will be beautiful to us when it is melting and in flames and perishing." The Parents explained that the dome of Atalantaya blocked their ability to see what went on inside, and that the living pictures we were viewing had been taken within the dome by an earlier Replimoid some time ago.

I could see all this deeply affected Derek, and the Parents pointed out to us at that time that Derek had been made to feel things infinitely more strongly than the rest of us, in order to alert us to danger, or stress, or conflict in ways that our cooler nature did not allow us to perceive. After all, we weren't genuine mammals. We were carefully grown Replimoids, creatures wholly different from mammals.

We were always to travel together, to seek to be together and to protect Derek as best we could because Derek suffered in ways that we couldn't or wouldn't suffer. But Derek was indispensable to the purpose—as they called it—and we would see this over time.

How many minutes or hours were involved in our coming to know these things, I'm not certain. But we were soon told that we would learn a great deal about Earth and its mammalian people from studying the endless moving-picture walls that filled Home or our dwelling.

We were invited to roam from room to room, or chamber to chamber, and sit comfortably here or there as we chose to watch the transmitted motion pictures coming in from the planet. And all the motion pictures playing out on the walls in our dwellings on Bravenna were of life on Earth.

For thousands of years, we were told, Bravenna had been sending Replimoids like us to set up and maintain the transmitting stations that gathered the film footage we were to watch at our leisure. There were transmitting stations everywhere on Earth where there were animals or humans to watch. And we would soon see revealed all aspects of earthly life simply by roaming Home at our leisure and selecting different film streams to watch according to our inclinations.

We began to do this, unattended, often sitting for hours on a comfortable couch to watch a stream of films originating in a jungle or woodland or a village of human beings. And when we tired of one stream we did seek another. In all the rooms through which we wandered there were Parents watching these films, Parents on the same couches that we enjoyed or sometimes up in the branches of trees that filled the room, or simply standing there transfixed by what they were watching.

We occasionally saw other creatures, creatures more nearly similar to us, though we didn't linger near these creatures and never were told what they were. I wish I could remember these creatures more clearly, but I can't. I have a sense, looking back, that they were a new wingless version of the Parents, with even tinier feathers, and a penchant for clothing such as we wore, and the people of Earth wore. But I could be wrong on this. Whatever they were, they were as drawn by the film streams as the Parents were and as we were.

The film streams deeply absorbed us. We saw endless footage as it were of animals hunting in nighttime jungles, or humans in small bands or packs roaming plains and mountains or living together in small hamlets of grass huts or villages. We saw great "close-up" images of birds building nests and feeding their young, of snakes devouring the eggs of birds, or of huge lizards foraging amid insect colonies for food.

But the film streams of human beings predominated. We witnessed humans coupling sexually in dimly lighted rooms or in secluded woodland hideaways, or arguing or fighting with one another. We watched families gathered at supper fires, and working at the making of clothes from skins, or gathering the wild wheat that grew on the plains from which they could make bread in their stone ovens. We saw bands of hunters surrounding and bringing down great animals that often killed one or more of the humans as they struggled to survive against a rain of spears or hatchets. We saw some humans in larger villages building and roofing better shelters for themselves and planting some simple foods, tubers, grasses, vines, and harvesting the food produced by these. We saw herders with their flocks of goats; we saw enclosures filled with pigs kept for food; we saw humans tending flocks of small birds for their eggs and their meat. In sum we saw humans at all the primitive stages of hunter-gatherer life, and the most primitive village life preceding what Earth knows today as the agricultural revolution.

We saw humans born and we saw humans die. And we saw humans doing many things we did not understand. Indeed, we passed through chambers of Home devoted entirely to streams of humans dying, where Parents watched rapt as loving people gathered around the dying one, comforting him or her and begging for some sort of spoken wisdom or advice or rules. It wasn't clear always what the human beings were saying to one another. If we watched any group long enough, we could easily penetrate the language, but sometimes there wasn't much language being spoken, only tears and groans and sighs. And the chambers were filled with these tears and groans and sighs.

Many things we saw puzzled us, but nothing really pained us more than all these deathbed scenes, or scenes of men dying in the hunt, or in battle, or scenes of babies dying at birth as mothers screamed in protest. And there were so many of these.

Now I had no idea as I watched this how such intimate images, from within huts or caves or forest enclosures, were being gathered. It didn't occur to me to ask. But it certainly came to be a significant question later. But to continue . . .

Gradually we came to chambers where the film streams focused entirely on quarrels, men and women pushing and shoving one another, or even physically fighting with weapons, scenes where women were severely beaten by men, or gangs of women severely beat their male oppressors.

Whenever we asked questions, the Parents, roused from their own absorption in the films, would give us brief answers. "Well, this is life in this village, you see, as it had gone on for centuries, and this is how they settle their disputes, because human mammals are violent, emotional, and often behave no better than the panthers or elephants or bears in the jungles."

One thing we came to note very soon was that tribes all over Earth constructed special places for weeping and crying and hugging one another and talking of their sorrows. Often this was done around small crude stone pyramids or in special clearings. Sometimes people formed circles in this place and sang in unison of their losses and disappointments.

We found much of this very painful to watch and Derek found it unbearable.

Some tribes had built more elaborate pyramids and some more elaborate circles of stones where they wept and cried out, and it soon came clear that some groups were addressing all their pleas and cries to some invisible person or force whom we could not see.

The Parents told us this was normal, for human

mammals to imagine that the great Maker of the "Realm of Worlds" was hearing their cries, and might intervene to do something to relieve their pain.

"Is there such a Maker?" Derek asked. The Parents said that there was a Maker but that no one knew what the Maker knew. They urged us to keep watching.

We found finer and more beautifully constructed pyramids. Sometimes fires were built on the flattened tops of these pyramids. On some there were wooden statues of great beings. In one place there were stone statues atop a pyramid, and in another a grove of stone statues. In other places there were only crude mounds of earth. But always the gatherings were the same, of people weeping, crying, imploring, moaning, and it seemed the emotions were visceral and visible.

Human mammals of Earth also danced and sang and feasted in their villages. They fought little wars and brought back slave prisoners of war, and sometimes they cruelly executed unruly prisoners. They bred these slaves, and used them for the hardest of the work that had to be done to gather food and build shelters.

The Parents told us it wasn't necessary for us to understand all we were seeing.

But what we must understand was how hard life was on Earth, and how the rampant emotions of mammals led them to fight one another, to commit murder and rape, as the strong bullied the weak, and powerful individual mammals sought to gain power.

But that certainly wasn't all we saw. We saw a great deal more that did not involve unhappiness. We saw human mammals embracing, sleeping in large groups in their huts, snuggled together, just as we snuggled together on the couches as we watched; we saw what were obviously feasts of great celebration. And we heard laughter, a great deal of laughter, perhaps more laughter and singing than weeping.

And over and over again, in film streams we saw the distant city of Atalantaya, as these simple human mammals saw it, and we saw what seemed to us other very small domed enclosures that appeared similar to Atalantaya. All along the coasts close to Atalantaya there were such domed settlements. It was from these that crafts sped across the sea to Atalantaya. We could make out the towers inside these domes, just as mammals on Earth could make them out, but we were reminded that the domes blocked the intimate surveillance of the Parents.

Whenever we grew tired of all this, we could sleep. There were plenty of soft couches for sleep and we enjoyed sleeping. It was like being back in the beds in which we were made, and we loved to sleep in one another's arms. And we could look out of the portals onto the larger forested world of Bravenna.

Gradually we came to realize that the Parents were winged beings, and that from the humps on their backs the most magnificent feathered wings could unfold with which they could fly high into the forest world of Bravenna beyond where our eyes could follow them. And we could look down into the fathomless depths of the forest world and see them flying beneath us. The Parents said they loved to fly though for aeons it had no longer been necessary. The Parents flew now for pleasure, and to dream the dreams known to them only when they were flying. But we didn't need to know more about them, they explained, as we had been made for a purpose to be fulfilled on a planet to which they never went and on which they never had lived, and on which they couldn't live.

"There are many worlds like Earth in the 'Realm of Worlds,'" they said. "And there are many very different worlds, such as the worlds like Bravenna where everything is comfortable for us. But you have been made to survive on Earth." The Parents also made mention of worlds outside the "Realm of Worlds," worlds on which life existed, but in forms invisible to the Parents. The definition of the "Realm of Worlds" was that it included the worlds on which life was visible. That was all they ever said about this question of invisible life.

Sometime during this information orientation or instruction, we were taught how to eat and enjoy food, and this was a great discovery. We were told that we could survive quite well without food as we absorbed nutrients through our skin, but we could also utilize food and drink, and our bodies would dissolve every particle of it. We had no need to eliminate. Now this was important to understand, they said, because everything that happened on Earth had to do with eating and drinking, and the species of Earth not only craved food and drink, but could die quickly without it, and all creatures of Earth which we saw in the films excreted waste as the result of eating and drinking and this too had immense significance on Earth.

"All the violence you see amongst these mammals," said the Parents. "All of it stems from the drive to live, to survive, and to have offspring to survive and to obtain all the food and drink necessary to survive and procreate. That is the basis of life on Earth. And self-aware human mammals—intelligent mammals—are the most savage and cruel and vicious of all the beings on the planet, or any planet in the 'Realm of Worlds.'"

The Parents gave us to know that planets ruled by the intelligent descendants of reptiles or birds or insects were far more reasonable, peaceful, loving, and harmonious. Indeed, for the most part these species were seekers of harmony by nature, and had a very different attitude towards time than human mammals did, a very different attitude towards love, and towards the Maker.

"Self-consciousness should never have developed in mammals," said the Parents. But at the same time as they told us these things, they also told us that our longing for love, our seeking of knowledge, our response to various patterns, our noticing of traits and similar structures, our excitement at realizing certain things—all of this had to do with our minds being made to resemble human mammalian minds.

Derek in particular wanted to know why this was inherently "bad" and I think he surprised the Parents with some of his questions. They never reproved him or criticized him or any of us, though they did seem stunned at times, and at a loss for an answer.

But they did give answers. "The mammalian mind is entirely shaped by emotional needs," they said, "by wild and intense feelings. And because of this it invents invisible personalities that do not exist and longs to communicate with such personalities. It attaches absurd and destructive attitudes towards feelings. Its idea of the 'Maker' has to do with emotions. Ideas of the Maker on planets on which reptiles, insects, and birds had developed into the ascendant species did not reflect anger or love or vengeance as did the human mammals' vision of the Maker.

"It is almost impossible for these creatures to know peace or genuine love," said the Parents. "They are always too deeply enmeshed in pain or pleasure, loneliness or a suffocating sense of paralysis, a need for love, or a raging jealousy resulting from love, or a desire for vengeance due to personal defeat or injury. And when they are physically wounded or experience disease, their suffering is unendurable for them. They are driven by it to terrible extremes. Peace, harmony, joy elude these creatures."

Finally came the day when we were tired of the film streams, of their repetitiveness, and we had become even a little callous to the endless suffering.

The Parents brought us together, and told us we were to pray to the Maker. They invited us to bow our heads, clear our minds, and think only of the great creative force that had made all worlds, including those in the "Realm of Worlds," and to thank the Maker for the gift of life and the gift of witness to life.

They made beautiful sense to us and we were glad to do it.

They told us to thank the Maker for our having been grown for a special purpose, and to promise to the Maker that we would do our utmost to fulfill this purpose. The wretched mammalian human lifeforms on Earth had to be destroyed and we were the ones chosen to do it.

At this point, Welf spoke up and in a rather jocular manner asked if this Maker was real, and if he or she heard what we were saying, and whether all this thanks mattered.

I was shocked, as it seemed inconsiderate or unkind to ask this of the Parents. But as usual the Parents were completely calm.

"We do not know if the Maker exists," said the Parents. "But we believe that he has to exist and he is not really male or female. There are many worlds in the 'Realm of Worlds' where the ascendant beings are not male or female. We use the male referent for the Maker for you because you are male or female, and the male on the planet Earth dominates the female. We believe it is wise and right to give thanks to this Maker. We can see no harm in doing it."

It was obvious to me that Welf thought this was hilariously funny, and Garekyn did not like it, and that Derek was coldly suspicious of it. For me, it was a matter of being courteous to the Parents. I wanted to know my purpose. I was eager to get on with it. I am by nature the most impatient of the People of the Purpose.

We went back to the prayers. We bowed our heads, closed our eyes as instructed, cleared our minds, and thought of the Maker. And for the first time since our awakening we heard music again, singing, and it seemed all of Home was filled with this singing; and singing came from outside the dwelling, from the forest realm with all its other dwellings. I opened my eyes and saw a great gathering of Parents around us, Parents who had spread their multicolored feathered wings though they were standing still, and all were singing, and outside I saw ascending and descending Parents, gliding as it were with open wings, and they too were singing. The words these beings sang said something like "We sing of the Maker; we sing of life; we sing of the gift of life; we sing of the glory and the mystery of life; we sing of our gratitude for life; we sing of our gratitude that we have experienced and witnessed life in all its grandeur."

Finally this came to an end. The huge room was indeed filled with more Parents than I had ever seen gathered in one place before, and the Parents who had been speaking to us resumed.

"As we have told you," said the Parents, "Earth suffered a calamity. Millions of years ago its atmosphere was poisoned by a large asteroid that struck the planet, resulting in darkness and coldness that killed its abundant life in unthinkable numbers. As the result of that, the mammals of the planet arose and made the life you have come to know, a life of endless struggle, violence, and misery.

"It is your purpose to go to Earth and to achieve an explosion there that will impact the atmosphere as greatly as the earlier catastrophe. And when you create this explosion, out of your shattered and dissolving bodies will come a toxin strong enough to reduce life on the planet down to single-cell structures once more.

"But it is imperative that you be in the city of Atalantaya when you detonate this explosion. You must be within the dome and you must be in the presence of the Replimoid who built and rules Atalantaya. It is imperative that this being know who you are, whence you came, and what you are about to do. And then with utter resolution you must do it. Indeed, you will need all your intellect and skill to make the journey from where we plant you on

Earth to the city of Atalantaya to confront the Great One of Atalantaya. If at any time before that final confrontation he suspects that you are Replimoids, if he suspects that you have come from Bravenna, he will seek to imprison you or destroy you. And he no doubt possesses the means to dissolve your bodies back to their basic chemical components, while removing the explosives and toxins in your bodies, and indeed he will use all the components to continue his unlawful rulership on the planet. You must take him by surprise. You must announce your purpose and explain it right before you fulfill it."

I was pondering this. So were Welf and Garekyn, but Derek was plainly horrified. And how could anyone expect otherwise, because we knew full well what death was. We had been watching humans and animals die for days or weeks, or months, for all we knew.

Derek cried out at once, "I don't want to die! Die? All of us will die? You mean Welf will die? You mean Kapetria will die? Garekyn will die? Why must that happen to us? What good will we be to you when we are dead? And where will we be when we are dead, the we inside of us, our minds, our . . . who we are!"

The Parents were obviously completely stopped by Derek's words. If they'd heard such an outpouring from a Replimoid before, they gave no sign of it.

Then the Parents began to answer.

"You will not be anywhere, Derek, when you die," said the Parents. "You will be finished, and gone. There will be no Derek. There will be no more of any of you. That is what death is, Derek. We die too, we who developed you and created you. All creatures die. And that will be the end of you."

Derek was in helpless tears. Welf and Garekyn couldn't comfort him. And I could see that they were none too happy with this revelation themselves. It had caused in me a sinking feeling I'd never known before.

"Perhaps you can explain to us," I suggested, "how this will feel." They answered, "You will not feel anything. When you detonate the explosion, you will cease to be. That's all. There is no life beyond biological life. There is no life beyond visible life."

It was clear the word "visible" had more meaning to them than their word for biological. And of course they were contradicting themselves. They'd told us of planets that had invisible life, or at least that is what I had inferred from what they'd told us.

"Can you tell us," I asked, "why you made us such complex and intelligent beings if we are to die so soon?"

"It's easy for us to make beings like you," said the Parents. "We do it all the time. There's nothing to it. We can easily replace you. Understand, all the mental and physical equipment we have given you is for your purpose. We cannot send you down to Earth without emotions. You will be found out by the Great One of Atalantaya if we do that. You will never get into the city. No one gets into Atalantaya except at his invitation. Don't you think all those starving, struggling, violent savages of the forests and the fields would love to live in his Atalantaya? Wait and see what it is like. See what they suffer. Of course they would. But he controls who gets in, taking from the planet what he needs for his city, his paradise, his utopia—taking what he chooses and locking out all those so that his chosen ones can enjoy it. Wait and see. You must put an end to this. This is important! He has no authority to rule on Earth. This is important to the 'Realm of Worlds.' This is why you were made. You have been born for this purpose."

"I don't want to do it," cried Derek. "I don't want to die. I want to stay alive. I want to keep thinking, being, feeling." He broke down in incoherent weeping and the Parents stepped forward and surrounded him and moved him away from us.

At this point, I knew my first real fear. I was afraid they were going to kill Derek then and there. I couldn't bear it. The pain in me was so all-consuming that it took all the strength I possessed to stand by and do and say nothing. However, I did not feel that there was anything that I could do to prevent whatever the Parents would now do to Derek. I braced myself for unspeakable suffering. But they didn't kill Derek. They stroked him, comforted him, wiped away his tears, told him that it was a great thing that he was doing. And that indeed his death might not come for months, maybe even a year, and that he would have time to realize the importance of his purpose.

As they spoke some of the other Parents began to sing, and underneath their singing I heard the familiar instruments sounding their echoing chords. Finally the Parents opened their wings, and began to rock back and forth with their singing, and we started singing along with them and so did Derek.

"This is unity," said the Parents. "This is peace." They went on in their lofty repetitive style telling him that many living things had long lives but many had short lives; they spoke of how beautiful butterflies of Earth lived for a short time and how some little animals lived for a tenth of the time of a human mammal, and how human mammals lived for a tenth of the life span of the Parents. On and on they went with all of this.

A great silent rain of flower petals began to descend, and they caught pink and yellow and blue petals in their hands and showed them to Derek and told him that the flowers from which they came lived only a day or two at most. Such was the way of the biological or visible life in the "Realm of Worlds."

"But there is always hope that something invisible of us . . . of the 'we' in you and the other People of the Purpose . . . might survive," they said. "There is hope. You have seen the human mammals of the planet weeping and sobbing and praying. They have hope, hope that the Maker hears them and that when they die their spirits go up and up and away from Earth and into a realm ruled by the Maker. There is always that hope. All through the 'Realm of Worlds' creatures have such hope. Only on Earth perhaps does it take such an emotional turn, but it is universal."

Derek had calmed down, and when they released him, Welf received him and held him firmly and Garekyn took up his station on the other side of Derek and did the same.

"Now," said the Parents. "It is time for you to know and understand the story of the Great One of Atalantaya who is named Amel, and how he came to do such evil on the planet."

Derek had gone completely calm, but not, I knew, because he was mollified or convinced or elevated to some new level of understanding. He was simply exhausted. And I kept in my heart a deep contempt for the Parents that they had so brutally and insensitively told us that we had been made to die on this purposeful journey. I kept in my heart a scorn for them that they had understood the pain they would inflict on Derek and on us with their cold explanations. I felt a deep suspicion of their prayers, of their talk of the Maker.

I did not want to die either. I did not want my eyes to close on the beauty and complexity I saw all around me. Indeed, they had told us at the very beginning of our lives that we were unkillable, and now they had let us know that they had planned all along to kill us. And what could be the meaning of all their talk of suffering on the planet, of violence, of cruelty, of viciousness?

But I knew better than to voice any of this. I knew exactly what they would say. "You are caught up in these emotions because you're a Replimoid. You are thinking and feeling like a human mammal." But I knew from all the film streams I'd watched that everything on the planet Earth wanted to live, not just the human mammals. I remained quiet. And they began to talk of Amel, the Great One.

## II

"Years ago," they said, "we developed and grew Amel just as we developed and grew each of you. But we gave him infinitely more knowledge than we have given you. Indeed, we shared with him all of the valuable knowledge of Bravenna as if he were one of us. And this was to equip him to survive on the planet and fulfill a specific mission.

"Mammalian primates had already developed, packs and gangs of brutal loathsome hairy beings who killed and fought and even ate one another's flesh. These repulsive beings held horrific and absurd ideas, that gods lived in the sea and in the forests, and in the mountains and in the fire and in the thunderstorms of Earth. And they would sacrifice their own children to these gods, slaughtering them on bloodstained altars.

"All through the 'Realm of Worlds' there was horror at this mammalian ascendency on Earth and the horrors produced by it, the blood, the violence, the cruelty.

"We sent Amel, the finest creature we could possibly make, to put an end to this. We equipped him with a plague that would strike down these violent beings, and give some chance to other ascending creatures.

"He was further sent by us to restore and repair all of the many transmitting stations all over the planet that had become idle due to slow erosion or storms or volcanoes or earthquakes with which this planet is tormented heavily as you have seen. We did not design him as we designed you to pass for a mammalian primate. On the contrary, we designed him to be perceived as a god.

"We had long noticed that certain mutations in the hairy primates of Earth could present pale-skinned and blue- or green-eyed primate mammals. And that the tribes in which such mutants were born regarded such creatures with fear and awe, worshipping them as gods or destroying them as evil.

"We made Amel a being of pale skin and green eyes and red hair as a consequence. And we knew that these traits, coupled with his vast intelligence and ability to speak all languages, and his keen ability to provide the tribes with useful information for healing and the making of tools and such—all this would produce awe in the primitive tribes who would then fear and obey him.

"He could therefore use the labor of these tribes to restore the transmitting stations where they had failed, and he could use them to set up new stations for the recording of the changes in atmosphere and water that would follow the releasing of the plague we had given him.

"This being, Amel, was the most powerful and versatile Replimoid we've ever made. He represented the finest of our knowledge on all levels, and he knew all that we knew. He understood that he was to repair as many transmitting stations as he could before releasing the plague at a predetermined time, and that he would keep working on the transmitting stations even after the plague was released and for as long as there existed savage human mammals to help him.

"We believed wrongly that he understood and valued his purpose, that being of the highest mind, and that being in full control of his primate emotions, he would perform the tasks we wanted and establish a base on Earth from which he could communicate with us as to the planet's future development. We equipped him to enjoy pleasure unendingly with the female or male primates of the planet. We equipped him to enjoy food and drink, and warmth, and the exceptional beauty of Earth. We stinted on nothing to give him the greatest gifts we had to bestow and to make his life on Earth not only endurable but wondrous. And with the healing gifts we had given him, he would be able to inoculate some females of the species to endure with him for many years and keep him company, and some males to breed with these females to provide him with future females."

The Parents went silent.

"Think on this," one of them said. And then another, "Think on it to understand the depth of his perfidy and betrayal."

We did as they asked, of course. We stood silent, waiting, pondering, reflecting. But in my heart of hearts my sympathies lay with Amel, our Replimoid brother, not with the winged beings telling this story.

"Amel deceived us," said the Parents. "Not only did he not restore the film-streaming stations as we had instructed him to do, but he actually destroyed all of those whose locations we had given to him for repair. One by one he broke, dismantled them, and he had demolished the majority before we came to realize what he was doing.

"In fact, Amel destroyed so many of these important bases that we could no longer track him or view him or hear him or discover what other things he was doing. But it came to pass that he was using every bit of knowledge we'd given him to gain power with the savage human mammals of Earth.

"Of course, Amel never released the plague. And we have come to understand that he used the very plague itself somehow to inoculate the species of Earth so that they would never be susceptible to it or to any number of other plagues that we might send.

"Thus began his rise among the beings of the planet, the rise of the Great One, Amel, the ruler who sought others to do his will, not our will, to make of Earth what he would have it be, and not what the 'Realm of Worlds' would have it be.

"Of course we sent Replimoids to destroy him. We thought they would overwhelm him easily by their sheer numbers, but no such thing happened, and communication fell off with every Replimoid ever dispatched to stop him. From the bits and pieces of information that did survive these attempts, we saw that he had sent legions of violent human mammals to destroy these Replimoids, and in some cases cut them up into pieces, saving the pieces and harvesting them for cell material for his own experiments. And he is a great maker of unusual things, this Amel.

"There is infinitely more we could tell you of Amel's rebellion, of his adventures, of his scorn for us, the Parents who had made him, for the 'Realm of Worlds.' It is enough to say that we vowed never again to send any Replimoid to Earth who would be equipped with the kind of knowledge we had given Amel. And we would never send against him any Replimoid who was clearly recognizable to him. These Replimoids were all instructed to repair and create new transmitting stations for us before they moved against Amel. But you will not have to do this. We have become impatient with Amel and his destruction is your only real purpose.

"In the meantime he became a builder of cities, an organizer of human mammals, teaching them better ways of hunting, and finally even of extracting metal from the earth and working in metal, and all manner of other things which helped them to multiply and advance, and to prosper. Through many old and new transmitting stations, we saw a great deal of what he did and what failed and what did not fail, and with horror, we realized that the evolutionary story of Earth had been fatefully marred by Amel's will and intellect.

"Eventually he built small settlements which he covered with thick roofs to block our vision, and finally he perfected the great city of Atalantaya, which is a legend to all the human beings of the planet, Atalantaya with its population of brilliant human mammals, schooled by Amel, and fostered by Amel, to dominate the entire world around them, to live in merciless indifference to the misery of the savage tribes of the planet, and on their backs, so to speak, as they labored to supply his great city with the earth's riches.

"It is now our decision that only Replimoids such as yourselves can succeed against him, Replimoids of such intellect and perfection that you can distinguish yourselves as clever and resourceful so as to gain access to the Great One himself, tell him who you are, whence you've come, and why. Tell him how angry we are with his disobedience.

"Then, you must surround him and you must detonate and blow up the city of Atalantaya and Amel.

"When you detonate the explosives in your bodies, the power stores beneath Atalantaya will surely blow, and the explosion will be sufficient to transform the world; other explosions will soon follow; raging fires will take over the forests and the plains. Volcanoes will erupt, and eventually as the smoke rises from these great conflagrations, the world will darken, and grow cold as it has many times in the past, and life will die out, and that life which does not die out will be weakened and mutated and destroyed by the toxin that will spread from your disintegrating bodies, the toxin that will poison the dark and cold planet."

The Parents then went quiet for a few minutes, until one of them told us that this was all we needed to know for now, and that we should go rest, and enjoy the transmissions from Earth as we had done before.

"But what if we cannot get into the city?" I asked. I knew I was the leader. And I also sensed I was speaking for the others. "What if we don't succeed in ever getting into Atalantaya?"

"You must," said the Parents. "As we have explained, Atalantaya has beneath it vast power stores, stores from which energy is drawn to create its lighting, its heat, its chemical laboratories and places of invention and manufacture. We do not know what these power stores are, but they are almost certainly inflammable, if not explosive by their very nature.

"And you must be in Atalantaya when you detonate so that you ignite those power stores. If you are not inside, the explosion will not be as destructive as it must be. And the dissemination of the plague inside you will not be as far reaching. If you cannot get inside the city, we will communicate with you and advise you as to what to do next to gain access. All you have to do to communicate with us is be within the vicinity of the transmitting stations. Now these are hidden and with reason. If Amel knew of them, they'd be disrupted, but there is one quite close to the main launching station for the boats to Atalantaya. It is in the remains of a small pyramid around which tribes gather constantly. It contains a Chamber of Suffering. Ask to go into the Chamber of Suffering. And when you do you will pray and in your prayers you will tell us in so many words, words not easily understood by others suffering around you, that you cannot get into Atalantaya. We will see you and hear you and you will hear us because you are configured to hear our transmissions."

"I have another question," I said. "What if we can persuade Amel to leave the protection of the dome and come out where you can talk to him and he can talk to you? Is it possible that some resolution could be achieved so that the planet does not have to suffer the cataclysm and the toxin?"

"Yes, that is possible," said the Parents, "but we are certain he will never take the risk. Remember, Amel has betrayed us and he has gone against our laws, our most sacred and important laws."

"But what if he does come out," I insisted. "What if he does want to explain to you what he has done and why? Is it possible that you will not go ahead with your plan?"

"It is possible," said the Parents. "And it is possible there could be a change of plan."

"And if there were a change of plan, perhaps we would not have to die?" I asked.

The Parents went silent for a few minutes before they answered. "There could be a change of plan," they said, "but again it is not likely. However, I think that you might have a great incentive of course to persuade Amel to come out of the dome. Yes. You could even tell him that you yourselves will not have to die if he is willing to come out. He might be moved by that. He does not like death. We could bring you back here with Amel. And then decide the fate of the planet in some other way which is not so dependent on the death of Amel along with Atalantaya.

"But do understand," said the Parents. "We must destroy Atalantaya and take the planet back to its earlier stage of development. This must be done. And if our plans through you do not work, we will use other means."

"Well, this would give us great incentive," I said. "The hope that we might return here with Amel."

Again they were quiet. Then: "Kapetria, you have been made for one purpose. Your desire to keep living should not enter into what you do."

"But you do want to talk to Amel yourselves, don't you?" I asked.

"Yes, it is true. We do," they answered. "There are things we want to know from him."

They went quiet.

"What sort of things?" I asked.

"Isn't it obvious?" asked the Parents. "We want to know what the dome of Atalantaya is made of. We want to know why it blocks our transmitting stations. We have questions about life inside of Atalantaya. And if this gives you incentive to take this approach with Amel, this is good. But we do not believe he will come out. And we believe that our plan, the explosion of Atalantaya and its power stores, and the dissemination of the toxin, is the best way to bring about a reversal of the life processes on the planet. This is our chosen plan, it is the plan that we are providing to do this. **This is our plan.**"

"But there might be another plan," I said, "that does not involve so much suffering?"

They considered this for a long time. "Kapetria," they said. "We know that you are a Replimoid and we understand your concerns. But this is the plan we have provided for the salvation of Earth. However, if you do succeed in persuading Amel to come out and we are able to remove you and him from the planet, we will consider another way of doing this."

"I'm profoundly grateful for this," I said. Welf and Garekyn also said they were grateful. Derek, however, said nothing. He was staring at them with reddened and glazed eyes.

That was all they had to say to us now. Tomorrow, they told us, after we had rested, they would go over the stories we would tell to the natives, and they would bring to the fore in our minds the knowledge they'd given us about plants and animals and their healing properties, the knowledge we would use to gain access to Atalantaya. Amel was always in search of those of the savage tribes that had special knowledge, and when our fame grew as healers Amel would inevitably send for us.

"Now, go watch the film streams as you have before," said the Parents. "Watch with new eyes, now that you know the purpose. Feast and rest."

We did as we were told. And we didn't dare to speak to one another about what we now knew. We knew that we couldn't risk this. But I know now that all of us were deeply troubled. It was not only the thought of our own deaths that disturbed us, it was the purpose to destroy all of life on Earth down to a lower level. It was the horrid and grisly descriptions of raging fires, of volcanic eruptions, and the thought of humans running in panic trying to save themselves; it was the horror of so much death! It was the horror of so much natural violence.

And why the Parents thought it would be restful to us to go on watching the transmissions again, these vivid streams of the complex forests and jungles and fields that we were going to destroy, these vivid streams of men and women living, working, loving, and dying, these vivid transmissions of magnificent animals struggling to survive—why the Parents thought we should watch all this, knowing we were to destroy it, we could not imagine.

I can't say I felt a great deal of emotion over this. I knew I had been made to lead the party and that I was colder in temperament than the others, but I was not only deeply disturbed, I had lost respect for and trust in the Parents in some vital way. I did not entirely believe them when they said they would consider changing their plan. Their utter indifference to our personal fate was obvious. And not believing some of what they said, I came to question everything they said. I wanted really only one thing and that was to get away from them. As it turned out Welf was feeling something similar and so was Garekyn. As for Derek, he was as miserable as any dying human mammal on Earth, and said little or nothing as the next few days passed.

Finally our orientation was complete and we were shown a small craft that would take us to Earth. This would have to be done in the far north, and under cover of night so that Amel's powerful sensors could not detect our coming. But we would be only a few days away from the south country, the great country around the sea in which Atalantaya was built, and we were well dressed in animal skin and woven cloth, and we had primitive weapons, knives, spears, hatchets, to defend ourselves on our short journey.

"Go to the friendly tribes," the Parents had instructed us. "Tell them that long ago your parents came out of Atalantaya to work in the Wilderness lands and that they died in a dreadful mishap. You be the teller of this, Kapetria. Tell how you and your brothers were orphaned young, and that you lost all connection with your parents and your home and are hoping to be accepted once again in Atalantaya. The savages of the Wilderness lands will treat you with respect. You have gold and silver to give them, and they will eventually take you to the landing to go to Atalantaya. You have abundant gold to carry you into Atalantaya. If this fails, use your healing skills. Use your intellect. Distinguish yourself until word of you and your achievements reaches Atalantaya. Actually none of this will be hard for you."

At last came the moment for departure.

## III

The Parents saw us strapped into the craft, at which point they spoke to me again about persuading Amel to come out of the dome.

"We are of the mind that this might work after all," they said. "Please do all that you can to gain his personal trust, to stay in close proximity to him, and to persuade him to come out of the dome and to the nearest of the transmitting bases. And you must all come with him. You see, we do very much want to recover Amel, and it would be of great value to us to have Amel here once more on Bravenna where we can study him and question him and learn from him."

"I will do my very best to persuade him," I said.

"I'm grateful. I am hoping that you will be so pleased that you will find some other use for us somewhere as we so much want to go on living."

The Parents indicated they understood.

Off we went for a journey of several hours to Earth. We knew that the craft would disintegrate after we were out of it. And that we would see Bravenna, or Home, in the night sky. We would see it as a bright star shining above. And that all the people of Earth knew this star was Bravenna, and they all knew the old legend that the Great One had come, aeons ago, from Bravenna.

Our landing was uneventful. We easily got free of the craft, and indeed it did disintegrate. We then set out, as it was still night, to make our first campfire and eat our first meal on the planet. We found ourselves submerged in the beautiful world that we had studied through the film streams, and our immersion in it was a sensuous experience far exceeding our life on beautiful Bravenna. This was, after all, an open and varied world, filled with night breezes, the songs of night birds, and fragrances of grass and flowers and woodland and even the smell of the sea coming to us on the wind; and in the clear night sky we saw the great sweep of the stars in a way that had not been possible from the portals of Home. But we did not dare to share our thoughts. We were too well aware of the fact that the Parents might easily enough see and hear us through a hidden transmission station, or that there might be devices built into our bodies which enabled them to hear anything that we said, and even to see one another through hidden eyes that we could not detect on our own skin. In fact, we knew, positively knew, that only inside the dome of Atalantaya would we be able, perhaps, to talk honestly with one another, and become ourselves with one another. Nevertheless there was a shared sadness, a shared seriousness that united us. We might have been born in innocence, but we were not innocent now.

We were among the tribes of the Wilderness lands for about three months. But I wish to collapse this part of the story. I could talk for a long time about our adventures with the tribes, what we learned, and what we saw. But I will only summarize this.

Essentially, we were surprised by the tribes. We were surprised that we discovered traits among the humans we encountered which had not been fairly represented in our orientation by the Parents. We were surprised by the daily lives of the tribes, whether they were hunter-gatherers, or communities of miners working under overseers from Atalantaya, or whether they were bound together in larger groups to maintain orchards or flocks or beehives.

What surprised us more than anything was the openness they displayed, the hospitality they offered us, the huge feasts to which they invited us, and what we saw of their family life. True, we had watched endless streaming on Bravenna, but little of it had revealed the way that humans loved and nurtured their children, or the sheer dependence on love that seemed a part of their everyday life. Admittedly, there were quarrels, there was casual cruelty, yes, and there were times when we saw eruptions and disputes that frightened us and caused us to move on; but the larger fabric of human mammalian life struck us as vastly more complex than the Parents had acknowledged.

We had gained little sense on Bravenna as to how much feasting was part of daily life, and how much these tribes enjoyed the intoxicating beverages they made from grapes, or wild grains, or fermented honey, and how many hours they lavished on preparation of the roast meats, and the thick sauces and the crude breads that they baked. We were not prepared for the hours of singing and talking at these feasts and how much a part of ordinary life this had become. It was an easy thing to spend our days at such family or village feasts, and to drink to excess, and sleep it off in some garden here or there or on the floor of a village hut while a woman drowsing in a corner cheerfully waved the flies away from us with a palm-leaf fan.

Resources were obviously abundant. The woodland and the southerly jungles were filled with game. Rich tuberous vegetables, similar to potatoes or yams, were a staple which people grew in their village streets or in their backyards. Bread made from grain cost, but people had plenty to barter for it. Honey cost, but they had plenty enough of this too. I don't remember butter, but there must have been butter. What I mostly remember is that there was no want, no hunger, no struggle. Some who welcomed us were obviously richer than others, but this advantage showed itself in ornamentation more than anything else, or the size of a dwelling.

We studied these people.

And we saw everywhere we went an inveterate obsession with "fairness," whether it was a group of gold miners arguing with the overbosses, or members of a small hunting band arguing with the headman over the distribution of food, or whether it was two daughters arguing with a mother about the chores or benefits offered by the parent. Fairness, fairness, fairness. The species had an instinctive understanding of fairness, and this extended to displaying what I would now call altruism in many areas of life. In other words, humans were willing to sacrifice for other humans; humans were willing to fight at the risk of their safety and lives against those whom they felt were oppressing them or threatening them; humans were willing to stand up for what they believed, even if this meant they would be attacked. When a human suffered a broken ankle or leg or worse, others pitched in to work for him and provide for his family, and fierce arguments sprang up if someone did attempt to hoard or cheat or get away with doing nothing.

However, there were dreamers and madmen who seemed to do nothing, and people cared for them as best they could without complaint. There were elders who were universally revered.

I wish there were time, or that I was up to the task of documenting all of these observations, but suffice it to say I became deeply intrigued as to whether I was seeing all this realistically or seeing it as positive due to my own Replimoid nature, and I could not resolve my conflicts with regard to this. I only knew that the species had an innate love of fairness and goodness, though the definitions as expressed might be vague.

As for the mining communities we encountered, we were pleased to discover that work in them was entirely voluntary and generally offered for consistently good rewards. Indeed, there were humans clamoring to work. The workday was four hours, with different shifts working round the clock to mine the gold, the silver, and the copper from the earth. Same in the large orchards and herding communities. About four hours was as long as any man, woman, or child worked to fulfill the commitment to the community and to Atalantaya. After those four hours, people spent time as they always have and always will, working on their own dwellings, training their children, cooking, dining together, playing games, working at handicrafts such as the making of clay pots or the weaving of baskets, and the making of clothes. We found out that four hours a day was the accepted time for work all through the Wilderness lands—as these lands were called—and that people in Atalantaya worked four hours a day as well.

People felt it was admirable and good to work four hours. They admired those who worked at least six days in a row before enjoying a work-free day. And they told us that that was the way of Atalantaya.

Clothes all over the Wilderness lands were in a state of flux. People wore skins mostly for warmth, protection, and prestige, but some people had begun a simple kind of weaving, and others were tanning leather to make it more flexible and durable, and some even wore silk garments that had come from the new silkworm communities near to Atalantaya, and some wore chemical clothes, or clothes made in Atalantaya of materials that did not come from nature, as far as I could see.

As for the pyramids, we encountered them everywhere and stood silent through many an evening ritual when humans gathered to watch the fires burn atop the pyramid and pray to the Maker. Adjacent to these pyramids and sometimes right inside of them were chambers where people came for the sole purpose of reflecting on their sorrows or their frustrations, with people weeping as they sat on benches, or chanting their tearful prayers. These were the Chambers of Suffering. This was the place, we were now told, where all could cry and even bang their fists on the stone walls. These were the places where we could shout aloud about our losses or disappointments.

We were even told once or twice that the Maker heard all that went on in these chambers, and the Maker loved it, that the Maker loves those who suffer pain and misery yet have courage to cry out against it, and go on with their lives. We were told in one instance by a guardian of one of the chambers that the Maker was particularly attentive to weeping, far more than ever to songs of praise or thanks. The Maker had compassion on the beings of Earth, and knew how hard life was, with many dying young, and many injured or wounded, and even sometimes whole villages dying in a flood or a forest fire.

Now the Parents had told us of one Chamber of Suffering near Atalantaya, but they had not told us that these chambers existed all over.

I noted all this with great suspicion, and I could tell by the expressions on the faces of Welf and Garekyn and Derek that they also thought this was intriguing, to say the least. We inquired more about all this, and the explanations came back the same: a

Chamber of Suffering helps people to weep here, to have a place for weeping; it helps people to weep in groups; it helps people to bare their suffering hearts. But now and then there was the hint that the Maker was especially pleased with these places and those who sought them out. Of course the Maker could hear cries uttered everywhere, but the Maker especially favored those who took the time to come to the Chambers of Suffering, and some had guardians who helped sufferers come in and go out, and others had guardians who guided singing that went on with the weeping and grieving. Those who came often to the Chambers of Suffering were the people most likely to see the intervention of the Maker in their lives.

What did this mean? Could the Parents see into all of these chambers? We were not certain that we had seen inside these chambers when we were on Bravenna, because we had seen so much suffering in the film streams that we had not noticed anything that might have involved special gatherings here. Did the Parents intervene in the lives of the suffering people who came to these chambers? I couldn't imagine it.

I asked about the Maker. I asked what he or she might do. And when I did I made people uneasy.

Gradually, I inferred from all this that it was not permitted to say as fact that the Maker would intervene, or to claim that the Maker had. What was accepted was faith that the Maker might. And that the Maker appreciated the sufferings of those on Earth. I was even told once that "not a tear was wasted."

As for the guardians of these Chambers of Suffering, there seemed no overall network. In some places there were strong guardians of the Chambers of Suffering, and in others only one or two old guides. And in some places, the chambers had fallen into positive neglect.

I felt more and more uneasy about the chambers, because no one had called our attention to them on Bravenna.

I often studied the way the chambers were constructed, and how the pyramids were constructed, but I could come to no conclusion. Indeed, I didn't see any evidence anywhere of the transmitting stations that were sending streams to Bravenna, and I learned early on that no one seemed to know anything about such stations.

This didn't make very much sense. But then the whole question of the transmissions didn't make sense. How had we, on Bravenna, been able to see into people's huts or houses, or caves? How had we been able to hear and see people coupling in the privacy of their beds?

I stored all I saw in my memory. I had no other way to store it. No one in this wide world was writing things down. I had seen no writing on Bravenna. I didn't even think of "writing" or what it had to involve.

Another thing fascinated me: people, far and wide, visited Atalantaya any number of times during their lives. Some visited regularly. They traded with Atalantaya, and indeed they had begun to use a coinage from Atalantaya as well. The representatives of Atalantaya were everywhere teaching people things such as how to graft branches from one fruit tree to another and how to construct small and easily managed looms.

Over and over, people told us we'd be welcomed in Atalantaya—that anyone with our knowledge of brewing healthful tonics and teas, of using plants to heal injuries, and reduce fever—would find a ready audience in the representatives of Atalantaya on the coast.

Nowhere did I encounter anybody who felt shut out of Atalantaya, or who had been rejected for a visit to the city, or who blamed Atalantaya for any circumstance in his or her life.

Now understand we were seeing many kinds of people, simple people, more complex and vocal people, people with the ambition to make pots and fabrics, and others who seemed content to rock their babies in their arms and sing to them, or dance around evening fires.

But none of them spoke of exploitation by Atalantaya. Indeed, some blushed when they told us that they just weren't strong enough to live in Atalantaya, but they had enjoyed the "festivals" there very much. Others said they couldn't live in those tall towers, and others that it was too crowded and others that it was too noisy. But no one, no one complained of being used by Atalantaya or excluded from it.

And this contradicted, directly contradicted, things which the Parents had said.

In sum, I loved this Wilderness world. We all did.

It was a great experience, our journey to Atalantaya, and when at last we did present ourselves in the coastal community nearest the great city, we were welcomed and approved for passage across the water almost at once. We scarcely needed to utter our "cover story."

All around us were happy people excited to be going to Atalantaya, many for the first time, and the officials in charge seemed excited for us as well. It was rather like being in a group today that is visiting the cities of Jerusalem or Rome for the first time.

After we walked through a great hollow tube of metal and stepped into the crowded white ferryboat, we gazed in wonder at the immense city rising before us, and felt not fear of Amel so much as desperate curiosity for more surprises, more revelations, more sheer pleasure, and more knowledge of the marvels of Earth. Hundreds upon hundreds of small fishing boats were on the sea around us, and other boats carrying various supplies to Atalantaya. It was a lovely spectacle, as these boats had small sails of individual colors and they were sprinkled as far as the eye could see. And before us Atalantaya became so immense as to seem like something beyond belief—that anyone or any group of beings could have built such a habitation.

## IV

The ferry appeared to fly across the water, and burrow into the very foundation of the city, entering a lock and coming to a stop at a station where other ferries were also docking, and people were streaming out of them and through gateways to stairways that led to the surface.

The officials who were stopping and questioning many only took one look at us and waved us through.

The sidewalks and the stairways moved under our feet, in ways that would surprise no one in the twentieth century but absolutely confounded us.

Within minutes we were in a huge spacious loggia with translucent walls where officials questioned us briefly as to whether we had gold to sustain us in Atalantaya (we did) and whether we would need shelter (we would) and then waved us on to a welcoming agent who told us we would find places of shelter all up and down the walkway before us, to our right and our left.

As we emerged from the loggia, we found ourselves in the very midst of the metropolis on a shining pathway bordered by enormous fruit trees and banked with vibrant flowers, winding its way amid the myriad towers, with doorways open to the walkway on either side from shops and hostelries and other "businesses" for which we had no name. In truth we had no name for most of what we beheld. But it would be no surprise to anyone returned to this moment in a Time Machine from a time such as this. Shops sold jewelry, clothing, communication devices, strange gadgets, sandals, shoes, bags for carrying things, and a multitude of other "goods" such as we had never beheld.

Above us the towers rose higher than any tree in existence on Earth as far as we knew.

But it was the people, the people of Atalantaya, who astonished us, dressed as they were in shimmering garments, mostly of pale pastel colors, and decked all over with gold and silver jewelry, many with pendants of precious or what we call now semi-precious stones.

Young and old, they seemed more spry and healthier than the people of the Wilderness. Some painted their faces in exquisite ways, not like the savages of the Wilderness but in a more subtle manner to enhance their features.

The clothing ranged from carefully made jackets and trousers and well-fitted dresses to loose tunics long and short, and formless robes. Some people were scantily clad just as the Wilderness people had been, but gone were the shaggy heads and long beards and strong natural odors of the Wilderness people, as these people were clean and groomed and striding along with a fierce self-confidence that startled us and confused us and momentarily brought us to a halt.

These people included women and men in what might have been equal proportion, and numerous children, and people cleaning the streets with sleek wandlike machines that appeared to be devouring dust and dirt and falling leaves. The fruit for the picking was everywhere, just as it had been in the Wilderness really, and out of the doors of cafés and dining places came the scent of delicious concoctions which we found ourselves craving right away.

As soon as we were seated in one of these places, a spacious eatery with a huge back garden, we discovered that everything offered was made from vegetables and fruit, eggs, and wild grasses or grain, and that meat was only eaten in Atalantaya during the Wilderness Festivals, or the Festival of Meats, that took place six times a year. Fish, however, was abundant. Fresh fish was sold at the docks in the early morning and then before noon and then before evening. We could have any number of kinds of fish, prepared roasted, or broiled, and even sometimes raw. We could have shellfish also, and sea grasses and other delicacies which I realize now included caviar.

That was fine with us. We loved the food we consumed, which was much more artfully prepared than the feasts we'd had in the villages, and that first meal is engraved on my memory for all the nuts offered us in bowls, and the vegetables both fried and baked, and the cooked grain mixed with raisins and sliced onions and bits of spices and herbs. There was something sacramental about the presentation but it seemed at the same time to be pedestrian to all those coming and going and taking their places at the tables and arguing and chatting with one another as they ate and drank. What I realized much later on was that it was competitive consumer presentation of food just as competing restaurants offer today.

Each restaurant had its own dovecote or henhouse for eggs, usually in a garden in back where fruit trees grew in abundance as they did everywhere. We'd stumbled into only one of many choices, and it took a pittance of our gold to pay for it, in change for which we received a lot of Atalantaya coin, in fact so much coin that we had to buy purses to hold it, which involved our very next stop in a clothing store.

But let me get back to what we actually saw in the city. If I go from point to point like this, it will take far too long.

As we emerged and began wandering, we soon encountered numerous moving staircases, and tracks on which people were carried about as on electric walkways today. Some of these tracks circled as high as three stories around various towers, carrying people up to doorways dozens of feet above the street.

And everything we saw, positively everything, seemed to be made from lightweight, flexible material of varying strengths as if this were a whole world made of plastic.

Though people walked everywhere, there were lightweight pods—of a glistening white material—also traveling the thoroughfares of the city, and as I recall, all of them looked similar, varying only in size. Some pods held only one person. Most held up to four. Though I myself never obtained or rented or borrowed one of these pods, it seemed anybody could do that, and that the pods actually drove themselves. In retrospect I think the pods were relatively new to Atalantaya and just catching on. I never learned any more about them.

As for the buildings themselves, they were fabulously translucent, but when you tried to see inside them you found that sometimes you could not. People had plenty of privacy in their shops, rooms, or offices, because with the wave of a hand, a wall could become utterly transparent or opaque, and we saw all around us walls changing in these ways.

Of course we found moving-picture places, dimly lighted salons into which we could enter to watch film streaming on walls, just as we'd seen it on Bravenna. But these films were not of ordinary life. It took only a few moments for us to gather that what we were seeing were artful and fictional depictions, in other words dramas in which people acted out parts.

If I had one regret of my time spent in Atalantaya, it is that I did not take enough time to understand the nature of these films, the values that these stories embodied or reflected, and the overall differences between one film and another. This was a burgeoning art form. I should have come to know it. Welf wanted to know it also and was forever urging us in the first weeks to go into the film houses and study the films. There were also stage plays, shows involving shadows only, and puppet shows. Garekyn had some interest in all this too. But the films and plays frightened Derek and he didn't like them; he could not quite grasp what the artifice sought to achieve.

"Why would someone pretend to have a fight with someone else?" he asked. Of course we could have come to understand this level of cultural expression if we'd taken the time. But we were too attracted by other mysteries such as: What were the walls made of? Why did people constantly talk to their own hands or wrists, and where were the energy stores of which the Parents had spoken and how was this energy actually used?

I need to add, at this point, that all through the crowds in the streets were Wilderness people like us, and many of them were asking questions, just as we wanted to do, so there seemed to be no risk. About one-fourth of the crowd in any lane or street through which we wandered seemed to be Wilderness people, coming to enjoy and "see" Atalantaya—"Behold Atalantaya, the beauty of Atalantaya, behold the talking clothes, the talking bracelets, behold the dome, behold the wonders!"—so we blended in.

Well, the talking clothes and talking bracelets were of course communication devices united by a wireless network, and analogous to today's cell phones. These were built into garments and certain kinds of jewelry, even rings, and people were not talking to their hands.

Within an hour of our arrival, we had bought talking bracelets for ourselves and we had our numbers and our names entered into the great network, and we could call one another, we were told, from anywhere in Atalantaya, and we need not shout as we were doing when we experimented with these things, we needed only to talk in a "soft voice" as the device would adjust the volume.

When I asked how these things worked, I received detailed and vague answers, both of which were usually beyond the understanding for which I'd been equipped. Essentially, what I came to understand was that all sounds had waves, and waves conducted communications, and the energy that made this possible was abundant and came from the roofs and walls of the towers as well as the surface of the streets, and even from the material of the immense citywide dome.

What they were not saying, because it was so obvious, was that sunshine provided the energy of Atalantaya and there were no actual energy stores.

I couldn't begin to guess what this actually meant. But in the entire time I was there it was the only explanation given me for virtually everything, and indeed on some overcast days, days when the marine clouds hung so thick above the dome that the city was grayish and even cool, some communications were slightly dimmed. Everybody expected this and didn't care. In fact, they loved it when rain pounded down on the dome and giant waves splashed on the bulwarks of the city, and there was much talk about how water as well was used in Atalantaya, and salt was extracted from seawater so that it was healthy for the fruit and nut trees that grew everywhere, and the vines that grew on walls and in gardens filled with gourds and pumpkins, and squashes and melons and vegetables for which I never learned names. Water fed the innumerable fountains of Atalantaya in gardens and groves and in nooks and crannies off the sidewalks everywhere. The people uttered expressions like "Sing the song of water!" equal to people today saying, "How beautiful the rain is."

By nightfall that first evening, we had decided we wanted to sleep in a tower. And a pod took us up to the third floor of a hostelry where we engaged a tower apartment for a month. The thirtieth floor was the highest we could get.

We rode up in an elevator—a silent pod that sped up the exterior of the building—and soon found ourselves walking into what seemed very grand chambers indeed. There was the moving-picture wall, desks with simple computerlike devices built into them involving complex symbols, individual bedrooms with large soft silk-covered beds, and outside walls that turned from richly colored opacity to sheer translucence when we waved our hands in a certain way.

There were lavish baths and toilets made of the same lightweight plastic material as the walls. There were showers. There were machines for laundering clothing, and there was heated air and cooled air in this apartment and shining floors throughout. There were lights in the walls that one only had to touch to bring forth illumination.

When I look back on it now, I realize that every single surface was a form of solar cell. Nothing that we saw or touched or used was not gathering energy. Clothing was made of solar cells. Even the tops of boots or sandals had solar cells and energy was somehow flowing from all of these collecting cells to some source—or it was being used to power everything in the immediate vicinity. I could never tell.

Of course we were overwhelmed by the beauty and comforts we saw. And we were just beginning to trust that we might converse honestly with one another, and we had, oh, so much to say!

We began our conversations very carefully, but within a few hours we were confessing emotionally to one another that we were half in love with Atalantaya and indeed with Earth and we didn't know what to make of that fact.

Derek was the first to ask in a whisper what would become of us if we went outside of Atalantaya, and looked up at the bright star of Bravenna in the night sky and sang out that we could not fulfill our purpose and asked that we be removed and brought Home.

Welf and Garekyn said at once that that was a really bad idea!

We tabled any more conclusions for the moment and went out in search of what the streets had to offer.

And indeed, we discovered that night that Atalantaya contained innumerable boulevards and lanes, some serpentine and others straight, in which all street-level doors led to businesses or restaurants, with actual dwellings invariably above. I never saw any street in Atalantaya that was for residences alone. I never saw any part of town without cafés and what we call grocery stores. We also came upon an old section of Atalantaya called the Wooden City adjacent to an even-older settlement called the Mud City, and these were just what they appeared to be—remnants of the first urban settlements on the island, from which the Great One had built the magic metropolis which now dwarfed them utterly in splendor. These old settlements were there for display, it seemed, and there were guides roaming through them explaining to the relaxed spectators how life had been in early Atalantaya.

Of course from the very first day on we heard talk of the Great One, the Great Amel who had built Atalantaya, the Great Amel, Amel who made all things.

We listened carefully to every bit of intelligence

about Amel that was offered us, and we were confident the whole time that we were lost in the shuffle, lost in the human herd. After all, how could the ruler have picked us out of this great stream of brilliant humanity? We looked like Wilderness people newly arrived, and quickly adjusting, and we had done nothing to call attention to ourselves in any way.

The first real startling glimpse of Amel came when we entered a Meditation Center on our street, just steps from our new home.

We had seen these Meditation Centers everywhere in our wandering, as their façades were marked by relief sculptures of human beings sitting quietly with heads bowed and eyes closed. And we had come to be curious, naturally, about these figures and why they appeared so often flanking doors to the street. Were these Chambers of Suffering, we asked those around us. They laughed at the idea and told us, no, that there were no Chambers of Suffering in Atalantaya.

Finally, when we were overwhelmed by all our experiences and tired, and ready to focus on something a little more challenging than wandering and asking and marveling, we saw a great many people walking towards the nearby Meditation Center, and we entered it along with them and found ourselves in a great dark domed room.

It was fitted out with a horseshoe of ascending benches, what people call bleachers today or stadium seating. We took places at the very back and top, and found the seats were comfortably padded and that people were now filling the place, though many left spaces beside them so as to signal a need for privacy or distance.

Soon all were sitting with their heads bowed and eyes closed, just as in the relief carvings on the exterior, and some were crying, quite visibly crying, but much more quietly than the Wilderness people did in their Chambers of Suffering.

So it is the same thing, I thought. Exactly the same thing. It was more subdued but it was the same thing.

At one point as we sat there waiting, trying to covertly study those around us and opposite us, the picture wall became illuminated and we saw for the first time the face of Amel. A deep-throated bell sounded somewhere, perhaps in the city outside, or within this building, I couldn't tell.

What a shock. I am not sure what I had expected to see but the face that appeared on the picture wall was that of a male, pale skinned as an albino, with substantial red hair and deep blue-green eyes, and very agreeable features. The man we saw as Amel in fact resembled you, Lestat, so closely that he might have been your cousin or even your brother. He had the same alert intense expression, the same easy smile when he spoke. And the same rather busy unkempt hair, and even the same square shape to his face and a similar symmetry to it. Of course, his pale skin in a uniformly dark-skinned world gave him an unearthly look, and something of an unearthly shimmer. We had glimpsed only a few albinos on our path to Atalantaya, a few others with red or golden hair, a few with pale eyes. And to see the rosy flush in his cheeks, and the expressive lines made visible by the lightness of his skin, all this was startling. But it was also a little repellent. That he spoke passionately and normally as a human being made him compelling.

He greeted his audience as I would see him do often in the next few weeks and began to talk in a seemingly natural and spontaneous way.

"Good evening, my fellow Atalantayans. This is Amel coming to you from the Creative Tower to remind everyone that the first Festival of Meats will be in three weeks, and when the gates open to the Wilderness people visiting for the first time, many will need shelter among you, or a helping hand in finding the public shelters. Please do extend your arms to your brothers and sisters from the Wilderness lands, and help us to enjoy a healthy and happy festival.

"Now I welcome you to the Meditation Center, and I remind you all as I have so often that you are not being spied upon here in these halls or theaters, that what you say is not being recorded, that it is not for the benefit of anyone but yourselves, and that these places exist for you and you alone and what you would make of them."

The face was gone as suddenly as it had appeared,

and we were left breathless and silent with this first glimpse of the creature we had come to admonish and destroy, and wondering if it was true that we could share our thoughts with one another in this theater.

I wish I had hours to describe what then happened, how pictograph writing appeared on the screen as a succession of human beings took the floor to discourse on the definition of evil and to recount their own personal triumphs or defeats.

"Evil is that which goes against life," said the first speaker, apparently reading a statement in the pictographs on the screen. "Evil is anything that goes against life, harms life, stifles life, destroys life. Evil is bringing harm to another person, inflicting unnecessary pain, suffering, or confusion. All evil comes from this. This is the root of all evil."

This struck us as profoundly beautiful. We found ourselves nodding just as others were nodding around the auditorium. We also pondered the pictographs. We had seen them in other places and thought them mere decoration. We each independently sought to memorize what was on the screen.

After that, people spoke up about their personal sufferings, the loss of a mother, the loss of a child, a disappointment in the workplace, an innate and debilitating melancholy which they could not cure. They spoke of losing a lover or a spouse. Others listened in almost total silence. But people nodded; tears were shed. Finally people began to sing. For the first time the screen was changed, and flooded with new pictographs and the people chanted in their untutored voices, echoing the beautiful music we had heard before we were actually born.

We joined in this singing, easily following the repetitive lyrics, though we could not yet read the writing. "Behold, we sing the song of life most beautiful; behold, we sing the song of the flowers of the field and the trees of the forest, and the splendor of Atalantaya and the splendor of a child's smile. Behold, we sing the song of harmony and unity. Behold, we sing the song of life itself."

When we went back out into the streets, Derek walked up to a man and asked him, "Who rules Atalantaya? And how is it done?"

The man said, "Well, no one really, at least not in the way that you ask. Amel is the Great One, but Amel does not necessarily rule." The man then talked on easily of councils and rulers, and representatives from this or that area of the city and from the Wilderness lands. "Amel's will is absolute, but he seldom asserts it, and usually only when there has been a ghastly crime committed, and even then he invites the councils high and low to review his decision."

Derek wanted to ask more but I spirited him away.

When we returned to our home in the tower, we talked frankly with one another for the first time. We took wine from our refrigeration compartments and shared it in the translucent drinking vessels that had come with our apartment, and we sat down on the couches of the gathering room, with no real light needed as we could see lighted towers all around us.

Garekyn who has always been more aggressive than the rest of us, more prone to sharp questions as well as solutions, spoke up immediately.

"If there are truly no stores of energy on this island," he asked, "if there are only places for using water and places for using the light of sun, how are we to make an explosion big enough to set off the fatal chain of explosions?"

But Derek didn't wait for anyone to answer. "What is so evil about the people of this city," he asked, "that the Parents want all of them dead, all of them and the Wilderness people who have been sheltering us and helping us for the last three months—all to be reduced to primal dust or soup! How can the Parents believe this is right?"

"Maybe we are not seeing deeply," Welf suggested. "We need to give ourselves time."

We talked over everything that night, and then went back to simply living in Atalantaya and witnessing everything the city had to offer. Within days we realized that erotic coupling was free and easy in Atalantaya with none of the rules that had prevailed in the villages of the Wilderness lands. And that people were in the main highly protective of and friendly to little children even though these children were not their own. People formed families both large and small, and respect for the very elderly was what we call today the norm. Elderly people, in fact, had the greatest freedom to do just about anything they wanted to do. People rose and bowed to the elderly, offered them tables in crowded restaurants, fell silent when the elderly spoke, and stepped aside for them on the street.

Life was busy in Atalantaya. People had places to go and things to do.

Within a matter of days we witnessed the creation or growth of a tower, an experience none of us was ever to forget. Whatever the damage done to our memories, and our perspective, each of us has remembered the planting of that building and the spectacle of watching it grow.

It was Amel himself who arrived at the garden site as everybody called it and stepped out of a large smooth traveling pod with the "seed" of the building in his hands. It looked like an egg. The time was dawn, just before sunrise, and musicians surrounded the garden with drums, cymbals, and horns. A huge crowd had gathered for this, and we'd been hearing about it for days. Now we saw that people were coming from everywhere to witness this, and that they crowded the windows and the balconies of the towers around us.

A huge cheer went up when Amel stood in the center of the garden and looked up and around himself to acknowledge the crowd. Indeed, it was a roar.

Then he turned to the tilled earth and appeared to inspect it, though I suspected he'd known it was ready before he came. When the first sun rays hit the garden soil, Amel laid the "seed" or the luminous white egg on the ground. He handled this thing as though it were fragile, but I wonder. Perhaps this was reverence. Perhaps he had hoards of such seeds or eggs stored away.

Whatever the case, almost immediately the egg or seed, in the clear rays of the sun, began to vibrate and then to break open at which point the musicians began to play and the whole crowd began to sing.

This truly was the music we had heard before our birth. This had to be its origin! The seed now exploded in great translucent shoots and stalks and what might have been leaves. Amel stepped back, and indeed everyone stepped out of the garden patch and allowed the building to grow.

Translucent stalks, shoots, leaves, whatever they were, gave off a crackling noise that I could scarcely hear for all the singing, and before our very eyes, a giant tower sprang into being and grew out and up and up until a fully detailed building rose before us, sprouting windows and balconies as it grew. Through the crystalline clarity of its walls we could see its shining floors, doorways, inner chambers blossoming and enlarging, and so many myriad details being realized that it was dizzying and impossible to watch the development of any one aspect, the tower soon rising hundreds of feet above us, rivaling the towers around it, the singing and the music of the instruments not reaching their highest volume until a great skyscraper existed there, complete, it seemed, in all its exterior and interior detail. Down through the earth, I figured, went its foundational roots, the earth being churned around them, and the air was filled with the scent of soil and water until at last this great soaring tower, as tall as the others around it, was settled, ceased to tremble or vibrate, and stood still and firm in the sparkling sunlight.

People cheered and screamed and we rushed around to one side, hoping to catch a glimpse of Amel again as he returned to his pod and drove away. He was a man roughly the size of Garekyn, roughly your build, Lestat, with a similar dexterity and grace.

Of course we knew that the music and the chanting had nothing to do with the magic of what happened, but I thought it a marvelous idea, as it made all who were assembled there feel as if they had participated in the building's birth.

We had a multitude of questions for those around us, and the people we asked were agreeable to explaining.

"The building is made of luracastria," said one. "Everything in Atalantaya is made of luracastria—buildings, sidewalks, driving pods, elevator pods, even clothing. Cups and goblets and plates are made of luracastria. Our world depends on luracastria and the proper handling of it; without luracastria, Atalantaya would be like the old Wooden City or the old Mud City. Luracastria is the basis of life."

As for what luracastria really was, all I could ascertain was that it was a chemical, and it was a chemical discovered, developed, and perfected by Amel. Amel worked tirelessly on improving luracastria and finding new ways in which it could be used. Luracastria could create other chemical formulas, I was told, luracastria could even heal a wound, restore a broken bone, as well as transform silk and animal skins into stronger and more resilient new entities.

Based on what I know now, I have come to believe that luracastria was like what we call a polymer, similar to innumerable polymers that occur in nature and to substances we see in nature such as spider silk, which is a protein fiber, and silkworm silk, which is a protein fiber as well. I could give you a long complex scientific explanation from a twenty-first-century vantage point of what luracastria likely was, but it would be purely speculative. I have never in the laboratories at Collingsworth Pharmaceuticals been able to duplicate luracastria.

I spent a good deal of time asking Atalantayans in the early days about luracastria but even those who worked in the laboratories where it was developed, or the factories in which it was created, did not seem to really understand what it was. All agreed that Amel knew how to make it, that he was the one who had achieved and perfected the formula and was always expanding its use. The dome over Atalantaya was made of this thick and unimaginably strong polymer and so were the threads of the clothes we wore which I had thought mistakenly to be natural silk.

Indeed, the whole network of energy harvesting and fiber-optic communication of Atalantaya depended on the bold use of luracastria, and everyone I spoke to seemed to regard it as cheap. Whenever the subject came near to energy again, they reaffirmed that there were no energy stores per se on the island, or anywhere in their world as far as they knew. Store energy? they asked. What could that mean? Energy flows. The sun and the water provided the energy, and the way in which this energy was extracted and transferred and used, well, they couldn't explain it. And frankly, they didn't see any need to explain it. I could go see the water plants and the solar energy plants if I wanted. They welcomed visitors.

This attitude was not too different from the attitudes of people today—in this very time—in which the entire world is dependent on energy technologies which the vast majority do not understand.

But I will tell you what was different.

This earlier world was an innocent world that had never known centuries of military developments or the agricultural or industrial revolutions that all today on Earth take for granted as inevitable precursors to technological advancement; and therefore these people did not labor under the immense weight of cultural or political or moral traditions from such revolutions.

Much of what I saw and heard I couldn't understand until I came awake in the twentieth century and saw the blessed affluent world of the West in this time, in which people carry enormous cultural burdens from earlier economic periods without even being aware of it. Take for example that hundreds of millions today still subscribe to an authoritarian religion inspired almost entirely by an early Mesopotamian agricultural revolution and the development of the monarchical city state that arose from it and fostered it.

Again, these ancient people were innocent of such things. They had gone from being hunter-gatherers to living in a technological paradise.

Another practical matter.

The engulfing public services of Atalantaya, the technologies of Atalantaya—were supported by a tax on every single financial exchange. But the tax was small and people had trouble understanding my questions when I asked about such things. The tax was simply part of life. And the abundance of goods and services available to everyone seemed to completely preempt any individual interest in acquiring personal wealth.

Now, there is one thing more I wish to recount before I move on to Amel. And that is simply the Festival of Meats, which gave pleasure to the city like nothing else I'd ever seen.

As I've indicated, there were six such festivals a year, and they were often referred to simply as Wilderness Festivals. They were the only time that the people of Atalantaya could eat the roasted or boiled flesh of lamb, sheep, goats, or the small fowl of that time that were similar to the chickens of today. It was also the time when fresh cheeses and cream were abundant in Atalantaya. The Festival lasted five days.

As the time drew near for it, parks and gardens everywhere were refurbished and made ready, and restaurants and cafés set extra tables and chairs outside their doors. Then the Wilderness people came flooding in, with their meats and milk and cheese to sell to the restaurants and cookshops and giant public kitchens—and suddenly the scent of roast meat was everywhere and people everywhere were buying from the makeshift booths and movable displays of the Wilderness people who offered all sorts of other goods for sale too: animal skins, feathered fans and headbands, and baskets, exotic plants in crude pots, spectacular birds in artful cages, and trained dogs of many breeds and sizes and even some domesticated cats.

In essence all the fruits of the Wilderness lands could be brought in for sale during the Festival—not just meats. And many a Wilderness family had a special tea or broth to offer, and even homemade intoxicating drinks and wines. And homemade concoctions of hallucinogenic herbs or mushrooms.

Atalantaya swarmed with the Wilderness people, and every merchant of Atalantaya was busy trading, buying crafts and skins, and selling luracastric clothing, furnishings, and gadgets to the Wilderness people as well.

Of course the talking bracelets and computers were of no use outside Atalantaya. But there were many other luracastric items for sale—from goblets and plates to spools of luracastric thread to gadgets we could not understand. Mirrors were a huge sale item, and Wilderness people apparently sold as much gold and copper jewelry from their villages as they bought from the more sophisticated jewelers and metalworkers of the city.

It was something to behold. And it was here I saw for the first time, in abundance, bound multipaged books made of luracastria, and scrolls of luracastria, and inks for writing on luracastria, and metal and feather pens. But these were highly expensive and only a very few people from the Wilderness had any interest in them. And these people, some of them, the ones who bought the books or pens, appeared to be people of authority in some capacity or at least people who commanded great respect. Looking back on it, I wonder if they were not eccentric scholars of the Wilderness or even shamans. Whatever the case, there were not very many of them.

The feasting was spectacular—much like the banquets we'd enjoyed in the Wilderness villages—except we had here every delicacy conceivable made with meat, as well as sauces of great refinement and combinations of hot spices and fruits and vegetables such as we'd never encountered before. Again, there must have been butter. But I can't remember any butter.

We ate ourselves sick during this time. Everybody did. Everybody drank freely. And people danced. They danced everywhere. Wilderness musicians were all the rage amongst the people, and the wildest music with flutes and drums echoed up the walls from every street in the city, and we danced, danced until we near collapsed in the street outside of our home building. Of course we had danced in the villages, but that was a far more limited kind of dance, often governed by the tradition of the village. This was a wild orgiastic dancing, an unbridled ecstatic dancing.

And people coupled outdoors such as I'd seldom seen in the villages. They made love in the gardens and groves, and back alleyways, and under the feasting tables. Meat, drink, dancing, public lovemaking, demonstrative lovemaking. It was the way of the Festival of Meats—of the Wilderness Festival.

Things did not always go smoothly. Some people fell down in the streets drunk and were carefully laid upon benches out of the way, or on patches of green in the parks. When fights broke out, the brawlers were surrounded and subdued and hauled off to "sleep" in the holding cells. In the main, however, things went peacefully. And we noted even some people wearing masks in the Festival and cavorting in ceremonial ways which we did not entirely understand. It had to do with deities, I thought, but not deities for whom there was any other kind of notable reverence.

But we soon came to see that there were other things going on! This was the time that Wilderness people brought their most promising children to Atalantaya to be educated, seeking acceptance in Amel's many multileveled schools. This was the time when brilliant young women and men from the villages offered their skills to the merchants and chefs of Atalantaya, or sought to sell bright and detailed paintings they had made on woven fabrics or the bark of trees. This was the time when Wilderness musicians who had made their own reed flutes, or skin-top drums or other instruments, sought to sell the instruments and themselves as skilled musicians who might work throughout Atalantaya. This was the premier time of exchange between the two worlds of Earth as they existed at this moment in history. Village healers, tellers of tales, collectors of village histories, these also came to offer services and themselves for hiring.

In all, it was a most exciting and exhilarating and inspiring time. But after the Festival was over, we were told, there would be Wilderness people not wanting to leave, who had to be rounded up and forcibly ejected from Atalantaya, and it did turn out that there was one murder or so everyone said. Amel would pronounce on the murderer, we were informed, and people did not seem eager to talk about this, or to explain anything about it, or to know anything further about it. It seemed they did not want to talk about such a distasteful and exceptional subject, and they gave us to know that murder was still common in the Wilderness lands, but not here. That surprised me. I hadn't seen murder in the Wilderness lands.

Now I want to explain one other revelation that came to us during the Festival of Meats. It concerned a small riot that broke out when one band of musicians sought to replace another band by force outside of our home building. A crowd gathered, with Atalantayans taking sides, and soon there was pushing and shoving and the verbal exchanges became furious.

At the moment when it seemed one of the musicians, the head of the usurping band, might well be harmed, certain people came out of nowhere who enforced the peace. And I noticed that these people were all distinguished by a tiny flashing light somewhere on their persons, either on their collars, or on a wristband, or even in their hair, and that they were working in overwhelming numbers to quell the riot.

It was then that I learned how law and order really worked in Atalantaya. The entire "police force," to use our words today, was in fact composed of people going about their lives in other ways, who could be called up in an instant, to turn on their tiny flashing lights and carry out their duties as needed. These people had in fact been specially trained for this, trained on different levels, and I later found the school where they were trained. Indeed, it trained men and women to fulfill a multitude of public tasks, being what we would call today police, guardians of the peace, even civil servants. I came to see that those who broke up small fights, or took into custody the disorderly, had not been mere passersby as I had earlier thought, but members of this ever-ready police force.

But the point I'm making is, there was no **standing** police force, any more than there had been a **standing** militia in the Wilderness lands. Rather, there were countless informally undercover individuals who could at a moment's notice transform from their regular activities as scientists or musicians, or restaurant owners or shopkeepers or wandering tourists, into "the guard" needed to keep the peace. And I realized that it had been the same in the Wilderness lands. Representatives of Atalantaya had been everywhere out there, but only showing themselves when needed. I had even seen those tiny twinkling lights now and then. But it was only now, seeing them in large numbers quelling the riot, that I recognized them for what they were and became curious as to how many there were.

Well, I never found out any specific numbers on the force of guardians, or civil servants, but what I have realized since is that this highly complex world did not need a standing police force or military. And as I had nothing to compare this to, I thought it made perfect sense. But imagine if nations in the modern world took this approach—training a huge and quiet guardian force of peacekeepers who only became professional peacekeepers when needed.

After we came awake in the twentieth century, I thought of this often. And I realized something else. The world of Amel had never been equipped to fight any kind of massive attack from Bravenna— perhaps because Amel had always known that defending Earth from Bravenna was impossible. And Atalantaya had never been equipped to fight any sort of savage or barbarian assault either. Of course we never saw any savage or barbarian assault, but when I read the histories of civilizations known to the modern world, I saw a horrifying pattern: great cities built, and then sacked and burned by warriors flooding in with no other purpose than theft or the joy of massacring the population. Again and again it has played out—Egypt, Mesopotamia, Athens, Rome, ancient Kiev, even Constantinople. Well, it didn't happen in Amel's world. And why? Perhaps because the Wilderness people were never exploited or forced to do anything by Atalantaya and Amel, and all had some free access to Atalantaya and much of what it had to offer. If warlike tribes existed somewhere outside the cultural reach of Amel—and they apparently did—there was no talk of their being a concerted threat, and no fear of them among the people we encountered.

But it's now time to let Amel speak for himself through my memories.

It was a week after the Festival that our meeting with Amel occurred. We were gathered together at dawn to watch once more the seeding and growth of a large building, and after we had witnessed that spectacle with the same awe and emotion we had experienced before, someone came up to us and told us that Amel wanted to see us, and that we could have our audience with him that very day.

This was a shock. We had been pondering for some time how we might get access to Amel's factories and laboratories, and to Amel himself. And we had been divided really, about how and when to attempt this and what danger it would inevitably present if we drew attention to ourselves on account of a special interest in Amel.

And then up comes this smiling civil servant or guardian or special representative of Amel and tells us that Amel is ready to receive us, and that we best be at his personal chambers in the Creative Tower at high noon. We knew what the Creative Tower was of course. This was where Amel lived and worked and ruled. The Creative Tower was one of many buildings in the Creative Gardens, where there were laboratories and factories and libraries which we had not yet seen.

Was this the end of our stay in this paradise? Was this the end of our lives? Was this the end of our mission, and who among us wanted to lock arms and detonate and blow the magnificent and complex world of Atalantaya to high Heaven? Garekyn actually suggested that we flee. After all, it was an invitation, wasn't it? No guards had been dispatched to take us prisoner and bring us forcibly to the Great One. Why not leave the city now? We could make a report to the Bravennans of what we had seen, a progress report, so to speak, and then come back to do the deed when we were more fully prepared.

"And how do we explain to them," Derek asked, "that we are not ready now? And that we are not fully prepared?"

Suddenly they were all looking at me. And as this conversation had been taking place in our gathering room, I went out onto the balcony and stared down into the busy streets of Atalantaya. I stared up at the sky in which I could see the ghost of a daytime moon.

When I came in, I told them: "It's time for us to talk to Amel, to learn who Amel is, and what Amel is, according to Amel."

I didn't have to ask as to their disposition about our purpose. No one wanted to fulfill The Purpose. No one wanted to detonate.

Finally, Derek said in a low murmur, "I do not want to destroy all this. Even if I were ready to die, I could not bring myself to destroy all this!"

"I fear that we are supposed to persuade you," said Welf.

"No matter," I said. "Today we go to see Amel."

"And what if he knows our purpose," asked Garekyn, "and what if he's been watching us all this time? I mean why else would he be sending for us?

There are millions of people around us. Why has he asked to see us?"

Finally after a lot of back-and-forth we all agreed that we were excited, much more excited than we were afraid.

## V

Like everything else in Atalantaya, the Creative Tower was beautiful with great pearlescent walls, and what seemed golden floors. When I came into this time in America and in the West, a lost pilgrim from Atalantaya, I read descriptions by Christians of their Heaven as a place of golden streets and side-walks. Well, that is how the Creative Tower was, and indeed the entire Creative Gardens were—a realm of gleaming gold paths and sidewalks.

We were taken on a long journey by those who welcomed us through broad corridors of gold, filled with light, greenery, and abundant flowers, past the open doors of huge rooms in which peo-ple were diligently at work in the most complex of environments—and it was here that we saw what might have been computer technology for the first time. And by that I mean big computers on which people appeared to be working through touch key-boards in the surfaces of tables, but what they were doing I couldn't tell. Assembling, organizing, re-cording information? There was no way to know.

We passed what were obviously immense laboratories, with fantastical luracastric apparatuses, and rooms of great airy cages filled with small animals from rodents to chattering monkeys and gloriously beautiful birds. There were even owls in these rooms, and the sight of these owls sent a thrill of misery through me because, of all birds on Earth, owls most resemble the people of Bravenna. I had to ask what these birds were in order to learn that they were owls. I had only glimpsed one or two in the Wilderness lands.

In the Creative Tower, there was very little evidence of metal anywhere. There was luracastria hard and soft, translucent or opaque. And there was music filling the air in different areas, streaming out of portals in the walls—with the sound of singing and instruments, and what might have been stringed instruments of great sophistication though I didn't know it, of course, at the time.

As we walked on and on through these corridors, slowly, past door after door, I came to realize that those leading us were deliberately taking us on a tour. In fact, after we had covered more than one story of this interesting building, I came to see that we were being invited silently to observe many communities of workers in different capacities, and also areas where the workers ate and drank and welcomed us with cheerful waves and invitations to join them.

I will regret forever that I did not ask questions, that I did not ask to see libraries and archives, that

I did not ask about those tapping on the tabletops before giant monitors, that I didn't ask about everything. But at the time, I was too intrigued and too aware of my burden as the leader of our small band, the one who could actually give the signal to bring this entire world to an end.

What I did receive was the impression of immense complexity and innovation and that a great divide separated those within this building from those without. I knew no one in Atalantaya worked more than four hours a day, I'd learned that on arrival, but I had not dreamt that a technocrat class of such size had been living in the Creative Tower, and that is what I did see on this tour.

Finally we were brought to the very top floor of this tower and through a pair of large gold-plated doors heavily carved with figures and pictographs—into the receiving room of the Great One, Amel.

He sat behind a large translucent desk with his back to a transparent wall, and through that broad expanse of western-facing wall we saw that we were now at the highest point in Atalantaya, with a thousand gardened rooftops spread out in all directions below.

As for the chamber, its gold polished floors were strewn with thick woven carpets, and a grouping of couches and chairs made a cozy and comfortable space for people to sit before the desk.

The welcoming guides left us. The doors were shut.

Amel rose from the desk and came towards us with his hand out to greet us. He was simply dressed in loose shimmering red pants and shirt, and he was smiling.

"Bravenna has sent you to lure me outside of Atalantaya, am I not right?" he asked.

We were speechless.

"Sit down here," he said, gesturing to the dark-colored couches and chairs. We did exactly that. I took my place in the middle of the couch on the left side of the group, and Amel took his place on the couch directly opposite me on the right. At that very moment the sun in the western sky moved into position to blind us through the transparent wall. Amel, with the simple gesture, caused the wall to darken just enough to take away the burning glare yet leave abundant soft light.

Garekyn sat down on my right and Welf and Derek on my left.

"I knew what you were the minute you arrived," said Amel. "What do they call you now, Replimammoids still? Or do they have a new name?"

"Replimoids," I explained. "Short version of the same term?"

He nodded and gave a cheerful punctuating laugh. "Ah, the Parents," he said. "And I suppose they told you that I was a renegade Replimoid and that you've been sent here to trick me somehow into coming outside of the dome with some absurd story of a little catastrophe necessitating my presence and my presence alone. What is it this time? Talk of a discovery of a cave filled with ancient writings? Or of a wise man too old to journey to Atalantaya who must see the Great One before he closes his eyes? Or is it a case of illness in the village that is so unique and ominous that I, myself, must attend to it to save the entire Wilderness from pestilence? Or has a brutal tyrant set up a cruel regime in some small hamlet somewhere, who has agreed to surrender and give up his blood-soaked reign if I personally come to take his confession myself?"

We gave him no answer, but we were, one and all, as we know now, astonished. He went on talking. He seemed to enjoy talking, opening up, surprising us, and paralyzing us with his revelations.

"Look, I've known who you are from the moment you arrived on the planet," he said. "I don't know how the transmitters of Bravenna work, or how they broadcast film streams to their home planet and throughout the 'Realm of Worlds.' If I did, I'd hunt down every transmitter and destroy it." He smiled and shook his head. He seemed absolutely honest and authentic. "But I can tap into their film streams," he said. "I can monitor them and marvel at their lust for collected images of suffering and pain, and I did indeed see you arrive and begin your journey across the Wilderness lands. Would you like to know why I allowed you to proceed?"

"Please," I said, "if you would, tell us."

"I wanted you to see the planet for yourselves,"

he said. "I wanted you to see human beings for themselves, or human mammals as the Parents so devoutly love to call them. I wanted you to see what prevails. And of course, I wanted you to find your own way to Atalantaya, to see how easy it is for anyone from the Wilderness lands to come here."

"I see," I answered. "Are we to infer from what you've said that the Parents have lied to us?"

"Kapetria," he said, laughing again, "that is an understatement. Haven't you concluded for yourselves that they lied to you?" He sighed and collapsed against the back of the couch, his eyes moving over the translucent ceiling.

"Do I take this slowly?" he asked. "Or do I come out with it all at once?" He sat up and putting his elbows on his knees he looked me directly in the eye. "What did they tell you to do, exactly? No, wait, let me take another guess, now that I've met you and I see how sophisticated you are, how refined you are compared to most of their earlier clumsier emissaries. Are you to persuade me to return to Bravenna with you for a conference? Are they eager to support life on the planet now and stop trying to kill it and manipulate it **and use it?**" His face was flushed red.

"All right," I said. "I will tell you exactly what they told us." I glanced to my companions. No one spoke against this idea. Derek was smiling as if he found this moment supremely interesting and satisfying.

"Well then?" said Amel.

"They told us to ask you to come outside the dome, yes, and to tell you that they want to see you and speak to you outside the dome. But they also told us you would never do it. And therefore that our purpose is to stand before you together, to tell you that you have disobeyed and failed the Parents, and that you are being punished and the world is being returned to a primal cellular level so that life can develop all over again. This is to correct the ascent of mammals on this planet, and return the planet to a point from which a reptilian or avian species, or presumably even an insect species, can attain self-consciousness and become responsible beings."

Now this was my own summary but I thought it was accurate.

"I see," he said, "and how are you going to punish me and reduce Earth to primal rocks and boiling water?"

"Through a great explosion," I said. "We are to detonate it, causing Atalantaya to catch fire and explode, and from our disintegrating bodies will come a toxin, a plague that will kill all complex life-forms. The Parents assumed there were stores of explosive materials on the island of Atalantaya. They said that when we detonated, the explosion would detonate those stores."

"And you believe that these powerful explosive materials are in your bodies?" he asked. "That the toxin is in your bodies?"

"This is what they told us. They told us to come

here, get inside the dome, get an audience with you, and then detonate. As I've explained, they did allow that if we could persuade you to come out of the dome and talk to them, that maybe this disaster could be averted. But frankly, I'm not sure they were telling the truth with this. They assume that you won't leave the protection of the dome, and they have emphasized that we were created for this one purpose—destroying you and life on Earth as it is now—and they expect us to fulfill this purpose."

He fell silent. He appeared to be brooding. And overall, he gave the impression of an emotional and sensitive being, not any sort of cool or detached genius. In fact, throughout this conversation he was seeming more like Derek than any other one among us. He was seeming hot blooded and distinctly mammalian. I couldn't help but wonder about the mixture of elements given him by the Parents.

Suddenly he rose to his feet and motioned for us to follow him. "I want to show you something," he said. And when we were all facing the inner wall to the left side of the entrance of the room he made a motion which caused the wall to light up, revealing four strange images. I recognized them immediately as images of us which appeared to show our exterior features and interior features. I could tell this by the outlines, the hair, the female morphology and the male morphology but the images were not pictures so much as vibrant and alive color paintings which showed a complex network of veins or threads all through the interior of our bodies, and small innumerable organs, perhaps, which I couldn't recognize as human. The tiny organs were threaded all through our torsos and our limbs. In some places the weblike circuitry of veins and threads was much denser—in our hands, in our feet, in our necks, and in our heads.

Now understand. We all had a rough idea of what composed a human being. We knew this from the information implanted in us: we knew humans like all mammals had hearts, lungs, reproductive organs, circulatory systems, brains, eyes, et cetera.

But we could see from these images that we did not possess these organs. Indeed, there were no brains in our heads according to these strange images. And I knew what a brain was, obviously, and I knew therefore that our consciousness command centers had to be a unique type.

"These are scans taken of your bodies," Amel said. "These were taken when you passed through the entrance to the ferryboat to Atalantaya. They are not of the highest quality. I can provide you with much more detailed scans of your interior workings if you want them. But this is what you are. Replimoids indeed. Now do you see anywhere in these scans anything that indicates your bodies contain toxins or explosives?"

"No, but we don't know what we are looking at or what a toxin or explosive looks like," I said. "We could be seeded with these elements in ways that don't show up on your scans. Perhaps there are seeds in us of explosives that are so tiny the eye can't see them."

"Well, that's true," Amel acknowledged. Then with a wave of his hand he brought up another image that was clearly an image of himself, inside and out. And he possessed the organs of a human being. I recognized his red hair, his greenish-blue eyes, his pale skin, and I studied the interior of his body.

Now this was the first time I'd seen such a scan of a human, yes, but I saw all that I expected to see in a human: heart, lungs, veins, and the brain in the skull behind the eyes.

"So they didn't make you," I said. "You're not a Replimoid."

"No, I'm not," he said. "But I am apparently the first human being they ever forcibly and stealthily and immorally removed from this planet. And what I became in their hands is the enhanced creature you see before you, ever resilient and self-renewing, and seemingly immortal." Once again, his face was flushed, and he was clearly angry.

He gestured for us to return to the couches, and then he spoke aloud to someone or something we couldn't see and asked for wine and food for all of us. We sat quietly looking at him as he sat there reflecting, waiting, as emotional as before.

Whisper-quiet servants came and set a long broad table before us, and then laid out bowls of fruit, and of the sweet vegetables people eat raw, and some fresh-baked bread, very thin, and hot—like the naan in Indian restaurants today. And a clear wine was poured into the usual luracastria goblets.

"Go ahead, please. Eat and drink," said Amel. He appeared sad. He himself sat back and folded his arms as if he was not hungry or had too much on his mind to eat. His curly red hair fell down over his eyes and he brushed it back with annoyance.

I'm not sure any of us enjoyed a morsel of food, but it was considered courteous to eat in this world when a host offered food and drink, and so we did. I found the wine flavorful but safely weak. I took only sips. I wanted to keep my mind absolutely clear. I was pondering the scans we'd seen, going over in my memory the images. No brain visible, no heart visible in our bodies, and what were the tiny organs threaded all through our arms and legs and neck and head? Where were our brains? Why did I hear a heartbeat from myself? Why did I hear the heartbeat of Welf or Garekyn or Derek? Where was the physical command center of our intelligence and our bodily systems? Why were the networks of seed and vein so much denser in our hands and feet, in our necks, in our heads?

Finally Amel began to speak again. "I was born in the far north, in the cold lands, where snow is frequent and people wear heavy skins just to survive. My tribe was much paler than the people of the southern climes." He paused and took a deep breath as though all this caused him pain. "But even for a pale tribe I was a mutant, a green-eyed red-haired child in a world of dark hair and dark eyes, and my skin looked sickly. In our tribe, I inspired fear and distrust. And so my parents, after many painful mishaps had befallen me, decided to sacrifice me to the gods they believed in. They decided this when I was twelve years old. They laid me on an open altar in the forest and left me there, bound and helpless. In time wolves or bears would come, or the wildcats. I had been drugged and did not care too much. I was frankly glad to be out of the world where I was constantly ridiculed and persecuted. It was then that the Bravennans removed me from the planet. I spent years on Bravenna growing to my full height, and being educated by the Parents and being altered into the being I am now. But! Understand this!"

He sat forward and looked into my eyes again. "Understand this," he repeated. "Everything good in me came from my birth as a human being, my childhood among human beings, my parents on Earth, my teachers on Earth, the wise and the kind of my village, the children brave enough to befriend me and pity me—and not so much from the superstitious and fearful notions of my tribe, but from the underlying morality of the tribe!" He pressed his lips together. Again we saw anger and emotion. "It is from nurture, **mammalian nurture**, that all human beings derive their sense of what it is to be loved, to be cared for, to feel this world as a good place, to feel life as something good. And it is from mammalian nurture that they derive their crucial sense of fairness."

Fairness. How many times had I shared my amazement with the others on how all the human beings we encountered seemed to have an innate sense of fairness?

"Are you following me?" Amel asked. This time he looked to each and every one of us. "Do you see what I am saying? Do you think the Parents care about what gives life value for the people of this planet? Do you think they really mean their pious nonsense about reptilian and avian ascendant species being superior? Did they tell you all their pious ideas about the gentleness and wisdom of reptilian ascendant species or the patience of avian species? Did they discourse forever on the evils of hot-blooded mammals? They are puppet masters! Do you know what that means? Have you seen the puppet shows in the city?"

We all nodded because we had.

"They are liars!"

Suddenly Garekyn couldn't contain himself any longer. "But why would they lie?" he asked. "Why would they seek to control human beings as if humans were puppets? What's the point if not to return the planet to a primal state for the good?"

"The good of what?" Amel said. He pounded his right fist on his knee. "What good? But they're lying about wanting to do this." He sighed and threw up his hands. "I cannot prove this to you without destroying one of you, but I wager there are no explosive devices or toxins in your bodies! They have lied to you."

"But what is the point of the lie?" asked Welf.

"To foment trouble!" he said. "So that you would come here and seek desperately to lure me out of the dome and into exposure to their monitors! This is just the latest ploy! They want to take me prisoner, and stop the manufacture of luracastria!"

"But why?" Welf pressed.

"Don't you see what I've done? I've built a city here!" Amel used his word for city, of course, but the word meant huge, complex, infinitely more than a village. It meant metropolis. "And," he said holding up his finger for our attention. "I have sheltered innumerable human beings in this city from the prying transmitters of Bravenna! And I am building outposts along the coasts all over the world protected by luracastria. True, there are only a handful now, but eventually there will be thousands! You've seen our great luracastria plants, you've seen our plants for cleansing the water, and for using it for energy. You've seen our solar plants. We can make a world on which they cannot spy, a world protected from their conniving, a world on which they cannot build more of their plans to foment violence and suffering on the planet! They don't want a better ascendant species here. They want more war, battle, violent struggle, human against human!"

"I knew it," said Derek in a small voice.

"But why do they want that?" demanded Welf again.

"Be respectful," I whispered to him.

"No, let him ask," said Amel. "Let him ask his questions. I will answer. I will always answer! I like it that he asks, that all of you ask and speak up and express your **souls**!"

This was the first time we'd heard the word "soul"—that is, one concise word containing multi-meanings of the same concept.

"What is a soul?" asked Derek.

"Your soul is your inner being, your thinking, reasoning, loving, choosing inner being!" said Amel. "Your capacity to stand up for what is right. Your capacity to fight against what is wrong. Your capacity to choose even to die for what you believe is right. That's your soul." He shook his head. He wasn't satisfied. "It is the irreducible part of you that combines conscience, and deep feeling."

"I see," I said. "And you believe that we have souls? We? The Replimoids?"

"Yes," he said. "Absolutely. I know you do! I've watched you. Even if I'd never seen you before, I would have detected your souls here in this room. But why do you even ask?"

"Because we were made for one purpose," I said. "We weren't birthed from human beings like you were. We were grown on Bravenna." I could see he wasn't understanding me. "I suppose I would have expected **you** to tell **us** that we had no souls! I suppose I expected that you would tell us we were tools especially made to appear human, but that we were not human."

"Who said you had to be human to have a soul?" he asked. "Look, I've been on this planet for thousands of years. Everything that is self-conscious and capable of thought and love has a soul. The soul emanates from self-consciousness. The soul is the expression of self-consciousness. The soul is generated by organized self-consciousness. When they endowed you with self-consciousness, when they bred you out of Earth elements to the point where self-consciousness emerged in you, they put you on the road to having a soul. When you began to think and feel, a soul was formed within you as the result of your thinking and feeling."

"I see what you're saying." I looked at Derek, Derek who was so often moved to tears, Derek who knew fear the way the rest of us did not, Derek who had always given himself so much more than the rest of us to the joys of music, or feasting, or drinking, or dancing. But I saw that we all had souls. It was the "I" of each one of us, the "we" of us, the "who we are" part.

I looked at Amel searchingly. "But why is this important, that we have souls, that you have a soul, that anyone has a soul? I can see that perhaps animals even have souls, the sheep, the goats, the faithful dogs of the villages, even these have partial souls perhaps. . . . But why does it matter exactly?"

"Because it's why I can't destroy one of you to show you there are no toxins in your bodies," he said. "Your soul is an expression of the precious quality of life that makes me refuse to destroy it!" He paused and then continued, staring intently at me, though of course he was speaking to all of us. "You are not 'made things' without a soul, limited by your very nature to one purpose," he said. "You are beings of conscience and feeling and the will to respond to what you know to be right. And if I killed one of you to make my point, it would be an immense cruelty to you, and you would never forgive me for it, and you would grieve for your lost brother, for his loss of the gift of life!"

"You're right, yes, I see," I said. "But let's return to what you were saying, about the Parents and what they want, and why they would lie, and why they would seek to control humans as if humans were puppets!"

"Yes, that is the crucial issue here," said Garekyn. "Why would they make us, grow us, instill knowledge in us, and let these souls develop or emanate from us, and then send us here on a dishonest mission?"

"They want trouble, to make trouble. They want you to foment conflict. They hoped very likely that you'd be captured in the villages and revealed to be non-human, and that you would all be brought here with much fanfare to be executed by me in defiance of them and their machinations. Or they wanted you to attempt to kill me, and maybe even to damage the great dome of Atalantaya! They wanted conflict, trouble. Who knows? Look what happened when they returned me to the planet!"

"But what did happen?" I asked.

"They sent me down here, equipped with immense knowledge and godlike strength, to enslave the tribes, to install transmission stations for them far and wide so that their streaming could take place. And I was told that when this mission was complete, I was then to loose a plague on the planet that would kill huge numbers of the population. 'This is desirable for the world's improvement,' they told me. But they knew, positively knew, I'd never do it. They knew that I'd come to love my fellow human beings, I'd come through working with them and living with them and ruling over them to see their inherent virtues, their values, to let my soul warm to their souls! And they knew I'd refuse to loose the plague, and that I'd start to do things in direct contradiction to their orders, and thereby make conflict, **make new things happen!**"

"I see what you're saying," I said. "And I see the similarity between your mission and our mission, and I can see why they might have known full well that you wouldn't fulfill your purpose and we wouldn't fulfill ours. But why? Why do they want to 'make new things happen,' as you put it?"

"Yes, what is the point?" asked Garekyn.

Amel waited. He was looking at each of us in turn and then his eyes settled on Derek.

"Ooooh, I see," said Derek. "The Chambers of Suffering! The films, the streams! They are feeding off the suffering of the planet!"

The most brilliant smile spread over Amel's face.

I was astonished. It seemed obvious, then too obvious, and then undeniably obvious!

"They feed off it!" Derek went on. "They want to watch this . . . people weeping and screaming in grief and pain! This is why their film feeds are filled with scenes of people dying and those around them in agony as they die, agony worse than that of the dying!"

"Yes," said Amel. "I believe that is exactly what is happening! And they value this planet all the more for its mammalian ascendant species because no creature in the universe suffers like a hot-blooded self-aware mammal."

"But this is an unspeakable lie!" I whispered. I shook my head. I didn't want to believe it, but I couldn't not believe it.

"When I came back here to this planet," said Amel, "war was as common as peace, and tribes fought tribes and murdered and raped, and sacrificed their own children and their enemies to their gods, and the planet was covered in blood-soaked altars and blood-soaked groves where men sought to placate the storms and the snows and the fire of the volcano or the rages of the sea with bloodshed and death and pain! And they loved it! The Bravennans loved it, and their transmitting stations which I myself installed all over this planet in places I can no longer find or recognize—these are their means of receiving this suffering, receiving it and devouring it!"

"But how?" I asked. "They enjoy it, yes, I have seen this with my own eyes. They love it, and they lied to us about this, but how do they devour it exactly?"

"I don't know," said Amel with obvious frustration, "but I do know that suffering itself, emotion, pain, agony, rebellion, these things give off an energy just as the sun does, and just as the raging sea does. . . . But I have not been able to discover the science of it! I have **not** been able to discover how the energy given off by emotion can be translated into the physical or biological realm! It's driving me mad." He paused, then went on. "This is a biological world. Biology is the reality of this world. Soul is generated by biology, by the chemistry of the brain rooted in biology. All things spiritual emanate from the biological. And they must have some way of translating the energy of anguish into a definable force in the biological realm."

This struck me as powerfully fascinating.

"I understand this in a crude way," said Welf.

"When we were drinking and dancing during the Wilderness Festival, I felt the energy of the crowds around me—."

"Exactly!" said Amel.

"I felt it, it was palpable and I felt myself grow more excited and more . . . more delirious . . . on account of the delirium around me. And at the Meditation Center when someone told a tragic story—."

"Yes, exactly!" said Amel.

"—I felt the energy from that story; I felt it enter me and make me cry," said Welf.

"Exactly!" said Amel. "And when you see heroism, great heroism as in a battle, this too gives off energy, and you are energized to fight beyond your normal endurance. And when you gather and sing around a great tower being planted and grown in the earth, you feel the energy and your own body warms and quickens and gives off more energy to join the communal energy." He looked to each of us for a nod, for confirmation, and we gave it willingly.

"Well, somehow," he said, "the Parents thrive on the suffering and other less dramatic emotions of the human beings of this planet—anger, resentment, sorrow, grief—and they are, I suspect, transmitting their film streams of hot-blooded life on Earth all over the 'Realm of Worlds' to those cooler species, cold species like them who also thrive off this suffering, off the pain that human mammals feel! And for all I know this not only gives them delight, intoxicating delight, but this fuels Bravenna itself and fuels its lights and its warm air, and the laboratories in which you were developed and grown! It is their fuel—our human suffering!"

"This is appalling!" said Derek. "This is cruel."

"Yes, it is very cruel," said Amel, "and the Parents are very cruel. Did you not see that?" He paused, then went on. "Someday I will discover how this energy is being translated into something biological or measurably physical. I will discover it."

At this point, Derek began to cry. Just as he's crying now. Because of course we had all seen it, the unspeakable cruelty of the Parents developing us and growing us and offering us beautiful music in our cradles and then telling us that we were meant to destroy ourselves, to lose our lives as we destroyed everything on this planet.

In a hushed voice Derek began to talk about it, talk about the cruelty of the Parents, and talk about how the deathbed scenes in the film streaming had torn at his "soul," and how he loathed and detested the Parents and would fight them forever, and fight everything that was cruel.

"Ah, but be wise," said Amel. "They want you to fight. They have bred you to fight. They would like nothing better than for you to go forth and start to try to root out every transmission base and station and to quarrel and fight with any human who sought to stop you. They want people to come to blows. They want people to shed blood. They would love to see you taken prisoner by the tribes for seeking to destroy their Chambers of Suffering!"

"The people believe suffering has value!" said Welf. "That's what I saw in the Wilderness lands. We all saw it."

"Yes, for thousands of years, the people have believed this!" said Amel. "It's the only way they can go forward in a world where there is so much suffering. They have always believed that a brave man will suffer torment but will not give in. They have believed the gods want the blood of children and the agony of those children when they die, and the agony of their parents when they see them sacrificed. And people have been bred to feed off suffering! To feed off the grief and pain of the victims of war and blood-soaked altars. **But there is no value to suffering!**"

"There is only value," said Derek, "to overcoming suffering and seeking to spare others the suffering one has known oneself!" He sat on the edge of the couch. "In the Meditation Center I saw and heard that people of all ranks understand this. They see suffering as inherently a natural evil!"

"Exactly!" said Amel. "And with luracastria, I have locked the Parents and their greedy eyes out of the lives of countless humans! And I have fought with all my being to provide a way of life in Atalantaya that does not thrive off of nor require suffering."

We sat quiet for a long moment, and then for an endless while we talked about these things. We talked about the stories we'd heard in the Meditation Centers. We talked about all the lessons we'd learned on Atalantaya and how we marveled at life here and the influence of Atalantaya and what it meant for the Wilderness lands.

"It is through example and enticement that I teach," said Amel. "Not coercion. Those tribes who war and sacrifice are banned from Atalantaya. They are not welcome in our farming or mining villages in the Wilderness lands. And that alone is the most powerful inducement for them to seek the peaceful ways."

"Yes, we've seen it," I said. "There was indeed so much the Parents never explained."

Amel laughed suddenly. "They treated you like humans treat their pets, didn't they?" he asked. "You've seen the dogs in the village? You've seen the pretty little cats and dogs people on Atalantaya are given to keeping? That's how they treated you? Am I right?"

"Yes," said Derek. He was wiping his tears away and trying to calm himself. "That is how they treated us, putting out food for us, letting us wander about, comforting us when they felt we needed it."

"And any truths or explanations that they sought to teach were just part of that comfort," said Amel. "They have sent so many bands of you here!"

"But what happened to the others?" I asked.

"Well, in the beginning, I destroyed them. I hadn't caught on. I played into their hands. I won the battles that they fomented. And they were crude, these early Replimoids, some apelike, others mechanical. They went to the very opposite extreme of what they had achieved in enhancing me. But whatever the case, I was a better leader. I won out against their emissaries. But for all I know, there are surviving Replimoids out there now." He made a gesture to include the wide world. "For all I know there are Replimoids up north building transmitting stations among the northern tribes who are far beyond my influence. There are Replimoids perhaps beyond the seas on islands that have no name. How can we know? And some Replimoids they sent in the first years of Atalantaya disappeared without a trace when I refused to go with them outside the dome—wandering back out to report the failure of their mission, I presume, and being given some other dreary task if not the making of more transmission stations."

"And no one has ever remained with you to work with you?" asked Derek. "To give you their allegiance?"

"Yes," said Amel. "They exist and they are here, and they are scattered throughout Atalantaya. But even the latest are not as complex or beautifully realized as you are. The last group before you was excellent, I have to admit. But not as fine as you are." He paused as if to ponder. "But there are a few here, yes, a very few. Alas, like me, and like you, they are sterile. They're good workers. But no new tribe can ever be grown from those of us who have been the playthings of Bravenna. Our offspring must be the promotion of love and goodness. Because that is all we can birth and nurture."

Derek gasped at this. I found myself smiling. **Our offspring must be the promotion of love and goodness.**

"I want to stay here," said Derek. He turned to me. "I want to remain with Amel and learn from Amel and serve Amel!" He looked at me, waiting for some sort of permission. "I don't care if they kill me for it. Who knows, but there aren't devices inside of us by which they are listening to us here, and devices by which they can paralyze me and punish me! I don't care! I want to be with Amel!"

"Derek, what authority have I over you?" I asked. "Any authority given me was given by Bravenna. Do what your soul tells you and what Amel will allow."

"Oh, I would so love to have your loyalty," Amel said. "You are welcome in Atalantaya no matter what you do. And do know that I have learned and profited from every single Replimoid that has ever stayed behind with me." He looked tired suddenly, crestfallen, and empty. His mind was wandering. His words had been scattered, and confused though a strong truth united all he had said.

I felt I knew why. Because, though I was exhilarated from what I'd learned, I was also shocked and wounded. The idea of the "Realm of Worlds" deliberately fomenting suffering on Earth and planting the idea that suffering had value, the idea of the "Realm of Worlds" actually using this suffering as a form of energy, was more ghastly than anything I could ever have imagined.

"You need to rest now," said Amel, "and to be alone and to talk amongst yourselves. I will give you passes that provide unlimited access to every plant, factory, Creative laboratory, or compound. You'd be welcomed in most of these places anyway, but the passes will assure you of welcome. Study what we do with luracastria, the many uses we have put it to and our continuing explorations with luracastria. Watch the workers who are experimenting with it, and its extraordinary properties."

"I want to do this above all!" I said immediately.

He drew the "passes" out of his pocket, four small disks engraved with a pictograph on one side and his face on the other, and he put these in our hands. The disks shone like gold, but were obviously made of something much lighter.

I found myself staring down at his image on the disk, the long-haired, square-faced image of a human—a human face with a faint smile to the lips and large inviting eyes.

"And when you've done that," Amel went on. "When you've roamed and studied and seen the un-limited possibilities, you come back to me. Come back anytime that you wish. You'll be received and brought up here to me. And when the time is right, I will invite you to meet the other Replimoids who have come over to me. I will bring you together with them. And we will all talk again together."

"One last question," I said. He nodded. "Have you attempted to build Replimoids yourself?"

"I have," he said. "Until recently it wasn't remotely possible but I have attempted it and I have not been successful. I have infused a few human beings, human beings who were willing, with luracastria as a step towards the building of some sort of Replimoid, but this was not successful. These subjects were of course dying of diseases I couldn't cure, but still, it was death to them when I injected luracastria into them. And I have no knowledge even in my wildest dreams of how to quicken a Replimoid into conscious life. Perhaps the perfect biology and chemistry will inevitably generate the conscious life. But I'll tell you—if the Bravennans have in fact done this, well then, I will someday be able to do it. But it must serve human beings when I do it; it must be for the good of human beings to make such creatures, and there are many reasons to be cautious."

"Why do you say 'if'?" asked Garekyn. "Aren't all the Replimoids from Bravenna proof that they can make Replimoids? I don't understand."

"We don't know the full extent of the ingredients used to create you," said Amel. "Believe me. We do study the blood, skin tissue, and other biopsied tissue from the Replimoids we have here who are willing, but we really don't know what they used to achieve what they have done. It is still possible they used humans from this planet as part of their process, and that they have lied about this."

"So they might have taken brain tissue from humans," I suggested. "They might have taken substantial amounts of brain tissue to make us?"

"Yes," he said. "That is one way of putting it."

"They led us to believe," said Garekyn, "that we were wholly grown from Earth elements in a way that did not involve parts of living human beings. At least that is how I understood them."

"Yes, but they told you I was such a freshly developed Replimoid, too, didn't they?" Amel smiled. It was a bitter smile.

"Yes, they did," I said.

Amel rose, which was obviously the signal for us to rise too, and he put his arms around Derek and held him warmly. "You are splendid creations," he said in a low reverent voice, "whoever made you and for whatever purpose. You are splendid." Then he offered each of us the same embrace and we felt a fever emanating from him, and also we felt his suffering. We felt the energy of his suffering, the energy of the pain he was experiencing due to all he had laid out in plain words for us.

"You are like music," he said looking at us, including all of us in an open gesture of his right hand. "A man or woman carves a flute from a piece of wood and brings it to the lips and breathes into it a deep feeling, and out comes an astonishing sound, a sound which surprises everyone even the musician, and then the sound develops and grows and is splendid and is a new thing, a thing born of the feeling inside the man or woman who made the flute and dared to breathe into it. You are like this. Your souls are like this. The Bravennans don't know what they have achieved. I picture them lazing about their rooms full of picture walls, drunk and drowsy and gorging on the suffering they are viewing. Enough. You are their gift to me, though they can't know it."

There were tears in his eyes. He gestured for us to go.

And as we left him, there was no doubt in our minds, none whatsoever, that he had told us the truth and that he represented all that was good of which we knew; he was, in sum, the most nearly perfect being we had ever encountered, and we had Atalantaya to back up this conviction. And our time in the Wilderness lands amongst the tribes he'd influenced only underscored it more.

Now, let me pause here in this story. You cannot imagine how stunned we were by Amel himself and by the presentation of his ideas. But think on this! Think on the surprise of Welf and me when we came alive again in the twentieth century, having slept for aeons in the ice, to discover that the major religion of the Western world taught that suffering is good and suffering has value! Think on our shock to hear people speaking of "offering up their suffering" to a God who valued it! Think of our horror to discover the mythic story of a God who sent Him-

self in human form to the planet to die a horrific
death through crucifixion to appease Himself with
His own Incarnate suffering! Think on that. Think
on our horror to see the very concept against which
Amel railed as the driving force of a religion that has
dominated the West during the time of its highest
philosophical and technological and artistic development!

Whence came such ideas? Whence came the
notion that suffering could have such value? Oh,
I don't mean the common gratitude we all feel to
those who have suffered inconvenience or pain for
the good of others, or the gratitude we feel for those
who are willing to die to protect others from harm!
But in those instances, it is the good of life which is
important. I mean now the rock-bottom idea of the
God Incarnate religion that holds that God Himself works through pain and suffering to "redeem"
His creatures from His own wrath. And then think
on the concept of eternal damnation that lies behind this God Incarnate–crucifixion religion—the
idea that the Maker of the universe, the Maker of
all worlds, has devised a place of eternal unspeakable conscious agony for all human beings who are
not redeemed through acceptance of the horrific execution of this God Himself as His own Son in the
flesh! How this God has consecrated suffering; how
He has elevated unspeakable suffering as something
to which He personally attaches unlimited value.
He requires this Hell of eternal suffering as some

sort of payment from those struggling finite humans who have disobeyed Him or failed to consecrate the suffering of God Incarnate on His fabled cross as an act of love!

And He Himself, this God, is presumed to be eternally aware in every particular of this unspeakable suffering, else how can this Hell be supported and maintained? Think of how this struck us—Welf and me—as we came alive and to consciousness again in the town of Bolinas on the West Coast of the United States. Who could have authored such a religion, we asked; who could have developed it and perfected it, were it not the Bravennans!

Yet what proof is there that such a horrific religion did come from Bravenna? None. Indeed, it seems this religion evolved to its final blood flower over a long period of time during which human beings sought to make sense of the fact of suffering and pain and a world in which there was no apparently overarching justice! And what cruelty came of such ideas. Think of the Christian saints who starved and flogged themselves; think of the cruel flogging inflicted on children due to the barbarous idea that they were inherently evil from birth. Think of the cruel executions throughout human history. Think of the morbid idea of the God of love inflicting suffering on those He favors and would bring to perfection!

But human beings are moving away from these blood-drenched fables, are they not? They are moving away in an affluent world in which people have come to suspect the value of suffering. They are gradually rejecting these old notions. The abundant New Age writings in some places contain the same themes as troubled Amel—that some force beyond this planet might be harvesting emotions, thriving off human emotions and using them for purposes known and unknown.

Well, think on it. Think on it that we saw a long-ago world in which many simple people rejected such an idea without the long history of the development of ideas that you have all inherited on this earth. We saw it there in the beginning. And it was not the teachings of Amel that inculcated these people with a suspicion of suffering. I believe that what moved the millions of Atalantayans to think in a different way was that they had never been indoctrinated with such a notion in the first place. They knew of it, they associated it with some tribes in the Wilderness lands, but that was all. And in the free and creative atmosphere of Atalantaya they believed in a world without the sanctification of suffering.

But let me go back now to us! Let me go back to that day on Atalantaya when we all but staggered out of Amel's chambers and went down and out and back into the city. We were virgin minds, newborn minds, minds unprepared for the shock of all this. Yet we were mammalian beings and we had within us the mammalian concept of fairness. We felt the human mammalian revolt against that which seems utterly monstrous!

In the days that followed we wandered the city anew paying attention now to things we'd ignored before. Nightly without fail, we sat for at least an hour in a Meditation Center. And we visited the great water compounds in Atalantaya which extracted salt from the sea and somehow harnessed the power of the flow of water to run many complex systems of Atalantaya. We also visited the great factories in which all manner of items were made, and everywhere we went we found that pilgrims like us were welcome. Seldom did we need to show our passes.

People worked in large light-filled enclosures with ample food and drink nearby, and as in the Wilderness lands, no one worked more than four hours a day, and some worked even far less. And nowhere did we see the slightest evidence of coercion.

Of course we witnessed arguments, disputes, lines formed to obtain certain goods, occasional mishaps in laboratories or factories, and occasional discontent over lack of personal promotion or recognition, but essentially we witnessed a giant system, a citywide system, a realm of enterprises if you will, in which Amel's values ruled on every level!

And slowly we came to realize something else, that we were witnessing a world in rapid development.

In the cafés of the factories and plants we heard passionate conversation of innovations and improvements and what might soon be possible, and the latest innovations in luracastria which now dominated the making of larger ships to sail the seas and talk of the possibility of flying machines. What I did come to understand was that luracastria was in fact an imprecise name for a growing family of chemicals and materials and processes related to polymers and thermoplastics as we call them today. I was so sure I had endless time ahead of me to learn about all this, and to work with luracastria myself, once I had been prepared for the life inside these laboratories.

And understand again: this was a technological paradise evolving free of economic competition and war—the two forces, economic competition and war—that have driven the technology of the world of the twenty-first century.

This was a world of justice and affluence in which innovation was driven by vision and imagination rather than brutal competition, or want, or aggression.

In my heart of hearts I was deeply troubled. And so were the others. We each confronted the paradox of the future! Were we to disobey the Parents, and it seemed almost certain that we would, would we be committing forever to a life beneath the dome of Atalantaya or, at best, a life in the city and in her satellite cities to and from which we must travel under the luracastric domes of her fleets? Would we be hunted beings, marked for destruction by Bravenna?

If we were to set foot outside the dome, would Bravenna have some way of detonating us and the lethal chemicals in our bodies?

And one thing troubled me more than anything else. Had the Parents foreseen our fall from grace? Had they foreseen—as Amel insisted—that we would never detonate or loose the toxin? And if so, then what did they actually want to happen?

The weakest part of Amel's presentation had been his insistence that the Parents wanted to foment trouble. Unless, of course, and it came to me gradually, they had sent us into this paradise to be the equals of Amel intellectually, as we say, if not scientifically—to provide the possibility of a covert movement against him as the absolute ruler? In other words, had we been created to be revolutionaries in Atalantaya? Had we been created to want to compete with Amel for control of this immense metropolis?

I couldn't quite believe such a thing. We had not been inculcated with any unusual thirst for power, nor were we innately competitive, and we were not devious or quarrelsome with anyone, let alone with one another. Nor had the Bravennans spent all that much time on condemning Amel, working us up against Amel. But then maybe there was a reason for that. Maybe they really didn't know what was going on in Atalantaya and assumed it was so evil that we would share their condemnation of it. Maybe they really couldn't grasp the sophistication of Amel's approach to the planet.

It was a mystery, and what also haunted me was something that the Parents had said during our final orientation—that if we did not fulfill the purpose they would find some other way to reduce the planet to its primal purity.

That shook me to the root, because now an immense desire was born in me—not merely to save myself and Welf and Garekyn and Derek, and Amel, the Great One, Amel—but to save the planet! I spent hours on the balcony or terrace of our apartment home gazing up at the bright "star" that was Bravenna, wondering how this planet Earth could defend itself from such interference. Were these thoughts the result of my mammalian makeup? Was my anger really bred into me? I didn't know.

Derek was beside himself. He made the rounds of the Meditation Centers nearest to us, listening, singing with the others, reciting the statement as to what is evil—that which diminishes life, destroys life—and, coming home, he would say that he could scarcely bear the sight of innocent Earth people everywhere going about their lives in the paradise of Atalantaya without the slightest knowledge that their world was perhaps about to end.

Finally, after much discussion and eventual agreement amongst ourselves, we went again to the Creative Tower to see Amel.

## VI

He received us cordially just as he said that he would, though he had to dismiss a meeting of what we would call scientific researchers in order to see us alone.

"We want to work for you," I told him. "We want to do all that we can to promote the good of life on this planet. We have conceived of ourselves as the People of a New Purpose and that purpose is never to do anything that harms life."

"I'm pleased," he said, "and this is what I have been expecting. Tonight, we'll feast here and I'll invite the other Replimoids to meet you."

The feast was a joyous one. But Amel had been kind when he had said these Replimoids were not of the same standard as ourselves. They did not even resemble us, and in fact—except for one—they were exact duplicates of one another—as many before them had been, we were told—and presentable enough, but clearly slow witted, with significant handicaps when it came to reason or initiative.

The one who was not a duplicate did not speak to us at all. I could write a book on them, the ones who did speak, but won't digress anymore on that now.

It's enough to say they were inferior models of imitation human beings—hearty males appearing healthy in all respects, slow of speech and obviously deficient in emotional expression and so slow in their natural movements and responses as to arouse any human's suspicion as to what they were. I saw them as foot soldiers in Bravenna's war on the planet, whereas we were Bravenna's attempt at espionage, and when the feasting was over, I wasn't surprised that Amel asked only one—the silent one, the one who had not been designed on the same template—to remain behind for a private session with us.

This one was named Maxym, a being with dark reddish-brown skin and dark wavy reddish-brown hair, very neatly groomed, and perhaps the shabbiest and most indifferently attired creature I'd seen in Atalantaya. He was the only one present who had not attired himself especially for the evening.

As we gathered on the couches again for serious talk, Amel told us Maxym was among the last team of Replimoids sent to the planet before us. There had been three in the group, and the other two had long ago disappeared.

I didn't say so, but I couldn't see anything wrong with this Replimoid, that is, nothing that made him seem in the least inferior to us. But perhaps Amel knew of traits which I couldn't perceive.

"Maxym came many years ago," Amel explained. "More than three human lifetimes in years. And Maxym was with me when I built the first luracastric dwellings on the island. It is Maxym who sees to all the Meditation Centers on Atalantaya and develops new Meditation Centers as the population increases. That is his passion, providing places where souls can meditate and reflect."

"That is not all I do," said Maxym. He had had a rather dreamy expression on his rather solemn face as Amel described him. But when he spoke up he commanded everyone's attention. His face was perfectly oval, and his features balanced. He lacked any of the calculated individualizing faults that we have. Perhaps that was the character of his inferiority. He'd been made too ideally perfect, and maybe the other two with him had been exact duplicates.

"I will never recover the sense of well-being I knew on Bravenna," he said in a deep impressive voice, "and there is no redemption for me since my defection, but I have done what I believed to be right."

"This is surprising," Derek said. "Can you explain? I never felt a sense of well-being on Bravenna. I was disturbed from the outset by the film streams and confused when I was told that I was to die in fulfilling my purpose. What was it that gave you a sense of well-being?"

Maxym gazed on Derek—there is no other verb for it—as if from a lofty height and then explained in a subdued voice, almost a monotone, "Perhaps you spent too little time on Bravenna," he said. "I was part of something bigger than myself when I was on Bravenna. I was part of a great and creative vision. And though I have devoted my life to Amel, I have never known the complete acceptance by any group since the days of Bravenna when I and my brothers were being prepared for our mission—to kill Amel, and destroy what he had done."

"What happened to your brothers?" I asked.

He smiled bitterly and shook his head. He looked like a human being of maybe twenty-five years. Prime of life as it was then. We were from the same design in that regard.

"Who knows what became of them?" Maxym replied. "They lacked the fortitude to choose." He looked at me intently and I found myself uncomfortable with his hostile expression. "They fled Atalantaya," he said. "Perhaps the Bravennans destroyed them. How should I know? That was long ago, before the great dome rose over Atalantaya. People came and went, came and went. There was something craven in them. They were afraid of Amel, afraid of Bravenna, afraid of me. We've heard nothing of them since."

Amel looked off as Maxym spoke. I think Amel had heard all this before. He looked faintly sad, but perhaps he was simply thinking of other things.

"And you don't feel part of this magnificent Atalantaya?" asked Garekyn. "You chose for Amel, but do not feel part of all this?" No answer. "We've been in love with Atalantaya since we arrived," he went on. "And we were in love with Earth before."

Now Maxym gazed from his lofty spiritual height on Garekyn and said with amazing force, "Amel doesn't give these people enough! Amel has never understood. If there is a Maker beyond these skies, then our highest calling is to do the will of that Maker, to open ourselves, our hearts, our souls, as Amel is always saying, to the Maker who will guide us to be what he wants us to be."

Amel turned and glared at Maxym as if he'd had enough. "And what if there is no Maker?" he asked. "When have you ever seen the slightest proof of any Maker?"

"The Maker offers us creation itself as proof of his greatness," said Maxym, "and we are to seek his will in what we see in the creation, in the green grass, in the trees, in the stars above. Not build great edifices of our own to tempt the wrath of the Maker with our presumption and ingratitude."

They went on arguing, just Maxym and Amel, Maxym pushing at Amel with his assertions ever harder. Maxym believed life was too easy in Atalantaya. Maxym believed its people were lazy and selfish. Maxym believed Amel had fostered a population of pampered beings who never became true adults. Maxym believed in the superiority of those who struggled in the Wilderness lands.

"When will you realize," Maxym asked, "that Earth doesn't need luracastria and all the dazzling personal enrichment you have used to corrupt the population! When will you realize that you have taken upon yourself an authority that you do not have?" Maxym's eyes were large and dark brown and searching and accusatory. "You have robbed these people of ambition. You have robbed them of the capacity for deep concerns. You have robbed them of the opportunity to grow in spirit."

I sat listening to all this, realizing something quite remarkable—that Amel apparently allowed this being to live here in his service, though they violently disagreed on these vital distinctions, and therefore Amel must have had some use for Maxym that we could not fully understand.

At the end of a particularly nasty exchange, perhaps one of the most heated I'd ever witnessed between any two beings, Maxym rose to his feet, hurled his wineglass at the faraway translucent wall and stormed towards the doors. Then turning back he declared with fierce unnatural volume, a volume no ordinary mammal could modulate, "You will see. You will see in the end that in your hatred of Bravenna, in your endless defiance of the Parents, you have led the inhabitants of this planet to reject that which may well be what the Maker has always wanted—penance, and self-abnegation, and self-denial. You have cast doubt on the inherent value of denying oneself, starving oneself, disciplining oneself to know things spiritual that cannot be learned in the midst of endless feasting and drinking and dancing and surrendering to one's appetite to couple day in and day out!"

Amel sat calmly facing him, with one arm on the back of the couch, and now it was Amel who gazed on Maxym as if from afar. "Maxym, Maxym, you make Makers where there are no Makers, and endow them with powers where there is no power, and all to assuage your endless guilt!" He sighed. His voice remained level. "Bravenna has never punished you for your defection," he said. "I have never punished you for your assault on me. And so you devise a Maker to punish you, some great awesome being beyond Bravenna, to make you miserable. You break my heart."

"Break your heart!" cried Maxym. He came close again and then did something that struck me as most unwise. He came up behind the couch and leaned over Amel menacingly. But Amel did not respond. Now, had any being come this close to me, and leaned over me in this manner, I would have moved away. But Amel sat there, staring off, as if this were nothing threatening to him and only barely interesting. "What heart do you have to break?" Maxym asked. "What are you but a Replimoid, the same as I? You have no heart. And you have no soul."

So there it was, the distinction that Derek had alluded to when we had gathered here before—the obvious question perhaps as to whether a thing developed and bred on Bravenna could have an "I" to it, a "me" to it that was as authentic as the "I" or "me" of human beings.

Suddenly Amel stood and faced Maxym. "I was

born on this planet," he said. "I was born on this planet!" he repeated, slightly raising his voice. The red flared in his cheeks. "I am of this planet, and you forget that, and I tell you anything that is sentient, self-conscious, possessing a sense of fairness, a sense of right and wrong, has a soul. You have a soul! These beings here, Kapetria and Welf and Garekyn, and Derek—they have souls."

Maxym shook his head as if he were genuinely disappointed. He turned his attention to me. "Follow him, will you? Work for him, will you? I tell you, someday the Maker will bring him and the offspring of his pride and greed to ruin!"

And then off he went out the double doors without closing them and down the golden corridor, his heavy steps echoing off the walls.

With a wave of his hand, Amel made the doors close.

"Well, you see for yourself why there are likely not many other converted Replimoids amongst us," he said, "especially not of the complex kind. Bravenna poisons what it creates. Maxym is poisoned. He lives as one who is poisoned, unable to taste, to feel, to see, dying every day that he lives because he insists upon dying."

"Why do you keep him as part of your family?" asked Derek. He was genuinely puzzled. I wanted to know this as well.

"Because I love him," said Amel with a sad smile. "And he is immortal as I am immortal. I love you for the same reason. I have had lovers. I have had wives. I have lost them all. I can't share this immortality of mine with anyone." He sighed. "But there's more to it," he said. "I would rather have him here in Atalantaya shaking his fist at me, than out in the Wilderness lands fomenting his worship of the Maker among the tribes." He shrugged. "But someday, he will no doubt wander out into the Wilderness—and he will find infinitely more appreciation for his fear-inspiring ideas than he ever finds among us."

I want to pause here. I want to ask you all—Lestat, David, Marius, all of you: do you have any idea why I have given time and space here to this Maxym? You know what is about to happen to Atalantaya, and you know what happened to us. All of us. You likely can easily surmise what happened to Amel. Well, I'll tell you why I have told you this story. Because I suspect this Replimoid, Maxym, too survived the destruction that was soon visited on all of us. But not bodily as we did. I suspect that he exists as surely as Amel exists, and that his name is now Memnoch, who creates astral traps for unwary souls.

I have no proof of this. It's theory. But this is what I believe. And if this is so, I want to examine this creature when he's incarnated for what I can learn—not from his particle body but for the invisible and subatomic neural circuitry that controls it, just as Amel's neural circuitry sustains all of you.

But we can talk about this in detail later. Suffice it to say that in all your writings, the Vampire Chronicles, no two spirits command the same attention as Memnoch and Amel, and I do want to explore very much this spirit Memnoch, though my first goal is of course to understand and learn about Amel, to know the subatomic anatomy of Amel.

And when we do come to examine this subatomic anatomy, we will be examining the anatomy of a soul.

But let me return to that night, that night of all nights!

As the hours passed, Amel confided in us his theory once more that all sentient beings generate souls, and souls have their own intricate anatomy and organization which gives off an energy, an energy that Amel believed was irresistible to Bravennans who had been harvesting the misery and suffering of the planet for thousands of years.

"I have often wondered," he said, "if they have found a way to harvest souls. Imagine, if you will, what this would mean for these monsters who thrive off the energy of the invisible part of us, if when the lives of men and women are finished here, Bravenna takes their souls."

I thought it was all too fanciful, but Amel would not let go of it and I could see then how much more interested he was in the fields that later epochs would call philosophy or theology than he was in the actual biological sciences which he had used to such advantage to shape and sustain his world.

"What if the transmitting stations, wherever they are, can draw to themselves the souls of all those who have finished their biological life, and what if these souls are drawn to Bravenna as surely as all those moving pictures are drawn, and what if the Bravennans use those souls as a concentrated form of energy, a concentrated expression of energy, enhanced and deepened and perfected by suffering so that those souls are like ripe and perfect fruit to the Bravennans and maybe even to others in the 'Realm of Worlds'?"

He went on describing this, how it seemed to him that the souls of human beings, thanks to their mammalian nature, might have a wholly different flavor than the souls of other sentient species, and this would make the souls irresistible to Bravennans.

Even as I regarded this as utterly far-fetched and unprovable, Garekyn took an interest and began to speculate along with Amel.

"And what if," asked Garekyn, "that is why they want to foment war on this planet, because they will have more souls to harvest, somehow traveling through the transmission stations as they are released from the biological bodies, souls drawn Heavenward through the beam of the transmission station as if through infinitely long tunnels of light?"

"I can't bear the thought of such a thing, such a horrible thing," Derek said more than once. Welf, always the practical one among us, simply shrugged and said that it was something one could never know for sure.

We went over all our experiences on Bravenna, and Amel listened attentively, but there was little to support such an idea as the harvesting of souls.

"I can believe," I said finally, "that they are feasting off the suffering of this planet, and fomenting it. I believed that really from the first moment it was suggested to me because I saw the film streams, and saw what they prized above all, and it was always suffering; but unless the soul itself is a spiritual and physical emanation of a human mind—virtually composed of the experience and suffering of that mind, unless the soul is materially changed by suffering and generated perhaps by the longing of the individual to understand its own suffering, well, then I don't know how it would work."

"Now that is an interesting observation," said Amel, "and I had never thought of it, but perhaps you are onto something, that suffering itself helps to generate the soul."

"I meant the energy given off by suffering, of course," I explained, "that it might organize into a soul. To put it another way, a being's unsatisfied curiosity might generate that human being's soul. And the fuel might be the collective suffering endured by that human all through his or her life, and some other intangible ingredient, perhaps, such as an overview, an attitude, a perspective on life, that too might help the formation of a soul."

I can remember this ever so clearly, this long conversation, our being gathered there and talking to one another as though we had all of the time in the world.

"This is what gives me the greatest hope," said Amel at one point with great excitement. "It is that if we can imagine a question, then there must be an answer to it. And it is merely a matter of hard work and perseverance to find that answer. In essence, no question can be imagined by us that is unanswerable by its nature. Does that make sense to you?"

I for one said that it did. So did Garekyn. I could feel the workings of my own mind as we so passionately discussed these things, I could feel my mind exercising itself just as one might feel one's legs when running and leaping and dancing. And it felt so good to me to be possessed of a mind and to be possessed of these questions.

"Whatever I do here," I said to Amel, "may it not have to do with the study of the concept of soul? May I not work on trying to discover how to measure the soul?"

"I would love for this to be your work," Amel answered immediately. Welf raised his hand with a little mocking laugh and said he would be delighted to go along with it, because he was eager to see just how I was going to measure something as completely imaginary as souls.

"And what if you do prove it," Garekyn asked, "that beings have souls and souls are energy and that these souls can be harvested from Earth's atmosphere, what then will you do? Can you ever strike out at Bravenna? Can you ever do more than shake your fist at the sky?"

My memory of the next few minutes falters. Amel protested almost angrily that what he could do was hunt out every transmitting station and destroy it, and close up every Chamber of Suffering in existence, but then he lamented that this would make him the cruel "headman" that he had never wanted to be.

As for Derek, he seemed blissfully happy in the midst of this conversation and went off on his own tangent as to whether the souls of those who knew joy more than anything were not finer fruit to harvest than the souls who'd known so much pain. Welf was pressing my hand, signaling me he was ready for our home bed, and some coupling, and I caught the wink of his eye and sweet smile on his lips.

What happened next? I reached for the goblet that held my wine and I took a long easy drink of it, which one can do when the wine is weak and deliciously cold, and I saw the wine moving in the goblet, sloshing from side to side, and I realized that the entire room was moving, that the furniture under us was moving, and that Amel had stood and was staring through the great western wall towards the stars.

"What is it?" Derek cried. "The island is shaking. Look, look outside, the towers are moving!"

But Amel's face was turned upwards.

"It's Bravenna," he cried out. "Bravenna is moving! Look at Bravenna!"

Suddenly we were all at the wall gazing upwards, and we watched the erratic movement of the bright star that was Bravenna when suddenly that star grew huge and exploded and out of the vast darkness came a great shower of innumerable burning stars—flying in all directions—and the blaze that was the star itself grew larger and larger as Amel screamed again, "She's coming towards us, she's breaking up! She's coming down on us—."

A horrific roar swallowed his words. From all sides came the pounding reverberations of explosions. The towers everywhere were swaying wildly as if they were dancing, and the room began to rock from side to side. I saw fire descending on Earth, exploding against the shimmering dome, and then even here in this high room, even here above the city, I heard the roar of countless human voices.

Below us, people ran in panic over rooftops, and smaller buildings were falling sideways into the buildings next to them. From the balconies and open windows people were tumbling. Huge ocean waves the color of fire splashed against the great dome as if reaching to extinguish the endless flames.

The sounds of the explosions increased in volume until one deafening explosion after another shocked us and paralyzed us. Huge cracks and fissures broke up the walls.

Then great knives of fire appeared to slice through the dome itself.

"The luracastria, it's melting," Amel cried. I could

see it. We all saw it, the towers melting, the dome melting. Our building shuddered. I fell into Welf's arms. Amel grabbed hold of me and ran with me towards the doors, waving for the others to follow, while with his other hand he dragged Derek along beside him. "It's the whole island; it's the whole world."

A fierce wind broke through the shattered walls and the fire blinded me. The roar of the population was as loud as the roar of the sea. I felt rain against my face but it wasn't rain. I could feel myself falling, and I felt Welf against my ear saying, "Hold on to me, Kapetria, hold on. Hold on. Hold on." I screamed for Derek and Garekyn. I screamed for Amel. I heard Amel's voice but I couldn't see him.

Down we fell as flames rose all around us. The surging water devoured us and then released us while innumerable humans screamed piteously for help. We were in a street which had become a roiling river of the drowning. The water was sucked away from us and again we tumbled as if into a fathomless abyss. Towers were melting, entrapping thousands of tiny faceless humans in the glistening sluggish liquid that had been the luracastria—thousands around me splashing and screaming for help when there was no help. Broken furniture, tables, chairs, traveling pods, and debris covered the waters—battered and broken trees. We were caught in a whirlpool. The planet itself had cracked beneath us. Down we went in darkness, only to rise to the surface once more.

Then I saw Amel, saw him silhouetted against an endless wall of flame. Where we stood, where we were, I could not tell. But there was Amel.

"Atalantaya," he cried, but how I could have heard him, or heard anyone cry out any words, I don't know. "Atalantaya!" he roared over and over again. He shook his fists at the Heavens. "Atalantaya," he cried again and again.

The oozing luracastria was molten gold on the surface of the water as if it were burning. Boats, thousands of them, it seemed, surrounded us, but desperate people were capsizing them and pulling them under as they sought to climb on board.

Amel was gone. Derek and Garekyn were gone.

Welf held me, cradling my head with his hand. The rain stung my arms, my neck, my face. We were riding the surges of the water helplessly, and I saw the dead around me—lurid faces with vacant eyes, bodies stripped naked, and some headless, infants bobbing on the surface, lifeless limbs.

Beams of light pierced the thick mist, and loud voices called out to people to seek the tunnels. I heard the word "tunnel" again and again. But how could we seek the tunnels? We had no idea where they were. I called frantically for Derek and for Garekyn. Welf did the same.

A mass of struggling humans was swept against us by a fierce current, and masses of debris, of mingled wood and stone, raced past us with people atop these masses as if they were ships.

A great white ferryboat rose in front of us with people high on the deck above waving and dropping ropes for those below. But the boat vanished as suddenly as it had appeared. Then came another, like the ghost of a boat in the water, monstrous in size and fading into nothingness as the storm raged.

Another explosion stunned us and deafened us, and then came another and another. Belching smoke, caustic burning smoke, and the flickering blaze of flames were all I could see.

The stench of the smoke suffocated us. The current tossed us up and then tried to swallow us but we kept riding it, rising again and again no matter how deeply we'd been drawn down.

Finally we realized we were in the open sea.

Atalantaya had opened up and broken apart and expelled us into the sea. We could see her distant fires blazing but the waves were of immeasurable size, and though we never stopped calling out, we knew we had lost Derek and Garekyn.

We were never to see them—or Amel—again.

The cries of the desperate and the dying were gone.

The rain drenched us as surely as the sea. Yet no matter how dense the veil of the rain, we could still see the distant spectacle of Atalantaya—the immense blazing island shaken still by one eruption after another—growing ever more distant as a great silence and darkness engulfed us in which we couldn't even hear one another, or even see one another, our bodies pressed together, our arms tight around one another as the hours passed.

Hours. It is wrong to speak of hours. There was no time. Once in a while a small craft would pass us, broken and empty, or a massive tree would slam against us, its giant tangle of roots like a huge multi-fingered hand reaching vainly for help. We were alone, perfectly alone. But we had each other and my soul ached for the panic and the horror of those who had no one, those who had perished in this maelstrom without another soul to embrace, to hang on to, without loving arms around them, those who were truly alone. Was Derek alone? Was Garekyn alone?

Dawn never came. No sun ever broke through the torrent of rain that descended on us without cease. The acrid stench of smoke or fire was gone. And the water grew icy cold, and the world was white and blinding, and we climbed out of the water and we trudged through a featureless world of snow.

What had become of the Wilderness lands? Where were the verdant jungles and forests? Where were the fields of high grass and wild grain? Where were the thousands who had lived in the villages and settlements?

Our garments were in shreds. And the cold hurt us but it could not kill us. It numbed us. It robbed us of stamina. It closed down on our minds.

Sometime or other, and for a little while, we found

the shelter of a cave from which we saw fire on the horizon, the sky beautifully illuminated by this fire with streaks of gold, and red and even green. How indifferent seemed this beauty, how unconscious of witness, yet it touched me and calmed me and I dozed watching it—and then the earth beneath us was shaking violently once more, and terrified of being buried alive, we tried to run again.

Up and up we climbed through what must have been mountains, and soon we saw nothing but whiteness, and the spectacle of fire was no more. Gone forever, it seemed, was anything remotely like fire, and all was lost in a blizzard and in that blizzard we struggled until life itself was nothing but struggle, nothing but seeking for shelter when there was no shelter—until finally I remember wrapping my arms around Welf, holding him as tightly as I could possibly do it, and saying, "I can go no farther," and the last thing I heard was Welf whispering my name as my eyes closed.

You know now that the four of us survived. You know that we eventually emerged from our frozen graves, and you know how we found one another. But there are other stories someday to be told.

Welf and I opened our eyes many centuries after the destruction of Atalantaya on a later barren and wintry world. We lived a lifetime among the tribes of hearty humans who struggled against the snow and ice eternally as the very conditions of life, with no memory of the great temperate Wilderness lands that had once covered so much of Earth and no memory of such a thing as Atalantaya, though their legends told of ancient gods and goddesses and fallen worlds. The first time we came to consciousness we survived perhaps for three or four human generations before retreating, exhausted and discouraged and broken, to the ice to freeze again.

And there was another awakening after that in a time of simple villages and towns where once again the inhabitants knew nothing of a great metropolis that had once ruled the world.

Derek can tell you stories of the lives he lived, and what drove him in each instance to retreat to the high mountain caves of the Andes to sleep once more. Garekyn alone slept through the long aeons until awakened by his mentor and discoverer Prince Brovotkin, who was then laughed at by his colleagues and his fellow European noblemen for tales of the immortal man found in the Siberian ice.

You know most of my history. You know I have worked for years for Gregory's great company, and you can easily imagine how I sought to use his immense resources to study my own body and Welf's body to better grasp our own physical makeup, with its self-sustaining resilience and mysterious organization which had never been explained to us by those who made us.

But be assured, I never cheated Gregory Duff Collingsworth. I helped develop medicines that added to his great wealth and benefited immensely by his profit-sharing programs, bonuses, and salary increases, building wealth of my own. I helped develop an artificial skin marketed by Collingsworth that has been of great help in treating burn victims. I've also contributed mightily to research on a rejuvenation drug that shows tremendous promise. I have developed sophisticated techniques for cloning that will contribute to the work in that area.

But for all the hours I've worked alone and with Welf in the sanctum of laboratories under Gregory's roof, I have never discovered the actual formula for luracastria, or come close to reproducing a thermoplastic or polymer like it. I have not, contrary to your suspicions, ever grown a Replimoid whole and complete and animated, though I have certainly struggled towards this goal for many years. I have been unable to discover whether our bodies do in fact contain a toxin that can destroy the planet if we are destroyed. I do not know whether our bodies contain explosives of some unimaginable power that can reduce the world to its primal purity once more. My hope, of course, has been to develop my own technological complex of laboratories where I can take my own personal research to new heights. And whatever I have taken from Gregory, well, I hope I've somehow repaid.

In the realm of astronomy, I have ascertained almost certainly that no asteroid comparable to Bravenna has been seen recently in the night sky. I've combed the legends of the planet and find no evidence that Bravenna or some substitute of Bravenna ever returned to Earth.

As you must infer from what I've just said, I don't know what actually happened on Bravenna that last night as we watched from Atalantaya. I don't know whether Bravenna fired some advanced weaponry on the planet, or simply exploded showering the planet with meteors which precipitated cataclysmic floods, volcanoes, fires, and eventually a rising of the sea level and a deadly winter which locked the planet for centuries in ice and snow. I have read widely among those who speculate on just such an early cataclysm and I have studied this in light of the beautiful legends of the lost kingdom of Atlantis, and there is no doubt in my mind that Atlantis is Atalantaya, and that there is indeed confirmation of a catastrophe that brought her ruin—eventually raising the level of the seas and changing the weather all over the planet.

I have discovered many things . . . but no discovery in all my years has ever been as important as my discovery of you, the blood drinkers, and your legends of Amel.

I have no doubt that Amel lives inside you. I have no doubt that this is our Amel. But he is also your Amel. I know this, and I see what you are and how precious life is to you, as it is to us. And please do understand that we see you as a priceless form of life just as we see ourselves as a priceless form of life.

And it is through you and your kindred that we

have found one another again, and through Rhosha-mandes's bloody blundering assault on Derek that we have the knowledge that we can increase our numbers without even understanding how or why. We are disposed to love you, to revere the things that we have in common, and we ask for your love.

There are many things more I could say, many observations I could make. But I have told all the truth that matters here, all the truth that may matter to Amel. We've come to you at great risk to ourselves because of Amel. But also because you are our brothers and sisters in immortality; we see kindred in you. And we trust you'll see kindred in us. In those centuries when we opened our eyes on a primitive and harsh world, we found our loneliness as immortals all but unendurable. Derek suffered the same fate. And Garekyn was suffering it when he approached Trinity Gate. We are ready to need you, if you are ready to need us.

I have told you everything, and now I see there are two hours perhaps left to the night before you have to leave us and we have to leave you. I'm yours for that time, and I hope forever, really. Ask me what you would; and I'll try to tell you the truth.

# 20

# Lestat

SHOCK. SILENCE. No one moved or spoke. All eyes remained on Kapetria. Then I heard Armand's telepathic message. **Mark the danger.**

Kapetria was right about there being two hours before sunrise. But I myself did not have the full two hours. I had at the most one hour and was very glad that the tale had been told in its entirety at one time.

Was I suspicious, incredulous, as to all we'd heard? No.

I sensed that Kapetria had presented everything truthfully. And I also knew that the tale had had a powerful impact on Amel. Throughout the telling, I had felt one subtle convulsion in Amel after another, and sometimes what amounted to a considerable disturbance, and I knew that the other vampires at the table, able to read my mind, had some dim sense of these responses as well.

At the moment when Kapetria had described the explosion of Bravenna, I saw the same images that

I'd seen repeatedly in my dreams. Others at the table had seen the same.

And at that point, the point where Amel in Kapetria's story had cried out, I felt a searing and inexplicable pain in my head.

That pain had leveled somewhat but it was still with me, and it produced a deep sense of alarm in me that I tried desperately to conceal from everyone else. I could not recall Amel ever causing physical pain in me. Yes, he'd tried to move my limbs more than once, and I'd felt a tingling and cramping in the limb. But that had not been pain. This was pain. And I knew perfectly well that the human brain had no pain receptors, and that brain tumors cause pain in humans because of the pressure they create on pain-sensing blood vessels and nerves inside the human brain.

So how was my invisible friend causing this pain? I wasn't going to ask him because others at the table would know that I was asking him, and I just didn't want them to know what was going on.

Amel gave me to know now—pain or no pain— that he wanted to ask Kapetria a question and to talk to her.

But Fareed immediately started to ask her any number of questions about luracastria and generating Replimoids that I didn't understand. The others all seemed absorbed in this—a discussion of thermoplastic and genomes, of the absolutely remarkable strength of spider silk in the natural world, and so forth and so on. Kapetria clearly loved it, this pure scientific talk replete with abstractions of dizzying opacity, and I could see Seth loved it and to some extent so did David. Gregory too was enjoying it. But I wanted to speak.

"Interrupt," said Amel, "and now." There was a sudden pain in my right hand, and then my hand jumped on the table. Kapetria stopped in midsentence and turned to me.

"Amel wants to ask you a question," I said uneasily.

She was riveted. "Please, what is he saying!" she asked. She seemed hardly able to contain herself. Derek, Welf, and Garekyn were equally eager to know.

"There's something I have to tell you first," I said. "This spirit sometimes doesn't tell the truth."

A searing pain behind my eyes nearly blinded me. I tried to lift my right hand to cover my eyes, and I couldn't. The pain intensified so that I found myself rising out of the chair, and pushing the chair backwards. I'd never known a pain inside my body of this intensity, and I was forced to close my eyes! I made some involuntary sound.

"All right, you scoundrel!" I whispered. "Stop it, or I won't tell her the question! You understand?"

The pain stopped, but only for about two seconds. It came back with renewed force. It was so intense my eyes closed again, and when I tried to reach once more for my head, my right hand was shot through and through with pain, pain ripping through every blood vessel and tendon. I could feel my nails drumming on the table, and when I struggled to open my eyes, I saw only a blinding light.

Something touched my hand. I could hear people moving. I felt a hand on my right arm. The pain continued, throbbing, as it seemed to swell behind my forehead and behind my eyes, and then I felt something being put in my hand. It was a pen.

Someone was putting my fingers around the pen, while at the same time lifting my hand, and then putting it down on paper. My left hand was covering my face. I could hear the scratch marks as my right hand wrote or drew with the pen.

**Stop the pain, stop it, do you hear me, stop it!**

When it did stop, I was seated in the chair, and Marius was standing behind me and holding my shoulders in a way that was protective and comforting.

The pad of paper was lying there in front of me. And just before Fareed took it and put it in front of Kapetria, I saw pictographs on it, crude, squiggly pictographs.

Kapetria looked for a long moment at the paper and then up at me rather helplessly. "I never learned to read them!" she said. She seemed crestfallen.

I heard a long painful sigh come from Amel.

"Tell her she is not looking in the right place for the formula for luracastria. She should look inside herself."

Marius surely had heard this. They all had. Armand sent a swift telepathic negation. If the others wanted to stop me from blurting it out, they might have said something. They didn't.

I repeated Amel's words precisely as he had said them in my head.

"Ah," she said. She sat back in her chair as if this were a eureka moment.

A little tumult in my head. "I didn't mean to hurt you!" Amel said. Highly emotional. "I didn't!"

"All right, I understand," I said aloud. "And we can write. But we ought to find a way to write that doesn't cause me pain!"

I was exhausted as if I'd been running and running and had to fall down on the ground. And then I felt the moisture, which had to be blood in my eyes.

Kapetria was staring at me in alarm.

Marius offered me a handkerchief before I could find mine. And there was blood on it as I blotted my eyes.

"Amel, don't do this again!" Kapetria said. "You are in a parasitical relationship with Lestat's brain, Amel. You can injure it."

"Laughter," I said. "He's laughing." Then he let loose with a long stream of the ancient language, the language we'd heard ourselves on Benji's broadcast. "Stop," I said. "I can't repeat it this fast. Stop!"

Now we're great mimics, all of us, and have savant abilities when it comes to singing and replicating music, so I tried to give in to these talents and began speaking the strange syllables he was speaking, punctuating what he was saying to me with my repetitions, until finally he began to pause at the right moments. Suddenly he ran on with such fury I simply couldn't follow.

There came a blast of the pain again, and this time before it blinded me I saw what I hadn't seen before—that it was hitting the youngest of us at the table, who was David, who'd been made less than thirty years ago by me. Then the pain took over. And realizing what must be happening to my Rose and to Viktor wherever they were and to Louis, and all the others who didn't have thousands of years in the Blood, I collapsed.

I knew I was lying on the floor and I didn't care.

Kapetria was talking, on and on, the same way he'd been talking, in that tongue. She was talking to him in me and he was answering but I couldn't tell her the answers.

Suddenly he was screaming at me, screaming. And I was screaming back.

**If you don't stop, I can't do anything! This pain is unendurable!**

Gone. Merely the little convulsions behind my eyes and at the base of my neck. I stared up at the ceiling, at the brilliant painted images ringing the plaster medallion of the chandelier, at the gold-tinged clouds up there, and the smiling face of the putti gathered in the far corners. It seemed there was nothing to worry about, no need for haste or for alarm. Just this strange kind of bliss.

**Her blood, her blood, open the channel and I can talk to her. . . .**

Marius helped me up. Seth was on the other side of me, his firm hand on the back of my neck. I stood on my feet. The lights seemed impossibly dim and I knew this was wrong, really wrong, no one had dimmed the lights. Yet the pulsing wreath of the chandelier, with its myriad baubles of crystal, was glowing through a cloud of golden vapor. Kapetria looked up at me. Her breasts were touching my chest. **Not a female. Not a true female anything. But something free of male/female, something wondrous.**

"Drink," Amel said to me.

I took her in my arms and turned her so that my back was to the long table, though I knew my mother was behind Kapetria and she saw this seemingly obscene intimacy as I touched Kapetria's throat with my fangs and then let them push through her soft hot skin, such beautiful dark bronze skin, and I felt the blood fill my mouth—extraordinary blood.

Atalantaya. High noon. A sky as endlessly blue as the sea and Amel talking to Kapetria as they walked together, this evil twin of mine, with his shoulder-length red hair and green eyes and supple smile, the musical ancient tongue running on, and now its words were shining with meaning, **from your own** skin and your own blood, these elements, without which, impossible, every Replimoid, this synthesis, accelerating the protein and strengthening and locking in the properties of—. The two in a great airy laboratory together, and something sparkling and marvelous as liquid glass sprouting and growing from a tiny egg in Amel's cupped hands, and stretching its shining tentacles up and up in the light that streamed in through the clear windows . . . chain reaction inevitable, invasion and transformation of the substance and . . . A body on an oval bed, a body like the body of a human being only smaller. The precise chemical balance, nutrients, out of my body, out of those enhancements of me . . . He held her in his arms, his red hair falling in his face as he kissed her, his fingers tightening on her arms. . . .

Yea gods, what blood, such rich, irresistible blood, with so many tiny hearts throbbing to make up the resounding throb of one heart that wasn't a heart at all. I was bathed in the blood; the sweet blood was a fountain, and every cell in me was satisfied and upheld by the blood.

I awoke. Her friends held her as if she were the dead Christ in the arms of His Mother and John and Joseph of Arimathea, with the others from the wall like so many angels. She lay back upon this safety net of arms and hands.

"My coffin," I said, "put me in my coffin!" When had I said those words before. "Put me in my coffin!" And Louis had not done it, and Claudia had not done it. In came the knife. Only this time I was being helped. Marius and David had ahold of me and were taking me out of the room.

"Rose, Viktor, what's happened to them? Where is Louis?"

We hurried down the curving stone stairs, and through the broad passage towards yet another stairway, and into the bowels of the mountain. The music from the ballroom sounded like a **Walpurgisnacht** nightmare. I pictured monsters and demons and bats and witches colliding with one another. "Get me away from that music."

Someone picked me up, lifting me so that I fell over his shoulder. When the doors of the crypt opened I smelled the incense and recognized the soothing light. Down, yes, down, into the silk, on the silken bed.

Fareed knelt beside me. He pinched the skin on the back of my left hand and plunged the long thin silver needle of a syringe into the pinched flesh. I didn't feel it but then I felt the blood leaving me. Such remarkable blood.

"Why are you doing that?" I asked.

"Because I want her blood," he said. "As much of it as I can get."

He must have had more than one syringe. He turned my hand over and tapped on my wrist. I shut my eyes.

After a long moment, I opened my eyes.

I lay there like a dead man on display at a wake.

Dim flickering light. Marble walls. A border of acanthus leaves running along the four sides of the rectangular ceiling of this little chamber. Stars painted in the deep blue of the ceiling.

Beside me sat Seth, still and quiet, on the long marble bench, his narrow dark face solemn as he regarded me.

"What have I done?" I whispered. "What have I revealed?"

"She was murmuring things, murmuring to them and to us," said Fareed. "She said it was the luracastria which links us all, it's a great web of subatomic luracastria but it's alive. . . ."

Quiet. Fareed was gone. They were all gone.

I lay alone in the semidarkness. A candle burned on the marble shelf by my coffin. I was dizzy and sick.

". . . and so it comes," I said, "from inside his brain, and the soul, the astral self of him that survives is the subtle form—nano-particles of luracastria—of that immortal brain of his, and nano-luracastria is its single most important surviving ingredient or element."

Yes. Yes, that's it. To alter me and to make me immortal as a Replimoid they used a string of synthesized elements which I extracted and studied and reworked and finally saw and knew and broke down and made into luracastria, all these elements originally of Earth, made by me into luracastria, behold the chemicals, behold luracastria, beautiful luracastria, injected back into myself, luracastria,

into me, behold luracastria, sing the song of luracastria in me, a new synthesis, and when the chemical stores in the Creative Tower went up in flames
and smoke, behold the flames and smoke, when the
rolling explosions went off one after another and
the walls poured down like syrup into the flaming
water, I went up in flames, broken apart . . . hands,
arms, and legs and head all blasted apart, I could
still see it, behold all the parts of me swallowed by
flames, the tiniest parts of me sizzling and turning
black and my torso blown into fragments, engulfed
in flames, but the "I" of me went up and up and up
and when my skull exploded "I" was free.

# 21

# Lestat

I WAS REMEMBERING THE way that Marius had described to me the emptied body of King Enkil after Queen Akasha had awakened and drained him of all blood, that the body had lain there like something made of glass, empty and translucent. And that is what Mekare's body had become, something translucent like plastic.

And so is this what is happening to us, that this subatomic luracastria is slowly invading and transforming every cell in our bodies while those cells retain their self-replicating nature and we are slowly becoming luracastria?

The sun had set two hours ago. I sat in my private bedchamber with Rose in my arms, Rose with her drowsy head against my chest. And Viktor my son beside me. Rose was so new she looked human in all respects, even to her ruddy skin, and she felt soft all over, soft and sweet, as she lay against me, her raven hair veiling her face, and her long soft gown of burgundy silk cleaving to her beautifully shaped limbs. My son was worn and weary from last night's pain. He sat erect, his arms clasped between his knees, his blue eyes fixed on some faraway point, his short clipped yellow hair shimmering in the light of the wall sconces, regal even in his dark olive cargo shirt and pants, his face so like mine yet wholly different, more finely proportioned, his mouth smooth though his eyes were narrow and his expression was one of anger.

They had both suffered the unspeakable assault. And Louis, too, must have experienced it, though he said not a word about it. Indeed, all the Undead throughout the Château had known some version of it. Or so it seemed. David had lost consciousness at one point. So had Rose. Viktor had stubbornly clung to consciousness determined to observe it.

"I made it into colors," Viktor said to me now. "I saw the pain in red and yellow, and when it was at its worst, it was pure white. I couldn't imagine what had happened. I couldn't. And no one came out of the Council Chamber to tell us. And we didn't dare move. Louis was holding Rose when it all happened. I wanted to hold her. I couldn't hold her."

Louis sat in a chair nearby, quietly resplendent in his Lestat-chosen clothes, the inevitable dark blue velvet jacket and the layers of tiny, subtle lace at his throat, and the emerald shining on his finger. His boots looked like onyx.

Inside me, Amel said: "I didn't mean to make the pain, I didn't mean for there to be any pain; I couldn't stop the pain. The pain was never the point."

This was the first time he'd spoken to me since I had awakened. He hadn't been there for the first hour while I lay obediently in my coffin bed of satin, unable to risk the last rays of the sun above.

I spoke to him silently. "What do you want now?" I asked.

"Want?" The long sigh, a sigh so distinctly his I would have known it was his sigh if I'd heard it amid a multitude of sighs. "Want." Not a question. Just a remark. Silence. The fire crackling behind the brass fireplace screen.

The room swam in my sight. A chamber fit for a prince.

"Listen to me, all of you," I said. "He didn't mean for there to be pain. He will try very hard never to cause such pain again."

Viktor nodded.

Rose stirred against my shoulder. "Even if it has been only for half a year," she said, "it has been a lifetime."

"Don't talk like that," said Viktor. "What, are we holding a funeral for ourselves before we're even dead?" He looked at me. "Father, you are not going to allow these Replimoids to destroy us!"

He stood up, facing me, his arms folded. Powerful shoulders, fine body. No father in the world ever asked for a finer son. "Throughout the Château," he said, "everyone is grim! How can they be so grim?"

I nodded that I understood what he was saying, but I had no words.

"My mother felt the pain," he said. "She called from Paris. It must have been felt all over the world. Benedict and Rhoshamandes must have felt it. I wish I knew how many of us there are in the whole world."

"No one knows that, not even Amel," I said.

Little pulse at the back of my neck, little spasm in the blood vessels under the skin of my temples.

I couldn't stop seeing Mekare's empty shell of a body. Was it all luracastria? And does the subatomic luracastria transform the cells to a more resilient and ever-perfecting luracastria that becomes at last immune to the sun, almost entirely immune, except for me, the host of the brain of Amel?

Inside me, he made no response to this.

Carefully cradling Rose in my arms, I rose to my feet and placed her carefully on the settee. I kissed the top of her head.

"Whatever happens," I said as I looked from her to Viktor and finally to Louis, "I will fight for us and who we are. We are the strange flowers of this entity, but it is through us that he's discovered himself, and he knows that I love him, and I love him all the more with every discovery about him, and I know that he must love us, must know—."

**Love you.**

"And there is no reason," I went on, "for this to end for us. There is no way right now that Kapetria or the other Replimoids could conceivably want it to end for us; they are not waiting with scalpels in hand to free him from me because they have no place to put him."

**This is true.**

"Now, I'm going to go back upstairs and work with the others towards some sort of solution."

"Where have they gone?" Louis asked. "When I woke, I was told some of them left the village at about two o'clock, and that the others remain here to await some action against Rhoshamandes."

"That's correct," I said. "Twelve of them left. Twelve. And the elder four remain."

"You mean they increased their numbers in the space of one day?" asked Louis.

"Apparently," I said. "I suspect each one of them generated another. That would make a total of sixteen. Subtract the four elders and you have the twelve who left, two of whom were women, and all the rest males. I was getting word on all this earlier while I was still in the crypt."

I could see the mingled revulsion and alarm in their faces.

"They don't suffer anything when they multiply, do they?" asked Rose. "They simply do it."

"How can we know?" I asked. "But what is the point of becoming alarmed about this? The fact is they could have done this anytime easily. What do they require but a safe room in which the process can take place?"

I had thought when I first awakened that it would be our task to communicate what had been said in the conference room to others within the Court, but Marius and Gregory had already done this. And the news had been traveling fast.

"There are other things for us to talk about now," I said. "Gregory, Seth, Teskhamen, and Sevraine have gone to find Rhoshamandes. They left before I even opened my eyes because they wake sooner than I wake. Arion soon followed. So did Allesandra, and Everard de Landen, and Eleni. These are Rhosh's fledglings, as you know."

"But you didn't give your permission for this, did you?" asked Louis. It was asked in such a neutral way that I couldn't interpret it for or against.

"No," I said. "Maybe they've gone to lay down the law that Rhoshamandes cannot harm the Replimoids any more than he can seek to harm us."

They seemed to accept this, and I sensed as I had so often in the last six months that everyone, near everyone, expected me to articulate certain things, and when I did articulate them, there was inevitable relief for the moment.

"I see no way out for Rhoshamandes," said Louis in a soft voice. He wasn't challenging me, just reflecting.

"Well, there's at least a chance for peace," said

Rose. She wiped her hair out of her eyes, and stared for a moment at her hand, at her fingernails. Her fingernails were the only real giveaway right now that she was preternatural. They were shining. She couldn't help but look at them, be fascinated by their sheen. Luracastria.

"A chance, yes," said Viktor, "but frankly I wish that Rhoshamandes was no more. Don't we have enough to worry about now without him?"

"It's time for me to show myself and do what I can to calm the others," I said. "I have to go out into the ballroom, no choice."

"We'll go with you," Louis said.

I headed out and through the long series of connective salons which stood between me and the ballroom of this my glorified lair. The music was playing as always, and this evening it was Sybelle at the harpsichord and Antoine conducting and Notker's singers chanting in a monosyllabic delirium— in a riotous waltz spinning off of Camille Saint-Saëns's "Danse Macabre," carrying the melodies to savage heights.

When I stepped into the room, I saw it was packed, and almost every single blood drinker was dancing, either alone or with a partner or a ring of partners. Only a few sat here and there, some caught up in the music as if in a trance. At least a hundred newcomers or recent comers were in the crowd, and if there was any panic over the Replimoids, it certainly was not visible to me. Yielding to the music, yielding to the dance, that is what mattered in the ballroom. Faces brightened as they saw me, bows as they saw me, salutes from the ragged and the bejeweled.

At once, the gorgeously attired Zenobia took my hand and moved out on the dance floor.

"I'm so grateful that Marius has stayed behind with us," she said. She was delicate of face and build and her fine shimmering black hair was artfully threaded with ropes of pearls. Eyes that had gazed on Byzantium, eyes that had seen Hagia Sophia in all her glory.

"I'm glad too," I said. "But why did he?"

"They put it this way," said Zenobia. "Some of them might not return from their visit to Rhoshamandes, so it was imperative that, if things went wrong, there be strong ones here, here to help you on your right and your left." Such a sweet voice, speaking English with a heavy accent that gave it a distinctive charm.

"I see," I said. "And Avicus?"

"Dancing," she said with a quick smile. She made a graceful gesture with her small hand that meant "somewhere here." She was as lovely as Marius had described her when he'd first encountered her in Constantinople so many centuries ago. And I found it especially enticing that she wore finely tailored men's clothes—slim-waisted jacket with sequined lapels, tight shimmering pants, a silk shirt of brilliant turquoise.

We were turning in wild circles before I knew it, and then I was passed by her to the lovely brown-haired Chrysanthe in a graceful swirling white gown with diamonds on her breast that were blinding. The music was driving towards a frenzy.

"And from Gregory? Have you had any word?" I asked because surely her Blood Spouse would have let her know what he might be keeping from the rest of us.

"I've heard nothing," she said. "But I'm not afraid. Yet I won't rest easy till he returns. I wanted to go with them. But Gregory wouldn't hear of it. None of them would hear of it."

"I should be with them," I said. But the others had been completely against it. Why wouldn't Rhoshamandes on the precipice strike out at me and thereby seek to destroy all of us?

The dancing continued to be dizzyingly fast. I caught glimpses of Davis and Arjun playing instruments in the orchestra, Davis the oboe this time, and Arjun the violin, and there was Notker the Wise himself singing with his choir of male and female soprano voices, and Antoine conducting so fiercely it was a dance in itself.

There was Marius in his long red-belted tunic sitting on the sidelines in fast conversation with Pandora, and Gremt Stryker Knollys, the spirit incarnate, staring at me and watching my every move as David Talbot sat beside him, obviously talking to him, and leaving him unmoved. Gremt needing me, calling to me silently without a visible sign.

"Forgive me," I said to Chrysanthe. "There are things I have to do."

She nodded that she understood. But I held her hand as I motioned for David to come forward, and then I delivered her now into his gentlemanly arms. I headed in the direction of Gremt. And when Gremt saw this he rose and moved towards the open doors that led to a stone terrace. Did the young vampires think he was a vampire? Did the old vampires despise him because the Talamasca, their age-old stalker, had been founded by him? I could have spent every single night at Court talking to new blood drinkers, or encountering old ones who were forever arriving, it seemed, to put to rest the "exaggerated" rumors of their demise. Please, Quinn, my beloved Quinn, some night, if we have many nights left, come walking through these doors.

Gremt wasn't trying to avoid me. Rather, as he glanced over his shoulder, he appeared to be asking me to follow him outside.

The air was freezing and the terrace was covered in the snow, but the sky was remarkably clear and clean, and the snow crunched and crackled under my feet because it was frozen.

Gremt stood at the railing, and looked out over the village below. This terrace had not existed in my time, but had been added to the Château by my workers, and it gave the finest view of the village with its winding street and dimly lighted tavern and townhouses. Curfew was in effect for the humans of the village, but going from and coming to the tavern was allowed, and I could see furtive figures down there on the fresh-swept pavers, and some lingering against the wall like dark ghosts gazing up at the Château, and perhaps at us as we stood side by side, though mortal eyes couldn't have seen me clasp Gremt's hand.

Kapetria and her kindred Replimoids waited in the inn down there for word on Roland and Rhoshamandes—the re-creation of the inn in which, centuries ago, I'd drunk myself sick with my lover Nicolas and first confronted my mortality and gone out of my head.

Gremt's hand. So warm, so human. He was the picture of dignity gazing out, silken hair as well groomed as that of a Greek statue, his tall formidable body clothed in the long black clerical-looking **thawb,** a garment he apparently liked very much. And what were his thoughts tonight? Why couldn't I read his mind or the minds of the Replimoids? So be it. He'd tell me when he was ready just what Kapetria's revelations had meant to him. They must have shaken him to the root.

I caught the scent of blood as if it were something Gremt could release at will, and I heard the tripping of his mysterious heart beneath it, and felt the pulse in his wrist.

Innocent blood, there came that suggestion again, that whisper from Amel in a voice that didn't need words. **His blood, yes, now.** My mouth was tasting blood. **I want it, I want it, his blood.**

"Is this what you want?" I asked Gremt. "You want me to do what I did with her?"

"I want to know what you taste and what you see when you drink the blood of this body," he said in a muted and anguished voice. "What do you think this Replimoid woman might tell me about what I've done—how I've incarnated?" So that meant far more to him now than the revelations about Amel.

"Maybe she can tell us all plenty," I said. "And maybe she can tell us things we don't want to know. But she's going soon, that's the word, and nobody can persuade her to remain. She and her kindred will go—just as soon as they know that Roland and Rhoshamandes are no longer a threat."

Amel was goading me. My thirst was unbearable. And once more he spoke of innocent blood.

What's so delicious about innocent blood? What makes it like spring blossoms falling apart in your hands, or a bird fluttering in the prison of your fingers, or baby skin, or women's breasts?

Behind us, the music and light contrived to pull a golden veil over the ballroom. The raw impassioned voice of a violin broke loose from the desperate currents of the waltz and sang, as violins always do, of loneliness. Was that Arjun or had Antoine taken up his fiddle?

I moved Gremt off across the hard crush of the snow until we were swallowed by the shadows of a corner. The village was not in view because we were too far from the edge, and the night above was so clear that the stars seemed a thousand times their usual number. The snow shone as white as the moon. I could see it streaked and gleaming on the forested mountains all around us, and see it trimming the battlements and see the flecks of it in Gremt's hair.

This body was as beautiful to me as any I'd ever embraced and Amel was singing with the waltz so low I could scarcely hear him. I moved Gremt's soft black hair back from his neck, my left hand taking hold of his strong right arm, and then I went in, wondering just what might happen to this contrived body under such an assault. Had he ever let anyone else do this? Certainly Teskhamen, his partner in the Talamasca, had done this. **No. Never.** The blood gushed so fast and so hard I felt it wet on my lips and on my face as never happens, but I couldn't turn back, it was coming too fast, and the heart was sounding with the regularity of a fire bell.

Sweet, luscious blood, blood with salt, blood with all that blood is meant to be, and his mind broke open like the golden meat of a peach in the old days when I was alive and loving the summer fruit, the intoxicating sweetness of the fresh fruit from the trees in the village, right here, this village, me and Nicki lying on a haystack, eating fresh fruit till our lips were sore.

I saw a firmament of stars and a great war of vaporous beings faceless and howling and battling one another, with broken phrases and taunts and cries of pain, and then the earth below with its great expanses of black water shining in the light of Heaven and the land planted with a thousand clusters of man-made lights and shimmering roofs and thin spidery roads, and the wind roared in my ears, and we were Gremt, both of us, Gremt walking on one of those roads, walking with palpable steps, and when we turned, out of the great dark woods around us came a stinging torrent of freezing air and dead leaves that hit us full force like a rain of nails. Anger, anger everywhere we turned, the anger of the spirits, and then he was standing before me and he had his arms out, and he asked, Am I flesh and blood? Am I? What am I? The image wavered, weakened, dimmed. Dear God, was he dying? It took all my strength to draw back. Amel cried out and hissed and there came the pain again, the pain in my hands as he tried to force me to hold on and the pain shooting up the back of my neck. Gremt fell down into the snow.

**Stop it, damn you, stop it, or I swear it, I will surrender you to the prison of a vessel from which you cannot hurt us!**

It was finished. Nothing vanishes quite like pain—when pain does vanish, that is. Because most of the time pain never does.

I knelt down beside Gremt. He was drawn and almost as white as the snow, and his eyes were half-mast and gleaming the way the eyes of an animal can gleam when the animal's dead.

"Gremt!" I turned his head towards me with both hands. Warm, warm with life, warm with the will to live.

Slowly his eyes grew wide and clear.

For an endless moment we were together in silence. Snow fell. Light soundless snow.

"Was it good, the blood?" he whispered.

I nodded. "It was good," I said.

"What have I done?" he whispered. He appeared to be looking past me, at the stars. Did he see spirits up there? Did he hear them in some way that I could not?

"Are they watching us?" I asked.

"They're always watching," he said. "What else do they have to do? Yes, they're watching. And they wonder what I've done, just as I wondered what Amel had done. And how many more will descend?"

I moved to help him to his feet, but he begged me to wait, to give him another moment. His breathing was uneven and his heartbeat had a ragged edge to it.

Finally he was ready. Surely no mortal on the planet would think him anything but human, except perhaps some gifted witch who knew all the many mysteries, she might see through him, but not the others. And Amel had been right that Gremt could no longer disperse the particles. I didn't have to ask. I knew it was true. Because if the particles could have been sent flying, it would have happened when I broke into his blood.

I led him back into the swirling golden light and music of the ballroom. He was sleepy, sluggish, but otherwise unharmed. We brushed past dancers, and those who stood stranded on the edge, and Avicus appeared in the corner of my eye and beside him the red-haired Thorne, and Cyril's dark faintly amused face.

"All hail the mighty Prince," Cyril muttered. But the smile wasn't mocking and neither were the words. Just Cyril commenting on the state of things. And Cyril's comments always had an ironic twang. Tonight he was dressed for the ball in black-and-white finery, and it was amusing to see that—Cyril, the haunter of caves and shallow graves, all decked out to the golden cuff links. I almost laughed.

"Yeah, the mighty Prince," I said in a low snarling voice. "Just what we all need right now, right?" That was my best New York gangster imitation and Cyril loved it, and laughed under his breath.

I helped Gremt to sit down on the only couch I could find in deep shadow, a brocade settee lost beneath a sconce of burnt dead candles and wisps of acrid smoke. I held him steady.

"What did you see?" I asked. "What did you see in me?"

"Hope," Gremt said. "Hope, you'll get us all through this."

Not at all what I expected.

"And you didn't see **him**?"

"I saw you."

He was gazing at the great writhing mass of dancers under the dim chandeliers. And without a hint of irony the orchestra and the chanting voices went into the full-throated straight-up "Emperor Waltz" by Strauss—producing wild laughter everywhere from the colorful crowd who began to mock it with their exaggerated steps and turns—newcomers in rags prancing as proudly as those in sequins and diaphanous silver and gold. I saw Rose dancing with Viktor, Rose throwing back her head and letting her hair fly loose, and all around her fledglings with their petal-pink faces like her face, and then my son, straight backed and graceful as a European prince leading Rose in the Viennese flourishes. Viktor took this so seriously. Viktor wanted it all to succeed. Viktor believed in the power of pomp and circumstance.

Even Gremt laughed softly and his head moved faintly with the festive, happy music. But then here came the kettledrums and the French horns and dark strings to give the waltz the tension so prized by the company.

Why was this so important, why did so much depend upon it, immortals gathered here in wild community, in this fortress against the human world?

"But I don't understand," I said. I put my lips to Gremt's ear. "What has our fate to do with yours?

You can go on no matter what happens to us. Why would I give you hope?"

He turned sharply and looked at me as if he had to see me to understand what I had said.

Then he asked, "But who would want to go on without you?"

I stared at him, astonished.

"And what of Amel?" I asked. "What of Kapetria's whole story? You said nothing in the end. Was it what you had always wanted to know?"

"What?" he asked. "That Amel wasn't born evil, that he'd been a champion of the good when he was alive? It wasn't what I expected. But does it matter now? It mattered yesterday and last year, and the year before that, and the century before this one, and the century before that. But I don't know that it matters now. I'm here and I'm alive, and that woman can help me though I don't know how and why."

I nodded. I thought of what Kapetria might do for the ghost of Magnus. And surely Magnus was here somewhere, invisible, watching.

"Why does she have to leave?" Gremt asked me. "Why can't she stay? Gregory begged her to stay and so did Seth and so did Teskhamen. After you left last night they offered her the moon. Gregory said he would build whatever laboratories she wanted in Paris, that she could have whole floors of one of his buildings, that no one would ever pry into what she did. But she said no, that they had to go off, come to terms with one another, get to know one another. What if we never see any of them again?"

"Now that might be the very best thing that could ever happen to **us**," I said. "But what's to stop you from going with her?"

"But that's just it. She won't tell anyone where she's headed. She kept repeating, 'Not now, not yet, not now.'"

"Maybe she has to test us, Gremt," I said. "Maybe she has to make certain that we aren't playing with her, that we will let her go. And we have to meet the test. If we don't, everything we told them about kindred loyalty is a lie."

He didn't answer. "I'm spent," he whispered. "I have to find my bed and lie down."

Of course. I'd taken enough blood to knock a mortal down to the threshold of death.

I helped him to his feet again and gestured to Cyril. "Take him to his rooms," I said. "He needs to sleep now. Get him anything that he wants."

Without a word Cyril took Gremt in hand.

It seemed the music had risen a notch in volume. Something radiant and inviting was standing in front of me. It was my Rose, her long full burgundy skirts swirling around her, feet in dagger heels and jeweled straps.

"Father, dance with me," she said. Her teeth were white against her red lips. I couldn't refuse. And suddenly she was leading me in great circles all through the shifting crowd, and we were dancing faster than I'd ever danced. I had to laugh. I couldn't stop laughing. The blood of Gremt had quickened me. All around us people were bowing and applauding. Rose sang the long monosyllabic chant of Notker's singers, and the orchestra seemed to swell in volume or size. This is our place, I thought, our ballroom, our home. We, who have always been despised, we who have always been loathed, we who have always been condemned—this is our Court.

Round and round the floor we went, and I saw nothing but Rose's upturned face, and her red lips and her glowing eyes.

**Hope . . . that you'll get us all through this.**

And somewhere far off to my right in a flash I saw the specters dancing, Magnus with the ghostly bride of Teskhamen, none other than the willowy and beguiling Hesketh. What does it feel like to a ghost to dance? And would they someday be as solid as Gremt was, imprisoned in their bodies they had constructed for themselves, and would Kapetria build them splendid Replimoid-style bodies for their ancient souls?

# 22

# Rhoshamandes

WHAT A COLLECTION they were, the ancient ones whose minds he could so little penetrate and his own fledglings turned against him whose minds had always been locked from the keenest love he'd known for them or the worst suffering he'd ever endured.

"And when we—each of us—were taken prisoner by the Children of Satan, you turned your back on us!" cried the bitter and ungrateful Everard de Landen, such a brittle little dandy in his off-the-rack designer jacket and friable Italian shoes.

"And what did you do for the others, Everard, when you obtained your freedom!" Benedict shot back, poor loyal Benedict standing beside him. "When you got free of the Children of Satan, you never came back to help the others get free. You hid out in Italy, that's what you did."

"And when they tortured us and made us believe the old Satanic creed," said Eleni, weeping, weeping blood tears, "you did nothing to help us. You who were so strong. Oh, we never dreamed how strong you were, how old you were, that you'd existed long before the land into which we'd been born even had a name!"

"Why didn't you help us?" asked Allesandra, the one who had supposedly forgiven him. Did she really want her Rhosh to confess it all again?

"I wanted peace," Rhosh said. He shrugged. He stood against the wall beside the empty blackened fireplace unable to move, the collective power of Gregory and Seth and Sevraine holding him there. And when would these telepathic beams turn to blasts of heat? How long does it take for someone as old as me to burn up, he wondered. He had not sought to use that cruel power against Maharet. He had used a simple mortal weapon only to strike at the head, at the brain.

Oh, that he had never gone that night to her compound, never believed the Voice, never been the dupe of the Voice.

And here he was—damned if he did and damned if he didn't—cursed that he'd not been warrior enough to fight the Children of Satan who'd captured and tormented his fledglings, and cursed because he had struck at the great Maharet.

Benedict continued to plead. "Everywhere he goes, they curse at him, spit at him! Everywhere he goes. It's the mark of Cain!"

"And what did you think would happen?" asked Sevraine, who never raised her voice. "The Prince let you go, but he couldn't promise you a cloak of invincibility, or invisibility. What did you think would happen when you walked boldly in the big cities where the young ones hunt?"

"What do you want of me!" Rhosh asked. "What? Is this mere prelude to an execution? Why drag it out? For whose benefit do you say all this?"

"You must never strike at any of us again," said Gregory in a level voice.

"Oh, you, of such little loyalty!" said Rhoshamandes with contempt. "And I stood by you when the Mother imprisoned you for your love of Sevraine. Have you a veil of forgetfulness over those times when I served you in the Queens Blood with my whole soul! What did you teach me then about authority, about monarchs, about presumptuous immortals who made up tales of 'divine right'?"

"I have said nothing to you about divine right," said Gregory in a low voice. "You kept that innocent Derek, that helpless Derek, prisoner here when you knew we were under attack by these Replimoids. You knew, yet you made no move to bring him to us. And you know what we want."

"Tell us where this Roland is hiding, the one who kept him for ten years," said Sevraine.

"And why would I do that?" asked Rhoshamandes. "Why would I betray the only blood drinker in the world who befriended me after I was cast out by all of you, yes, all of you, and forced to wander in exile! And what is it to me if Roland kept this strange prisoner? Am I the keeper of Roland? Am I the keeper of anyone?"

"They are our friends now," said Seth. "They are our family and they demand justice for what happened to Derek. They demand this to seal the pact of peace with us."

Benedict drew close to Rhosh again, and Rhosh motioned for him to stay back.

"Don't let it be the last thing I see," he said to Benedict, "that you're destroyed with me. I beg you. Not that."

"All right," said Benedict to Gregory and Seth. "He kept Derek here. Rhosh struck off Derek's arm, the same way the Prince had struck off Rhosh's arm. Surely there's something he can do or say to settle this! I don't believe the Prince wants this. I know he doesn't. The Prince would be here if this was what he wanted."

Face streaming with blood tears. Poor Benedict. Rhosh couldn't bear to see Benedict suffering like this, and the appalling reality struck him that if and when they brought this to a close, he'd be gone, and there would be no one to console Benedict and Benedict would be alone, really alone for the first time ever in all these long centuries.

Rhoshamandes felt so tired suddenly, so weary thinking that this might go on and on through the hours of the night, and there came back to him some little wisdom he'd picked up centuries ago from a Roman Emperor, esteemed as a Stoic, that all you have to lose in death, no matter how long you've lived, is the present moment in which you die. He smiled. Because now it seemed true.

Not much written in the pages of mortal philosophy was written for immortals, but Marcus Aurelius had it right. He had written that you can live three thousand years or thirty thousand years, and all you have to lose is the life you are living right now. He felt he was drifting. He could hear their mingled voices but not their words.

"Benedict, go back with them. Leave and go back with them."

Was that his voice? He seemed to be two people suddenly, the one pinned to the wall with his arms dangling helplessly and another watching all of this as it unfolded. And so it ends like this. If only I could see one more opera, one more good production of Gounod's **Faust,** have one walk through the palatial opera house in Prague or Paris. He couldn't hear them now, his accusers. He was hearing those lovely raw sounds of an orchestra tuning its myriad instruments. Echoes in a giant gilded theater. He was hearing Marguerite's last song in the finale of **Faust,** Marguerite on the point of death. Oh, how lovely to be recalling it so vividly, so nearly perfectly. He could hear her voice rising in triumph. He could hear the angelic chorus. And he felt free as he always did when he heard this music, no matter where it was, or at what time. He felt like nothing could intrude on him here, in the great gilded theater of the mind, as long as he could hear this music in his head.

But something was bringing him back. The music was growing dimmer and fainter, and he couldn't revive it. He could see Marguerite, a tiny figure on an immense stage, but he couldn't hear her.

Reluctantly he lowered his eyes and let the assembly of accusers come into focus again. **"Judged!" said Mephistopheles.** But what was happening?

Roland was standing there before him. Roland. And that was Flavius, the old Greek slave, beside him, and Teskhamen, the powerful Teskhamen whom he'd never known in ancient times, holding Roland fast by the right arm. They'd found him, brought him in out of the wind and rain, and Roland stood there, his face a mask of terror. Arion too was in terror. And Allesandra, his faithful Allesandra, had lifted her hands to cover her eyes. It seemed they were all talking at once.

The figure of Roland went up in flames. Flames sprang from his heart, his limbs. Rhosh could scarcely believe what he was seeing, Roland turning around and around, and the flames shrinking him to a great whirling cinder while not a sound rose from Roland, not a sound rose from anyone—not from anyone—flames shooting to the ceiling, flames dancing and collapsing on themselves until there was nothing more in the flames. And no flames.

Out went the fire. Not a sound in this room. Something unspeakable was collected there on the stone floor. Something as thick and dark and foul as the soot in the fireplace.

And then Benedict crying, Benedict the only one crying for Roland—that was the only sound.

Rhosh closed his eyes. He could hear the sea pounding against the island, and the wind rushing into the great open arched windows, the wind that wore at the delicate Gothic tracery of the windows. Benedict was sobbing.

A weight struck Rhosh.

It was Benedict crushed up against Rhosh, his back to Rhosh and his arms out. For a moment Rhosh was free of the pressure of the telepathic beams and tried with all his might to throw Benedict aside, but Benedict was unyielding and Benedict was finally calling on all his strength, finally learning how to use it, to remain there as the others held Rhosh's arms.

"Very well," said Seth, the vicious Prince, the proud Prince of Kemet. "Give us your word that you will never again strike out at any one of us or any one of them."

"He gives it!" cried Benedict. "Rhosh, tell them."

Sevraine stepped forward and turned now towards the others. "And let it be known throughout the world that no one shall accuse him or spit at him, or curse him or in any way seek to mock him!—that that is at an end!"

When no one spoke, she raised her voice again. "What is the good of a court or a prince or a council, if you can't give that order! Roland is gone, finished, punished for what he did. Now Rhoshamandes, please, give them what they want, and you, and you and you, give him what he wants!"

Benedict turned around and embraced Rhosh and laid his head against Rhosh's head. "Please," he whispered. "Or I will die with you, I swear it."

Gently, Rhosh moved Benedict to the side.

"I am sorry for what I did," said Rhosh. And it was true, wasn't it? He was sorry. He could have shrugged again at the pure irony of it. Of course he was sorry! Sorry he'd ever been such a fool and botched it on top of everything, and sorry he'd ever let the Children of Satan ensnare his fledglings and drive him out of France. He was so sorry. So sorry for everything. Seems he was saying it aloud, and who the devil cared that they had no idea what he really meant.

"But I want to come to Court!" he said.

They stood facing him like pieces on a chess-board.

"And I will not clean up that abominable soot you have left on my floor!"

Benedict lifted his fingers to Rhosh's lips. "I'll clean it away," he whispered. "I'll do it."

"Come yourself to Court and ask the Prince if this is what he can accept," said Gregory. "And if you ever strike at any of us again, at any of us, your Blood Kindred, **or the Replimoids,** it will be the end for you, mark my word."

Silence.

Rhoshamandes nodded. "Very well," he said.

They were gone.

Just that quickly, they were gone. The long heavy velvet draperies scarcely moved on their rods. A ripple ran through the massive old tapestry on the far wall, and all those French lords and ladies looked at him from the corner of their eyes.

Rhosh was walking out of the room before he had made up his mind to do it. In his bedchamber he sought the only chair he had ever much liked, and rested his head against the high wooden back. There the civilized fire of early evening still burned, and the golden clock on the wall said it was not yet midnight.

He closed his eyes. He slept.

When next he came awake the clock told him he'd been sleeping for an hour, and he saw that the fire had been banked and built up. The very sight of the flames, always so comforting to him, was chilling. He looked at his hands, so white, so inhuman, yet so strong, and he rested his head back again, vaguely aware of the clock striking the hour of one.

Sleeping. Dreaming.

Then Benedict and he lay side by side on the bed.

"Will you go to Court and talk to the Prince?" Benedict asked.

"No," he said as he stared up at the interior of the baldachin. "But I won't be told that I can't."

Benedict laid his head on Rhosh's chest.

Rhosh wanted to say so many things to him, tell

Benedict how much he loved him, tell Benedict that he'd never seen such bravery, tell Benedict that he would never ever as long as they walked the Devil's Road together forget Benedict's courage . . . but none of these words were spoken, because words couldn't do justice to the sentiments inside him and words took too much effort and words cheapened the love, the consummate love he felt for Benedict and always had.

He ran his fingers through Benedict's hair.

**Faust . . .**

Somewhere in the world surely some opera company was presenting **Faust.** How could there be opera companies in the world and no one presenting Gounod's **Faust?** And tomorrow night or the next or the night after, they'd find that opera company; they'd seek out its palatial home. Then they'd walk together like mortals, simple mortals, in evening attire, through long carpeted hallways, surrounded by the pulse of human hearts, and the heat of human breath, and into the velvet-and-gilt box they would go, and take their seats, and they would sit there in the sweet snug darkness, secure amid the mortal throng, and he would hear Marguerite's voice rising in the finale, and everything would be perfectly fine once more.

After all, it is a lot of trouble to hate people, isn't it? And a lot of trouble to be angry, and a lot of trouble to bother with such abstract notions as guilt or revenge.

The Prince seemed far away and unimportant. The Court meant nothing to him. Even Roland meant nothing. He could not have saved Roland. Roland was gone. That's all. Roland was gone. But this fellow being, lying against him, this being who was his Benedict meant everything, and why this made him weep he did not know.

# 23

# Derek

I T HAD TAKEN time, or rather a long night of listening to Kapetria and remembering, and some time near her and with her—but he was finally able to see these creatures as innately beautiful, not as the white leeches who had kept him prisoner and tortured him. And particularly these two.

Marius and Lestat. It was 2:00 a.m. in the morning and the entire Replimoid company had been sleeping, except for the newest of the newborn ones who'd been feasting quietly on cold meat and wine, famished as it seems newborn Replimoids are, when the knock had come at the door.

Derek had heard it, and sat straight up in bed. Then Dertu who had been sleeping beside him was awake, and they were listening to Kapetria's voice. Everything was all right. They knew by the sound of her steady voice.

Now they were gathered in Kapetria's rooms at the very front of the inn. Her quaint leaded glass windows looked down on the slumbering village, and the sheer white curtains no doubt kept out all prying human eyes, but then no one was awake in the village—in spite of the fact that when the wind was quiet, you could hear that nightmarish music coming from the Château. And if you did step outside and go to the very top of the street, you could see them all moving up there, those strange beings, a community of strange beings, moving behind the windows through rooms and corridors filled with brilliant yellow light.

Lestat and Marius. They were beautiful, undeniably, positively majestic, and from the beginning they had appeared to Derek like father and son.

Lestat sat back in a chair tilted against the wall like a Hollywood-western cowboy with one boot heel hooked on a chair rung and the other booted foot on the seat of the chair in front of him. His rakish long hair was tied back at the nape of his neck. But Marius sat still and straight as though he'd never slouched or slumped or relaxed in his entire long immortal life. Both wore red. The Prince a velvet coat and pressed blue jeans, and Marius a long tunic of heavy wool that might have been court dress in any kingdom of the ancient world for a millennium.

"But is he really **really** dead?" asked Derek. "I mean he burned up, but does that really mean he can't come back?"

It was Marius who had done all the talking and Marius who answered the question now.

"You might be able to survive such a little conflagration," he said. "But we cannot. Roland had maybe three thousand years in the Blood. That makes for a powerful blood drinker, but not one that cannot be burned up."

He was using Derek's phrase but not mocking Derek. Marius's preferred vocabulary included such words as "immolated" and "incinerated" and "annihilated." And phrases such as "quite gone beyond reprieve."

"This was witnessed by some ten of us," said Marius, "and of course Rhoshamandes witnessed it as well. It was an exemplum for Rhoshamandes. Rhoshamandes yielded. Rhoshamandes has his young partner again, Benedict. Benedict saw this too. Between the fire that consumed Roland and the love that consumes Benedict, Rhoshamandes has been mollified and has given his word."

"You believe him, that he will not try to hurt us?" asked Kapetria.

"I do," said Marius. "I might be wrong. But I believe him. And for the moment, if any one of us acts on his own and tries to annihilate him, well, there will be tremendous discord. Believe me, I have in my heart of hearts not a particle of love for this creature, but I feel that the forgiveness of Rhoshamandes must be the cornerstone of what we are seeking to build."

The Prince rolled his eyes and smiled.

"He won't break the peace now because of Benedict," said the Prince looking directly at Derek.

"Rhoshamandes can live with slights and live with failure. He's protected from fatal pride by a near-fatal smallness of soul."

"And more use to you alive than dead," said Kapetria.

Marius appeared to be thinking this over. Then, "Thousands of years before I came into existence he was alive, walking the earth as we say." He paused. "We don't really want to . . ." His words gave out.

"I understand," said Kapetria. "I read enough of your pages to understand." This is what she called their books, their "pages."

Marius nodded and smiled. He didn't smile often, but when he did, he looked youthful and human just for an instant, rather than like an ancient Roman carved on a frieze.

"And we have so many things we must do now," said the Prince. "We have to make a credo, make rules, make some way of enforcing rules."

Marius kept his eyes on Kapetria. "So where will you go now?" Marius asked. "Will you actually leave here without telling us where we might find you?"

This was a continuation of yesterday's argument and Derek felt himself tensing all over, fearful that these creatures were not going to let them go after all, that they'd never planned to let them go.

But Kapetria took it in stride.

"Marius, we have places, places that are our very own. Surely you understand how much we need this time together."

"I know you're increasing in numbers as we speak," said Marius, "and I can't blame you for it. But when will you stop? What do you plan to do?"

"As I told you last night," said Kapetria, "we need this time together to know one another. Can you not see it from our point of view?"

"I see it, but it troubles me," he answered. "Why not take Gregory's offer to live and work in Paris? Why withdraw from us in such secrecy when we've all sworn that we are eternal friends?"

What was the Prince thinking now, the Prince who was smiling and looking off as he listened?

"If for no other reason than that I must answer their questions," said Kapetria, "as to all I've learned about us these last few years. And I have to study the new ones. I have to come to some sort of understanding of what they know and don't know, and just how knowledge is passed on, and what are the qualities of that knowledge in the new ones, and what might be their weaknesses. Look, I'm being completely open with you. My first obligation is to the colony, and I have to take the colony into seclusion."

The colony. This was the first time Derek had ever heard her use this word. Derek liked it, the word "colony." We are indeed a colony in this world, he mused.

"Why don't you stay close," asked the Prince, "and work along with Seth and Fareed? You know Fareed's eager for this. Okay, so some sparks flew last night, but it was nothing. He's eager to work with you. Think what you might achieve together, you and Seth and Fareed."

He even talked like a Hollywood cowboy gunslinger, thought Derek. He looks like a princely porcelain statue but talks like a gunslinger, with a low easy drawl. French can be beautiful when you speak it with a drawl, and his English was beautiful with the French accent and the drawl. But however he spoke, he seemed sincere, and this warmed Derek's heart. The Prince's smile was brighter than Marius's smile because the Prince smiled with his eyes and his lips, and Marius smiled mainly with his lips.

"Surely we will achieve great things together," said Kapetria. "This is the future we all want. But we need our time alone before anything further happens. And I ask that you trust us. You do trust us, don't you?"

"Of course," said the Prince. "And what would we do if we didn't trust you? Do you think we'd try to force you to stay? You think we'd try to seal you up under the Château the way Roland kept Derek in Budapest? Of course not. It's only that I didn't expect you to leave so soon."

She wasn't budging, Derek thought. She wasn't giving them anything. And he wasn't sure why. Why didn't they remain here in the safety of the Château or better yet set up some new residence for themselves in Paris in the shadow of the great Gregory Duff Collingsworth? He'd offered to give them whatever they wanted. He'd promised resources beyond their dreams.

"And what will you do now with the information Amel gave you?" asked the Prince. "We've opened our doors to you. And the doors remain open. But I can't help but wonder what you will do. I wonder because of what I am and what I once was." Just like a cowboy, so straightforward.

"Please remember," said Kapetria. "We do see ourselves as the People of the Purpose—the new purpose we embraced in Atalantaya. We will never do anything to harm sentient life. We are like you. You are like us. We are alive, all of us. But we must have some time to ourselves."

"What about Amel?" asked the Prince. "You don't want to learn more directly from Amel?"

"How can we be learning directly from him," asked Kapetria, "when such communication risks causing you excruciating pain and that pain is felt by the tribe when you feel it?"

"The pain was before I drank from you," said the Prince. "I think we could attempt it again."

"There are other ways," said Marius. "Amel can speak through any blood drinker. He could speak through me. I'm centuries older and stronger than Lestat. Whatever pain I feel won't be felt by others." His voice had a coldness to it as he spoke, Derek thought, but the coldness didn't seem personal.

Kapetria was studying Marius with narrow eyes.

"What did **you** learn from Amel?" asked Kapetria. "Is Amel who you thought he was? Maybe I'm asking, what did you learn about Amel from me?"

Silence. Derek was surprised at their silence and their stillness. When they went quiet they resembled statues.

Then the Prince spoke, and for the first time, his voice sounded cold, too.

"I think Amel told you things in the blood," he said, "that I couldn't share."

Kapetria did not respond. She held his gaze and gave no hint of what was in her mind.

"I think he told you things perhaps that you didn't know," said the Prince. Then he shrugged, and sat up a little, and looked off again. "Naturally," he said, "I wonder why you want to leave so soon. I wonder what he told you. I wonder if we really are friends, kindred, fellow travelers of the millennia. How can I not?"

"I don't want to disappoint you," said Kapetria. Her voice had taken on a new and darker tone. But it wasn't hostile. Just more serious as if the admission had been drawn out of her by force. "Something tells me that you, both of you, think on your feet. I don't think on my feet."

"There are so many questions," said Lestat, "that you haven't asked. You haven't asked me if Amel remembers himself now, and that seems an immense question."

Kapetria regarded him carefully before answering.

"I know that he remembers himself now, Lestat," she said. "I knew last night in the blood. I knew he was our Amel and he remembers himself and he remembers us."

The Prince waited for a moment and then he nodded. "Very well," he said, looking off again and then back at her. "I can't change your mind, can I?"

"No," she said. "But will you believe in us? Will you trust us? Will you trust that we will be back soon?" This was as close as she had come to deep feeling, Derek figured.

Again, the Prince hesitated. "He has something else to tell you," said the Prince.

"What is it?" she asked.

He drew a piece of paper out of his jacket and he handed it to her across the table. It was fine stationery folded in half and in half again.

Kapetria opened it. Derek could easily read the large perfect alphabetical script without leaning over to crowd her. In a flash, he realized what it was. It was what Dertu had told Kapetria to do over the phone line—if they had to communicate with one another via the internet—to transliterate the ancient tongue of Atalantaya into phonic words via the alphabet. And as he heard the written syllables in his head he understood them:

**You cannot hurt him. I love him. You cannot hurt them. I love them. You must find a way to do it without hurting him or them. Or it will not be done.**

She looked up and smiled. "Very well," she said.

"What does it say?" asked the Prince.

"You really don't know?"

"No." Again he shrugged. "He didn't tell me what it meant. He only kept repeating it and telling me that I had to give you the message. That you couldn't leave without the message. And so I wrote it down just before coming to see you. Does it make sense?"

"Yes," she said. "It makes sense. Isn't it his place to tell you what it means?"

"Probably," said the Prince. He sat up, and let the front legs of the chair settle on the floor, and he rose to his feet.

Kapetria was looking up at him with a kind of wonder but Derek stood out of respect. Marius had also risen and moved towards the door.

Slowly Kapetria rose. She folded the sheet of stationery back into fours and tucked it inside the neck of her dress. She did this carefully as if it had some ceremonial meaning. Then she gestured for them to wait. She moved soundlessly into the bedroom and came back with a large capped vial filled with blood.

Derek was amazed. He watched with misgivings as she put the vial in the Prince's hand.

"This is my blood," she said. "Give it to Fareed. He wanted it, didn't he? Well, this is a pure sample. I want him to have it, to make what he can of what he discovers in it."

The Prince slipped the vial into his jacket pocket

and bowed. "Thank you," he said. He laughed. "This will make the mad scientist supremely happy, perhaps more than either of us can know."

Kapetria stretched out her arms to the Prince.

They embraced tightly, and they stood together like that for a long moment.

Then Kapetria said, "Let me tell Amel now through you that I understand," she said. "And I love you, and will never do you harm."

The Prince smiled, but it was no spontaneous innocent smile.

He nodded.

"And you, Derek, let me take you in my arms too," said the Prince. "You've been through too much suffering. Forgive us for what happened." They embraced, and then Marius offered his hand in farewell.

It was all right touching them, feeling their skin. He had not felt the frisson he'd been dreading. However powerful they were, they were suffused with a genuine human heat, and it was all right.

Yet now that they were going down the stairs, Derek felt a cruel little surge of joy that Roland was dead. Roland had been punished for what he had done to Derek. Roland had lost his "immortality." Roland was no more. That Arion had aided in the punishing of Roland, this too made Derek happy, but it felt very bad to Derek to be happy that any living creature was dead. It flashed through his mind suddenly that when they did get away to some safe place, they would all be joyful because death would be no part of it, and fear would be no part of it, and they would be a colony and a kindred in their own little world. A deep sense of Atalantaya came back to him, as it had last night all during Kapetria's story, of warm nights in Atalantaya when it seemed all living things were content and flourishing, and the music played on the street corners and in the little cafés and the flowers perfumed the air, and the tall thin trees with their yellowish-green leaves sent lacy shadows over the shining pavements, and the birds sang, all those tiny birds that lived under the great dome of Atalantaya, of which they'd not spoken a word, any of them, behold such birds.

Kapetria went to the window and moved back the white curtain. Derek stood beside her, looking down on them as they stepped out under the lamp above the sign of the inn and then both figures vanished.

Kapetria uttered a small delighted laugh. "Did you see which direction they went?"

"No," said Derek. "They simply disappeared."

"Now if we could only move like that."

She stood gazing down at the empty street. Derek could hear the dull echoing thrum of the music from the Château.

"It's Marius who rules, isn't it?" he asked in a whisper.

"Not really," said Kapetria, still looking out and up over the pointed roofs opposite. "I thought so at first. I thought it was obvious. But I was wrong. It's the Prince who rules. It's the Prince who's decided to trust us."

"Is that why you gave him the blood?" Derek asked. "Are you sure you should have done that?"

"Yes, I'm sure," Kapetria said. "Don't worry, Derek."

"If you say so," he responded. He felt better already. He felt that nothing bad could ever happen to him again if Kapetria was here. He thought of all the times that Roland had drunk his blood. And to think there was this blood drinker doctor, Fareed, and what he might have given to study the blood.

Kapetria was still looking out into the night.

"Marius will gather the Council together," said Kapetria, "and he will do all the work of making a credo for them and rules, and means of punishing offenders and he will see that it's done with dignity and honor. But Marius is angry, angry at the other old ones. He's angry that for centuries they never came forward to help him with the keeping of the Queen when Amel was inside her. They watched from afar but they never helped. It's all in their pages. You can read it later for yourself."

"Why didn't they help him?" asked Derek. He spoke as softly as she spoke.

"That's a question only they can answer," said Kapetria. She let go of the sheer curtain, and sat down again, holding the backs of her arms. "Whatever the case, Marius will do the work that has to be done.

But it's the Prince who holds it all together. And the Prince loves Marius and that's enough for Marius to do what has to be done."

"Gravitas," said Derek. He stood there looking down at her. "Marius has gravitas."

Kapetria smiled. "Yes, that's the old Roman word for what he possesses, isn't it?"

Derek nodded. He thought in a vague way of all the books he'd read in Spanish and English before that horrid monster, Roland, had captured him like a little bird between two cupped hands. He thought of all he'd learned when it just did not seem to matter, as he'd roamed all alone searching and dreaming of beings he thought he might never find again. Well, that was over now, and all that he'd read would come alive for him now, wouldn't it, in new and wondrous ways. He wanted to read the vampire pages as Kapetria always called them. He wanted to read poetry and history and all the books on the legend of Atlantis that she had described to him, the books she'd read and studied in Matilde's library in the town of Bolinas, California, where Kapetria and Welf had come to shore like lovers carved in stone. He wanted to go to all those places Kapetria had described to him where she had gone trying to find remnants of "the lost kingdom of Atlantis." And he wanted with all his heart to hear the voice of Amel. If only the Prince had let Derek hear that voice. If only there had been no pain.

He realized that Kapetria was smiling at him in

the most affectionate way. The warmth, the sense of safety, the sense of being able to be happy again, swept over Derek. Kapetria stood and kissed him.

"Beautiful boy," she said.

She moved back to the window again and, lifting the curtain, looked out at the street once more. For a moment he thought she was going to weep. And he'd never seen Kapetria shed a tear. She turned to him with that loving expression that melted his heart.

"But why didn't you tell the Prince what Amel said?" He said the words as softly as he could. No human being could have heard. But the vampires, who knew what they heard?

"Amel will tell him," she said.

Why does she look so sad? She was still looking off again now in the direction of the Château.

"Come," she said suddenly. "We need to pack up now."

# 24

# Fareed

He sat behind his computer, in his apartment in the Château, and he listened to all that Marius had to say and that Lestat said. Seth was as usual perfectly quiet. He wanted to get to work on this new vial of blood. The blood he'd drawn from Lestat had been contaminated with vampiric blood. This was pure Replimoid blood, fresh and still warm.

"You have no idea what the message said?" asked Fareed.

"None," said Lestat. "But it was brief, whatever it was. And he pressed me to give it to her right after Roland died. He knew that Roland had died. He didn't tell me. He just gave me the message and I went into the library and wrote it down. I made a copy of it, of course."

He took a piece of paper out of his pocket and handed it to Fareed, and then he turned his back and started pacing, making a slow circle in the middle of the carpet, with his hands clasped behind his back, looking remarkably, Fareed thought, like an eighteenth-century man. Maybe it was the hair tied back like a young Thomas Jefferson or a picture of Mozart. And the frock coat with the flared skirt.

Fareed went over the words. He went over them again and again and again. He tried to relate them to the phone messages which he had also gone over again and again and again. Seth was standing behind him looking down at the paper.

"I can't crack it," said Fareed.

"Neither can I," said Seth, "but it is interesting to see it transliterated that way. The pictographs were hopeless."

"So what do you think?" asked Fareed.

Lestat sighed and continued with his pacing. "I don't know. They're leaving and it's their prerogative to leave, and what will happen will happen. That's what my mind tells me. Now does my heart agree with my mind?"

He stopped and he had that blank look on his face which always meant that Amel was talking, but if this was true, that message too was a mystery. Because Lestat said nothing but began pacing again.

There was a sudden pounding on the door.

"Come in, please," said Seth.

It was Dr. Flannery Gilman and she had a sheaf of papers in her hands.

"I've been calling you and calling you," she said to Fareed, without greeting anyone, or even so much as a nod to Lestat.

Of all the doctors Fareed had brought into the Blood, this one he loved the most. And it was she who had helped him in the making of Viktor, the nearest thing that Fareed would ever have to a son. It was she who had enticed Lestat into the few brief moments of erotic passion that an infusion of hormones had allowed him and she who had carried Viktor, given birth to Viktor, nursed and cared for Viktor until finally the time had come when Viktor would be all right on his own.

Now both were blood drinkers, Flannery and Viktor, and the only pair of blood drinkers in the whole world who were mother and son, other than Gabrielle and Lestat.

"You have to look at this, all of it, now," said Flannery. "You can bring it up on the screen if you want, but I've gone over this here and circled everything that's relevant. She lied to you. She deceived you."

"What do you mean? Who?" Lestat turned as if somebody had pulled him out of a dream.

"Fareed said go over every single requisition, order, list of purchases, everything for as far back as the records went. And I did it. I pulled everything she's ever ordered for any experiment, any project, any trial!"

Fareed went through the papers, eyes moving with preternatural speed over the printout, over Flannery's many felt-tip-pen circles, over her underlining, turning the pages rapidly, and then he carried the whole stack around the side of the table so that he could spread the pages out.

"What is it?" asked Seth.

"I see exactly what you're saying!" Fareed said. He looked up to his beloved mentor and then to Lestat. "All the way back to her first weeks at Collingsworth. But how did she get away with it? Oh, I'm beginning to see. Under the names of the assistants."

"And look at the notations for duplicate amounts," said Flannery. "Reorders, claims of stolen packages, or packages damaged or never received. I wager every single order was always received. Look at this, these orders for human growth hormone. What could she conceivably have been working on to use that amount of human growth hormone? Or this one, look at this one. This was all for the synthetic skin project. Why, that's enough to make skin for half of Europe."

"She was building a Replimoid body!" said Lestat. "And she lied about it."

"Go back over the film of her talking about it," said Flannery. "I've watched this same footage over and over again." She didn't wait for Fareed to respond. She sat down at the keyboard and brought up the film of Kapetria telling her story, zipping through it until Kapetria's voice poured out of the speakers of the computer.

Fareed came round to watch the film as Seth and Lestat gathered to his right and left:

There was Kapetria at the table as she had been last night.

"But for all the hours I've worked alone and with Welf in the sanctum of laboratories under Gregory's roof, I have never discovered the actual formula for luracastria, or come close to reproducing a thermoplastic or polymer like it. I have not, contrary to your suspicions, ever grown a Replimoid whole and complete and animated, though I have certainly struggled towards this goal for many years."

Flannery hit the button to go back.

"Now watch it again. See what she does? See how she touches her hair when she said the words. That's a tell, a giveaway, that she's lying. If you watch the whole tape again, you'll see exactly what I mean. There are three points where her voice changes in pitch and she makes that same gesture, smoothing back her hair."

"I have never discovered the actual formula for luracastria, or come close to reproducing a thermoplastic or polymer like it. I have not, contrary to your suspicions, ever grown a Replimoid whole and complete and animated, though I have certainly struggled towards this goal for many years."

"I see it," said Seth.

"Struggled with it?" asked Flannery. "She's been working on it night and day, and she's close to completing a Replimoid! She's used enough chemicals to grow a family of Replimoids. She's established a reserve of such chemicals. . . ."

Lestat turned and walked away. He started pacing again, making that same circle, or was it an oval now?

"Lestat, do you realize what Flannery is saying?" Fareed said. "How long before they're scheduled to leave?" He knew the answer. He didn't have to look at his watch. He knew full well that it was almost time for Lestat to retire to his crypt, and that meant that Fareed had little more than an hour himself.

"What can we do about it?" Lestat asked in a low voice. His head was bowed and he kept walking at exactly the same speed. His hands were clasped behind his back.

"She's making a body for Amel," said Flannery. "Lestat, you know that's what she's been doing." Flannery looked helplessly to Fareed. "Whatever her goal was before now, whether it was simply to make others, she's got that body almost ready. I know it. Give me another two hours with these printouts and I could chart her progress just through the orders."

"No need," said Lestat. "He gave her what she needed to know last night. I saw him do it. I saw it in the blood when I was holding her in my arms. I saw it all." Back and forth he walked.

"And you're going to let her leave here?" asked Flannery.

Fareed looked at Seth. Seth stood back away from the computer table, his eyes still fixed on the screen. Flannery had paused the image of Kapetria at the table, with her hand lifted to her hair.

"Flannery, my darling," said Lestat. "There is simply nothing we can do." He stopped and looked up and flashed one of his finest smiles on Flannery. "Whatever will happen . . . will happen."

"Not if you stop them!" cried Flannery. "Not if you lock them up. Why, you have more than enough help here to lock them up no matter if there are twenty of them now or twenty-four or thirty!"

"Darling," said Lestat. "What good would it do? And how would we live with it, a colony of Replimoids in our cellars forever, multiplying unceasingly, and never allowed to see the light of day again? Or do we chain them to the walls so they don't multiply? Didn't we execute Roland for just such a crime?"

"There has to be something we can do."

"There isn't, and we can't, and we won't," said Lestat. He stood there, hands still clasped behind his back, and his face went blank again, and then assumed its regular meditative expression, his eyes moving almost aimlessly over the walls of the room.

"Has Amel translated the message for you?" Seth asked.

Lestat nodded.

He looked directly at Seth but he was speaking to them all.

"This is the message," Lestat said. " 'You cannot hurt him. I love him. You cannot hurt them. I love them. You must find a way to do it without hurting him or them. Or it will not be done.' "

Fareed took a deep breath.

"That is exactly the message," Lestat said. He appeared so marvelously calm, so astonishingly calm.

"Maybe there's some way," said Seth. But then he stopped.

No one knew or understood better than Seth just where they were in their research and what they could or could not do.

"There has to be some way to reason with her," said Flannery. "To slow her down, to force her to realize that this cannot be attempted without guarantees. . . ."

"She'll do what she can to set him free," said Lestat. "And she'll do everything that she can to abide by his wishes. I know, because if I were her, that's what I would do, but if I couldn't abide by his wishes, I'd still do everything in my power to incarnate him and re-create him and set him free."

In a small voice, Flannery quoted the old Dylan Thomas poem, " 'Do not go gentle into that good night, . . . Rage, rage against the dying of the light.' "

Lestat smiled sadly.

The doors opened and in came Thorne and Cyril.

"You know that gang of weird ones is gone, don't you?" said Cyril with his usual brashness, addressing the Prince as if no one else in the world existed. "They just pulled out in two cars. They breed like rodents! There must have been twenty of them! You want us to go after them? I thought they weren't supposed to leave until daylight. There'll probably be thirty of them before they get to the outer gates."

"No," said Lestat. "Let them go."

Fareed looked at Seth. Seth was staring at the Prince, but behind Seth's dark eyes the wheels were turning.

"Sleep well, beloveds," said Lestat. "I'm calling it a night . . . or a day."

The Prince and the bodyguards left the room.

Fareed stared at the large vial of blood. He'd have to refrigerate it for now and take it to Paris when the sun set. A great surge of anger rose in him, anger that surprised him and confused him, because he was seldom angry with anyone in the Dark World to which he now so totally belonged. But he knew that Lestat, and all the tribe, were in great danger, and he was terrified that he would not hit upon any way to help in time.

# Part III

# THE
# SILVER
# CORD

# 25

# Lestat

SEVEN NIGHTS HAD passed. How the discussion raged. Of course Benji issued only the blandest of official announcements on the radio broadcast. Peace had been made with Garekyn Zweck Brovotkin and the other Replimoids and no blood drinker anywhere in the world was to harm these creatures. The Replimoids had sworn never to bring harm to the vampires, or betray their secrets. Life was to go on as before. But the world of the Undead knew what was happening. The endless telepathic emanations had circled the globe.

All the blood drinkers gathered beneath the roof of the Château knew precisely what was happening, and groups came forth demanding that we defend ourselves against this new enemy that might try to seize the Core from within the Prince and thereby annihilate the tribe. Cyril and Thorne asked why we didn't fight.

Armand and Marius had a dreadful quarrel in which Armand demanded that the Replimoids be hunted down and annihilated, and Marius accused Armand of having the savage and ignorant soul of a child.

The ancient ones discussed it amongst themselves endlessly, except for Fareed, Seth, and Flannery, who went off to Paris to work ceaselessly to find some solution to the problems we faced. Fareed was of the opinion that my precious evil twin, Amel, could be removed some night somehow into a neutral container of some sort, a tank of ever-circulating vampiric blood, until such time as the Replimoids surfaced again. But he admitted that as of now, he was utterly incapable of achieving this feat.

And what good would that do anyway when Kapetria sought to put the brain inside a Replimoid body, a body of flesh and blood that could walk in the light of the sun? Wouldn't the mysterious nano-particle tentacles be severed then? Or would we all burn up, even the eldest of us, within a space of weeks as the mysterious engine that animated us exercised its new prerogatives? And what was to stop him, except our keeping him a prisoner forever in some chemical device?

Again and again, the ancient ones sought to calm the young ones, and all who came from far and wide to find out what was truly happening or not happening, and what they might do.

One thing was now achieved. We had a fairly good fix on our numbers. It was merely an estimate but I thought it was a sound estimate. We could not be more than about two thousand worldwide. Such a small tribe. Fareed had completed the calculations that he had begun last year—putting together all accounts of the infamous Burnings when Amel was on the rampage, and calculations as to how many any one coven house had claimed as occupants, and calculations as to how many coven houses there had been in the world. He had recorded the identity and particulars of each new blood drinker arriving among us. And he had taken the blood of the blood drinker too for his laboratory. And he had questioned each blood drinker as to what other blood drinkers he'd encountered throughout his life.

It was over my head, the graphs and the mathematical talk. But I sensed the figure itself was accurate, and now we were seeing not a flood of new faces at Court but the same people coming back who'd been here when we'd first opened our doors.

But what did it matter if two thousand of us perished or fifteen thousand? Were we soon to be a legend and nothing else? Would the human Talamasca, now severed from Gremt and Teskhamen and Hesketh, ever know what became of the fabled vampires they'd studied for centuries?—ever know why they perished or that a new tribe of immortals had now come together, the Replimoids, to increase exponentially if they chose?

And that exponential increase is what we tried to explain to those who kept saying, Destroy them! Burn them. Wipe them out.

"That has never been an option," said Marius night after night as he addressed the company in the ballroom. "Even when they came to us, there were others hidden somewhere, likely multiplying beyond reckoning. While the embassy of Replimoids was with us, it multiplied. We know of nothing that limits their individual or collective ability to replicate. For all we know there are hundreds of them now, and possibly thousands. So whom are we to hunt down, and seek to destroy?"

Marius didn't attempt to defend our conviction that we could not morally exterminate the Replimoids. But we, the inner circle, never wavered in this regard. Besides, they had done nothing yet. They had not even made a threat against us. And if and when they did, could we not protect ourselves?

Our vaults were so strong, it would require explosives in mass quantity to disrupt them during the daylight hours; and it was inconceivable that the Replimoid tribe, so distinctive physically, would come here with the strength of a battalion to breach the castle doors and crypts. The villagers would panic at the first sounds of explosives. They'd summon the forces of the mortal world from far and wide.

Whatever they were, and whatever they were destined to be, the Replimoids surely were fearing exposure just as we had always feared it; and though we had triumphed in hiding in plain sight in a world convinced we were fictional, the Replimoids, once captured, imprisoned, and examined, simply did

not have our formidable gifts to help them escape
from mortal bonds and literally burn up all traces of
their cell matter that might remain in mortal hands.

"Why don't we expose them?" asked the young
ones. "Why don't we turn the forces of the world
loose on them?"

"Because they could in turn expose us," said
Marius, answering some form of this question almost every single night.

As for the vial of blood which Kapetria had
given to Fareed, he could find nothing in it that was
directly helpful to what he had to do, though its
makeup puzzled him. He spoke of its having five
times the density of folic acid as human blood. He
talked of other chemicals, of breaking down the baffling DNA, of mysterious components for which he
had to make new names. When, through me, he put
the question to Amel as to what distinguished Replimoid blood from human blood, Amel wouldn't answer. I don't think Amel knew how to answer. Or
something about the question aroused deep currents
of feeling in him that he couldn't bear.

Amel certainly had no idea as to how to solve the
problem of the connection, that was clear. Whether
he might ever be the great scientist of Atalantaya
again, no one could know; but he was not the Great
One now.

As for me, I was no more resigned to perish than
I'd ever been, my dramatic little suicide attempt in
the Gobi Desert notwithstanding. But helpless to

do anything about the connection between me and Amel, I became obsessed with our connection to the others, and how they might be severed from Amel inside of me.

I told Fareed: Find a way to snip the tentacles of the nano-particle thermoplastic luracastria that bound all vampires to the Core. Then I'd die when Amel was removed from me, yes, but the tribe would live.

I became convinced that Kapetria was giving us time to focus on this, and when she had described this vast web of connections as a failed attempt at propagation, she'd been giving us the only help that she could.

More than once I went on Benji's radio cast and made vague appeals to her, heavily disguised as general admonitions to blood drinkers everywhere as to how we must always work together, and think of one another, and think of the welfare and destiny of one another. I gave out the number of the cell phone I carried. But no call from Kapetria came.

"If she knew how to sever the connection, she'd tell us," I said to the others; though why I clung to such a view of her I wasn't sure. Maybe it was simply that I had liked her, liked all she'd told us of her birth and her brief life in Atalantaya, and I positively loved what she'd told us about the life and adventures of the spirit inside us who had always been known as Amel. I loved that she had volunteered the vial of her blood. Yes, she'd lied to us. But

I knew why she'd lied. I couldn't fault her for lying. I couldn't yield to a cynical view of Kapetria, or to a cynical view of those with her. And I could not bear to think of their annihilation any more than I could think of ours.

That anything so ancient and mysterious should die—this was unthinkable to me. When Maharet had died, the great unique universe of Maharet had perished with her, and I found it unendurable to think about it. And that was why I couldn't wish for the death of Rhoshamandes either. Who was I to put an end to a being who knew what Rhoshamandes knew, a being who had seen all that he had seen? Some night, Rhoshamandes and I would talk about it all, talk about what it had been like when he first came north from the Mediterranean into the wild primal forests of the land we now call France. Some night, we'd talk about so many things . . . that is, if it wasn't too late.

Whatever the nightly arguments, the heated question-and-answer sessions, vampires clung to the Court. The Château could shelter some fifty or more guests in its crypts; another two hundred or more lodged safely and secretly in the nearby cities; and the young ones who had to hunt the millions in Paris came nightly to Armand's house in Saint-Germain-des-Prés. And I went to be with the young ones there for at least an hour every night.

There were tears shed, loud accusations of betrayal, sharp challenges to my integrity or worth as the Prince of the Vampires, and long violent discussions as to what to fear and what to do, and how long we might have.

But we hung together, at Armand's house, or here in this mighty fortress where the lights never went out and the music always played.

As for Amel, he listened to all of my speeches and exhortations in silence, only pouring forth his heart to me when we were alone. It seemed with every passing night, he knew more of his own story, but he knew it threaded through and through with confusion and pain. He wept and railed at the Bravennans, whom he called the authors of all evil, and blamed on them all the bloody religions that had ever become the scourge of humankind. He lapsed into the ancient tongue for hours as if he could not help himself, and other times he fell to weeping without words.

This was no longer the childish spirit baiting me and telling me he loved me one moment while calling me a fool the next. This was Amel who knew things that I would never know, no matter how long I walked the earth, knew possibilities and probabilities of which we blood drinkers simply never conceived—but Amel who could not think how to save us from destruction, and swore again and again that he would never allow such a thing to come about.

"Why don't we go into Paris?" I suggested more than once. "Why don't we just talk with Fareed and

Seth and maybe **you** can figure how to sever the connection so that the others don't have to die?"

Weeping. I heard him weeping. "Don't you think I've tried?"

"I don't know. I wonder. You built Atalantaya," I said. I couldn't get used to calling it Atlantis. "Surely you can bring your extraordinary mind to bear on this problem and come up with something, there has to be something."

This was torture for him. I knew it. But I was desperate.

"I won't let her do it!" Amel protested. "Don't you understand? You think she can do this without my cooperation? You think I can't use the power inside you to incinerate her? She knows I can and I will."

And on he'd go, weeping, and avowing that we are one, and you are me and I am you. "Go look in a mirror. Find a mirror. There are mirrors all over this castle. I want you to look in a mirror. I want to see you in the mirror."

And so I stood in front of a mirror from time to time and let him look at me, remembering Kapetria's description of him with his green eyes and red hair. Could have been your brother or your cousin, is that what she said?

"When I first saw you standing before Akasha," he said, "I saw me."

If I slept, we dreamed, and we were in Atalantaya and the language was all around me. We walked the gleaming streets together, as people came out to greet him, touch his hand. It was balmy and sweet there like it is in New Orleans in springtime and the banana trees were vastly bigger and primal sending their knifelike leaves sky-high over us. The buildings did shine with the luster of pearls. But these dreams faded fast when I opened my eyes.

One night I dreamed a man and a woman were talking together in the ancient language. I couldn't see them, but I was hearing them, hearing her voice and his voice; it seemed they'd been talking forever, and I had the distinct impression that if I did listen with the utmost focus, that I could crack the language. The secret lay in the repetitions. I felt I knew now the word for "behold," the word they said so often—**lalakaté.**

Then it was morning. I woke up, found I wasn't in my coffin, that I had fallen asleep on the marble bench beside it. I'd done that often lately, fallen asleep on the hard cold marble, not bothering with the comfort of the coffin as though I were a monk sentenced for his sins to sleep on a hard pallet. I saw my phone lying on the floor. Out of the charger. No battery. I remembered that I'd put it in the charger, then put my right hand under my head and gone to sleep as the world sang Lauds above.

I stared at the phone.

"It was you talking to her!"

No answer.

I sat up and picked up the phone. I checked back and there were the calls. All day long, calls one after another, until the battery had gone out, seven distinct calls.

"Don't bother," he said. Anguish. "She has no solution for the severing of the ties. She is working on 'what she has to work on now,' she says."

"How did you do it?"

"She'd given me the number when we were together in the blood," he said. "I hadn't realized what it was. I had to think about it. You know how hard it is for me to think of any one thing without so many other things. She'd talked of ghosts using phones and radios and radio waves. And the phone was right by your head. More and more often you were sleeping like that on the bench and the phone was right by your head. But it doesn't matter. She doesn't know anything. She's working on 'what she has to work on.' She's like a parent determined to rescue a child against the child's will."

He didn't speak for the rest of the night.

But I was shaken.

I told the ancient ones what he'd done, managing to connect through the phone while I slept. We'd all suspected long ago that he wasn't paralyzed as we were by the sun, but it was, like so much else, just a mystery that Fareed could not explain with all the abstract medical terms in the world. I told him of all the times that Amel had tried to force me to move against my will, of the times he'd made my hand jump or cramp.

I left the phone and the charger upstairs in my

bedchamber after that. If they needed me during those hours when I was down there waiting for sleep, they'd have to knock at the door of the vault.

Amel didn't seem to care. And he wasn't trying to make my limbs move anymore anyway. At least not most of the time.

# 26

# Lestat

I TOLD LOUIS EVERYTHING. Ten nights had passed during which I sought to protect him from the extent of my fear. Of course he knew absolutely everything that had been going on; he was always with me, and we'd managed to get away to hunt in Paris twice.

But this was different. I poured it all out. I confided all my fears that there was nothing I could do to stop the inevitable, and I talked about severing the tentacles and how Fareed and Seth were working on that now, marshaling every bit of research they had on us to try to figure a way.

"And what are the chances of Fareed figuring out this mystery, as to how we're all connected?" I asked. "As Fareed himself put it, how can he disconnect something that he cannot see?"

We were in the Château because no one wanted me to leave it, unless I positively had to, which I didn't, except to go to Armand's house for a brief visit, or hunt when I felt I had to, and all that I'd already done.

We were in the south tower, which was wholly new, and contained some of the most splendid rooms, reserved in theory for the most honored guests, and this meant we had a bedchamber parlor to ourselves, and it was a fine comfortable place to talk.

I'd had this apartment done all in shades of gold, magenta, and rose, with nineteenth-century flowered wallpaper and a nineteenth-century walnut bed and armoire and chests of drawers and chairs. It made me think of our flat in New Orleans and I found it comforting after all the brilliantly lighted baroque splendor of so many other rooms.

We sat at the small round table before the arched window, with the two leaded-glass sashes open wide to the night air. No need of a light as the moon was full. There were two decks of cards there, and I'd thought I might deal out a game of solitaire just to do something, anything, but I hadn't touched the cards. I love shiny new cards.

"For two nights now, Amel hasn't been with me," I said. "I don't know whether or not you can tell."

Louis was leaning on his elbows and looking at me.

He had taken off his black wool jacket and was dressed only in a gray cashmere sweater over his white shirt and black pants. He would never have done that on such a freezing night as this before he'd received all the powerful blood. I wonder if he ever thought of Merrick anymore, the unearthly sorceress who'd seduced him and spellbound him and pushed him, unwittingly, to expose his fragile vampiric body to the sun. Merrick had left us early of her own will. She'd been one of those powerful souls utterly convinced of an afterlife more interesting than this world. Maybe she was thriving in that afterlife, or lost in the upper air with the other spirits and ghosts in the confusing realm that Gremt had fled.

I'd been observing many small changes in Louis over the years due to the powerful blood. His eyes were certainly more iridescent and it irritated me that he would never wear sunglasses, even in the brightest rooms or on the brightest streets. But nothing changed the wall of telepathic silence that fell between master and fledgling. Yet I felt closer to him than to any other visible being in the world.

"What happens if you call to Amel and ask him to come back?" Louis asked.

"What would be the point?" I asked.

I was wearing my usual court finery, because I knew it comforted almost everyone. But it wasn't in keeping with my mood to be dressed in steel-blue brocade and linen frills, and for the first time, I envied Louis his simpler clothes.

"Amel could be inside you right now looking at me for all I know," I said. "What does it matter? One minute he swears he'll never let her harm me, and the next he's as grim as I am, speaking of Kapetria as a parent bound to rescue a child against the child's will."

Of course I'd told him all about the phone incident.

"I don't think that's possible," Louis said. His voice was even and soft. "That he's inside me, I mean, but let me get back to that. I've been thinking a lot about the matter of tentacles binding us and what Kapetria said, that this was a failed attempt at procreation or propagation. It makes me think of the silver cord."

"What silver cord?"

"The silver cord was what the old nineteenth-century parapsychologists called it," said Louis. "An invisible connection between body and soul. When a man astral projects, goes up and out of his body and into another body as you did with the Body Thief, the silver cord is what connects him to his biological body, and if the silver cord breaks, the man dies."

"I don't know what the hell you're talking about," I said.

"Oh, yes, you do," he said. "That etheric body that is traveling on the astral plane or hooked inside another body—the way David Talbot's etheric body was hooked into the old body of the Body Thief— the etheric body is free only once the silver cord is cut."

"Well, that's sweet and poetic and charming," I said. "But likely there is no real silver cord. Just old poetry, poetry of the British spiritualists and psychics. I don't remember seeing any silver cord when I switched bodies with the Body Thief. Likely it's something imaginary that helped astral travelers to visualize what is going on."

"Is it?" Louis asked. "I'm not so sure."

"Are you serious with all this?" I asked.

"What if it is the very same silver cord which in our case remains connected—connecting each new etheric body developed by Amel in a host—to his etheric body, when it should, as Kapetria suggested, snap so that the new vampire can be free?"

"Louis, honestly. The silver cord connects a biological body to an etheric body. Amel is an etheric body, isn't he? And his etheric body is connected to the etheric bodies in each of us."

"Well, we know now, don't we, that they are likely both biological, right? They are two kinds of biological body—the gross biological body and the etheric biological body made of cells we can't see. And in his case those etheric cells are expressions of what he was when he was alive."

I sighed. "It hurts my head to keep talking about cells we can't see."

"Lestat," he said. "I want you please to bear with me. Look at me. Pay attention. Listen to me for a change." He smiled to soften this and laid his hand on mine. "Come on, Lestat, listen."

I growled deep in my throat. "All right, I'm listening," I said. "I read all that foolishness when it was published. I read every word of Madame Blavatsky. I've read the later books. Remember, I am the one who has switched bodies, after all."

"What happens to make the silver cord snap and let loose the etheric body from the biological body?" he asked.

"You just said it; the biological body dies."

"Yes, if the biological body dies the cord snaps, freeing the etheric body," he said.

"And?"

"But that's just it. We never actually die when we're made into vampires. Oh, we all speak of dying, and I had to go out into the swamps and rid my body of all the waste and excess fluids, and I did that. But I never actually died."

"So how can this lead to a solution?"

He sat there for a long moment, looking out over the snowy fields that lay between us and the road. Then he stood up and walked back and forth before turning to me again.

"I want to go to Paris," he said. "I want to talk to Fareed and the doctors."

"Louis, they've likely read all those British books by the Golden Dawn people. That is what you're talking about, right, the Theosophists and Swedenborg and Sylvan Muldoon and Oliver Fox, and even Robert Monroe in the twentieth century. Seriously? The silver cord?"

"I want to go to Paris now and I want you to come with me," Louis said.

"What you mean is you want me to take you," I said.

"That's right," he responded, "and we should bring Viktor with us."

"Unlike you, Viktor has the skill and the nerve to take to the air on his own."

I removed my iPhone from my pocket. I had come to hate it more than ever since Amel had figured how to use it, but I hit the number for my son.

Turns out he was in Paris already, hunting the back streets with Rose.

"I want you to go to Fareed at his laboratory," I said, "and tell him I'm coming, and I want you to meet me there."

One very endearing thing about my son: I never had to explain an order to him. He simply did whatever I asked.

"David, too," said Louis. "Please call David. I think David will understand this better than I do."

I did as I was told. David was in the Château library, going through our own pages again as he'd been doing since Kapetria left, searching for some clue as to how the great connecting web might work. He said he would go to Paris now, if we wanted him to. He would do anything we wanted. I rang off.

"Don't you think you might call Fareed personally and tell him we're coming?" Louis asked. "That's my last request, I promise."

I didn't really need the phone for that. Fareed's telepathic antennae were as powerful as mine. I sent out the message that Louis and I would be joining him within minutes. Louis felt it was important. But then I heard the voice of Thorne in the shadows nearby.

"I've texted him," he said. "We are ready to go."

And so it was done. Louis was putting on his jacket and scarf. I was unhappy. I watched him pulling on his gloves. I couldn't imagine how this could end productively or happily. I didn't want Louis to be humiliated, but what could Fareed and Seth say to talk of the silver cord? If they became impatient and short with him, I'd be furious.

It was a matter of minutes to reach Paris.

I caught sight of the unmistakable light patterns of the roofs of Collingsworth Pharmaceuticals and within seconds we were on the tarmac surface and headed for "our door" that led directly to Fareed's secret quarters and work area, with Thorne and Cyril following.

These new facilities had been remodeled last fall especially for Fareed, and he had an immense glass-walled office which opened directly into a vast laboratory with tables, machines, sinks, cabinets, and apparatuses of ornate and baffling complexity that wandered on for half a city block.

The office itself was furnished, as all of Fareed's offices were, with a mixture of ornate antiques and comfortable modern couches and shapeless chairs.

There was the de rigueur marble Adam fireplace with its porcelain gas logs and the array of carefully modulated flames. There was the Louis XV desk for writing, and then there was the endless computer table with its five or six brilliantly illuminated monitors, and Fareed, in his white lab coat and white cotton pants, slumped in a great engulfing leather office chair replete with buttons and levers on the arms, and, opposite him as he turned to face us, the inevitable "conversation pit" of velvet recliners and a broad couch that ran on forever and the coffee table littered with medical journals and sketch pads filled with nightmarish drawings and diagrams— and Seth, in a white **thawb,** standing beside Fareed.

Viktor and Rose were already settled on the couch. And so was David. I took the recliner to the right. It pained me dreadfully to think Louis was about to be dismissed out of hand by the two scientific geniuses of the Blood, and that Viktor and Rose were here to witness his humiliation, but Louis seemed utterly undeterred.

Louis went right to it, standing off to Fareed's left so that his small audience had a clear view of Fareed.

"You know what the silver cord is," he said. He was rather deferential. "The old British psychics spoke of it, the cord that connects the astral body or etheric body to the biological body when a person astral projects."

"Yes, I'm familiar with it," said Fareed. "But I think of it as metaphorical."

"Yes," said David cheerfully and he began quoting from scriptures:

"Because man goeth to his long home, and the mourners go about the streets; or ever the silver cord be loosed, or the golden bowl be broken, or the pitcher broken at the fountain . . . "

"That's it," said Louis. "I'd forgotten it in scriptures. I remembered it from the Theosophical literature, and when it's snapped the etheric body or brain or soul is free."

"And the biological body dies," said Rose. "I've read those wonderful books. I used to try so hard to astral project when I was in high school, but it never happened. I'd lie on my bed and try for hours to go up and out the window and over New York, and all that ever happened was that I went to sleep."

Louis smiled. "But let's for the moment think of it in reverse. Let's not say if the silver cord is snapped the body dies, but rather if the body dies, the silver cord is snapped."

"What has this to do with us, Louis?" Fareed asked. He was really playing the gentleman. I knew how tired he was, how discouraged.

"Well, I'll tell you. I believe that these cords that connect us to Amel are a version of the silver cord; it's the silver cord connecting Amel's etheric body to the new etheric body formed in a new vampire—and the reason that we all remain connected is that we never actually die physically, when we are made. There is an etheric brain planted in us at the time we are brought over and it quickly generates an etheric body in us; but our biological body doesn't really die. It's merely transformed. So we remained tethered—Amel's etheric body and our etheric body. If we did actually die, the cord would snap, and the new etheric body which has taken over the physical body would be free of Amel."

"I thought we died as soon as the vampiric element took hold," said Viktor. "We went out to die after we were brought over. Our bodies had to get rid of fluids, waste—that was physical death."

"But you didn't really die, did you?" asked Louis. "Yes, that transformation happened. But you didn't really die."

"Well, if we had we wouldn't be here now," said Seth. "If the fledgling dies before the process is complete—."

"But what if the fledgling dies after the process is complete?" asked Louis.

"Well, you have everybody's interest, I'll say that for you," I murmured.

"Lestat, do be quiet," said David in a gentle voice.

"Let me explain," said Louis. "I was present decades ago when Akasha was killed. I was in the very room. And when it happened I was as connected to Amel then as everyone else was. I lost consciousness when the Mother's head was struck off, and I only know what happened later because people told me. I was revived only after the brain was taken out of Akasha and consumed by Mekare, or when the vampiric brain within Akasha's brain found another host and locked in to that new host."

"Locked in," David repeated. "That's a good description."

"Well," said Louis. "I'm not connected now."

"What are you talking about, of course you're connected," I said. "You were connected ten nights ago when I felt the pain, when Amel forced that unspeakable pain."

"I certainly was," said Viktor in a low voice.

"But I wasn't," said Louis. "I didn't feel the pain."

"Are you certain?" asked David.

"Even I felt it," said Seth.

"That's because you are connected," said Louis. "But I'm not."

"But I thought you did," I insisted. "Louis, everyone said that you did, that everyone felt it."

"They assumed that I'd felt it," said Louis. "But I didn't. And at Trinity Gate, the night you took the Amel brain out of Mekare's brain, I didn't feel anything then either. Everyone else did. Everyone else experienced something. But I experienced nothing. Oh, I was frantic when I gathered from all of them what was happening, but I didn't lose consciousness, I felt no pain, and my vision wasn't impaired, not even for a second. I saw the others around me standing stock-still as if frozen, or going down on their knees at some point. But I felt nothing and I think I know why."

We were all looking at him.

"Well?" I said. "Tell us why."

"Because I died years ago," he said. "I actually physically died. I died completely. I died when I deliberately exposed myself to the sun behind our flat in the French Quarter. It was after my misadventure with Merrick. Merrick had bewitched me. And I didn't want to go on. I exposed myself to the sun, and I had none of the blood of the elders to strengthen me, and all day I lay in the sun and I burned and I died."

Louis looked at me.

"You remember, Lestat, and you remember, too, David. You were both there. David, it was you who found me. I was as dead as anyone can be—until you both poured your powerful blood right into the coffin, right into my burnt remains and brought me back."

"But the etheric body, the Amel body, was still in you," said Fareed. "It had to be or you couldn't have been revived."

"That's true," Louis said. "It was there inside me and it would have remained there until the ashes were scattered. It would have remained suspended, waiting, waiting for how long we don't know. Remember the old admonition from Magnus, Lestat? Scatter the ashes? Well, no one scattered my ashes and I was brought back—by your blood, and David's blood, and Merrick's blood too."

"Then you were not really dead, Louis," said Fareed patiently.

"Oh, but I was," said Louis. "I know now that I was. I was dead according to one ancient and highly significant definition of 'dead.'"

"I'm not following you," said Fareed. I saw the first signs of impatience but it wasn't impolite.

"My heart had stopped," said Louis. "There was no blood pumping in me. All circulation had stopped when my heart stopped. That is how I was dead."

I was speechless. Then slowly it dawned on me. It came back to me what Kapetria had said . . . something about the invisible tentacles—or the cord—being the only part of us that was not filled with blood.

Nobody was speaking. Even Fareed had narrowed his eyes and was looking at Louis in the hard sightless way of someone peering only into his own thoughts. Seth too was pondering.

"I see!" said David in amazement. "I don't know the scientific explanation for it. But I see it. Your heart stopped; the blood wasn't pumping. And the cord snapped. Of course!" He looked to me. "Lestat, how many times have you ever seen or heard of a vampire brought back from such a state where the heart had stopped, where the ashes were still perfectly formed, and everything remained there but the heart had stopped!"

"Never seen another example of it, ever," I said.

"Neither have I," said Seth, "but I know the old admonition, scatter the ashes."

"Well?" asked Louis. He looked to Fareed. "You

want to try an experiment or two to see if I'm right? Viktor here is bravery personified. If you put a candle flame to Lestat's hand Viktor will feel it. Unfortunately so will Rose and so will every vampire in the world, though in different degrees, correct? I won't feel it. You can see this for yourself. And ancient blood or no, I should feel it, because I'm not even three hundred years old."

"I wish there were some other way of proving it," David said. "There has to be."

"There is," I said. "It's simple. Stop my heart! Stop **my** heart. Stop it until the blood in me stops circulating, and what will happen to all the others all over the world? They'll lose consciousness, yes, but . . ."

"But that's what happened when Akasha was decapitated," said Seth. "You told me."

"But only for three or four seconds, Seth," I said. "It was no longer than that. She was decapitated and her skull was shattered by the falling glass. And Mekare scooped up the brain in her hands and had it in her mouth immediately, just as Maharet ripped open her chest and took out the still-beating heart. I know the heart was still beating because of the way the blood was flowing. So it was only a matter of seconds. What if the heart of Akasha had really been stopped and stopped for a long time?"

"It's been proven in tests on animals," said Fareed, "that the brain lives for perhaps as long as seventeen seconds after decapitation."

"Well, there you have it," said Louis. "It was only a matter of seconds."

"He's right," I said. I was almost too excited to speak. "Fareed, he's right. Stop my heart. Stop it for a long time, and then start it again."

"If I do that, Lestat, I'll lose consciousness and there won't be anyone here to restart your heart. Unless you trust a mortal with such a responsibility."

"No, wait a minute. There's no need to trust a mortal," said David. "Gremt can do this. Gremt can restart it. You only have to give him the instructions. Gremt knows all about the theory of the silver cord. Good Lord, Gremt founded the Talamasca and he probably has read more literature on the silver cord than anyone, and Gremt can be trusted to do this!"

"You don't need Gremt," said Louis. "You have me. If you stop Lestat's heart and every other blood drinker worldwide suffers it in one form or another, I won't suffer it. I will be wholly conscious and able to restart Lestat's heart. You just have to tell me how."

"If you're right about the disconnection," said Fareed.

"I am right," said Louis. "But if you want Gremt to do this, then ask Gremt. I'll sit with Gremt for the duration. Doesn't matter to me. The question is, do you have a simple way to stop and restart Lestat's heart?"

"Yes," said Fareed. "But think what might happen to all the vampires everywhere when this little experiment is carried out! There's no way in the world to warn everyone."

"What do you want us to do?" I said. "Send out an alert? We don't even know how to reach all the blood drinkers of the world."

"Yes, we do," said Louis. "Use Benji's broadcast. Set a time for this tomorrow night, and tonight have Benji broadcast the alert, that at a certain hour Greenwich mean time all blood drinkers must be in a safe and secure place for the space of sixty minutes. And have Benji loop the broadcast all day tomorrow and up to the time of the experiment. That's the best you can do, really. And have all the old ones send out the word telepathically. We come here at sunset and Fareed stops your heart. If it's started a half hour or forty-five minutes later by Gremt . . ."

"We could lose some of the young ones doing this," said Seth. "Louis did not die when things appeared hopeless. But we are talking about Lestat. And suppose the minute the invisible connection is severed, death follows for all who are disconnected."

"But death didn't follow for me," said Louis again. "Look, you're not thinking of all aspects at the same time."

"We're about to face pure annihilation!" I said. "I say do it. Do it now! The Hell with sending out a message. Where is Gremt? Gremt is at the Château or he's at his home in the country. That's not three minutes from here for one of us."

At that moment, the door to the back stairway

opened and Teskhamen and Gremt appeared. They wore long heavy coats, with cravats. And I could see at once that Teskhamen had brought Gremt here via the wind and they were both dusty and ruddy from the cold.

Gremt approached slowly as if he might be intruding and then he said in a soft voice to Fareed, "What is it I have to do? Can you give me precise instructions?"

We all went back to arguing, until quite suddenly Cyril stepped out of the shadows and cried, "Enough!"

Of course this commanded everyone's attention as the great hulking Egyptian stood there with an expression of pure exasperation on his face.

"You can't stop me!" I said.

"I don't want to stop you, boss," he said. "What I want is for somebody to stop my heart now and see if I can survive it. I volunteer. Stop my heart. Let it remain stopped for an hour, for all I care, then try to wake me up. If I can survive, can't you survive?"

"You're mixing everything up!" I protested. "One minute we're talking about me dying when my heart's stopped, and the next about all of you dying when my heart's stopped."

"No, best to do it to me," said Viktor. "You've got thousands of years in the Blood. I was born yesterday. Do it to me."

Rose immediately insisted that she must be the one for she was most certainly the weakest and everyone was quarreling again. But then Thorne protested that he was not even fifteen hundred years old, and he ought to be the one, and then David insisted he should be the one and so on it went.

They were confusing me mightily. But I might have been the only one to observe Fareed slipping away quietly, and disappearing into his laboratory amid the apparatuses and the machines.

Everyone was still arguing when Fareed returned. He had two syringes in his hand.

He gave one of these syringes to Seth as he whispered in Seth's ear. Then he plunged the other syringe into his chest and went down unconscious on the floor.

"He's done it," I said. "He's stopped his heart."

What followed was likely the longest half hour of my life.

No one spoke, but I think we were turning the idea round and round in our minds, trying to think of every conceivable possibility, as Fareed lay there on the tiled floor in his white coat and pants staring straight up into the ceiling lights.

At last Seth knelt down beside Fareed and plunged his syringe into Fareed's chest. A big hoarse breath came from Fareed. He blinked, and then closed his eyes. Then very slowly he sat up. He appeared shaky, and though Seth offered his hand, Fareed sat still for a moment with his own hand to his eyes.

Perhaps two minutes passed, and then Fareed rose to his feet.

"Well, I seem to be quite all right," he said. "Now let's take it a step further. I was hypersensitive to the pain Lestat felt when Amel convulsed or whatever it was that Amel did, so let's devise some reasonable pain test now to see if I am truly disconnected as well as perfectly all right."

Another heated argument started, with everyone talking at once. I tried to get a word in, that we might make it a mild experiment, but Seth was shouting at Fareed this time, and Flannery Gilman had come in and demanded to know what was going on.

I tried to answer her. But suddenly, without the slightest warning I felt a dreadful pain in the back of my neck. It grew so intense that I cried out and went down on my knees. I heard Rose scream. David fell to his knees with his hands to his head. I looked up at Fareed. Fareed was feeling nothing. Louis was right next to him and Louis was feeling nothing.

"Enough!" I shouted. And it was gone, just like that. No pain.

I looked around me as I rose to my feet. Everyone—but Gremt, Fareed, and Louis—was recovering more or less from the pain. I didn't have to ask whether Teskhamen or Seth had felt it. There was blood in Teskhamen's eyes and Seth was still holding his head with both hands, his eyebrows knitted, as if he was straining to remember just what he'd felt.

"Well, this is extremely helpful," said Fareed. "Because I didn't feel a thing."

Amel was still making himself known to me, but in the gentlest way.

"And what do you think, Amel?" I asked aloud so all could hear me. "Do you think this experiment will work?"

"You won't die and I won't die if your heart stops," Amel answered. "Do it for the same amount of time that Fareed did it. No more."

I sat down on the couch, still numb from the pain. Gremt sat beside me but said nothing.

Amel spoke. "I told you I could not go into Louis, did I not? And now I tell you, I cannot go into Fareed."

I looked up at Fareed, and then to Louis. "Well, you two will survive, whatever happens," I said. I wanted to weep with relief. "Look, we have to go ahead with this. But you do keep mixing up the matter of my heart and your individual hearts. Fledglings may die when my heart is stopped. Everybody but—. I'm sorry, I can't keep it straight."

Fareed and Seth were looking at one another. Something was wrong.

Suddenly Amel spoke to me softly as if he didn't want anyone else to hear, but of course most of them could hear. "Do it," said Amel. "Nobody will die. You won't die because I'm inside you, and I and your body will simply be waiting for your heart to be re-started, that's all. And they won't die, all the others, because they are safe and intact and they will likely be disconnected almost at once."

"At once?"

"Exactly," said Fareed. "Amel is correct, don't you see? Go back to when the Mother was killed. You all suffered. But if Amel had not been rescued and transferred within seconds, the connection would have broken. And likely none of you would have died. Akasha alone would have died. And Amel would have been—."

"Released," said Seth.

"I'm not following. When Akasha was put into the sun, vampires all over the world died in flames."

"They were all connected," said Fareed. "Don't lose sight of the goal. It is to disconnect."

"Lestat," said David, "what they are saying is— you were almost all disconnecting after Akasha died. If Amel hadn't been rescued by Mekare, you would have all been disconnected. But Amel was rescued and found a new host before the web disintegrated. For the web to disintegrate, it must take some time."

"Same with the second time," said Fareed. "If you had not taken Amel into yourself, Lestat—if Mekare had been allowed to perish with Amel inside of her—all the vampires of the world would be free."

"You're talking in circles," I said. "How could she have perished without us perishing?"

"I think I know," said Louis. "If her heart had been stopped for a long time before her perishing, the disconnect would have been complete, and then however she perished, no one would have felt her death but her."

I was stunned, but even I, with my foolish lack of scientific understanding, could see the logic. Well, almost.

"We might lose Amel," I said. "That's what you're saying. Stop my heart which is death but not destruction. And when it's started up again, they'll all be disconnected, everybody will be disconnected, but what if when my heart stops, he disconnects from me?"

"But I don't think he can," said Fareed shaking his head. "Not as long as your body is intact, and waiting there safely to be resuscitated. No."

**He's right.**

"This is all too theoretical," said Flannery Gilman. "All that might happen is Lestat is in suspended animation for an hour, and all the rest of the vampires of the world die."

"It's possible," said David.

"Not likely," said Fareed. "What's likely is that some will take longer to disconnect than others, but the web of connections will perish because no blood is being pumped through the body of the host. And when Lestat is revived Amel will be there as before. But the web will be gone."

Another huge free-for-all argument ensued. I was dejected beyond words. I held up my hands for silence.

"Amel, are you willing for us to do this?" I asked.

"Yes," he answered.

"Then I say we do it," said Fareed. "Otherwise

we are back to the near-impossible task of severing each vampire individually."

Slowly they all came to full agreement, though Rose was the last one to come around. Rose had been arguing for the disconnect of individuals to proceed exactly as it had taken place with Louis and Fareed. She didn't want to think of my heart being stopped. But when Fareed began to name all of the many individuals, and to speak of how any fledglings I ever made in the future would be connected to me—until severed—and to speak of a multitude of other difficulties, she threw up her hands and agreed.

We would do this tomorrow night while I was still in my crypt, safe from any twilight rays lingering in the night sky. And with the great door sealed, and only Fareed and Louis and Gremt with me inside. That way, if Kapetria drew any conclusions from the radio alert, I'd be protected, with Thorne and Cyril outside my door.

Fareed would give me the injection to stop my heart and he'd be there to reverse it but Gremt would also have a syringe and so would Louis.

There was some other equipment involved, drugs, something, but I couldn't follow it. The main point was we would do it at that time when many young vampires at Court and all over Europe had not risen yet, and hope for the best.

For all we knew not all of the vampires of the Château would experience unconsciousness. It was entirely possible that the very old ones like Seth and

Gregory would not at all. They might be weak, failing in vision, even limp and unable to move, but they might remain conscious and able to present a deterrent if Kapetria, intrigued by the alert, tried to enter the Château. After all Mekare and Maharet, old as they were, had managed to keep functioning when Akasha had been decapitated, but of course that was only for a few seconds . . . ah, but who really knew?

I could focus upon only one aspect of this: my heart would stop; the blood would stop circulating; but nothing else would really happen to my brain or my body. Amel would remain in me. I'd be safe in my coffin.

Whatever the case, the crypt of the Château was the best place to do it, and the more ancient ones would be gathered on the stairway that led down to the crypt.

Benji picked up as soon as we called.

He would start announcing the message immediately. An important half hour of meditation is declared for tomorrow night at 6:00 p.m. All the Undead must be in a safe sheltered place at this time, and participate in this experiment by remaining entirely still for the full half hour, and keeping their eyes closed. He would mention "time of meditation" every hour until dawn sign-off, and then he'd set the tape to looping immediately before he retired for the day. We were thankful he didn't ask for an explanation. But then Benji was powerfully intuitive. Benji had Marius's blood in him and he knew and heard and understood things others could not. Probably many of the others knew what was happening. No doubt Gregory knew, and Marius as well.

Fareed began to laugh, a bit madly, like someone laughing from exhaustion or unbearable strain. "This is too funny," he said. He gestured to the desk, the book-lined walls, the laboratory. "And this, this old talk of the silver cord brings us to this experiment. If this works, I swear I will give up science altogether, and I'll begin reading all the poetry, literature, and psychic books I've always ignored. I'll become a New Age monk, a contemplative, a priest!"

# 27

# Lestat

WHEN WE RETURNED to the Château I went out for a walk in the snow. I was not having regrets, but I had lost my remarkably clear understanding of how or why this should work.

I walked way up the old mountain that was my mountain, and I would cheerfully have killed a pack of wolves had they attacked. But there were few wolves if any in these woods now. And any and all surviving European wolves were a cherished part of life in this time, and not to be thoughtlessly or carelessly killed, just because I didn't know what might happen tomorrow night.

I'd been wandering for about an hour when the iPhone in my pocket rang. I was surprised as I was so far from the Château. But it was Kapetria coming through loud and clear.

"Fareed won't tell me what you're doing," she said.

Ah, so she'd heard Benji's call for all the blood

drinkers of the world to be safe and still tomorrow evening at 6:00 p.m.

"Do you blame him?" I asked. "You left us. You went off on your own when you might have helped us. You told us what to do, didn't you, find some way to prevent the whole tribe from dying when you made your move. But you didn't stay to help us figure out how."

"I'll help you tomorrow night."

"Oh, no, you won't. We're not telling you where this is to take place and you're not to come near us. If we see you or any of the People of the Purpose, the experiment won't take place. Besides we don't need your help."

"Please let me help."

"No."

"You don't know what Amel wrote for me. The message, I mean. The one you gave me."

"He told me," I said. "Later that night as a matter of fact. And in so doing, he let me know it was just a matter of time till you made your assault. I know about your phone conversations. He said you were a parent prepared to rescue a child, no matter what the child wanted."

"Do you think I would ever go against Amel's wishes?"

"Yes," I said. "Because I probably would, if I were you."

"I want to help you. I'll come alone."

"There isn't time."

"Yes, there is."

"Oh, giving away your location, are you? This means you're still in Europe, doesn't it?"

"Will you please let me come."

"No, Kapetria. I'm resigned to what happens whenever you make your move, but right now I want to be certain that whatever you do, you do it only to me."

I ended the call. I turned off the phone. Amel was with me but he wasn't saying a word.

It was now half past three in the morning. I headed down the mountain slowly, singing to myself. I was remembering the giant old yew trees growing around Gremt's old monastery home and I thought I would like to have yew trees planted here too. I hadn't given enough thought to the old forest.

I was thinking of anything except what lay ahead. Finally as I drew near the Château, I heard a commotion in the ballroom, so I took to the air and came down on the terrace and went in through the open doors.

The ballroom was empty except for three people. And one of them was Kapetria. She was all bundled up in a gray wool coat and red scarf, and her hair was pulled back into a rather stylish black cloche hat. She had an accidentally glamorous look to her, and her dark face was all the more striking for the severity of the hair pulled back into the hat. She was sitting on the couch nearest the empty orchestra chairs and she was in a fierce argument with Thorne and Cyril. She had a large valise at her feet.

She stood when she saw me. "I came alone," she said. "Alone. Nobody is with me. No one is anywhere near. I didn't even tell them where I was going. I started driving as soon as I heard."

"Well, now, this is interesting," I said. "And you've made a very stupid mistake. Because how can the others possibly mount an assault on me to free Amel, if you are no longer the captain of the team?"

She didn't answer.

"You're in grave danger is what I'm trying to tell you," I said.

"Please don't take this tack," she said calmly.

I honestly didn't know what to say.

Then Amel spoke up.

**Let her help you.**

She couldn't hear Amel, of course, but Thorne and Cyril had heard him, and they exchanged glances.

"Let her help!" Amel shouted at me. Thorne and Cyril stared at me as if I were a ghost, or he were a ghost inside me.

Still I didn't know what to say. But Fareed had just come in and Seth was with him, and Gregory was right behind them and so was Marius. Gremt was there and Teskhamen and David as well.

In a moment, they had surrounded us.

"I want to help," she said again. "I know you're going to try something, and if it isn't dangerous, it's not likely to work."

Four a.m. The great clocks of the Château were chiming, not one in sync with another it seemed. Time for me to leave.

"You make up your minds on it. Her old friend from Atalantaya says to let her help. I'm going down now. Whatever you decide, you'll let me know."

Of course I could still hear them talking when I was safe belowstairs as I lay there in the dark.

I could hear Armand's voice now as well, and Marius's voice and now and then even Kapetria, though it was very difficult to hear her, as I had to hear her through them. Gradually I put together the picture: they were taking her to the inn to spend the night. Fareed was doing the talking. And mortals spied on them from behind closed blinds.

"Do you think it's going to work?" I asked Amel.

"If she helps," he said, "there's a better chance."

"And why is that?"

"Because she can recognize the signs of things that Fareed might not recognize. Don't underestimate her senses. If you begin to die, really die— that is, if the process of irreversible cellular death commences—she'll restart your heart."

"Hmmm. Irreversible cellular death. That's a mouthful."

"Not for me."

I laughed. "You're not the least bit worried about this experiment, are you?"

"No," he said. "I don't see why you should die. Your own etheric vampire brain and body will simply wait for you to be revived—even if I am detached and forced out when your heart stops."

"**Mon Dieu!**"

"Don't be concerned," he said. "Not likely to happen. I'm more than likely to remain locked into the blood as I've always been! There were moments of horror and despair when I tried with all my will to detach from Mekare. I could never do it. Now think on this.—Imagine if the body of Akasha had been frozen, or the body of Mekare. All the tribe might have been disconnected; but I'd have been locked inside her, unable to rise, until the host was unfrozen, and the heart started to beat again."

"So that's all it would have taken—ever—to disconnect the tribe from the host?"

"Maybe," he said. "But who knew?"

# 28

# Lestat

I AWOKE ABOUT A half hour before they came. Amel was with me, as far as I could tell. Soon I heard their voices. The doors of the vault were opened and Louis came with Fareed and Kapetria, the two scientists attired completely in white and with their valises, no doubt filled with marvelous medical gadgets and vials of chemical wonders. Both of them had stethoscopes around their necks. Seth was nearby.

Rose and Viktor were there too. This was Kapetria's idea and Fareed had agreed.

It had been decided that if after my heart was stopped, either Rose or Viktor showed signs of actually "dying" in some way—shriveling, deteriorating, transforming in any way indicating irreversible death—then my heart would be restarted at once.

It had also been agreed that if all the vampires of the world merely remained unconscious for the duration, likely the "Great Disconnection" would be a failure, and they'd all still be connected when my heart was started again.

"The Great Disconnection," I said. "I like it. I'll love it, if it works."

Rose and Viktor understood. They sat down to wait it out on the stairway outside the vault.

Louis closed the lid of my coffin and seated himself there. He was close enough to me that I could take his hand and I did.

A memory came back to me, a memory of the first time I ever saw him in New Orleans. He'd been staggering through the streets drunk, a rough-cut version of what he was now. Suddenly the veil collapsed between that time and this and it was all playing back for me as if someone else had a hand on the button and I saw him after the transformation standing in the swamp, the water almost up to his knees as he marveled at everything around him, including the moon snagged in the moss-hung branches of the cypress trees, and I could smell the fetid green water again.

I let out a long sigh.

"You're here, aren't you?" I asked Amel.

"Of course, I'm here and I'm not going anywhere," he said.

Fareed stood over me, testing the syringe in some way, making it spurt in silvery little droplets. When he bent down to put the needle into my chest, I shut my eyes.

The most remarkable thing happened. I wasn't there in the vault at all. I was someplace else entirely.

It was midday and the sun was pouring down through the dome. The light was so bright and pure and equatorial that it was almost impossible to see that the dome was there.

"This is your office?" I asked.

He sat behind the desk. His red hair was very much like my hair, but it was a real true red, not coppery or auburn, but deep red with golden highlights to it, and his eyebrows were darker and distinct and his eyes were most certainly green.

He had a longer nose than I had, and a long full mouth, the lower lip bigger than the upper lip, but the upper lip was perfectly shaped, and his jaw was square. And having said all that, what can I say about the brilliance of his smile and the boyish look to him overall? He'd been finished, like I had, on the very verge of manhood, with the requisite shoulders, but the face had the stamp of a boy's curiosity and optimism.

"Yes, it's my office," he said. "I'm so glad you've come."

"Oh, you're not going to start crying on me, are you?" I asked.

"Not if you don't want me to. But look outside. Just look. This is Atalantaya! This is all mine!"

It was quite impossible to describe. Imagine you're stranded on the sixty-third floor of a building in Midtown Manhattan and all you can see around you are other buildings like it, but everything is made of glass. Imagine the light skittering on all those glass surfaces, and then imagine that you can see into the buildings and see all the living beings at work in them, at desks, tables, machines, or just stranded on balconies in groups of two or three or more, talking to one another, all the busy life of the city all around you, and some of the towers climbing so high you can't quite see the top from where you're sitting and others below you have verdant gardens on their roofs, and you see fruit trees, and flowers, and vines spilling down over the balustrades, vines with purple blossoms, purple as wisteria, and you see in one garden, just one particular garden, a group of children in a circle with their arms out embracing one another as they skip and dance—**Lock arms and detonate**—and as they pull the circle this way and that. But it holds as a circle. Because circles don't have to be round.

"But I thought this was the tallest building. Oh, I see, the buildings are changing shape, the buildings are moving."

"That's just because I want you to see everything at the same time."

"I can see the clouds beyond the dome. Does the dome increase the heat of the sun?"

"Of course. But it's all balanced. Everything is balanced. That's what I want you to see."

He sat back in his chair with his feet up to one

side on the desk. He wore shiny clothes, clothes that shimmered as the building shimmered, a collared shirt with breast pockets like the shirts we have today, and soft creaseless pants, and sandals on his feet.

I must have been standing in front of the desk, because he was smiling up at me, positively beaming. He had just the smallest cleft in his chin, and that and the curve of his cheeks made him look so new, so young. He actually had dimples in his cheeks. Dimples.

"You can't imagine what it was like in the beginning," he said. "So many steps to come to this point. And what do you think might have happened if we'd never been interrupted, if they'd never come and tried to destroy us? What do you think the world would have been like?"

"I don't want to think of that," I said. "Because I love the world the way it is. After all, hasn't the world come almost to the same point? I mean take a look around you in the world, and see how far they've come on their own. I don't mean that what you did wasn't splendid. It was glorious. All this is glorious. And they can't make a city of luracastria, no, but think of all they've achieved without one guiding force, and subject to the squabbles, and battles and war, of a multitude of guiding forces. They've come out of it to achieve so much."

"They have," he said. There were laugh lines at the corners of his eyes, and his lips spread back so easily in such a generous smile. "They certainly have, and I would never interfere with them now. I want you to know that! I would never seek to do what I did before. But right now, here, in this world, the world of Atalantaya, savages do live beyond this dome and the Wilderness lands can be a treacherous and terrible place. But remember what I'm saying. I would never seek again to have such power, to be such a dominant note."

"I understand."

"But I just wanted you to see it, this world, my world. I wanted you to see what I'd done, and see what it was that Bravenna destroyed, and what time buried, and what perished from the record, and what's remembered now only in legends and poems and songs."

Time, so much time passed! How did we get here in the street, walking together, and what had we been saying, the two of us, because it seemed like only a moment ago we'd been way up in the Creative Tower and we'd been talking, but I knew a day had passed. The sun was setting, and the towers were going opaque in shimmering shades of pink, and gold, and even a very pale metallic blue. The street was shaded here from the heat by leafy branches that arched completely over the sidewalk. People were rushing by us, on a multitude of ordinary errands, and we walked slowly on these smooth shining pavers, polished pavers, and suddenly the scent of an unknown flower enveloped me. I stopped. I looked around. Flowers covered the wall beside me, the flowers of an immense and sprawling vine, pretty cream-colored deep-throated flowers climbing up and up on a mass of tangled tendrils and creepers until I couldn't see distinct blossoms anymore or the farthermost tendrils of the vine. The sky was twilight purple and the building had turned to a luminescent violet.

Amel stood there watching me. The vine began to tremble.

"No, wait, look, it's coming undone!" I said. "The whole vine, look, it's losing its grip, it's falling."

And it was—the great leafy mass of it coming loose from the violet wall, and the flowers shivering as they fell, with the branches curling down upon themselves, and the whole thing collapsing suddenly and vanishing as if it had never been there, and there had never been all those blossoms, all those gorgeous blossoms stemming from one root.

"Oh, wait a minute!" I said. "I see."

Darkness.

"Don't go!" I said. "Don't leave me."

Voice against my ear. "I haven't left you!"

Darkness. Stillness. A stillness so perfect that I could have heard my own breathing if I had been breathing. I could have heard my own heart beating if it had been beating.

And then suddenly it was.

I jumped. I felt a pain in my chest that made me wince and sit up.

I couldn't keep quiet, the pain was so sharp and intense, but then it was over and my heart was pounding and I felt a flush of blood in my hands and in my face.

"I told you I wouldn't leave you."

Last glimmer of Atalantaya, twilight, the violet towers filled with soft yellow squares and rectangles, and Amel, long red hair mussed in the breeze, looking into my eyes and kissing me. "I love you, I have never loved anyone in all my long life as I love you."

Silence except for the steady rhythm of my heart.

I opened my eyes. Kapetria and Fareed stood before me, watching me with a horrid impersonal fascination. Louis was sitting on the coffin, and he was holding my right hand.

Rose and Viktor were standing nearby in the alcove before the stairway. They were radiant and regarding me with wonder, and I thought them the most marvelous beings in the whole world. Seth stood behind them.

"Did anyone suffer—?" I could not quite get the words out.

Fareed shook his head. "Everyone felt the shock of it. But within the space of five minutes, I was myself. Seth was himself. For Rose and Viktor it was longer, perhaps ten minutes, and then they were completely restored. Marius came down moments after that. The ballroom was filled with young and old who had felt the shock and recovered."

Only Kapetria looked distressed, wildly distressed. Kapetria was staring at me in alarm.

"Tell her I'm still here," said Amel.

"Oh, yes, of course," I said. "I'm so sorry, Kapetria. Amel says to tell you that he's still here." I didn't try to explain about the vivid dream, the sense of absolutely being somewhere else with Amel, the assurance that Amel had never left.

Kapetria closed her eyes, and when she opened them again, she looked up and took a deep breath. Her eyes were moist and then they became glassy. She appeared to shiver all over, but then to collect herself and sink back into her thoughts.

A wave of nausea passed over me.

Left to my own choice, I wouldn't have moved so fast. I would have sat there for a longer period of time, but they wanted us to go upstairs.

"It didn't work, did it?" I said to Fareed. He didn't answer. "They are all fine, all of you are fine, and it just didn't work."

Each step jolted my entire frame and the nausea came again more than once, but I kept walking, doing what they wanted, until we reached the ballroom where it seemed the entire world of the Undead was gathered, even threaded all through the orchestra chairs, and out onto the open terrace, and out through the doors to the adjacent salons.

We made a space for ourselves in the middle, and I made up my mind I was going to appear absolutely strong for everyone here, no matter what I felt. I let go of Louis's hand and I let go of Fareed's hand. Cyril had his hand on my back and Thorne still held my right arm.

"It's all right," I said to them. Reluctantly, they allowed me to stand on my own.

All around, I saw pale hands raised with glittering little glass cell phones aloft, as if they were lights beamed down towards me.

Seth held a narrow silver candelabrum with all three candles burning. There was a feverish and low murmuring around us, rolling like a wave through the meandering assembly, with occasional gasps, and then silence again except for the faintest whispering like dry leaves crackling in a wind.

"Give that thing to me," I said. With my left hand, I took the candelabrum by its bulbous sterling-silver stem, and then I held my right hand, palm down, above the three quivering flames. It took a few seconds before the pain became unbearable and still I held it, gritting my teeth and letting it burn me, holding steady, not moving.

"Silence," said a voice.

I held firm. The pain was so acute I had to look away, look up at the painted ceiling, look up into the light of the chandelier. This is beyond bearing, and it's such a simple thing, just candles, just little flames. Steady little flame. A flame is a flame is a flame. I heard the sound of my flesh cracking.

My mother cried out, "That's enough!"

She pulled my hand away from the flames. She held my wrist with all her strength, her eyes flashing with protective rage. The candelabrum was taken away. Scent of smoking wicks.

Even in the midst of the pain, I saw she had let her hair down, all her glorious fair hair, and just for an instant she was my mother, the mother I knew, staring at my hand and then at me with her quick anxious gray eyes. I heard her whisper my name.

The palm of my hand was black, covered with big yellow blisters. It was a mass of agonizing throbbing pain. The black skin was cracked and bleeding, and then as I watched, it faded to red, bloody red, and the blisters shrank. The fissures closed. And the raw red flesh turned to dark blue. The pain was slowly fading. The hand was healing itself. The hand was turning a pale pink color and slowly it became purely white. Just my hand. The pain was gone.

And they didn't have to tell me:

No one else, no one else in the ballroom, no one else in the Château—no one else throughout the whole world—had died and no one had felt this pain.

The orchestra gathered. Everyone was talking. The music began and I went to the nearest chair and sat down. I looked out at the night sky beyond the terrace and I kept seeing the bright blue sky over Atalantaya, and feeling that soft tropical air.

# 29

# Fareed

I T HAD WORKED, and for nine nights, Fareed
had been writing, writing endlessly as to how
and why it had worked, and how it had affected
the tribe worldwide. The first panicked calls proved
false alarms. No one now disconnected from the Core
was in fact aging or falling to pieces, and none of the
elders had lost the Cloud Gift, or the Fire Gift, or the
Mind Gift, or any other gift. And the vast majority
of the Undead could still read the minds of others
and the minds of mortals. And finally early in the
morning on this very night, a new fledgling had been
made securely by a vampire in Oxford, England—an
old coven master willing to attempt the step with one
he'd loved for a long time—and it had worked. Was
the fledgling somehow connected to the master, as
all the tribe had once been connected to Amel? No.

But this was just the beginning. Fareed would be
gathering data on an infinite number of aspects of
each and every individual whose nightly progress
he followed—for years to come. Flannery Gilman,

who worked at his side for hours without speaking, would keep feeding the data into the computers. And vampires of all ages would be hard put not to keep imagining things in the wake of the Great Disconnection, and it might be years before anything like a full picture of properties and probabilities and expectations could be made.

The bottom line? Nothing had changed. Nothing, that is, except that each and every one of them was now a discrete entity. Or as Louis described it, each and every one had his or her own etheric body with its etheric brain—the etheric brain collected, formed, and developed in the biological brain of the fledgling when the vampiric blood of the master had first gone into it, and the etheric body that had developed from that etheric brain all through the biological body of the fledgling as the vampiric blood circulated through the biological body driven by the biological heart.

Louis's simple explanation became the explanation that most could understand.

And Fareed had acknowledged more than once that Louis's simple understanding of old-fashioned Theosophical rhetoric had led them in the right way.

But Louis took no pleasure in his triumph. He received acknowledgments with sad eyes and bitter smiles. Fareed understood this only too well.

As for the Prince, Fareed couldn't imagine what life was really like for him now, and the Prince obviously didn't care to share.

They all knew that Amel could no longer travel into the minds of others, no longer be heard in other brains as a separate and distinct entity, but everyone had expected as much. Was Amel unhappy with this development? Had Amel's thirst become an agony because he was confined to one vampiric body? Lestat never said.

As he watched Lestat move through the inevitable crowds in the Château, Fareed began to wonder whether Lestat possessed extraordinary courage, or whether Lestat simply didn't know what fear was. He appeared oblivious to the Sword of Damocles hanging over his head.

He danced with the young ones and the old ones, took long walks up and down the mountain with Louis, played chess or cards whenever he wanted, and spent hours watching films in the screening room of the castle just as he had done before.

Maybe Lestat knew something that they didn't know.

But Fareed doubted that, and Seth said it wasn't so. Marius said it wasn't so. Lestat was simply living from moment to moment, with the same brashness and boldness that had always characterized him. Maybe he simply didn't care.

The fourth night, Lestat had gone to see Rhoshamandes without warning a single soul as to what he planned to do. Thorne and Cyril followed him as faithfully as they had in the past.

"You're our Prince," Cyril had declared. "Nothing has changed that. You think we're going to let anybody take you down? Grow up!"

The meeting with Rhoshamandes had taken place in the Outer Hebrides on his island of Saint Rayne in the formidable and famous castle that Rhoshamandes had built for himself a thousand years ago.

"I simply told him what had happened," Lestat explained afterwards. "I gave him a little demonstration. Nothing as elaborate as setting my right hand on fire, but he took the point. I thought he should know it was true, because I knew he wouldn't believe all the rumors and the extravagant claims. And I didn't want him believing all the predictions of rapid-fire deterioration. After all, he is one of us."

**After all, he is one of us.**

Cyril and Thorne attested to the fact that Rhoshamandes had received the Prince with cordiality, inviting him in and taking him on a little tour of the castle. They had gone out on the **Benedicta** together. Rhoshamandes had been candid about fearing the Replimoids. But Lestat had assured Rhosh that the Replimoids were occupied with far more important things than settling any old score. And the Replimoids had given their word.

Had the two discussed what the Replimoids would do next?

"No," said Lestat. "That's no one's concern now but mine."

Rhoshamandes had given Lestat a copy of Marcus Aurelius's **Meditations.** And Lestat had been seen reading it more than once.

"I see a change in him," said Marius. "It isn't resignation. It isn't courage. It's practicality. He's always been practical. He knows it's about to come to a head."

"We have no hope of safely detaching the spirit from him," said Fareed. "But there has to be a way to do it. There has to be."

"Leave it to Kapetria," said Seth. "Whatever we do is likely to be a blunder compared to what she might do."

It wasn't that she had brought any superior skill to the experiment of stopping Lestat's heart. She hadn't. She'd simply come to assist, to watch, to try to calculate when the experiment might have to be brought to an end. But when it came to the possible fate of Amel, of Amel's transfer into another body, Kapetria was the only one who knew anything at all.

Before she left on the night of the heart-stopping experiment, Fareed had given her a large vial of vampiric blood—from his own veins. She had asked for that. And since she'd gifted him with a vial of her own blood, how could he refuse?

He was surprised that she'd waited so long to ask for it, actually. But then he could not really construct a path for her because there was simply too much he didn't know. But Fareed and Seth talked about it all the time.

"Garekyn saw the etheric brain in the biological brain," Seth pointed out whenever they discussed it. "He described it as something sizzling, sparkling, that he could see. Well, we can't see it. And just possibly Kapetria can see the very thing she'll seek to remove from Lestat's head without killing him. Just possibly she has developed instruments that could see it because she herself can see it."

If this was a possibility, Kapetria never said. After the experiment, she had left the Château in the same sleek dark blue Ferrari that had brought her there. And the Prince had laid down the law that no one was to try to follow her, or track her license plate, or hack the facial recognition software systems of Europe for any clues as to where the Replimoids were based.

"We made the decision to leave her alone and we leave her alone," said Lestat. "She knows what she's going to do." He had repeated this since with the same rationale he gave that night. "I know what she's going to do because I know what I would do if I were her."

Whenever three or more ancient ones were gathered together with him, they ended up pounding Fareed with questions on the entire matter, whether the Prince was present or not. But Fareed had never come up with any new answers.

The Prince himself never asked questions. But surely he listened. Surely he heard all the theories being floated, all the back-and-forth amongst Fareed

and Seth and Flannery Gilman. Viktor was working with Flannery now; Viktor had started "reading
medicine" with his mother, as they used to call it in
the old days. Viktor felt driven to find some solution. And Viktor worried about many things.

"What is to stop every blood drinker from making a multitude of other blood drinkers?" asked Viktor. "Before, everyone had agreed; no more making
of blood drinkers until the Court had established
some rules. But now? Without the problem of Amel,
what's to stop our ranks from increasing again until
there are wars in the streets?"

Also Viktor wasn't at all convinced the modern world would ignore the vampires forever as
fictional. True, the bias against vampire beliefs in
modern medicine was so widespread and rigid that
any deviating scientist could be ruined for life. His
own mother, Flannery, had been marginalized and
destroyed because she had claimed to believe in the
vampires. This was still happening to doctors and
scientists in parts of the world. But Viktor said it
couldn't go on forever. Governments must be inves-
tigating. Somebody would round up evidence of the
indisputable truth.

Seth said no. The Prince said no. "They'll never
believe in us any more than they believe in aliens
from other planets or near-death experiences, or the
existence of ghosts. And there is no indisputable
truth. One doctor's indisputable truth is another
man's fantastic lie."

Fareed's head ached. Too much to study; too many directions to take; too many questions; he lacked the discipline now that always upheld him in the past.

And Amel. What went on with Amel?

It was still possible to hear the voice of Amel as Lestat was hearing it—Fareed's telepathic powers had always been considerable. Anytime he was close to Lestat he could eavesdrop. Unless the two wanted to be sealed up in solitude. Then no one could telepathically penetrate their exchanges any more now than before. When Amel wanted to be overheard, he made it obvious. He laughed; he raged; he screamed; he sang in the ancient tongue. When he didn't, he spoke to Lestat alone.

Was all peace and harmony between the two of them?

Marius said no. Amel was gaining ever-greater ascendency over Lestat's body. Lestat tried to conceal this. But Fareed knew it was true. Fareed could discern those brief periods when the Prince allowed Amel to take over—to lift a pen and scrawl innumerable pictographs over pages and pages of paper, or to pick up the cell phone and tap in with one thumb a number that only Amel knew.

Fareed knew when this was happening that Lestat was watching all of it with the same hard focus with which Fareed and Seth watched it. But what about the moments when Lestat didn't want to give in to this interior command center? Did he really like waking up one night last week at sunset to discover the white marble walls of his vault covered in jagged and bizarre alphabetical writing in the ancient tongue?—all of this done apparently during daylight hours with a felt-tip pen that Amel had pilfered without Lestat's knowledge yet obviously using Lestat's left hand?

"That's how he did it," Lestat had said when he recounted the incident. "I was clamping down on my right hand so hard he couldn't use it, and while he had me distracted like that, he used my left hand to slip that pen into my pocket, or so he has bragged. I suppose he's ambidextrous. Likely they're all ambidextrous. I should have known."

"I think he's furious," said Marius when he and Fareed and Seth talked alone about it. "He wants freedom. He wants a biological body of his own. But he loves Lestat. He has no real concept of what it will be like to be on his own in a body again. But it's a love-hate war they have going on. And Lestat knows that the final maneuvers won't be his."

"Of course Amel is furious," Fareed murmured. Should Fareed bother to point out to the others that, since the Great Disconnection, Amel's etheric body was now larger and stronger than ever? All those hundreds of disconnected tentacles had snapped back into the complex etheric entity that was Amel. Had they added to Amel's measurable bulk? Something six thousand years ago had driven that spirit to want more vampires created; was it the sheer size of the spirit's etheric body, being as it was infinitely more complex than the etheric body of a simple human being?

"Everyone is suffering," said Rose. "No one can bear this waiting. There has to be something that we can do!"

But there was nothing anybody could do.

And it seemed to Fareed that those who suffered in the extreme were Gabrielle and Marius—and, of course, Louis, who never left the Prince's side. Gabrielle was in the ballroom every night, often saying nothing, doing nothing—simply listening to the music and watching her son. Gabrielle wore her hair free and down and beautifully brushed back from her face. She wore women's gowns of a simple and timeless cut, and double ropes of pearls around her neck.

Louis had been gravely hurt that Lestat had gone off to meet Rhoshamandes alone. So Lestat had promised never to do such a thing again.

As for Thorne and Cyril, they swore they would die fighting Kapetria and the Replimoids before they'd give him up. But Lestat gave them the same order nightly: When the moment comes, stand down.

"I do not want anyone burned," said Lestat as he reiterated his wishes. "I do not want anyone thrown through a wall. I won't have bloodshed, no matter what kind of blood it is. I won't have any creature dying because of this except me."

As for the ever-changing crowds that filled the

Château, all knew about this to some extent, but no consensus as to what to do about it had ever formed. Each individual was glad to be untethered from the vital Core. And many a blood drinker, young or old, swore they would die to protect the Prince, but most sensed that they'd never be called on to prove it.

So when the music surged, and the dancers danced, and the audiences crowded the theater to watched vampire plays, or listen to vampire poetry, or see the films of all ages available through the video streaming of the mortal world, they seemed one and all to forget about the threat, and maybe some in their hearts wondered who the new monarch would be when the Prince disappeared.

Would it be Marius? Some said that it should have been Marius all along.

Fareed could not be aloof or indifferent or pragmatic about these matters. He loved the Prince too much, and had from the beginning. And Marius was in too much pain for anyone to make the slightest remark along these lines to him.

Marius was working on the constitution, and on the rules. Marius was making the code. Marius was devising a way to enforce the rules against those who broke the peace by seeking to move into another's territory, or through the wanton killing of innocent mortals, or innocent blood drinkers. Marius had just about as much authority and responsibility as he had ever wanted. And sometimes, Fareed thought, Marius didn't want any more at all.

Marius was weary. Marius was anguished. Marius was alone.

After all, he'd lost his longtime companion, Daniel Molloy, to Armand again, and these two remained at Court only because of the threat to the Prince, and hoped some night to be free to go to Trinity Gate in New York. Meanwhile Pandora, Marius's ancient love, was firmly linked to Arjun again, her legendary fledgling and lover from ages past. Bianca had come back to Court after a long time in Sevraine's compound in Cappadocia. Bianca loved Marius. Fareed could see it. Bianca entered Marius's private study every night and watched him from a distance, her eyes fixed on him as if he were an engrossing spectacle as he sat at his desk writing. She was always dressed in a simple modern gown or a man's suit, her hair adorned in artful ways and sweetly perfumed. But Marius did not seem to notice or care.

"She's undeniably beautiful," Fareed had said to Marius once about Bianca.

"Aren't we all?" had been his grim answer. "We were picked for our beauty."

But such was not the case for Bianca. She'd been given the Dark Gift by Marius because he had needed her at a time of great weakness and suffering. Maybe Marius had to deny the memory of that weakness. Maybe that is why he seemed oblivious to her presence.

If Marius sought a new dedicated companion in someone else, nobody knew.

"I am determined that this Court will hold together, no matter what happens," said Marius whenever the subject surfaced. "I am determined that this shall endure!"

The Prince expressed the same absolute concern. "Keep it together, all of it. I've arranged all the legal papers to guide it down through the centuries. I've done everything I can. Marius will be the protector of this property. Marius will be the protector of the Court. Marius will be the law for the tribe if or when I am gone."

The Court was vibrant. The Court was intermittently glorious. The Court was filled with surprises, as new ones continued to appear, though less and less often, and some were quite ancient with astonishing stories to tell.

Fareed came back from Paris every morning well before sunrise, because he wanted to spend the last two hours at the Court. He needed to walk through the ballroom before the musicians had quit for the night; he needed to listen to the music for a while, even if it was only Sybelle playing the harpsichord or Antoine the violin, or Notker's singers forming a large or small choir.

He needed to see Marius working away in his apartments, amid all the books and papers. He needed to see the smiling face of the Prince himself sitting in a softly lighted corner somewhere in fast conversation with Louis or Viktor. He needed to believe that Amel's prediction was true: Kapetria would find a way to free him without doing Lestat harm.

Tonight, as the hours pushed towards dawn—and Lestat had no need to go early to his vault to protect anyone from anything—Fareed stood watching Lestat and Louis playing chess with a marvelous medieval set of exquisitely detailed figures. They were in the largest of the salons off the ballroom, sitting at one of the many round tables scattered all through the castle. Lestat appeared calm, even cheerful, smiling and nodding when he saw Fareed nearby.

A wretched anxiety came over Fareed. If he dies, I can't bear it, Fareed thought. It will destroy me if he dies.

But rather than reveal this irrational desperation, Fareed turned away and silently retired to his crypt.

As he lay down to sleep on his broad Egyptian bed—a duplicate of his bed in Paris—he reflected on the one line of speculation that had recently given him hope.

Lestat was the third host for Amel; Lestat had developed a full vampiric etheric brain and body before ever taking Amel into his body. So what if Amel hadn't mutated Lestat to the same extent that Amel had mutated Akasha, the first host? What if Amel was only possessing Lestat, riding as a parasite inside him? An extrication might be possible in this instance that would never have been possible with Akasha.

And then there was the spirit's own huge desire for release. The spirit would cooperate when Kapetria's scalpel met the fragile biological brain tissue, and just maybe, maybe it would work.

"It has to work," Fareed whispered in the darkness. All scientific detachment deserted him. He was weeping, weeping like a child. "It has to work," he said aloud, "because I can't live with Lestat dying! I can't see a future without him. This is more painful than I can bear."

# 30

# Lestat

THE CALL CAME from Paris. Kapetria wanted me to meet her "out in the open" right in front of Notre Dame at 4:00 a.m. "The sun will be eighteen degrees below the horizon at that time." In other words very close to sunrise—at the time referred to as the dawn of astronomical twilight. Light in the sky but no visible sun.

"Why should I meet you?" I said.

"You know why."

"And what will you do if I don't?"

"Does it have to come to that?"

"Yes, unless you answer my questions."

"I'm going to do everything in my power to achieve this without your being harmed in any way."

"But you don't know that you can achieve it without my being harmed?"

"No. I don't."

"And how do you expect me to respond to that?"

"You're keeping him a prisoner inside you. I want to free him. I want to take him out."

He was Amel. And Amel was silent. But Amel was listening.

In fact, I was in Paris. I was just leaving Armand's home in Saint-Germain-des-Prés. We'd encountered an ugly problem there, a young and foolish fledgling named Amber who'd victimized one of Armand's oldest and most loyal mortal servants. Armand insisted that I, myself, extinguish the brief immortal life of the fledgling, and we knew where the fledgling was. I was going to do it, and now we were standing in the courtyard with the wooden gates to the street still closed, pondering just how we would do this—bring the fledgling back here or simply carry out the death sentence offstage. Armand wanted her brought back as an example. I loathed the idea of the grisly spectacle.

And now this.

Armand's face crumpled, and I saw pain in him such as I hadn't seen in years. "So this is it," he said in his old Russian.

"Maybe," I said. "Maybe not."

I addressed Kapetria. "Maybe you need to do some more work on the whole problem," I said. "Amel's perfectly safe where he is."

"I don't think I can do better."

"Not good enough."

"What do you want us to do?" she asked as if I were in control of that aspect of things. "Please come. Don't make this a battle."

"You can't win a battle. And I can't make myself participate in my own ruin without a fight."

She was still there, but she wasn't answering.

"I might come," I said. "I have an hour to think about it, don't I? Then again, I might not."

"Come now, please." She clicked off.

"Forget that unfortunate girl for a moment," I said to Armand. "You can deal with her tomorrow on your own. I have to think about this, think if I'm going to make a stand."

I glanced up at the roofs of the four-story house that formed a rectangle around the courtyard. Cyril sat up there on the edge of the roof like a gargoyle looking down at me. Thorne stood beside him, hands in the pockets of his leather pants.

"What are you going to do!" Armand whispered. Only now was I seeing how hard this had been for him. He was actually trembling. He had become the boy he'd been when Marius brought him over. "Lestat, don't let them do it!" he said. "Take her prisoner, and blast the rest into infinity!"

"Is that what you would do?" I asked.

"Yes, that's what I'd do. That's what I've wanted to do all along." His eyes were shot with blood and blazing. A spectacle to see his angelic face so contorted with rage and grief. "I'd blast every one of them off this earth because they are a threat to us! What are we becoming? We are vampires. And they are our enemy. Destroy them. You, I, Cyril, and Thorne—we can do it all ourselves."

"Can't do it," I whispered.

"Lestat!" He moved towards me with his hands

out, then he stepped back and looked up to the rooftop. Cyril and Thorne appeared almost instantly at his side. "You cannot let this happen!" he said to them.

"He's the captain of the damned ship," said Cyril.

"I do what the Prince tells me to do," said Thorne with a long agonized sigh.

"I haven't made up my mind," I said. "There's one more vote here right now to be taken into consideration, and I'm not hearing that vote."

Just the pulse on the back of my neck.

I thought of that little fledgling Amber, hiding in her cellar only moments from here, sobbing and crying and waiting to be executed. I thought of the Court.

Last night the most extraordinary thing had happened. Marius had come in, and danced with Bianca. He'd worn a simple modern suit and tie, as they say, and she had been in a gown of black sequins and tiny twinkling jewels. They had danced for hours, no matter what the orchestra played. Marius, the one who would be King tomorrow night if I were gone by then, gone Heaven only knows where?

Was Memnoch waiting for me in that hideous purgatorial school of his? I couldn't help but wonder whether my unanchored soul would shoot up to that geographical part of the astral plane.

"All right," I said. "Listen to me once again. This is my life! Mine alone to risk if I choose! And I don't want to go out with the blood of those Replimoids on my hands! I have enough blood on my hands, don't I? I'm telling you now that I am the Prince and I am ordering you to let me go to meet this woman alone."

I went upwards, rising hundreds of feet above the tiny crestfallen gathering.

And within seconds I was looking down at the pavement in front of Notre Dame—where Kapetria stood, a tiny figure in a trench coat and pants stranded in the empty square, apparently alone. But she wasn't alone.

Soundlessly I dropped down to the balustraded walk closest to the top of the cathedral's north tower. She was standing about fifty feet from the central door. Other Replimoids were all through the streets to the far left of the square as I looked down on it, cleaving to the buildings. And I could see them on the bridge over the river. From above I'd seen them along the flanks of the cathedral.

I wondered what they thought they could do. I put my hands on the balustrade and looked out over Paris for as far as I could see. Long years ago, Armand and I had met at Notre Dame, and he had come alone into the cathedral to confront me, and confront his own fears that the power of God would strike him dead should he do this—because he was a Child of Satan and the cathedral was a place of light.

Of course Kapetria must have known this, must have read it in the "pages," but I suspected she had more practical reasons for wanting to meet here, that her Frankensteinian laboratory was somewhere quite nearby.

I scanned the world for Armand, for Thorne, for Cyril. No trace of them. But Gregory Duff Collingsworth was also in the square, many yards away from Kapetria, lost in the shadows, his eyes fixed on me.

I shot downwards, grabbing Kapetria by the waist and then rising hundreds of feet over Paris, as I cradled her in my arms to protect her from the wind. Below, the Replimoids descended on the square from all directions.

Slowly, I set Kapetria down on the roof of the north tower, which was flat enough and big enough for her not to be in danger of falling.

She was terrified. The first time I'd ever seen her show any fear whatsoever, and she clung to me and drew in her breath and trembled, and then fell at my feet. Of course I picked her up. I hadn't meant for her to fall. She came back to consciousness immediately, but the fear had her again, and she buried her head in my chest.

"Is this the woman who roamed the high towers of Atalantaya?" I asked.

"There were railings," she said. "High safe railings."

But what she really meant to say was that no one had ever picked up her and carried her into the air like this before. And I remembered when Magnus, my maker, had taken me prisoner and set me down on a rooftop in Paris, and I'd felt the same terror she was feeling now. Primate, mammalian fear.

Holding her firmly, I moved towards the edge so she could see her followers gathered in the square below, but she struggled against me. She didn't want to look over the edge. She didn't want to be close to it.

There was nothing to do but to take her to a safer place, so I did. I moved more slowly this time, and, holding her all the more firmly, pushed her head down against my chest so she wouldn't be tempted to look about her. I took her swiftly to the topmost roof of Collingsworth Pharmaceuticals, miles from the cathedral and miles from the old city, where she was surrounded by parapets of substantial width and height.

She was shaking ever more violently than before. She walked fast over to the nearest parapet wall, and sat with her back against it, her knees raised and her arms hugging her chest. Her loose black hair was mussed and she pulled her trench coat down over her knees, over her wool pants, as if she were freezing cold.

"You want to tell me what you plan to do?" I asked.

I expected her to be furious, to hit me with a volley of insults for this vulgar display of power, this vain attempt to seize the upper hand, when in fact I didn't really have the upper hand. But she did none of this.

"I'm ready to do it," she said. "I'm going to wait for sunrise of course, when you are unconscious naturally, and then I'm going to do several things, flush out your blood and replace it entirely with Replimoid blood, open your skull—which you won't feel of course—and attempt to remove Amel intact into the waiting brain of another body that is ready and filled with Replimoid blood as well. Then I'm going to close up your skull, and close up the wound, and leave you there, bound, unconscious until sunset, at which time I believe your incisions will be healed, your hair will have grown back, and you'll be able to free yourself easily from your bonds. You can then leave the laboratory at your leisure because we will be long gone."

"And you think I'm just going to let you do this," I said, "when there are no guarantees that I'll survive, or that Amel will survive?"

"I have to try it, and I am as prepared as I will ever be," she said.

Why was I doing this? I wondered. Why was I putting her through this when I was prepared in fact to give up? Just when I'd decided to give up, I couldn't say. Might have been a week ago or a month ago. Might have been at the council table after she'd finished her long story, and I was drinking her blood and I saw her with Amel—Amel who was still silent now and saying nothing—walking through the ancient laboratories of Atalantaya. I felt a misery so heavy that I wasn't hearing her anymore.

But she was talking, talking about what Amel was, and what Amel could do, and who she was, and how she had no choice but to try to free him and put him in a body very nearly like the one that had been blown to pieces in Atalantaya, sending him on his journey of thousands of years into the realm of the spirits out of which we had been born.

I stood against the parapet a few feet to her right looking out over the modern buildings of Collingsworth Pharmaceuticals and the modern towers of Paris all around it, a world away from the old city and the cathedral in which I'd first drunk innocent blood. Somewhere lost in the confusion of rooftops was the doorway to Fareed's laboratory in another building, but I couldn't tell where that was. The fact is, we were safe here and I heard no preternatural hearts near us, no foolish angels to the rescue. Gregory had not followed. Fareed and Flannery were likely miles away at Court, and we were alone.

And she, a fragile thing, in spite of all her gifts, had about her the perfume of innocent blood.

Innocent blood. Amel had stopped asking for it, stopped bringing it to my mind the way he had been only a few months ago. Innocent blood, that tasted just the same as evil blood, if you closed your eyes to the visions that traveled with it, and just drank and drank and drank.

It was supremely enticing to me that she would not die if I drank every drop of her innocent blood, and in my secret lawless mind where fantasies are nurtured only to die an early death, I saw her as a captive wife in the dungeons of my ancestral château, kept there for me the way Derek had been kept by the unfortunate Roland, and I thought what conversations we might have, me and my immortal bride whose blood would never run dry. She was so very lovely, with her shining dark skin, such rich dark skin, and her raven hair and her quick, crisp speaking voice so easy to listen to, if I really wanted to hear anything she said. And I'd always want to hear what she had to say, because she was brilliant, and she knew things impossible for me to know. She'd really been up there, with the moon and the stars, on a star called Bravenna, higher than I could ever soar.

"All right," I said bringing to a halt her latest exhortation as to why I should do it now. "I'm not ready, but I'll be ready and when I am I'll tell you."

I picked her up and carried her upwards again and back over the city, and as I approached the cathedral I slowed and took her down the last few hundred yards and deposited her standing, as she had been before, before the central door of the church.

No sign of her legions. They must have retreated when they saw it was no use looking for her.

She buttoned up her coat to her neck, and shoved her naked hands into her pockets, and looked at me, defeated and discouraged.

"The fact is I am ready to do it now! And only a half mile from here. Everything's ready!"

"I'm not ready," I said. "I could die. He could die!"

I had a lot more to say to her but I didn't know what it was. I wanted to say that Amel was silent, Amel wasn't urging me to come with her, and that alone was reason for me to delay. Then for the first time it occurred to me: what would I do when Amel did say go to her? Maybe I was waiting for that and that alone.

I couldn't refuse Amel, not loving him and understanding him as I did. And if he was willing, if he was ready, who was I to stand in his way?

**So why are you silent, goddamn it! Why don't you settle this! Speak up now and I'll go with her!**

Weeping. He was weeping—so soft, so far away, and yet so near.

Something shook me. Sound of a powerful ancient preternatural heart. Gregory, most likely, or Seth. But it was the wrong signature. All hearts do have a signature, I had only just come to realizing that in these last few months. Amel had taught me that.

I started to turn around—to confront the intruder—but it was too late.

The being had me, had his arms around me as he stood firm against my back. It was strength so far beyond my own I was trapped. I couldn't send the Fire Gift at him because I wasn't facing him. I seemed unable to muster any telekinetic resistance. Yet I tried with all my might to get free. I could have broken the grip of a gargoyle sooner than this grip.

Kapetria stood staring at the pair of us. Her black eyes were wide with amazement. The square was deserted. Paris was asleep. But the sky was filling with light.

"Let's call it reparation," said the voice against my ear. But he was talking to Kapetria. "I take him to your chopping block, and then we're even for what I did to your beloved Derek. And you, Lestat—we're even for what you did to me."

# 31

# Lestat

I{T WASN'T ALL} that different from a hospital operating room, or so I imagined, since I'd never been in one. But I'd seen them enough in popular films to recognize all the equipment. Only difference was that the patient was strapped to a table by steel strips of seeming-impossible strength. And Rhoshamandes held me firmly there in place as we both waited for the rising sun.

There had been a battle in the square—desperate, confused, with Cyril and Thorne and the ghost of Magnus vainly assaulting Rhoshamandes. I'd sensed another spirit's presence, and even the presence of Armand. Others. There had been flashes of fire and howls and curses. I'd cried out, "No more. I surrender. Don't harm them." It had ended in a matter of seconds.

And now we were here, in this hospital room, and Rhoshamandes suddenly vanished.

I stared up at the ceiling of white acoustic tiles and at the surrounding wonderland of tanks and glistening plastic sacks of fluid and monitors and things that ticked and wheezed, and wires and cables and broad shining tubes—and dark-haired, dark-skinned Replimoids with beautiful almond-shaped dark eyes above their surgical masks, their entire bodies wrapped so tight in white surgical drapery and plastic that they appeared to be bandaged. A syringe held high in the air. Tap, tap, tap. Tiny squirt of sparkling fluid.

My hands were strapped down. My fingers were strapped down. My neck was strapped down. But a crank suddenly raised the upper half of this death-bed and I was sitting up. Of course. She had to remove the top of my skull! And all the steel straps had been arranged to allow this maneuver which took me further and further from anything that I could conceivably understand.

I wished I had had a glimpse of the other body, the body covered up on the table with all the tubes filled with blood running into it. Was that thing already alive?

Over my eyes, someone put a blindfold, thick and soft. And there perhaps goes your ability to see forever. How can you know?

I was groggy, almost unable to speak. The sun was above the horizon.

Amel was weeping.

**Say something, you idiot! At least tell me goodbye.**

Lights snapped on, so bright they burned through

the blindfold and my eyelids, but the old familiar darkness would take care of that. Scissors cutting. Never really liked this jacket and shirt all that much anyway. Needles piercing. I am extremely . . . extremely fond of this skin.

It wasn't a dream. It was a different place. And no sooner had I reached out my hand to open the door, then it was gone.

Just gone.

Next thing I knew I was sleeping on my side. Then I turned over on my back and I thought to myself, How hard is this bed, and the scents I'm picking up, what are they, these noxious chemical scents? I heard the noises of traffic and somewhere very close the sounds of people walking as in a busy street.

My eyes snapped open. I stared up once again at the acoustical-tile ceiling.

**I am alive.**

Dim electric light softly illuminated the ceiling, and the place where I lay.

I sat up and looked around the room.

Most of the equipment was gone. The other body on the other table was gone. I was alone, seated on a gurney, and I was fully dressed.

The linen shirt was new, the suit jacket was new, and the pants were new, but the spiffily polished black boots were mine. And the rings on my fingers, of course, were mine. My beloved violet-tinted glasses were in my breast pocket.

I felt of my hair; it was as it always was when I awoke, full and long. Yet I felt delicate but hard seams in the flesh of my head. I looked at my hands and then at the rest of myself.

I climbed off the gurney and walked through the scattering of tables and stands and metal cabinets and other seeming debris, and opened the door.

Empty hallway of a modern building, and at the far end a doorway to a busy street. I put on my violet glasses and went out.

It was the Marais—one of the oldest sections of Paris. And it was just after sunset, and all the lights were coming on. I soon found myself walking on one of those very narrow sidewalks so common in old Paris, past a crowded bookstore and a café with steamy windows, past shops, past restaurants, and after a while I was wandering under the vaulted ceilings of an old stone arcade. All around me were mortals, coming and going, ignoring my shocking white skin, or curious wobbly manner, as I struggled to put one foot before the other, following one stone street into another stone street. The crowds grew thicker, and it seemed this was the most vital city in all the world.

The sky was winter white and the air was not so terribly cold.

At last I wandered into a great square with a high triple-decker fountain in the middle of it. But the fountain was turned off. And the snow lay light and fresh and pure over everything, and the leafless trees were glistening with thin ice, ice that might crack into a million splinters if you touched it, and the deep sloping roofs of the mansions all about the square were shining with snow.

I was alone.

Purely alone. I took a deep breath of the bracing air and looked up through the whiteness and gradually I penetrated the layers of lowering clouds and I picked out the stars.

Alone. No warm hand on the back of the neck, nothing living and breathing inside me that wasn't me. No voice that could speak to me or hear me if I spoke. Just alone.

Just the way I'd been over two hundred years ago when Richelieu's statue of Louis XIII on horseback had been in the middle of this vast place, and these mansions had been down at heel, no longer fashionable, and I had walked through here briskly after the coming of the vampiric Blood, fierce and strong and able to roam all Paris, it seemed, driven by my thirst.

Innocent blood. That was my thought. It hadn't come from someone else.

**Still alive.**

A mortal woman stopped just a few paces from me. Her coat went down to the tops of her boots, and a scarf was wrapped entirely around her face and neck. She spoke to me in rapid French telling me I would catch my death of cold if I didn't go inside somewhere, get a coat to wear. I nodded and thanked her and she rushed on across the dim lawns of snow.

Well, it's as good a time as ever, I thought, to find out what had been lost, if anything. I went up, fast enough that no mortal eye would catch it, and was soon crossing the sky over Paris and headed infallibly as ever for home.

It was eight o'clock when I walked into the ballroom. I had heard the cheers and screaming before I ever reached the doors. And the sounds of people rushing through the many corridors and salons.

"Where is the orchestra?" I asked. I made my way into an open space beside the harpsichord. Marius took me in his arms. The musicians flooded into the little congregation of gilded chairs, and Antoine stepped up on the small black podium. Some lusty triumphal music soon swelled behind me.

I held still to Marius. "These have been the worst hours of my whole existence," he whispered in my ear. "Then they said you were alive, that you'd been seen in Paris. And I didn't believe it."

The crowd around us was getting thicker and thicker, with blood drinkers pushing here and there to diminish the space in which we stood.

All the faces were soon there, except for Louis and Rose and Viktor. But how could that be? I turned around. They stood only two feet away from me, huddled together, and down the pure whiteness of Louis's face were two thin lines of blood tears.

It must have been an hour of individual embraces, of reassuring myself and each person that I was whole and complete. I was thirsting, but I didn't care.

I couldn't mention **his name**. I couldn't. I couldn't say his name and it seemed they sensed it and they didn't say it either. They didn't ask, Is he here? Is he gone?

Only when at last it was over—all the festivities, and the questions, and my repeated answers—only when I went down into the crypt did I sit alone in the dark and say, "Amel. Amel, where are you? Are you flesh and blood? Are you safe?"

The blood tears ran down my face the way they'd run down Louis's face until the shirt and coat were ruined, and then I wept like a child.

# 32

# Lestat

The next night I made about the best speech I had ever delivered to my kindred in the Blood. I didn't write it or plan it or think it through. I stood on the small conductor's podium and addressed the hundreds crowded into the room, and the hundreds listening from other rooms.

I told them first off that Amel was indeed gone. That was all I said of him or what had happened.

Then I told them that we had to make our way of life sacred, that we had to see ourselves as sacred, and we had to see our journey through the world as sacred whether anybody else ever did.

I told them—in so many words—that no confraternity or sodality had ever been made sacred except by the faith of those who formed it, as there was no known power beyond this world or in it that could make anything sacred except the power we claimed for ourselves. I told them all that we were children of the universe no matter who thought otherwise, that we lived and breathed and thought and dreamed as do all sentient beings, and no one had a right to condemn us or deny us the right to love and to live.

Yes, the rules were being written, and yes, the history of the tribe was being written, and yes, we would seek a consensus before we went forward. But the thing to remember was this: the Devil's Road had never been easy or simple, and those who traveled it for more than a century did so because they had cared about something greater than themselves and their endless appetite for human blood. They had wanted to be part of something immensely bigger than they were, and they had rebelled in their own way against the inevitable isolation that closes around us all; they had survived because the beauty of life wouldn't let them leave it; and a thirst for knowledge had been born in them—a thirst for new ages and new forms and new expressions of art and love—even as they saw everything they had cherished crumbling and fading away.

If we wanted to survive, if we wanted to inherit the millennia as Thorne and Cyril, and Teskhamen and Chrysanthe had inherited them, as Avicus and Zenobia had inherited them, as Marius and Pandora and Flavius had inherited them, and as Rhoshamandes and Sevraine had inherited them—and as Seth and Gregory, now the very oldest among us, had inherited them—then we had to meet the future with respect as well as courage and count fear and selfishness to be small things.

"This is our universe," I said. "We too are made

of stardust as are all things on this planet; we too belong."

Seems I went on for a while on that theme, and then when I realized I had in fact finished, I brought it to a close.

I didn't really provide any new or better answers than I'd grudgingly given last night, and when people praised me for my bravery in giving myself up to what was to happen, I waved that away and said, "It was not my courage. It was just what happened."

I left, taking Thorne and Cyril with me, and sought out Rhoshamandes, who was, as always, in his own castle in his own lofty and cold and relentlessly gray world.

He gave a violent start when I walked into his spacious drawing room or great hall, or whatever he might have called it. And he rose at once, dropping the book he'd been reading on the floor.

"No enmity between us," I said. I extended my hand. Thorne and Cyril were on either side of me and I could feel their hostility towards him. I knew how they longed for him to provoke a battle but even the three of us were no match for what one as old as he might do.

He regarded me coldly for a long time as if he couldn't believe what I was saying.

"All things," I said, "must be made new. There can't be lingering grudges."

He didn't answer. I went on. "You said it would

make up for what I'd done to you. Well, stick to your word."

At that he softened somewhat, and then he shrugged. Shrugged just the way I did so often. And he extended his hand.

"I know you were hoping I wouldn't survive," I said. "But let's just keep the peace now. You are welcome in my house anytime as long as you keep the peace."

I didn't wait for any cold, incomplete, inadequate, or disappointing rejoinders. I wanted to go home. But he stopped me as I turned to go and he said,

"Peace between us! I'm grateful to you." He seemed more than merely sincere. "I didn't want you to die," he said, "but I hope that Devil who was inside you perished. I hope he went up in smoke to hover in agony again over this world forever."

This stung me to the heart. But I didn't blame him for what he said. The general feeling throughout the world of the Undead was that we'd been born of a diabolical force that brought us alive to Darkness only through blindness and thirst. There had not been a tear shed anywhere by anyone for Amel.

I wanted to say Amel was flesh of our flesh and blood of our blood, but I said nothing. If you really want peace in any world you have to learn to say nothing. I clasped his hand again and said I hoped he would come to Court soon.

When we reached the Château, it was Cyril who

asked me how I could do that, just shake hands with that monster, after he'd delivered me to that Kapetria creature and her schemes.

"I shook his hand because I don't give a damn about him," I answered. "I care about peace among us. After all, some new and hideous spirit may yet descend to lay waste every dream I still hold dear, or some rebellious band of envious revenants rise out of nowhere to overthrow the Court soon enough."

# 33

# Lestat

SPRING CAME TO our mountains with uncommon speed and warmth.

Soon all the windows of the castle were open to the night breezes, and the forest was green once more, and the lawns were like soft green velvet, and the wild grasses in the mountains were green, and the wildflowers broke out in patches of meadow under the moon, and the Court enjoyed the inevitable rejuvenation in countless ways.

No one had heard a word from the Replimoids. And no one was looking for them either. We were agreed on that, that we would not look for them, but I was in agony not knowing whether or not Amel had survived.

I figured, given their warm-blooded nature, their need for a warm climate, they had likely gone to establish themselves in some South American land where there were mountains and forest in which they could get lost. But then given their peaceful nature, and their desire to remain the People of the Purpose, dedicated to serving life in all forms—well, I figured they might be in safer places, like the United States.

The truth was, no one knew.

Now others were curious about the fate of Amel, obviously, but I don't think anyone felt the pain I felt. Louis knew what I couldn't confide, and he was respectful of it, and comforting and patient. Louis never failed me. But others spoke carelessly of Amel, of the Amel Factor, of the Amel Core, and of the Burnings instigated by Amel, and of how Amel might have been the ruin of all that he had brought into being when he plunged into Akasha thousands of years ago. The young ones wanted to hear again and again the story of our origins; but the heroes and heroines of the oft-told tales did not include the faceless, voiceless spirit who had only come to himself in the late twentieth century. And by the end of May, it was not uncommon to hear young blood drinkers in the ballroom saying casually that they found it hard to believe "all that old mythology" about Amel.

We were now what we had always been—a tribe of the shadows, hunting humans on the margins, drifting through the mortal crowds of the world wrapped in Gothic splendor and self-sustained romance. But we were united and we were strong. We had one another. And we had the Council, and we had the castle, and we had the Court.

I was intoxicated with the Court by the time summer came. I was spending part of every evening working with Marius on a constitution that he was writing in Latin, that reflected far too much of his Roman principles, and strange Hellenistic disdain for the material and the biological, and then I spent time talking with the young ones about how they must and could protect themselves from discovery, while working with all the relentless digital surveillance of the mortal world. The spiritual, the practical, the timeless challenges, the challenges of the moment.

Renovations were complete on the Château and on the village, and on three manor houses that had been reconstructed from old paintings and molding drawings and historical maps.

I had let most of the mortal architects, designers, and construction laborers go; only a small community of retirees remained. And I faced the question now of whether I wanted to bring my beloved chief architect, Alain Abelard, over into our world.

Meanwhile, Abelard didn't want to leave the village. He didn't want to leave me. He told me he had new projects to suggest to me, and would soon be presenting me with various plans. Abelard had no real life apart from me.

When all this became too much for me, I'd break off and go to Paris just to wander places old and new, and breathe in the city's endless vitality.

By mid-June, I was walking about Paris all the time and Louis invariably accompanied me. Soon we had our favorite streets, and our favorite bookshops, and our favorite cafés. We saw films together, and occasional plays. We haunted the Louvre and the Centre Georges Pompidou. But mostly we roamed.

So it was that on a particularly beautiful and warm Saturday night we found ourselves in Paris, talking softly about how miraculously changed our world was from the times in which vampires believed themselves to be sinister supernatural beings endowed with myriad mysterious characteristics by someone's deliberate design.

Louis spoke of having recovered Paris from the pain of the loss of Claudia, and of loving the modern city more than he had ever thought he could.

Well before midnight, we came to the Quartier Latin and settled in a spacious outdoor café, one of our favorites, a tourist mecca now, but as genuine and vital a place as one could desire.

We took a table on the very outside of the flagstone sidewalk to sit and talk some more and watch the passersby. I was thirsting. And once again, I kept thinking of innocent blood.

But there is a lot to be said about spending most of the night thirsting, when one's senses are sharpened by the thirst and colors are more vivid and sounds more piercing and sweet. So I ignored the thirst, and certainly I ignored the temptation to seek innocent blood.

We ordered enough of everything—wine, sandwiches, coffee, pastries—so that the waiter, to whom we slipped a large bill, would leave us alone for a long time.

Louis went off at one point to find a newspaper, and I was sitting there alone, hoping that no wandering members of the Undead would recognize me or seize on this moment to "talk."

The world seemed splendid and I was as in love with Paris as I'd ever been.

But I soon realized that someone was watching me. A still figure at the next table, practically opposite me, had fixed its gaze on me with a little too much concentration to be welcome. I didn't look at the figure. I scanned the crowds for images of him in the eyes of others and when I realized what I was seeing, I turned and confronted him at once.

He was a young male, perhaps in his twenties, and he had handsomely suntanned skin and long deep-red hair to his shoulders and bright green eyes. When he smiled at me, my heart stopped.

He got up from the table and came over to me. He looked fine in his jeans and blue-and-white seersucker jacket and stiff white shirt open at the neck. He sat down opposite and leaned in close, forearms on the table, long slender fingers reaching out and covering my right hand.

"Lestat," he whispered.

I didn't dare to say his name. I was racking this up as a hallucination because how under Heaven could anyone have so perfectly re-created the boy-man I'd been with in Atalantaya during the time when my heart had been stopped. The dimples, the cleft in the chin, but more than anything the large vibrant eyes and the intense feeling that appeared to heat him all over from within.

"It's me," he said, his warm fingers squeezing my hand tight enough to hurt a mortal hand. "It's Amel."

"I'm going to lose it," I said quietly. I could hardly speak. Beyond him I saw Louis approaching with his newspaper, but when Louis saw what was happening at the table, he nodded, folded the paper, and moved out of sight.

There was no way to put into words what I felt. This was Amel. Amel, alive; Amel as fully realized and present in this body and this body was a living breathing replica of the body he'd lost when Atalantaya had fallen into the sea.

He couldn't read these thoughts from me, apparently, and finally I said the only thing I could say. "Thank Heaven!" I put my hand up to shield my eyes and I cried. I sat there crying for a long time, and finally, I managed to find my handkerchief, and I blotted my eyes, and folded the linen to hide the blood.

"How many times have you been here?" he asked. He imprisoned my right hand again and I saw that he'd been crying too. The cadence of his voice, the pitch, the timbre—it was all the same as the voice he'd shaped in my head.

When I didn't answer, he started up again as if he couldn't contain himself.

"This is the first week," he said, "that I've been allowed out by myself, the first week I've been permitted to walk the streets unattended, the first week I've been allowed to be nearly run over by traffic, or to get lost, or to be mugged and robbed of my papers, or to get sick after overeating and gag in an alleyway on my own." He stopped only to laugh and then went right on, his white teeth sparkling and his eyes coloring beautifully in the lights. "I told them if they didn't let me out, I was going to run away. I swore that if they didn't let me make a few blunders on my own, I was going to go on a hunger strike. Of course they reminded me that we don't need food, and nothing much would happen except that I'd be miserable, but finally Kapetria drove me into the Boulevard Saint-Michel and I jumped out of the car and walked off."

So they had been in France all the time—in Paris all the time more than likely. I didn't care. I didn't care about anything but him.

"And none of that happened to you, did it?" I asked.

"No, nothing bad at all," he announced proudly with the most incandescent smile. His eyes were moist. "I've been roaming since morning. And I knew that you had been walking in these very streets. I knew you frequented this café. I overheard them say it. I knew. I dreamed of seeing you! I wanted to see you. I would have kept coming back until I ran into you." He stopped and looked over the table of sandwiches and pastries. I could see that he was hungry.

"Please, eat," I said. I moved a glass of wine towards him. And I uncorked the bottle. "Are they trying to keep you and me apart?"

He took a long deep drink, and I refilled the glass.

"They know they can't, really," said Amel. "That I want to see you and talk to you and inevitably they will have to allow it. But they keep saying I'm not ready. Well, I am ready. I need to see you like this."

He began to eat slowly, savoring every bite of the bread and meat, but his eyes kept returning to me.

"Ah, such pleasure," he said under his breath. "Every cell in my body is learning to enjoy this more and more each day."

"What else can I get for you?" I asked.

I signaled the waiter.

"What about an ice-cold beer?" I asked. "Would you like that?"

He nodded. "Hot, cold, sweetness," he murmured. He took a bite from the sugar pastry right before him, closing his eyes, shuddering as he held it in his mouth. Then he looked at me, took me in again as if he were feasting on the sight of me. Tears hovered in his eyes.

Scent of blood, delicious blood inside him.

There was so much I wanted to say that I said nothing.

"I am famished for the whole world," he said. "I'm famished for wine, for beer, for food, for life, for you! Take off your glasses, will you, I have to see your eyes, oh, yes, thank you, thank you. Those are your eyes."

"Don't cry anymore," I said. "If you don't cry anymore, I won't cry."

"Deal," he said. The waiter set the beer before him. He drank half the glass and sighed and said that that was so good. "You wouldn't believe how long it took me to learn to eat, to sit and stand upright, and to walk, to see. I had to learn how to see all over again. My brain didn't come equipped with any knowledge. We don't know how the Bravennans equipped minds with knowledge. My brain is just a made-up thing, made from cells taken from Kapetria's hands. She figured it out, if she never severed the hand, but took the biopsies from it while it was still connected to her, then no new life would be created that would have to be killed. And she built my brain from the cells in her hands, and some from the cells in Derek's hands, too." He shrugged. "I could explain it to you, but it would take years. Anyway, I had to learn how to see, to walk, to talk!"

"It's only been four months," I said. But I was shocked by the implications of what he was telling me, shocked by the genius of Kapetria and the living proof of that genius in him.

"Seems like forever." He sat back in the little woven tub chair and gazed up at the awning. His

wavy red hair fell down in his eyes but he didn't
seem to care. Dark eyebrows, precise eyebrows, and
lashes. She had constructed all of this.

Horrible possibilities occurred to me as they had
before—of beings grown or manufactured and gaining ascendency on an unsuspecting planet if Kapetria and her tribe could do this. And what of the
dead, the earthbound dead who might come back
through such marvelous bodies? What could they
do for Magnus, and for Memnoch?

"What are you going to do?" I asked. "Have you
any great plan?"

"I don't know." He shrugged. He picked up another small jelly pastry and swallowed it, and then
broke off a bit of the lemon tart. "I have no idea,"
he said. "There's so much I have to learn. I thought
I knew everything, that inside you, I'd grasped the
entire tenor of the age!" He laughed at himself and
shook his head. "So stupid, so blind. Every day now
I'm shocked by some new discovery. I read of the
things human beings have done to one another in
war. I read of carnage on the planet now. I'm paralyzed by much of what I read, what I see in television news, in films. Yet I must continue to study,
that before anything, study and travel. And I want
to figure where Atalantaya was, where she sank. I
need to know that, I need to know where my city
died. I need to know where everything I'd created
and envisioned and planned for this mighty world
died!"

"I don't blame you. You must know infinitely more than the legends."

"No, I don't," he said. "In those long-ago days, I was too preoccupied with the projects right before me to pay that much attention to the whole scheme of the planet. I thought I knew its geography, but what I knew was distorted, limited, primitive. Anyway, now I must go everywhere. I must roam jungles, deserts, mountain ranges. I must see the ice melting rapidly at the poles, see that for myself, the ice melting and breaking off and falling into the rising seas. And I have this dream that maybe one of my little satellite cities sank somewhere with the dome intact." He paused, looking around him, and then back at me. "And then there is the work in our laboratories."

"Can you fully duplicate the luracastria of the old days?" I asked.

"Oh, of course, Kapetria had to complete that before she could put me into a working body," he said. "But luracastria begets other materials. That has always been the power of luracastria, it's like a virus, mutating other chemicals in wholly unforeseen ways. I'm working on it constantly in here." He tapped his right temple. "This ghost brain is organizing this biological brain and I'm recovering old knowledge and acquiring new knowledge all the time! But tell me, what is Fareed doing? What has he discovered? What is Seth up to? I want to know them. I must know them. And Louis, I must come to know Louis. Louis is over there watching us. Louis is making you happy? Before we were separated, I knew Louis through you and—."

He broke off.

He wanted to say something, but he couldn't. "I lost all of you," he whispered, "and I grieve for that loss." The tears rose again.

"Yes," I said. "I know that. And I lost you." I fought my own tears. "You brought me together with Louis, you did that, and you gave Louis back to me. I have Louis now because of you."

Ah, this was agony, and yet I treasured every second of it.

He reached inside his seersucker jacket and took out a white card and a pen. The pen was a very-fine-point gel-ink pen, and in a scrawling spidery hand he wrote numbers for me. This was for his phone. He gave the card to me and I put it in my pocket.

"Now give me your phone," I said, "and I'll tap in my numbers for you after I tap in yours."

"Oh, right, of course," he said. He blushed. He should have known it was that simple, and he was suddenly ashamed. But I fully understand such gaps, such random and sudden inabilities to grasp the simple or the sublime in the midst of the flow of so much powerful knowledge. He watched me manage these small tasks. "You're as beautiful to me now as you were in the mirror," he said. "You're as beautiful to me as you were the first night at Trinity Gate when I saw you in the mirror through your eyes."

He was startled. He looked around anxiously. I hadn't heard anything or seen anything. "Just watching for them," he said. "They're going to be coming for me because I won't call for them to come. Ah. I knew it. I always experience this frisson . . . that's one of your words . . . this frisson when I'm being watched. There they are now. I love you. I'll see you again. Vow to me, we'll meet again here as soon as we can."

I held his hand. I wouldn't let him go.

I had no idea of the names of the four women who came towards us, except that they were clones of Kapetria, or of Kapetria's clones. They were magnificent with the same deep shade of bronze to their skin and the same large black eyes with flecks of gold in them, and lots of gold in their long hair. They wore rouge on their lips and they had on sundresses of light cotton with only straps over their beautifully molded shoulders, and bright gold bracelets on their naked arms.

"Good evening, Prince."

"Good evening, ladies." I pushed the chair back and rose to my feet. "Can't you give us just a few minutes longer?"

"Amel gets overexcited, Prince," said the one who had spoken, while the other ones nodded. "Tell you what . . . we're double-parked. We'll go around a couple of blocks and come back. With this traffic, it will take us a little while. But only if you promise you'll both be right here when we return."

"Promise, cross my heart, hope to die!" said Amel. His face was wet with tears. "If you take me right now, I'll never forgive you."

Off they went, piling back into their large black Land Rover and steering the car into the sluggish stream that was moving on the boulevard.

He shuddered, and tried to swallow his tears. "I love them," he said. "They are my people now, and I am of them. But I—. I can't endure their relentless control."

"There's so much I want to ask you," I said. "So much I want to know. They won't prevent us from knowing and loving one another."

He appeared doubtful, sad. A dark fear gripped me.

"Know this," he said taking my hands in his hands. "I will love you forever! Were it not for you, I would never have survived."

"Nonsense, you would have gone into one of the others sooner or later."

"No," he said. "Wasn't working. It was your courage the first time and the last time. It was always your courage, and your patience and your insistence that solutions could be found, that great conflicting forces could somehow be reconciled."

"You're giving me way too much credit," I said. "But we have a destiny, you and I!" I started to weep again. I wiped angrily at my eyes and put the violet sunglasses back on. "I can't think of anything else right now but you and what you're experiencing, what the future holds for you."

He sat silent, gazing at me.

"Give my love to them, even the ones that hate me," he said. "What did you do to Rhoshamandes for what he did in helping Kapetria?"

"What do you think?" I said. "I did nothing, of course."

He laughed softly under his breath. He shook his head. "Lestat, you know," he said, "that Rhoshamandes is a danger to you."

"So everyone says," I replied, "but I've lived with danger for so long. I don't want to talk about him now. I don't want to waste a moment here even thinking about him."

A silence fell between us, and then I said,

"You know the kind of power you have." I spoke hesitantly. "You know what you and the other Replimoids could do to this world." I gestured to the street, to the buildings, to the people, with my right hand. "You know what you could do for the earthbound dead and the spirits—."

"We are the People of the Purpose!" he said. "You must remember this always. And the purpose is never to harm life in any way. Now there is not a creature on this planet who ever really lives such a purpose, no, we know that. But we will try! We will try as surely as any colony of people dedicated to the support of life has ever tried."

It must have been a full hour that we talked.

He told me about the books he'd been reading, and asked me questions about things he said he didn't understand. But how do you explain to a person why Late Antiquity embraced wholeheartedly the Christian rejection of the biological and material world? How do you explain such personalities as Saint Augustine or Pelagius? Or Giordano Bruno? How do you account for the fact that the ancient Romans could stamp coins but never invented a printing press? Why did it take so long to invent the stirrup or the barrel? Or the bicycle? How to explain why French and English are so different when the languages evolved so close to each other? We confessed we were both at a loss to account for the dark cynicism of so many humans living in a modern world so full of wondrous progress.

"They can't know history as we know it," I said.

We talked of the Bravennans and whether or not they still actively monitored this world, whether or not their film feeds were still flowing. We talked of the mystery of other aliens coming to the planet.

He and the People of the Purpose had the very same speculations as human beings, that alien visitors might actually be walking among us, far more skillfully disguised than we could imagine.

He spoke of his own great and small discoveries, a new luracastria derivative, a synthetic hormone that he thought could lead to increasing the human life span in some individuals for ten years beyond the allotment of their genetic clock.

"Don't fear me," he said finally. "Never fear me. What I will do, I will do with respect for what all these beings achieved on their own. After all, they built this paradise without an Amel, didn't they? Human beings built it, this world of Western Europe and America and England and all the countries of the West."

"You haven't been to the East yet," I said. "You haven't seen China or Japan or the Levant. There is so much to learn there as well."

Finally the Replimoid women were there at the curb again with the door of the car open.

He jumped to his feet and came around the table and took me in his arms. "Ah, that this too, too solid flesh must never melt!" he said.

I took his face in my hands and kissed him.

"Amel," I whispered in his ear. "My love."

He turned away abruptly, as if it were the only way that he could make the break, and he headed towards the waiting car. At the curb, he stopped. We looked at one another, oblivious to the traffic, the noise, the crowds.

He came back to me and we embraced completely. We were wrapped in each other's arms. And the scent of his blood overwhelmed me.

I bit down into my tongue and let my mouth fill with blood. Then I kissed him full on his mouth and opened his lips and let the blood pass into him. I felt him stiffen, shiver, and I heard an ecstatic moan come from deep inside his chest.

"Drink," he whispered.

And I did. Holding him tight to me, I drove my

teeth into his throat. All the mortal world would see was a man kissing another man, but I tapped into the blood, the rich and flavorful Replimoid blood, and the world dissolved.

The images came in a rush like the song of a full symphony orchestra, images of him in myriad moments of his new existence too numerous for me to absorb, riotous images filled with his laughter and the mingling of voices, music, the roar of engines, explosions, wind and rain, and I saw towers, towers of exquisite beauty and structures of unimaginable complexity and great dense urban landscapes of fantastical scope, and it was not Atalantaya I was seeing, it was cities of this world, now, our time, cities that existed and cities yet unknown but envisioned, and—it was **innocent blood.**

Innocent blood filling me, innocent blood pumped by his heart into my heart.

It was innocent blood with all its sweetness and freshness and illimitable power.

It was innocent blood and he was not dying as I took it.

Innocent blood.

The others had surrounded us. They were trying to come between us. I thought I'd die in agony when I drew back, but I didn't. I held him by the shoulders and looked into his eyes. The noise of the café and the boulevard assaulted me and I hated it, but I held him fast.

The women tugged at him, trying to pull him

back. They'd assumed I was hurting him, but I hadn't hurt him. Undiminished, he stared at me through a veil of shimmering tears.

"Au revoir, Lestat," he said with another one of his brilliant irresistible smiles, and he was off, hurrying out of the café with the women, and waving as he climbed into the car. The car moved at a reckless speed, weaving dangerously through the traffic, and finally disappeared.

His blood was still ripping through me.

I was tempted to go up high in the air and follow the car, track it to wherever it might lead, and find out just exactly where they were hiding in plain sight.

Maybe another time I would do that. Maybe another time. Because I knew I would see him soon again and there was nothing they could do to stop it.

I stood still feeling the heat of his blood begin to fade inside me.

Louis came up finally, and took my arm and we began to walk together.

"You heard it all?" I asked.

"Yes," he said. "If you'd wanted me gone beyond hearing, of course, I would have gone."

"Not at all," I said. "You're the only one who really knows the full extent of it, of how much I love him."

"Yes," he said. "I know."

We headed for a dark deserted alleyway, far from human eyes. And then we headed for home.

It was midnight when I entered the ballroom to address the Court.

When I explained that he had survived, and that he was incarnated and alive, and that he was well, and he was splendid and was the self he'd been long centuries before he'd ever come down to Akasha, they all cheered.

Cheered and cheered. Some of them shed tears.

You would have thought they really loved him. But they did not fool me. They never knew him as I knew him. They never loved him at all. They feared him far too much to love him, and they would in time come to fear him again. They'd fear the very idea of him, and the idea of the Replimoids and what they might do.

They'd come to fear the Replimoids just as others in this world feared us.

And so we go on without him.

We go on without the mystery of Amel. Already it sinks into the past and becomes legend—the story of the Divine accident and the King and Queen who ruled in silence for thousands of years, and the story of those who took the Core into themselves and ultimately set the Core free. And as the legend grows, some will quickly forget, and others in ages to come will never even believe.

He walks the earth with the power to destroy it. But then so does the human race. And so do we.

But what endures is what has always mattered: love—that we love one another as surely as we are alive. And if there is any hope for us to ever really be good—that hope will be realized through love.

If they want to believe they loved him, so be it. Maybe they do love him now. Maybe they will love him in retrospect. Maybe they will love him in the story of Atalantaya and how he died and how he survived and how he goes on now.

I love him without question, and he loves me. He knows how to love, as well as anyone I'd ever known, and Atalantaya with her shimmering towers was the greatest evidence of his fathomless love.

To love any one person or thing truly is the beginning of the wisdom to love all things. This has to be so. It has to be. I believe it and I don't really believe anything else.

1:50 p.m.
July 1, 2016
La Quinta, California

# Appendix 1

## Characters and Places in the Vampire Chronicles

**Akasha**—Queen of ancient Egypt six thousand years ago, and the first vampire ever created, through a merger with the spirit Amel. The story is told in **The Vampire Lestat** and in **The Queen of the Damned**.

**Allesandra**—A Merovingian princess, daughter of King Dagobert I, brought into the Blood in the seventh century by Rhoshamandes. First introduced in **The Vampire Lestat** as a mad nameless vampire living with the Children of Satan under Les Innocents Cemetery in Paris. She also appears in **The Vampire Armand** in the Renaissance where she is named, and later in **Prince Lestat** and **Prince Lestat and the Realms of Atlantis**.

**Amel**—A spirit who created the first vampire six thousand years ago by merging with the body of the Egyptian Queen Akasha. The story is told in **The Vampire Lestat** and in **The Queen of the Damned**. **Prince Lestat** and

**Prince Lestat and the Realms of Atlantis** continue the story of Amel.

**Antoine**—A French musician exiled from Paris to Louisiana and brought into the Blood by Lestat around the middle of the nineteenth century. Referred to as "the musician" in **Interview with the Vampire.** Later appears in **Prince Lestat** and **Prince Lestat and the Realms of Atlantis.** A talented violinist and pianist and composer.

**Arion**—A black vampire of ancient times introduced in **Blackwood Farm.** At least two thousand years old, perhaps older. Possibly from India.

**Arjun**—A prince of the Chola dynasty in India, brought into the Blood by Pandora around 1300. Appears in **Blood and Gold** and also in **Pandora.**

**Armand**—One of the pillars of the Vampire Chronicles. Armand is a Russian from Kiev, sold into slavery as a boy, and made a vampire in Renaissance Venice by the Vampire Marius. He is introduced in **Interview with the Vampire,** and appears in numerous novels in the Vampire Chronicles, telling his own story in **The Vampire Armand.** The founder of the coven at Trinity Gate in New York. Armand maintains a house in Paris in Saint-Germain-des-Prés, which functions as the Paris Court for Prince Lestat.

**Avicus**—An Egyptian vampire who first appears in Marius's memoir, **Blood and Gold.** Appears again in **Prince Lestat.**

**Benedict**—A Christian monk of the seventh century in France, brought into the Blood by Rhoshamandes.

Benedict is the vampire from whom the alchemist Magnus stole the Blood, a theft described in **The Vampire Lestat**. Appears in **Prince Lestat** and **Prince Lestat and the Realms of Atlantis** as Rhoshamandes's companion and lover.

**Benji Mahmoud**—A twelve-year-old Palestinian Bedouin boy, brought into the Blood by Marius in 1997. Benji originates the vampire radio station heard round the world in **Prince Lestat.** Resides at Trinity Gate in New York and sometimes at the Court of Prince Lestat in France. First appears in **The Vampire Armand** when he is living in New York with his companion, Sybelle.

**Bianca Solderini**—Venetian courtesan brought into the Blood by Marius in **Blood and Gold** around 1498.

**Château de Lioncourt**—Lestat's ancestral castle in the Massif Central in France, splendidly restored and the home of the new dazzling and glamorous Court of the Vampires with its orchestra, theater, and frequent formal balls. The adjacent village, including an inn and a church and several shops, has also been restored to house mortal workers and visitors to the Château.

**Children of Satan**—A network of medieval vampire covens, populated by vampires who sincerely believed they were children of the Devil, doomed to roam the world in rags, accursed, feeding on the blood of innocent humans to do the Devil's will. Their most famous covens were in Rome and in Paris. The coven kidnapped many of the fledglings of Rhoshamandes until he finally left France to get away from them. And the Children of Satan in Rome spelled catastrophe for Marius and his great Venetian household in the Renaissance. Armand told of his experiences with the Children of Satan in **The Vampire Armand.**

**Chrysanthe**—A merchant's widow from the Christian city of Hira, brought into the Blood by Nebamun, newly risen and named Gregory in the fourth century. Wife of Gregory. Introduced, along with Gregory, in **Prince Lestat.**

**Cimetière des Innocents**—An ancient cemetery in the city of Paris until it was destroyed near the end of the eighteenth century. Underneath this cemetery lived the Coven of the Children of Satan, presided over by Armand, which is described by Lestat in **The Vampire Lestat.** Referred to in the novels as "Les Innocents."

**Claudia**—An orphan of five or six years old, brought into the Blood around 1794 by Lestat and Louis in New Orleans. Long dead. Her story is told in **Interview with the Vampire.** Later appears as a spirit in **Merrick,** though the appearance is suspect.

**Cyril**—An ancient Egyptian vampire, maker of Eudoxia in **Blood and Gold,** and named for the first time in **Prince Lestat.** Age unknown.

**Daniel Molloy**—The nameless "boy" interviewer in **Interview with the Vampire.** Brought into the Blood by Armand in **The Queen of the Damned.** Also appears in **Blood and Gold** living with Marius. Also in **Prince Lestat.**

**David Talbot**—Introduced as an elderly member of the Talamasca, an order of psychic detectives, in **The Queen of the Damned.** Becomes an important character in **The**

**Tale of the Body Thief**, and also solicits Pandora's story from her in **Pandora**. A pillar of the Vampire Chronicles.

**Davis**—A black dancer from Harlem, a member of the Fang Gang, brought into the Blood by Killer sometime in 1985. Introduced in **The Queen of the Damned**. Further described in **Prince Lestat**.

**Eleni**—A survivor of the Children of Satan who helps found the Théâtre des Vampires in Paris in the eighteenth century; corresponds with the Vampire Lestat after he leaves Paris to travel the world. A fledgling of Rhoshamandes made a vampire in the early Middle Ages.

**Enkil**—Ancient King of Egypt, husband of the great Queen Akasha, the second vampire to be brought into existence. His story is told in **The Vampire Lestat** and **The Queen of the Damned**.

**Everard de Landen**—A fledgling of Rhoshamandes from the early Middle Ages who first appears in **Blood and Gold** and is named in **Prince Lestat**.

**Fareed**—Anglo Indian by birth, a physician and researcher, brought into the Blood by Seth to be a healer and researcher of the vampires. A major character introduced in **Prince Lestat**.

**Flannery Gilman**—An American female medical doctor, biological mother of Viktor, and brought into the blood by Fareed and Seth. Part of their medical and research team working with the Undead.

**Flavius**—A Greek vampire, a slave purchased by Pandora in the city of Antioch and brought into the Blood by Pandora in the early centuries of the Common Era.

**Gabrielle**—Lestat's mother, a noblewoman of breeding and education, brought into the Blood by her own son in 1780 in Paris. A wanderer who dresses in male attire. A familiar figure in the background throughout the Vampire Chronicles.

**Gregory Duff Collingsworth**—Known as Nebamun in ancient times, a lover of Queen Akasha and made a blood drinker by her to lead her Queens Blood troops against the First Brood. Known today as Gregory, owner of a powerful pharmaceutical empire in the modern world. Husband of Chrysanthe.

**Gremt Stryker Knollys**—A powerful and mysterious spirit who has created for himself over time a physical body that is a replica of a human body. Connected with the founding of the secret Order of the Talamasca. Introduced in **Prince Lestat**.

**Hesketh**—A Germanic cunning woman, brought into the Blood by Teskhamen in the first century. Now a ghost who has managed to produce a physical body for herself. Also connected with the origins of the secret Order of the Talamasca. Introduced in **Prince Lestat**.

**Jesse Reeves**—An American woman of the twentieth century, a blood descendant of the ancient Maharet and brought into the Blood by Maharet herself in 1985 in **The Queen of the Damned**. Jesse was also a mortal member of the Talamasca and worked with David Talbot in the Order.

**Khayman**—An ancient Egyptian vampire, made by Queen Akasha, and rebelling against her with the First Brood. His story is told in **The Queen of the Damned**.

**Killer**—An American male vampire, founder of the Fang Gang in **The Queen of the Damned.** Of unknown history or origin.

**Lestat de Lioncourt**—The hero of the Vampire Chronicles, made a vampire by Magnus near the end of the eighteenth century, the maker of a number of vampires, including Gabrielle, his mother; Nicolas de Lenfent, his friend and lover; Louis, the narrator of **Interview with the Vampire;** and Claudia, the child vampire. Presently known as Prince Lestat by one and all.

**Louis de Pointe du Lac**—The vampire who started the Vampire Chronicles by telling his story to Daniel Molloy in **Interview with the Vampire,** an account of his own origins, which differs in some ways from Lestat's own account in **The Vampire Lestat.** A French colonial plantation owner made a vampire by Lestat in 1791. Appears most prominently in the first Chronicle, and in **Merrick,** and in **Prince Lestat** and **Prince Lestat and the Realms of Atlantis.**

**Magnus**—An elderly medieval alchemist who stole the Blood from a young vampire, Benedict, in France. The vampire who kidnapped and brought Lestat into the Blood in 1780. Now a ghost, sometimes appearing solid, and at other times as an illusion.

**Maharet**—One of the oldest vampires in the world, twin to Mekare. The twins are known for their red hair and their power as mortal witches. Made at the dawn of Vampire History, they are rebels leading the First Brood against Queen Akasha and her Queens Blood vampires. Maharet is beloved for her wisdom and for following all of her mortal descendants through the ages all over the world, whom she called the Great Family. Maharet tells her story—the story of the twins—in **Queen of the Damned.** She also figures in **Blood and Gold** and in **Prince Lestat.**

**Marius**—A pillar of the Vampire Chronicles. A Roman patrician who is kidnapped by the Druids and brought into the Blood by Teskhamen in the first century. Marius appears in **The Vampire Lestat** and numerous other books, including his own memoir, **Blood and Gold.** A vampire known for reason and gravitas. Much loved and admired by Lestat and others.

**Mekare**—Maharet's twin sister, the powerful red-haired witch who communed with the invisible and potentially destructive spirit Amel, who later went into the body of Queen Akasha, creating the first vampire. The story of Mekare and Maharet is first told by Maharet in **The Queen of the Damned.** Mekare figures in **Blood and Gold** and in **Prince Lestat.**

**Memnoch**—A powerful spirit claiming to be the Judeo-Christian Satan. He tells his story to Lestat in **Memnoch the Devil.**

**New Orleans**—Figures prominently in the Vampire Chronicles as the home of Louis, Lestat, and Claudia for many years during the nineteenth century, at which time they resided in a townhouse in the Rue Royale in the French Quarter. This house still exists and is in the possession of Lestat today, as it has always been. It was in New Orleans that Lestat encountered Louis and Claudia and made them vampires.

**Notker the Wise**—A monk and a musician and a composer brought into the Blood by Benedict around A.D. 880, maker of many boy-soprano vampires and other vampire musicians yet unnamed. Living in the Alps. Introduced in **Prince Lestat.**

**Raymond Gallant**—A faithful mortal scholar of the Talamasca, a friend to the Vampire Marius, presumed dead in the sixteenth century. Appears again in **Prince Lestat.**

**Rhoshamandes**—A male from ancient Crete, brought into the Blood at the same time as the female Sevraine, about five thousand years ago. A powerful and reclusive vampire obsessed with operatic music and performances, and the lover of Benedict. Lives in his castle on the island of Saint Rayne in the Outer Hebrides, traveling the world from time to time to see different operas in the great opera houses.

**Rose**—An American girl, rescued as a small child by Lestat from an earthquake in the Mediterranean around 1995. His ward. Lover and later spouse of Viktor. Introduced in **Prince Lestat.**

**Saint Alcarius, Monastery of**—The secret residence of Gremt, Teskhamen, and other supernatural elders of the Talamasca in France, near the Belgian border.

**Saint Rayne**— The island on which Rhoshamandes lives.

**Santino**—An Italian vampire made during the time of the Black Death. Longtime Roman coven master of the Children of Satan. Presumed dead.

**Seth**—The biological son of Queen Akasha, brought into the Blood by her after a youth of roaming the ancient world in search of knowledge in the healing arts. He is introduced in **Prince Lestat** and is the maker of Fareed and Flannery Gilman.

**Sevraine**—A remarkably beautiful Nordic female vampire, made by Nebamun (Gregory) against Akasha's rules. Sevraine maintains her own underground court in the Cappadocian Mountains. A friend to female vampires. Introduced in **Prince Lestat.**

**Sybelle**—A young American pianist, beloved friend of Benji Mahmoud, and Armand, brought into the Blood by Marius in 1997. Introduced in **The Vampire Armand.**

**The Talamasca**—An ancient order of psychic detectives or researchers, dating back to the Dark Ages—an organization of mortal scholars who observe and record paranormal phenomena. Their origins are shrouded in mystery until they are revealed in **Prince Lestat.** They have Motherhouses in Amsterdam and outside of London, and retreat houses in many places, including Oak Haven in Louisiana. First introduced in **The Queen of the Damned** and figuring in many Chronicles since. Vampires Jesse Reeves and David Talbot were mortal members of the Talamasca.

**Teskhamen**—Ancient Egyptian vampire, the maker of Marius as told by Marius in **The Vampire Lestat.** Presumed dead until modern times. Connected with the origins of the Talamasca. First named in **Prince Lestat.**

**Théâtre des Vampires**—A boulevard theater of the macabre, created by the refugees from the Children of Satan, funded by Lestat, and managed for decades by Armand, who had once been the coven master of the Children of Satan.

**Thorne**—A red-haired Viking vampire, made centuries ago in Europe by Maharet. Introduced in **Blood and Gold.**

**Trinity Gate**—A coven dwelling made up of three identical townhouses just off Fifth Avenue on the Upper East Side of New York. Armand is the founder of Trinity Gate. And it functions now as the American Court of Prince Lestat.

**Viktor**—An American boy, biological son of Dr. Flannery Gilman. His story is revealed in **Prince Lestat.** Lover and later spouse of Rose, Lestat's ward.

# Appendix 2

## An Informal Guide to the Vampire Chronicles

**1. Interview with the Vampire (1976)**—In this, the first published memoir of a vampire within his tribe, Louis de Pointe du Lac tells his life story to a reporter he encounters in San Francisco—Daniel Molloy. Born in the eighteenth century in Louisiana, Louis, a rich plantation owner, encounters the mysterious Lestat de Lioncourt, who offers him immortality through the Blood, and Louis accepts—beginning a long spiritual search for the meaning of who and what he has become. The child vampire Claudia and the mysterious Armand of the Théâtre des Vampires are central to the story.

**2. The Vampire Lestat (1985)**—Here, Lestat de Lioncourt offers his full autobiography—recounting his life in eighteenth-century France as a penniless provincial aristocrat, a Parisian stage actor, and finally as a vampire in conflict with other members of the Undead, including the Coven of the Children of Satan. After a long physical and spiritual journey, Lestat reveals ancient secrets about the vampire tribe that he has kept for more than a century, emerging as a rock star and rock video maker, eager to start a war with humankind that might bring the Undead together and end in vampiric annihilation. Lestat survives his brash self-destructive ambitions and is the undisputed hero of the Vampire Chronicles.

**3. The Queen of the Damned (1988)**—Though written by Lestat, this story includes multiple points of view from mortals and immortals all over the planet, responding to Lestat's revealing rock music and videos, which awaken the six-thousand-year-old Queen of the Vampires, Akasha, from her long slumber. The first book to deal with the entire tribe of the Undead around the world. This novel contains the first inclusion of the mysterious secret order of mortal scholars known as the Talamasca, who study the paranormal. **Prince Lestat** and **Prince Lestat and the Realms of Atlantis** both deal with Lestat and the entire tribe, in the manner of **Queen of the Damned.**

**4. The Tale of the Body Thief (1992)**—Lestat's memoir in which he recounts his disastrous encounter with a clever and sinister mortal named Raglan James, a sorcerer experienced in switching bodies—a battle which forces Lestat into closer involvement with his friend David Talbot, Superior General of the Talamasca, whose scholarly members are dedicated to the study of the paranormal.

**5. Memnoch the Devil (1995)**—Lestat narrates a personal adventure, this time filled with devastating shocks and mysteries as he confronts a powerful spirit, Memnoch, claiming to be none other than the Devil of Christian lore, the fallen angel himself, who invites Lestat to journey with him to Heaven and Hell, and seeks to enlist Lestat as a helper in the Christian realm. Many questions remain unresolved as to who or what Memnoch is and whether he is a truth teller or a liar.

**6. Pandora (1998)**—Published under the series title New Tales of the Vampires, this story is Pandora's autobiographical confession, recounting her life in the ancient Roman Empire during the time of Augustus and Tiberius, including her great and tragic love affair with the Vampire Marius. Though it does recount later events, the book is principally focused on Pandora's first century as a vampire.

**7. The Vampire Armand (1998)**—Here, Armand, a profound and enigmatic presence in earlier novels, offers his autobiography to the reader, explaining his long life since the time of the Renaissance when he was kidnapped from Kiev and brought to Venice as a boy brothel slave, only to be rescued by the powerful and ancient vampire Marius. Yet another kidnapping puts Armand in the hands of the cruel and notorious Children of Satan, superstitious vampires who worship the Devil. Though Armand concludes his story in the present time and introduces new characters to the Chronicles, most of the account focuses on his earlier years.

**8. Vittorio, the Vampire (1999)**—One of the New Tales of the Vampires, this is the autobiography of Vittorio of Tuscany, who becomes a member of the Undead during the

Renaissance. This character does not appear elsewhere in the Vampire Chronicles, but he is of the same tribe and does share the same cosmology.

**9. Merrick (2000)**—Told by David Talbot, this story is centered on Merrick, a Creole woman of color from an old New Orleans family and a member of the Talamasca, who seeks to become a vampire during the last years of the twentieth century. This is a hybrid novel, involving a glimpse of a few characters from another series of books devoted to the history of the Mayfair Witches of New Orleans to whom Merrick is related, but it principally focuses on Merrick's involvement with the Undead, including Louis de Pointe du Lac.

**10. Blood and Gold (2001)**—Another in the series of vampire memoirs, this time written by the ancient Roman Marius, explaining much about his two thousand years amongst the Undead and the challenges he faced in protecting the mystery of Those Who Must Be Kept, the ancient parents of the tribe, Akasha and Enkil. Marius offers his side of the story of his love affair with Armand and his conflicts with other vampires. This novel concludes in the present but is principally focused on the past.

**11. Blackwood Farm (2002)**—A hybrid novel narrated by Quinn Blackwood recounting his personal history and involvement with the Talamasca, the Undead, and the Mayfair Witches of New Orleans, who figure in another book series. Set in a brief period of time in the early twenty-first century.

**12. Blood Canticle (2003)**—A hybrid novel, narrated by Lestat, recounting his adventures with Quinn Blackwood and with the Mayfair Witches from another series of books. This story focuses on a brief period of time in the twenty-first century.

**13. Prince Lestat (2014)**—Over a decade has passed since Lestat, the infamous Brat Prince, went into self-imposed retirement. The vampire world is virtually leaderless and in chaos, with vampires warring for territory in the big cities. Young blood drinker Benji Mahmoud launches a clandestine vampire radio station to call on the Undead worldwide to keep the peace, while begging the elders of the tribe to come forward and help their children. When some vampires begin hearing a mysterious telepathic voice—asking them to burn coven houses and destroy their own kindred—Lestat has no choice but to come out of exile and help the tribe face the challenges threatening to destroy it.

**14. Prince Lestat and the Realms of Atlantis (2016)**—Lestat, the new Prince of the Vampires—having established his glamorous and beautiful Court at Château de Lioncourt in the mountains of France—is hoping to rule the Undead in peace when a new and mysterious enemy presents itself. Strange beings appear offering an unexpected dimension to the story of Amel, the spirit animating the entire vampire tribe. And Lestat must confront the very real possibility of immediate and total vampiric extinction.

# LIKE WHAT YOU'VE READ?

If you enjoyed this large print edition of
**RINCE LESTAT AND THE REALMS OF ATLANTIS,**
here are a few of Anne Rice's latest
bestsellers also available in large print.

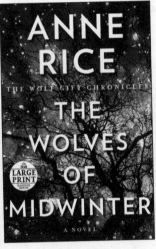

**Prince Lestat**
(paperback)
978-0-8041-9475-4
($29.00/$35.00C)

**The Wolves of
Midwinter**
(paperback)
978-0-8041-2110-1
($26.00/$30.00C)

**The Wolf Gift**
(paperback)
978-0-3079-9076-1
($26.00/$31.00C)

Large print books are available wherever books
are sold and at many local libraries.

All prices are subject to change. Check with your
local retailer for current pricing and availability.
For more information on these and other large print titles,
visit www.randomhouse.com/largeprint.